WHAT NOW, LIEUTENANT

A NOVEL

FRANK PORTER

RIVER GROVE
BOOKS

Published by River Grove Books
Austin, TX
www.rivergrovebooks.com

Distributed by River Grove Books

Design and composition by Greenleaf Book Group
Cover design by Frank Porter, author, and Greenleaf Book Group

Publisher's Cataloging-in-Publication data is available.

Print ISBN: 978-1-63299-544-5

eBook ISBN: 978-1-63299-545-2

First Edition

To: Ducks and our ducklings.

1

DR. E

W hile I am only a rumpled Latin teacher,[1] approaching the end of
a blameless though unremarkable career, I remain inexplicably
but incurably optimistic.

Yes, the honors I've received and the offices I've held have so far
been few and inconsequential. And yes, my scholarly publications
have not, as yet, received their deserved recognition. That said, I'm
excited about my soon-to-be-released Catullus monograph. The pre-
publication review is heartening.

Not to sound unhinged, but I liken myself to Spirit, the energetic, solar-powered robot NASA launched for Mars four years ago on
June 10, 2003. Quite a trip. It took me nearly seven months. Having
reached the Red Planet a few weeks before dear Opportunity, I, a
Senior Master[2] at a prestigious New England boarding school, wish to
be known as "Senior Rover."

The engineers who dispatched us were uncertain how long
Opportunity and I would survive in this challenging environment.

---

1   It wasn't always thus. Before it was unceremoniously dropped from the curriculum, I
    taught Greek as well.

2   There is a pernicious rumor circulating that we Masters may lose this time-honored
    title. What then? Rename the Masters golf tournament?

Maybe three months, they opined. Silly them. I'm still going strong, and so, I've learned, is Opportunity. I intend to keep trundling from crater to crater, sending back photos and useful data until I'm silenced, most likely by a dust storm that messes up—the science of this is beyond me—my solar panels and cuts off my power.

I anticipate my peregrinations will bring me into contact with some of my favorite Olympians. After all, one of the craters I intend to explore is Erebus, known to be the home of the Erinyes, aka the Furies. That cannot be a coincidence.

This is the perfect setting for someone immersed in the distant past. I have already discovered evidence of water that flowed here billions of years ago. Water on which Zeus may have paddled, when—as a swan—he had his imperious way with alluring Leda. And what significance should I attribute to the traces of methane I've found?

No, I am not deranged, or, at most, only slightly so. In fact, St. Matthew's, the school from which I graduated—at the head of my class, I might add—and at which I've been teaching since the middle, more or less, of the last century, just renewed my contract. Reluctantly, I have to admit. Not that they had much choice, since I'm undoubtedly protected under something akin to the Endangered Species Act. No matter. I was just granted another two years of complimentary, albeit shabby, faculty housing.

I say "reluctantly," because I fear my veneration of the true gods has brought me into conflict with the chaplain—Episcopalian, what else—and others of his stripe (virtually all of the faculty). There may be other outliers, but none, I fear, of my persuasion. That said, my covert proselytizing continues apace. And why not? Compulsory chapel is my unwitting ally. It breeds backsliding and rebellion among the more enlightened teenagers.

Allow me to be clear. I am not oppositional by nature, but it's self-evident that the Greeks—and even their Roman imitators—had an accurate grasp of the reality of the cosmos. Yes, I'd prefer a more congenial pantheon, but we must not sugarcoat the truth.

Will I be charged with heresy? St. Matthew's can be intolerant, and we know what happens to heretics. The flames—a foretaste of the hereafter. Far crueler than the axe in the hands of a competent headsman.

It's funny when you think about it. All this fashionable twaddle about diversity but show me anyone, even a so-called liberal, who will condone—let alone delight in—the notion of multiple gods. Monotheism's most notable achievements have been intolerance and strife. That is undisputed. Violence is enshrined in their sacred texts.

Should I feel personally insecure? Some of my colleagues refer to me, like Emperor Julian, as "The Apostate." I just beam harmlessly, look my advanced age (late eighties), and nod benignly. Thus far, I've not blotted my copybook or embarrassed myself or my school in any significant fashion.[3] Happily, my conscience is clear. There is no way my avuncular nature and affectionate behavior could be taken amiss.

Yes, there are those who consider me *difficult*, and, yes, I admit to a few habits (I am not referring to those scratchy garments worn by monks and nuns) that the narrow-minded might regard as "eccentricities," but surely they are not, singly or in the aggregate, disquieting. Likewise my togas, tunics, and sandals—or chitons if I'm feeling Attic—that so distress my conventional son, Frederick Elder, Jr. (he calls them nightshirts), but free me from worries about getting my cock caught in a zipper.

Freddy—he hates it when I call him this in public—misses the point. Despite the good-natured put-downs by the lordly D-B, I *am*

---

3 In fact, I am keeping a watchful eye on a cauldron of bubbling hormones. Unlike some of my colleagues who are amused by—or worse, sample—this steamy stew, I function like the control rods of a nuclear reactor. My role: prevent a meltdown and the rupture of the containment vessel.

something of a fashion plate. However, to soothe the conventional, I revert to the tedious mean in class, in the dining room, and gods forbid, in those endless, mind-numbing chapel services. Note to self: There must be some legal doctrine that exempts me from that daily—and twice on Sundays—ordeal. After all, I conscientiously object to that "onward Christian soldiers" claptrap.

On the credit side of the ledger, I still have scores of fans among the students, with the brightest clamoring to enroll in one—or both—of my classes, even though my uncompromising grading might jeopardize their admission to Harvard—my alma mater—if not to Yale. Every spring my most able student, whether male or female—yes, we're now coed—gets to carry my Corinthian helmet in the graduation procession.

And then there's Tom Chadwick, the track coach who sharpens my technique with the *pilum*.[4] And why not? Even the elderly served in the phalanx, though not necessarily in the front ranks. Another note to self: Remind the lads—oops, and the lasses—that Aeschylus himself fought at Marathon, Salamis, and Plataea.

I must, at all costs, remain true to myself. A few years ago, to ingratiate myself with the students while placating Freddy and Daniel Shaver, the man my son insists I prefer to him, I wore Levi's—with a coat and tie, naturally—to class. Evidently, they weren't the right color, cut, or brand because my frenemy—who says I am not au courant?—D-B referred to them as "recessive jeans."

Not to blow my own horn, but I *am* an engaging figurehead. In fact, I am St. Matthew's only presentable curmudgeon, and it's imperative for institutions like mine to have a functioning specimen it can

---

4 Familiarity with basic Latin is assumed at a place like this. Which reminds me, what's a centurion's favorite flavor? Answer: spearmint.

dust off and display. How else to deflect concerns about our relentlessly escalating tuition while reminding alums that their school's elite status assures them solvent, stimulating futures. That's so comforting to those who've made it and those who ache to make it, not to mention those who've lost it and can point to little else besides their distinctive accents and disintegrating school ties.

Since I am no longer struggling for advancement and have resigned myself to the blatant injustice of being denied the chairmanship of what once was St. Matthew's flourishing classics department,[5] I can be trotted out on ceremonial occasions with little fear I will be publicly incontinent or indulge in long-winded self-promotion. I am a reassuring reminder to major donors of their grand old school and the noblesse oblige it still endeavors, with diminishing success, to instill.

Enough maundering. I, the Senior Rover, intend to remain productive as long as my power lasts. Regrettably, dear Opportunity is on the other side of the planet. Were she here, I would polish her limpid solar panels and give her a gentle assist whenever she got stuck in the loose Martian soil. During the planet's harsh winters, we would hunker down, side by side, in a crater facing Helios, the source of all things. And when our power failed, we would spend eternity together under a comforting layer of fine-grained sand.

I shall keep these musings to myself. There are matters to attend to. Heading the list: dispel the rancor that exists between Freddy and the man he claims—erroneously, I believe—is his sworn enemy. That will be challenging.

I'm concerned for both of them. Each has experienced setbacks, and I've never been sure of their resilience. While *I'm* now in a "good

---

5   Now merged into, or should I say annexed by, the history department. The head of the language department was unwelcoming. "No dead tongues here," said he.

place"—stupid expression—thanks to dearest Polly,[6] I'll never forget my despair after being tossed aside by Helen. I didn't throw in my strigil, but I considered it.

The current mess is entirely my doing. What possessed me to take up Daniel Shaver, a promising lad from a primitive, disadvantaged family? Gentle Freddy was and continues to be a fine son. Why didn't I consider the effect of my obliviousness on him? Sons ache for their fathers' approval. Furthermore, who wants a reprise of Romulus and Remus?

Too late now. I will keep a watchful eye on both of them, employ my customary light touch, avoid becoming a tiresome Polonius, and offer the nuanced advice of the sort Lord Chesterfield gave his son. While I'm at it, I intend to figure out what these young men have against me, and why they ignore or, worse, make fun of me on—what I understand is known as—social media.

An acknowledgment before proceeding. I have few remaining contemporaries to gainsay me, should I choose to embellish or embroider my narrative. But know this. I am a Harvard man, and my alma mater's crest contains but one word—Veritas.[7]

---

6   We were destined for each other. Such a propitious name. Polly and St. Matthew's only polytheist. Perfect. Let me add, I reject the term "pagan," a pejorative ginned up by those shaggy, holier-than-thou monotheistic cultists to make us, the followers of the true gods, feel inferior.

7   Surely a translation is unnecessary, even for Yalies.

2

DANIEL

This time it's happening.

It's go time.

Into the glove compartment with it. On top of the registration. Impossible to miss, because he tossed all the other crap, including the maps and manuals, into the parking lot. Under the circumstances, the cops will overlook his littering.

Should he revise it further? It's somewhat terse and of no help in answering the questions everyone's sure to ask. It reads, "To whom it may concern: My secretary ("S") knows the location of all relevant keys, papers, and policies. I'm sorry for my lack of notice and apologize to any I've disobliged."

Gunny Pratt, his drill instructor, would have hated that last bit. He pounded it into his maggots that a Marine "never explains and never apologizes." Overall, however, the Gunny'd be pleased with his exit strategy. It was anything but indecisive.

No point in signing it. The handwriting was obviously his. Besides, he was uncertain as to form. Full name? Too stiff. Christian name only?

What else? He'd left a message on S's phone telling her where to find him. Was the note okay? You only get one shot—poor choice of words—at this, and he needed to nail it.

What about the airline cards and subway pass? He'd accumulated a lot of miles, and his pass was loaded. He left them on the dashboard.

Should he have selected a different venue? The bunker guarding the eighteenth hole? Comfortable. Good drainage. Or someplace more flamboyant? The Gettysburg battlefield? A tip of the hat to his New Hampshire ancestor who distinguished himself in the center of the Union line.

Why a decaying strip mall? Where should he park? Not out back near the overflowing dumpsters. Then it came to him: the handicapped space in front of the liquor store. Inspired.

Hard to explain how it turned out this way. You had to have been there. Now he was in a jam. Several actually, though everything still looked peachy from the outside. Nearly everyone he knew would still jump at the chance to be him. Christ, would they be in for a shock.

He was procrastinating. Fiddle-farting around. The way he did last night when he spit the bit and couldn't get it done. Literally and figuratively, he couldn't pull the trigger. Now it was Labor Day. A day of mournful endings. He'd be more reluctant to check out in September if he weren't sure the Sox would blow it in October.

Enough. Time to man up.

But wait, is this really necessary? There'd be no question were he Antony after Actium (thank you, Dr. Elder). Or a Jap admiral who'd lost his fleet. But they used what we now call "edged weapons." It can't have been quick. And it must have hurt something fierce.

If his difficulties leaked out, his detractors would claim he couldn't face the music. They'd put it about he was a coward. In fact, he was doing the right thing—for a change. His retainers, those who'd collect as long as he was alive, would be peeved he wasn't around to fleece. Too bad. This was proactive estate planning. He was conserving resources.

Some might attribute this to health issues. They'd be wrong, but perhaps the Feds would tread more gently if they saw him as a train wreck. Stop waffling.

Doors locked or unlocked? The former. He didn't want some homeless dude scoring his wallet, his Purdey, and his Patek Philippe, let alone his fire-engine-red Porsche 911. He couldn't do much about certain messy aspects of the undertaking, but he was damned if he'd climb into a body bag to accommodate an anonymous EMT.

Yes, there it sat on the back seat. Swaddled in its leather, fleece-lined case. Rust-free, with a light coat of oil. As he was taught in Officer Candidates School. A gift from Max.

A magnificent twelve-bore, side-by-side Purdey with a stock of the finest Turkish walnut. Full pistol grip. Double trigger. Matte finish. Handsome engraving on the receiver. Scroll work and game birds. Perfectly balanced. Such happy memories of potting grouse on the Glorious Twelfth.

Too bad his heirs and assigns weren't sportsmen. Assuming his executor wasn't hoodwinked, his Purdey would bring a bundle at auction.

Time for a wee dram. Never travel without a pick-me-up, in this instance a peaty single malt. Make sure it's a wee one. Not the time for a cock-up, and he wouldn't want anyone thinking he was gutless. That he had to get plastered first. Shotguns are not for the ambivalent.

Yes. Just what the coroner ordered. And maybe one more for . . . what? The road? Into the back it goes with plenty left for the guy who jimmies open the door. Same for his bespoke blazer. No sense ruining it. What the hell, off with his spiffy Tod loafers. Now he was getting chilly. Should have worn socks. How ironic—cold feet.

What about his watch? If he keeps it on, an EMT grabs it. If he hides it in his 911, some grease monkey gets lucky.

Does this really make sense? Aren't there less radical alternatives? Lord knows, he could afford the most expensive representation. The erstwhile prosecutors who were now cashing in by aligning themselves with their former prey. What about the shame? The unkind jokes? Imprisonment? Sharing a cell with some steroid-popping freak? What would be worse? The visits, or trying to remain chipper when nobody showed?

So unfair. Except for that incident in the grove, it was simply a few insignificant financial missteps. Anyone who had the opportunity would have done likewise. And everyone who could, did.

It would be a cinch to call in his markers. He could scare up a stack of letters demanding leniency and urging the judge to take into account his philanthropy and community service. Who was he kidding? His goose was cooked. He'd be dragged from his corner office in cuffs. A perp walk past S and the other secretaries—sorry, personal assistants—with a photographer waiting outside to capture him with lowered head.

No, he would not hang his head.

Then what? Manacled and wearing orange coveralls, unceremoniously hauled up before some grandstanding nonentity who'd peer at him over half lenses and drone on about remorse and contrition. Someone with more to hide than he. Not happening.

What about the mahogany and marble into which his name was carved and chiseled? Would he be erased like an unwanted tattoo? Like beefy Dennis Kozlowski whose alma mater sandblasted his name from a building he'd donated? Maybe not. There was still a Harvard museum with a now-reviled name over its front door.

Time to get on with it. Before S raises the alarm. No way to delete his message. If he was caught like this, he might be institutionalized. Involuntarily. Or worse, become the butt of savage Wall Street wit. His face on the cover of unkind tabloids.

What was Julius Caesar supposed to have said? Something or other *iacta est*? Where was his favorite Latin teacher when he needed him?

How about a pardon? Bubba handed them out like popcorn, and it probably served him well. Who did he know who was tight with

W? Wait! What he'd done, should it come to light, was too damning to pardon.

He got so pissed off when he thought of those maggots at AIG, Countrywide, Goldman, and Lehman. Those beady-eyed cruds blew up the world, kept everything they'd stolen, *and* skated. Even though the Feds had them dead to rights. They should've been dragged back from the Hamptons, sent to the slammer, and butt-fucked by gang bangers for twenty years.

But he'd done that and more.

Why didn't he have Max attend to it? He could have rung up Dignitas and concluded the matter with the efficiency for which those orderly clockmakers were so rightfully celebrated. His favorite Swiss Air stew could have repatriated what was left of him in the capacious Birkin bag he gave her. Duty-free, no doubt.

Would there be a memorial service? Would anyone come? His mantra had always been: If you don't go to theirs, they won't come to yours. Who'd be there besides a gaggle of development office dimwits? Would anyone speak on his behalf?

Would there be a reception afterwards? Sure. Where? Easy. On the verandah overlooking the eighteenth. Where he'd trolled for business.

Hell's teeth. He'd left no instructions about a stone. Or an obit that accentuated the many positives. The cheap, unmarked metal canister holding his—or someone else's?—clinker and bone fragments would find its way to a closet shelf where it would gather dust until its contents were dumped on a flower bed and it was repurposed. His remains would probably never make it to his family's bosky New Hampshire plot. Would he rest easy? Would he prowl forever? Was he, in fact, a "lump of foul deformity"?

Oh, shit. The wee dram was wearing off. And there was the sun.

Maybe he wouldn't be missing much. No more worries about losing it. No more terrors in the night.

Instead, he'd skip offstage in decent working order. No more lumps and spots to be biopsied. No more plastic bracelets. No pumps, pipes, and replacement parts.

Too bad. As a kid, he'd been certain his end would be glorious. He'd perish, his body miraculously intact, taking a hill in broad daylight. A steep, heavily fortified, fanatically defended hill. Never like this.

Hang in there. Oops, gallows humor. It would be over in no time. How funny, that's what he had left—no time.

So much for the Semper Foundation.

Get on with it.

Load both chambers. Buckshot? Roger that. That would guarantee finality.

Why not pills? They're for pussies, not Marines. A shotgun put him in good company. Papa Hemingway.

Damn! He couldn't reach either trigger. Should have ordered the shorter barrel. Wait! The ice scraper. Perfect. In the Crotch, this is known as a field expedient.

Enough.

Focus.

In park?

Affirmative.

Phone off?

Who gives a rat's ass?

Would he be discovered before he turned ripe?

Refocus.

Safety off?

Roger that.

Remember, maggot, squeeze it, don't jerk it.

Time's up.

Fuck you, Freddy!

Fire for effect!

3

DR. E

Somehow Freddy and Daniel Shaver believed and may still believe that I, an obsolete Latin teacher, am a war hero. Nothing could be further from the truth. If I'd guessed what they were thinking, I'd have told them how I came by my Purple Heart and that accursed knife. But I didn't. Maybe deep down I craved their admiration.

No, I wanted it all behind me. The terror. The shattered bodies. How could I have guessed they'd feel obliged to outdo me on the field of Mars?

Here's what really happened. I, a reluctant draftee, was coasting through WWII as an inconspicuous corporal in a high-IQ, far-behind-the-lines intelligence unit. Maybe I should have been, but I was not ashamed of having such a safe job. Most of us were Ivy Leaguers—if you're willing to include those not from H, Y, or P. We were stationed in London, where I spent my free time at the British Museum and the neighboring bookstores hoping to meet academic types who shared my interests.

I am not warrior material. Not for me the fighting and feasting on roast boar and mead with Odin in Valhalla, even if the Valkyries were obliging and literate. Too dark. Too cold. I wanted no part of the Hall of the Slain.[8] Sadly, back then we didn't have the option of making love *or* war.

Then came the Battle of the Bulge and the consequent shortage of riflemen. Those in charge cast about for fresh cannon fodder, and, without a by-your-leave, our cosseted band of softies was reborn as—of all unlikely things—an infantry platoon. The Germans—we weren't the only ones cracking codes—must have snickered. Even more absurd, I, Corporal Frederick Elder, became by default a squad leader. An authority figure. Would my former pals, now my subordinates, take me seriously? Negative. They were amused. I was not. Leaders of small units are often the first to fall.

After a sketchy briefing by a puffy staff officer, we were issued—reissued, actually—objects we hadn't touched since basic training. Even our most otherworldly couldn't help but discern that these unfamiliar items—BARs, rifles, and, most unnerving of all, bayonets—had once been carried by persons no longer with us. Many bore signs of rough usage. My bayonet was scary—fucking scary, in fact. It had a ten-inch blade with a blood groove on either side. I chose not to dwell on the purpose of blood grooves.

The briefing drew to a close. "Any questions, lads?" asked the captain, imitating a Brit and looking impatiently at his watch.

I had plenty. Among them: How could the Allies have been so stupid? Yes, it was winter, but hadn't the Germans swarmed through these selfsame woods just four years earlier? I deemed it imprudent to raise my hand and draw attention to myself.

"Dismissed!"

Then, with little ado, we were off to the Ardennes.

The situation, when we reached the top of a low, wooded, numbered

---

8   Norse mythology was an early interest, but *Furor Teutonicus*, as the Romans called it, put paid to all that.

hill and scratched out our shallow holes—they became deeper with the passage of time—was ominously described as "fluid." This implied we might be spending little time there. We should be prepared to "displace"—not flee—at a moment's notice. Next, we were fed into a rifle company that had been reduced to two understrength platoons and was short of NCOs and lieutenants. Thankfully, my dreaded promotion to platoon sergeant never occurred. I was sufficiently implausible as a corporal. I'll save for another day the story of how I attained that exalted status.

In an effort to imbue us with a smidgen of martial competence and elan, our three green squads were fleshed out—under the circumstances, an unfortunate phrase—with those who'd already been "blooded." It was like the classic melting-pot movie. My London roommate was a Yalie, which may explain why he was still an E-3. My foxhole mate was strapping "Ski" from Buffalo, New York. He could have stepped out of a Bill Mauldin cartoon. Ski proudly informed me that Buffalo was the world's second largest Polish city. Intuiting his feelings towards smart-aleck Harvards, I chose not to challenge that assertion.

PFC Ski's war ended dramatically during the third day of our less-than-harmonious cohabitation when a towering evergreen, deeply scarred by German artillery fire, uttered an unnerving groan and fell on us as we were sharing a cigarette in the hole—obviously not deep enough—that, in an act grossly prejudicial to good order and discipline, he'd made *me* dig. Everyone but Ski, who had his skull fractured, thought this was a hoot. Like the cautious fellow I am, I'd been wearing my helmet.

As he was being evacuated and without disclosing its provenance, Ski handed me an SS dagger wrapped in a stained—blood-stained?—undershirt, while muttering, "Don't let the fucking medics get their mitts on this. It's engraved and worth a mint." I nodded solemnly.

"And for Chrissweetsake, don't get captured with it. The Krauts'll use it to skin you. And make fucking sure you get it back to me in Buffalo! Got that, college boy?" I nodded again and smiled disarmingly.

Believe me, I tried, but, as I suspected, there were too many Skis in the Buffalo phone book. Pages of them and, Ski being a suffix, my search failed. What to do? Somehow, it wasn't right to sell the dagger. Who could tell what harm it would cause in the wrong hands? If I'd foreseen its malign influence, I'd have thrown it off the troopship ferrying me home. In the event—thinking it would never be discovered, or maybe hoping it would[9]—I interred it in my footlocker.

And yes, the nasty scrapes and bruises I received from the hostile tree got me a Purple Heart. And why not? As my lawyer friends might put it, German shellfire was the "proximate cause" of the tree's beaning me, but the forest gods intervened on my behalf. As a token of my appreciation, I brought home a twig, which, to this day, occupies a place of honor among my lares and penates.

Will fiftieth-century archeologists unearth potsherds, which, when reassembled, depict my wounding by that savage tree?

The next day Fortuna favored me again. Before I had to give the terrifying order, "Fix bayonets!"[10] (we were chronically low on ammunition, not that we generally hit much when we weren't) the weather cleared, and our eager pilots rejoined the fray. With that, the Hun executed an abrupt about-face and trudged east. Shortly thereafter, a bemedaled Corporal Elder, with a menacing SS dagger[11] concealed in his pack, returned to Blighty.

---

9   Enough. The examined life is overrated.

10 The first time I heard that ambiguous command I asked myself, am I supposed to repair my bayonet or attach it to my rifle? Anent that: A fixed bayonet implies a disturbing proximity to the foe.

11 I feared that dagger might play the same role in Freddy's life as the weapons Odysseus used to trick Achilles into sailing to Troy and his predestined doom.

Yes, I admit it. This condensed narrative omits certain graphic details often encountered in accounts of this nature. That is because I have chosen to unsee much of what I saw—an indelible exception being the sight of a shattered battalion stumbling back through our position. At least we didn't take them for Germans. The same applies to certain sounds and smells. But some refuse to stay buried, the most recurrent being the clang as your rifle ejects an empty clip. In nightmares, it's always your last clip.

Soon thereafter, I set sail—figuratively speaking—for comforting Massachusetts intending to cocoon myself in a life devoid of conflict.

Entering Boston Harbor, I likened myself to Odysseus returning to Ithaca. Thank goodness, there were, at that time, no suitors for me to dispatch with the bow that only I could bend.

So—to use the vernacular of this disheartening new century—what was the net-net of my military service? I believe it would be fair to say I did not bring discredit to the family. Put another way, like everything, my time in khaki was a test. While I can't claim my Harvard grade—a summa—I believe I earned what was once referred to as a gentleman's C. But perhaps I exaggerate.

4

FREDDY/FRED

First Lieutenant Frederick Elder, Jr., was the Officer of the Day, and as such, the safety of his unit, a Marine Corps artillery battalion, rested squarely on his not particularly broad shoulders. As OOD he was obliged to be vigilant until duly relieved. But, nearing the end of his days in uniform, he was nodding off, and why not? It was early 1965. He was stationed at Camp Pendleton in laid-back Southern California, and there'd been no reports of Mexican forces massing at the Tijuana border fifty miles to the south. As a soon-to-be-discharged reserve officer, he was "short," as in short-timer.

Gary Powers had been shot down when Fred was at Harvard, and for a while, it looked as though it might hit the fan. But it hadn't. Likewise, the 1962 Cuban Missile Crisis, a whole lot of nothing. Fred guessed that, despite the Tonkin Gulf dustup, the current ruckus in South Vietnam wouldn't amount to much either.

So far, his tour of duty had been a prolonged yawn, "a couple months of activity packed into three years," as he liked to put it. Last week's regimental mess night, from which many of the participants were still recovering, had been the high point of his enlistment. Those raucous tribal rites—they often concluded with imaginative feats of arms and/or projectile vomiting—could be a kick if you had no intention of becoming a lifer. It was dress uniforms adorned with every piece of cloth and metal the wearer earned or to which he had a semi-legitimate claim. All hands were expected to get entertainingly plastered, but never slip over the edge.

Upchucking—especially doing so on yourself, or worse, on someone of higher rank—or passing out, if observed by a sober superior officer, could finish a career in the Corps that was not subsequently resurrected on the battlefield. You had to cut it pretty fine, however, because moderation was also viewed with deep suspicion.

Fred had managed to thread the needle and, as a consequence, enjoyed and recalled every detail of the skit in which the protagonist, Colonel John Glenn, USMC, had gotten it on with the First Lady while the drawling Commander in Chief played Navy games in the showers. The skit drew roars of approval and a seemingly endless standing ovation.

To relieve his boredom, Fred volunteered for Marine Corps schools that taught him technical rock climbing (very scary), aerial observation, naval gunfire spotting, and what was called, with no irony intended, military justice. Though slow-moving, his time in California was not a complete bust. The local beaches, unlike those pinched, inhospitable New England strands, were awash in heart-stopping, if not wildly bright, babes. Keeping his mouth shut and playing the laconic warrior sometimes compensated for his lack of familiarity with the local patois about surfing, volleyball, and customized cars. These tanned, fun-loving creatures were such a relief from the pale, argumentative ones with whom he'd grown up.

In the meantime, he mimicked the most poised lieutenants. The hotshots with a pad on the Pacific, a fast ride, and, if they could trade for one, a flight jacket with name, rank, and USMC in gold letters over the heart. Pilots' sunglasses were also a plus. Quite wisely, those with Fred's lack of self-confidence allowed their uniforms—particularly the dazzling dress blues and sword—to speak on their behalf rather than opening their mouths and extinguishing the expectations those costumes aroused.

However, if Fred looked at things honestly, he had to admit his California forays differed little from his New England ones. Like agile goalies, the West Coast girls he longed for were equally adept at preserving the inviolability of the crease.

What next? Should he linger in this Eden?

Life is such a crap shoot. He'd never have wound up wearing the globe and anchor if he hadn't forced himself up to the sweltering attic and snooped around in his father's WWII footlocker. He'd noticed it was unlocked a year earlier when he was only eight but lacked the nerve to inspect its contents.

What he discovered, as a more confident nine-year-old—a Purple Heart medal and an SS dagger with "Wolfram Hube" engraved on its blade in creepy German script—changed everything. His father had led him to believe he'd sat out the war in London analyzing aerial photos. Nothing a boy could brag about to those of his friends whose fathers had been under—or within earshot of—enemy fire. Now he was among the elect. None of his pals' fathers had been killed or wounded. Not even nicked.

Though he could never own up to having gone through his father's gear, he was entitled to make an important assumption: In addition to earning a Harvard summa, his father was a war hero. This mild-mannered teacher, whose age had assured him of a safe posting, had, nevertheless, taken up the gauntlet, shed his blood, and returned bearing the spoils of war. How could he, this man's son and heir, do less? Shouldn't he at least put himself in what might possibly become harm's way?

In fact, his father's stubborn silence on this matter tended to confirm Fred's hypothesis. Elders were not braggarts. They were New Englanders.

From this flawed premise flowed serious consequences. If he hoped to measure up to Elder standards and beat back the aggressive Daniel Shaver, his father's latest protege, Fred owed Uncle Sam a few years. Preferably peaceful years, but if not, with any luck the conflict would be of short duration against an overmatched enemy. How about an amphibious assault on Bermuda? Then the movie—*Sands of Elbow Beach*?

What were his options? None. It had to be the Crotch, the insiders' pet name for the USMC.

After he'd served honorably—as evidenced by an honorable discharge—maybe he could sit down with his old man, grill him about WWII, and swap salty stories. He still recalled his initial attempt to break the ice on that subject. And why not? He'd just graduated from (he was not dropping "from") Harvard and signed up for the Corps. Before he'd barely started, his father grimaced and said, "Look, Freddy, your father's a colorless school master. End of story."

When would he learn how his father had gotten his medal and dagger? When would his father tell him what he knew about Wolfram Hube? When would his father stop calling him "Freddy"? When would he, Fred, have plunder to lay before his father?

———

Fred would be asleep in seconds if he kept staring at the hypnotic blades of the ceiling fan, or the familiar poster-sized photograph of the anonymous Marine lieutenant, carbine in hand, leading his men over the seawall at Inchon. Was he cut down moments later? Months later? Was he still in the Crotch? Was he making a bundle on Wall Street?

Nodding off could mean trouble. But wouldn't it be seen as outrageous to come down hard on a promising and otherwise squared-away first lieutenant who dozed off at his post in this stagnant California backwater? Who could say? Chicken shit was the order of the day when you weren't in the field. As things stood, he was unlikely to see the world or smite his country's foes, and he had to admit he was okay with that. If Uncle Sam didn't choose to pick a fight when Lieutenant Elder was on call, too bad for Uncle.

5

DR. E

Freddy was fourteen back in 1955. It was his first summer without the woman who remained his mother but was no longer my dear wife. Freddy and I were engaged in our Memorial Day ritual of opening and airing out my family's New Hampshire house that I, despite my ex-wife's not-so-gentle mockery, insisted on calling "Three Oaks."

The original Three Oaks had been a sprawling fifty-acre estate on the Connecticut shore that Marian Elder, my great-grandmother, was forced to part with shortly after WWII. Three Oaks was my Paradise Lost. I likened its meandering, quarter-mile driveway—lined with the marble headstones of terriers and polo ponies—to the Appian Way, while Freddy no doubt has fading memories of a stern woman in a houndstooth cloak, a stately porte cochere, and a formal garden in the center of which was a granite pool serving as a moat to protect the unclothed mermaid perched on a rock with water gushing from her mouth.

As for the taciturn Marian, I never discovered whether she took those sleeping pills by mistake.

Standing on a slight rise in the southeast corner of my four-hundred-plus acres of uncultivated glacial till and second-growth pulp wood—that, by the way, included no oaks—I shaded my eyes, ignored the threatening weather, and swept my left arm in what was probably an overly theatrical arc that took in the peeling farmhouse, its sagging ell, and the three sheds clinging duckling-like to its back. As I suppose I did every year with only minor variations, I proclaimed, "Someday, Freddy, all this will be yours. And maybe you can buy back the land we were forced to sell."

In what had become a predictable response, Freddy said, "You're always complaining about money and telling us we're land poor, whatever that means."

We both knew our lines. I cleared my throat, gathered my thoughts, and responded, "This land's our heritage, Freddy. It won't disappear like your mother, and it won't decline in value."

Freddy groaned. "Not again."

I ignored my son's rudeness and said, "How's our tennis court looking?"

"Rutted something fierce. Someone's driven a tractor over it. Just like last year."

Before I could say anything, Freddy added, "It's those Shavers."[12] I patted my son on his shoulder and said, rather solemnly I'm afraid, "We must not blame everything on the Shaver boys, particularly the younger one. Daniel strikes me as a good lad. He's worth trying to save."

Freddy replied angrily, "It's the Shavers' John Deere. I've checked the tread marks. And you're wrong about Daniel. He may be smarter than Gideon, but he's even worse. He knows how to butter people up."

Was I getting preachy—Freddy often claims I am—when I said, "We must try to understand the Shavers. They haven't enjoyed our advantages. Daniel might do nicely at St. Matthew's. You're two years older and could show him the ropes, and he could cut his teeth on my introductory course."

---

12 My dear Helen referred to them as "something out of Bruegel."

"No," yelled Freddy, perhaps wondering what was involved in showing ropes and cutting teeth. Before I could reply, Freddy added, "What advantages?"

I was, as usual, lost in thought and hadn't heard the thunder. "Admitting Daniel would improve relations with those who live in Lower Finley year-round. You could invite some of your St. Matthew's classmates here to meet him."

That was the wrong thing to say. Freddy picked up a rock and smashed it down on the anthill at his feet, saying, "Nobody who's been here ever wants to come back. Who likes being handed a hammer and told we're shingling before lunch and cutting brush afterwards? Besides, we've only got one bathroom, and the guestroom bed's busted."

It would have been wise to drop it, but I didn't. "If your classmates won't visit us, you can always play tennis with Daniel. If he played on our court, maybe Gideon wouldn't ruin it."

"You don't understand Gideon, and Daniel doesn't know how to play, and we don't have any extra racquets."

"Yes, we do, Freddy."

"We can't play with those. Everyone would laugh." Looking away from me and in a rising voice, Freddy said, "Are we turning into the Shavers?"

I could tell by Freddy's exasperated expression that I must have sighed or rolled my eyes. "No, we are not. I might agree with you about Gideon, but there's no reason you can't befriend his younger brother."

"Are we going to keep losing things, Dad?"

This was a new line of attack. "What do you mean, Freddy?"

"We lost the real Three Oaks, and now we've lost Mom."

It was colder. The thunder and lightning were getting closer.

"Why can't Daniel Shaver become a new friend? We all need friends."

"Lots of reasons."

Then I thought of something positive to say about the Shavers. "Didn't Ezra Shaver teach the three of you to shoot a .22 before his accident?"

"Mr. Shaver really scared me. He was always talking about the Japs he roasted with that flamethrower he kept in his barn. He stank and had hardly any teeth."

"That was ungenerous, Freddy. Sometimes Ezra drank too much, but he looked after our place and kept the road open in the winter."

"Promise me something, Dad."

I didn't care for my son's expression. "What, Freddy?"

"You won't retire early and make us live here year-round."

That hurt. "I wouldn't retire even if I could afford to. I love teaching."

Okay, new plan. This wasn't working. What if I took Freddy to Foley's Restaurant and bought him a frappe?

Freddy broke in, "Didn't you say hiring Ezra Shaver was like paying someone to look out for your car in Mexico?"

"For the last time, Freddy, we don't know the Shavers did it."

"Sure we do, but it's worse. They shoot things."

That got my attention. "Cans? Bottles?"

"No, living things."

The wind had picked up, and the first raindrops came pelting down. I hadn't noticed.

"Don't forget, Freddy, some of our neighbors hunt in order to feed themselves. Ezra Shaver's gone. Verna's doing badly with her diabetes. Mr. Flint's out of work, and, except for Mr. Rusher, the others don't have regular jobs. There are worse things than being a Latin teacher." That must have been the last straw.

"Yesterday they shot Cora."

"Cora?"

"The Flints' cat."

"Where did you hear that, Freddy?" Now it was pouring.

"I was there. They made me go with them."

"Why didn't you come home when you saw what they were doing?"

"You know those knives they wear? They said they'd skin me . . . and Marcus too. Now we'll have to keep him inside."

I must have looked frightened. "I'm calling the police, Freddy."

Freddy grabbed my sleeve. "Don't. Remember what happened to the Rogers's camp."

"Did they kill the cat?"

"Gideon shot her, but she wasn't quite dead. Then he laughed and said, 'I got an idea.' He picked her up—by her tail—and took her back to their house."

"Why didn't you leave?" That was a dumb question. "Why didn't Verna do something?"

"She was asleep in front of the TV. Or passed out."

The lightning was getting closer. Freddy ran for the house. I followed him, yelling, "Then what?"

Freddy shouted over his shoulder, "Gideon stuffed Cora into Mrs. Shaver's big meat grinder and held her there with a wooden spoon. He made me turn the handle till all of her came out. Then he handed me the bowl."

6

FREDDY/FRED

The overhead fan skipped a beat. Fred awoke with a guilty start. Drastic and immediate action was required if he planned to match, let alone upstage, his schoolteacher father. He'd made inquiries, submitted a bunch of forms, and waited to be contacted by the current incarnation of the OSS. As a single Marine lieutenant with an Ivy League BA and, he assumed, decent fitness reports, he filled the bill. He'd already been polygraphed. How could he miss?

But he still wasn't entirely sure of himself. You either had your shit together or you didn't, and Fred was beginning to think he did. His gear had come to feel like a second skin, particularly his pistol belt from which dangled his tools, each in its bespoke receptacle. Star billing went to his recoil-operated, magazine-fed, self-loading .45 caliber handgun. Ancillary items included two extra seven-round magazines; a lensatic compass; a pair of canteens, each nestled in its own clanking, heat-conducting, lip-burning stainless steel cup; and, for whatever illusory comfort it might provide, a tiny receptacle containing what he'd been told was a field dressing. The functionality of this item, which may have dated back to the Great War, had to be taken on faith since there was no way of confirming it without ripping open the metal container and contaminating its contents.

Not to be overlooked was the ensemble's one fashion variable: the helmet's camouflage cover. It had a green side to be displayed while in verdant climes and a brown one for arid, flora-free landscapes. Additionally, there were slits into which the wearer could stuff vegetation so as to confound ill-wishers by altering the helmet's distinctive silhouette.

In addition, those wishing to be seen as hyper gung-ho could accessorize their pistol belts with a menacing Ka-Bar fighting knife. Fred hadn't.

Finally, certain dominant members of his guild were authorized to distinguish themselves from others with a pair of 7x50 binoculars, a potent symbol of authority.

Yes, he was feeling self-assured in his new costume, and he'd finally mastered a troop leader's basic command, "Forward March!" The first word was pronounced "Fuh-Wud," with a distinct pause between syllables. Forcefully enunciated, "March!" could be mistaken for a violent discharge of phlegm.

As a commissioned officer, even seasoned NCOs were obliged to take him seriously, at least initially. From then on, it was up to him. Burned into his memory was the sight of an overweight, agitated second lieutenant named Nordberg standing on a moonlit California beach screaming, "I am a Marine officer!" at a staff sergeant who was muttering to himself as he strode away. Having been publicly neutered, Nordberg was immediately transferred, presumably to a faraway desk.

So far, nothing like that had happened to him. Perhaps he was not an imposter. After all, he and his three-man forward observer team had spent nearly a week on an isolated observation post in the Mojave Desert, where he'd been instrumental in winning the battalion competition for his battery. Initially, he'd been anxious. His CO had warned him his radioman, Corporal White, was "smart but insubordinate, a born troublemaker."

In fact, Fred got off to an outstanding start, registering his battery before the two others in the battalion. Then came his masterpiece, a fortuitous hit on a challenging target for a high-trajectory weapon: a rocky outcrop midway up a steep hill. Corporal White turned to him and, in front of the wiremen, said, "Fucking sweet shooting, Lieutenant." The wiremen grunted in agreement.

At that point, Corporal White took Fred under his wing and, with something bordering on affection, or maybe provisional respect, tutored him in the niceties of life in the field. Lesson one: Dig in carefully after dark, lest you unearth a buried latrine. Lesson two: If you have any choice in the matter, go for the fruit cocktail and avoid cans stamped "Ham and Limas." That evening, as Fred was heating what passed for supper, White reached into his field jacket and handed him a hot pepper and a switchblade to slice it up.

Fred's finest hour came two nights later, when, after the four of them removed their boots before crawling into their filthy sleeping bags, White sniffed loudly and declared, "Christ almighty, Lieutenant, your feet stink something awful." Tension.

The dreaded mutiny? No. Instinct asserted itself. With only a moment's hesitation, Fred shot back, "Officers' feet *never* stink, *Corporal.*" White roared approvingly. A split second later the wiremen did too.

In the meantime, Daniel Shaver was baying at his heels. At least his old man hadn't adopted him. It had started badly when Shaver, in his first year at St. Matthew's, walked off with the lower school Latin prize, a leather-bound copy of *The Gallic Wars*, affectionately inscribed by his father. Then came the Simulator. It transformed young Shaver into a star. The worst was yet to come. Daniel Shaver received a full scholarship to Harvard and signed up for NROTC with the express intention of joining the Corps and showing up the man he enjoyed calling "Freddy."

And here he was, Frederick Elder, whose namesake triumphed at Gettysburg, languishing at Battalion Headquarters like a doddering night watchman.

7

DR. E

Gossip, particularly gossip of a salacious nature, travels with the speed of light[13] through a place like St. Matthew's, always reaching the person least likely to welcome it—in this case, me. Thank you, D-B.

It seems my fifteen-year-old Freddy, while typically late to the party, reached the point where it was reasonable for me to hope he'd carry on our male line. I only wish he'd begun to *cherchez* somewhere else or, for my sake, been more circumspect.

Can I help Freddy choose a wife—a wife who won't leave him? A keeper. Left to his innocent devices and temperate desires, Freddy will undoubtedly set his sights on someone much like himself, a someone who'll look up to him. A Bostonian probably, or, if he's feeling venturesome, a Philadelphia girl who summers in Maine, New Hampshire, or Vermont.

Perhaps, with my guidance, Freddy can raise his sights. To the horizon, if not to the stars. Hold on, wasn't that just what I did? Have I learned nothing? All right, I admit it. I am unqualified to play Cupid. Nevertheless, I will coach inconspicuously from the sidelines. It would be irresponsible and uncaring not to. I have much to contribute.

---

13 Hermes, you troublemaker.

Yes, I'll accept my reduced role, but there's one verity. No drama. None of that Montague-Capulet or—to cite a more modern instance—Jets-Sharks business for my boy.

With luck, Aphrodite will champion Freddy, but that too can be fraught. Just ask Paris.

8

FREDDY/FRED

Freddy Elder was eager to develop his amatory skills but was damned if he'd give Daniel Shaver the satisfaction of witnessing and, worse, profiting from his ineptitude. He had a plan. It involved Cedric Douglas-Brown's secretary, a young woman named Jayne Hoskins, who possessed a bosom which, if it hadn't been artificially enhanced, looked to rival or maybe eclipse Mary Foley's. Plus, a huge plus, Jayne owned a car. Another positive was her secluded, private office where he could initiate his campaign far removed from those who would observe, snicker, and comment. Like Mary Foley, Jayne wore a modest silver cross. While Mary's swayed hypnotically in a shady dell, Jayne's sat primly atop her protruding lamb's wool sweater. Mary was Foley's Restaurant's blue-plate special. Boys, and older men who should have known better, crowded the counter to stare and ache and prolong their ordering. Why not? They moved so tantalizingly. Like gentle swells on a calm sea.

On the debit side of the ledger, Jayne's withdrawn personality and unfortunate complexion had put off St. Matthew's more accomplished swains. However, without articulating it, Freddy realized these apparent defects opened doors to the likes of him. Never having had to fend off the wolves, Jayne seemed trusting and pitifully eager to talk with almost any boy who bothered to seek her out. On balance, it seemed an opportunity worth pursuing. Besides, she smelled really nice.

Plus, he kinda liked her, not that he wanted that to be discovered.

Jayne owed her remote location to the introduction of a two-year Humanities program designed to expose the more precocious St. Matthew's students to music, art, and other matters beyond the ken of the less able. A cultivated alumnus had funded the construction—in an unused upper floor of the library—of a luxurious suite complete with sound system, projection facilities, and display cases for the priceless artifacts bound to be attracted by this ambitious enrichment program. The renovation included a palatial office for Dr. Douglas-Brown (Harrow, Cambridge, the Institute of Fine Arts) and a snug cubby for Jayne Hoskins, whom the doctor (known throughout St. Matthew's as "D-B") referred to as his "wee, sleekit, cow'rin, tim'rous beastie."

Despite outcries of favoritism from the faculty, Headmaster Ward was not about to offend one of his most generous donors by depriving D-B of his lavishly appointed hideaway and his seventy-words-a-minute secretary. Why bother? The faculty was always grousing about something.

Had he possessed the self-confidence gained as a Marine lieutenant, Freddy might have advanced with more verve. It would have been obvious to Daniel Shaver that Jayne would welcome all but the truly hopeless. But the rogue in Freddy was still dormant. So, wary of rejection, he proceeded tentatively, tamping down the fires he feared would consume him. He appeared. He hung around. He did his best conversationally, but never thought to ask Jayne about herself or favor her with gifts or compliments. His best lines occurred to him after the fact and were usually forgotten or inapposite the next time they met.

He might well have given up had it not been for Jayne's intriguing but ambiguous behavior. He'd been standing over her, perhaps closer than usual, trying to act suave (suave was everything in those days) and nonthreatening when Jayne lifted both hands from the keys of her Remington and, while arching her back, placed her fingers at the base of her skull and began doing something fascinating with her hair, pressing it upwards and outwards, while emitting puzzling but intriguing sounds.

Freddy, who was gradually transitioning to Fred, had never observed anything remotely similar. Nor had he encountered behavior of this sort in the steamy novels he'd devoured. Whatever was happening, he chose not to interpret Jayne's conduct as a hint for him to leave. Jayne, with her unfocused eyes, had withdrawn to some secret realm deep within herself. He'd loved to have joined her there, but the longed-for invitation never materialized. If anything, she reminded him of his father's description of the Delphic Oracle, drugged and transported by vapors wafting upwards through a tear in the earth.

Were all females so puzzling? He remembered his father saying, "Women are as difficult to decipher as Linear A." Whatever that was.

Freddy wasn't sure what to make of this metamorphosis and certainly didn't credit himself with causing it, but it occurred to him that if, at that very moment, he kissed Jayne or placed an exploratory hand on what certain racy publications referred to as an "erogenous zone"— wherever they were—he might not have been rebuffed. If there was any truth to that hypothesis, surely his suggestion of a ride in her car would not be taken amiss. That proved to be correct.

Freddy had no idea how to bring matters like this to a satisfactory conclusion or, for that matter, what a satisfactory conclusion might entail—certain outcomes being beyond the realm of the possible. Nevertheless, he sensed progress, however slight. He could tell by Jayne's shy smile when he appeared in her doorway. Having persuaded her to type one of his papers, the stage was set for a bolder move—a ride to the village Daniel Shaver referred to as Lower Bumfuck. That would be followed in short order, he fantasized, by illegal moonlit drives where opportunities to touch and be touched would, almost certainly, present themselves.

While he sourly admitted he would never rival Daniel as a Casanova, Freddy had come to hope, if not believe, he might develop an approach of his own. A recent issue of the school newspaper contained a feature about D-B, his suite, and Jayne, his thrall.

Eureka!

Taking a copy of the paper to a secure location, Freddy snipped out Jayne's picture. Before driving into town with her, he slipped it into his breast pocket and—upon reaching their destination—got Jayne's attention, held up the photograph, and, steeling himself, declared, "I carry your picture next to my heart." Jayne blushed becomingly.

Their first outing was quiet but successful. They visited Woolworth's, where Freddy impetuously bought Jayne a goldfish but didn't think to tell her that one day he would give her something really made of gold. She was visibly moved but wanted nothing to do with the slippery thing. That was fine, since it resulted in a trip to a nearby pond where "Goldy" was wished good luck and released, with Freddy boldly suggesting they must return now and again to feed "our baby." They lingered by the pond for a few moments without speaking. Would Jayne recoil if he touched her? He never found out.

The moment, if there'd been one, passed. They drove back to school with him, cowering beneath a baseball cap, feeling more Freddy than Fred. Jayne let him off behind the groundskeeper's building, gave him a bashful wave, and—driving her pre-war Plymouth in her tentative fashion—set off for the employees' parking area.

He was inclined to give the outing a "B plus." That was before Daniel bounded up to him in the dining room and trumpeted, "Just a heads-up, buddy. You were spotted in the five and dime with D-B's secretary. She may be a pushover, but what will your father say? Probably something like, 'Your reach should exceed your grasp.'"

"Cool it, Daniel. We're only friends." He could feel himself blushing.

"Never bullshit a bullshitter, pal. You're behaving like a catfish."

"Whadaya mean?"

"You're bottom-feeding, my boy." With that, Daniel sauntered off, saying over his shoulder, "You need a session with the Simulator. No need for a pickup line. No tedious prep work. No fear of her telling you to 'piss off.' How about I give you fifteen minutes, on the house?" Trying to ignore the sniggering at his table, Freddy snorted dismissively.

Two days later, he presented Jayne with a desk plant that had been on sale at Woolworth's and followed up with an assortment of flowers he'd snipped in the headmaster's garden. Drawing on something he remembered from a syrupy greeting card, he established eye contact and said, "These flowers are a symbol of our blossoming relationship."

Progress. The flowers were received with considerably more enthusiasm than the goldfish, and Jayne forbore from dwelling on his larcenous nature. While she was thanking him, he wondered whether he dared touch her shoulder, or maybe her arm. He opted for a shoulder, but she didn't seem to notice.

It was then that D-B stormed into Jayne's hideaway, tugged down his vest, glared at the flowers, and said, "Be so good as to accompany me to my office, Mr. Elder."

Freddy had the presence of mind to wink at Jayne before scuttling after D-B. Jayne looked terrified.

"Take a seat, Mr. Elder," said D-B, gesturing to one of the antique guest chairs facing his eighteenth-century desk. Freddy did so, but the doctor remained standing. "What do you have to say for yourself?" he asked.

"What do you mean, sir?"

D-B frowned as he stepped closer. "You know very well what I mean, Mr. Elder."

"Jayne's a friend of mine" was his lame response. However, he was unable to buttress this contention with corroborating specifics. Then D-B's interrogation took an unexpected tack. Only later did he get it; his perceived sin was larceny, not lust.

"You are, I presume, aware that Miss Hoskins works for St. Matthew's, and St. Matthew's has plenary rights to her services during normal business hours."

"Absolutely, sir. Why?"

"Are you aware I discovered Miss Hoskins typing one of your papers? She was contrite."

"I didn't know that, sir. I wasn't sure when she typed them."

"*Them?*" bellowed the outraged doctor.

"I'm afraid so, sir."

"Are you playing barrister with me, Mr. Elder? That's inadvisable," said D-B as he fondled one of the objects adorning his watch fob.

"Absolutely not, sir."

"That's fortunate, because you've been making improper use of school property. Lawyers, as you would say, have a word for that. It's 'conversion,' a common law tort. Should this behavior continue, it might properly be classified as 'theft,' which, as I'm certain you realize, is a crime."

"I'm sorry, sir."

D-B did his eyebrow thing. "I intend to express my grave disappointment to your father, and, in the meantime, I forbid you to have further contact with Miss Hoskins. Unlike the other Masters who must share secretaries, I share Miss Hoskins with no one, certainly not a student, much less an underclassman." Then the crusher, "You might consider modeling yourself on the bright, ambitious Daniel Shaver, who, I understand, grew up without any of your advantages."

Looking back, he was ashamed he never spoke again to the hopeful, sweet-natured Jayne Hoskins. In truth, he went out of his way to avoid her. Occasionally, he wondered whether wishing her complexion would improve did anything to restore his tarnished honor. Even worse, never would he disinter, admire, examine, and delight in what distended her lamb's wool sweater and whispered to him from beneath her plaid skirt.

But, far better a cad than how he'd felt after their last conversation when Jayne, just before hanging up on him, said, "Freddy, you shouldn't use people. It's unkind. Besides, you're not the greatest catch yourself." A pause to let that sink in. "And, just so you know, I've met someone from town who really likes me. Michael was three years ahead of me in high school. He has his own place, and he works at the bank."

Before he could formulate a rejoinder, Jayne continued, "Michael doesn't expect me to do things I'm not ready to do—at least not with you. Don't visit me anymore, Freddy. My job's really important to me and Michael."

Why couldn't she have called him Fred?

9

DR. E

No, I am not exaggerating when I say that on first meeting him in 1953, Cedric Douglas-Brown (aka "D-B")[14] struck me as a twit and a phony. It was all too much—the plummy accent, the hyphenated surname, and the charm he oozed like an incontinent geriatric. All he lacked was a fourth name. Spare me. Holden Caulfield would have seen through him in an instant.

His CV was too perfect. Like Byron,[15] he went to Harrow and Cambridge. That was followed by command, as a young subaltern, of a squadron of Crusader tanks in Monty's advance from El Alamein to Tunisia. Mentioned in despatches? So he claims. Did he bag a Panzer? He nods modestly. It amuses him to say he suffers from Turret syndrome.

D-B's favorite adjective: keen. A trait he feels he possesses in abundance given his many enthusiasms.

After being demobbed, D-B earned his fancy PhD, that being followed by a stint at his old school before St. Matthew's snaffled him away with heaven only knows what inducements and assurances.

---

14 Do I have a nickname? I dare not inquire.

15 And, perhaps surprisingly, that Old Harrovian, Jawaharlal Nehru.

Why, I ask, do institutions like mine feel the need to buttress their unassailable legitimacy by fawning over Oxbridge types? It utterly escapes me. Though callow by the standards of the institutions they mimic—Harrow was founded in 1572—schools like mine have been going strong for over a century.

And why, I wonder, would D-B leave Harrow unless something had gone badly awry? It took several years before I abandoned my attempts to discredit him.

I do not wish to appear smaller-minded than I am, so yes, I suppose D-B's handsome in that bland, sandy-haired—now dyed, I'm sure—English way. His eyes retain an audacious sparkle that must have galvanized his troops and has certainly endeared him to our female teachers, faculty wives, and a sizable number of the girls in the upper school. Even his English teeth pass muster.

Then there's his transformation of our soccer program from a refuge for the unmanly to perennial league champion. In the process, he's even managed to lure away some of our most gifted football players.

He best be on guard, though. The times they are changing. That twinkle and his single status—what could one deduce from that? Discarded women? Aberrant impulses? Yes, D-B bore watching.

All right then, I admit it. I felt threatened. D-B was trying to supplant me as St. Matthew's most engaging curiosity. Worse: what I mistakenly took to be his unseemly interest in my Helen. Worse still: He created his own course of study (some of which encroached on my preserve) and had a private suite plus an indentured secretary to do with as he wished.

10

FREDDY/FRED

A low-flying aircraft woke him. He, the Officer of the Day, must not be caught napping. Going to the coffee machine, Fred refilled his mug. Four hours to go.

Despite his commanding officer's belief—or was it hope?—that danger lurked in the shadows of every box canyon, Fred was certain Third Battalion, Eleventh Marines would make it through the night unscathed.

Enough inaction. He would arise, strap on his pistol, and jack up the sentries—his sentries. He hadn't done so in several hours. They needed motivation. Fred enjoyed this ritual but was concerned he cut an unmemorable figure with his pistol snugged up against his waist like everyone else. Not the nonregulation gunslinger's slouch favored by his commanding officer—the swaggering Virginian, Lieutenant Colonel Bruce McCleod—whose sidearm hung low on his hip. To top it off, he required his officers to stand watch with loaded weapons. So far, he hadn't ordered them to chamber a round.

What was that faint noise? He listened. Now it was clearly recognizable. The wop-wop-wop of insistent rotor blades. Not the repetitive clicking of the ceiling fan. A chopper or helipecker, as he had come to know them. Headed his way. Drowning out the crickets. Loud and angry. Why? It was the middle of the night, and his country had been at peace since '53. Thank you, Ike, for telling the French we wanted no part of their Indochina debacle. Even if they were commanded by men with such splendid names as Christian Marie Ferdinand de la Croix de Castries.

Had the Old Man been right to insist on live rounds? Was 3/11 under attack?

The helicopter surged towards Battalion Headquarters and went into a deafening hover, throwing up a storm of dirt, leaves, and twigs before settling lightly onto the empty parking area. The pilot cut its engine, and the crickets reclaimed the night. Fred was stumped. Yes, it was a HUS, the reliable Marine Corps workhorse, but this one lacked identifying markings and was painted a nondescript tan, a color he'd never seen on a military aircraft.

This incursion could hardly be ignored. But what was the protocol when an unidentified aircraft landed at O-Dark-Thirty in the area you were tasked to protect? There was no "book" on this.

Buck it up the line to regiment? The Duty NCO, who was awaiting his decision, looked anxious. Fred picked up the phone, thought for a moment, and set it back in its cradle. Not yet. This could be a ruse by regiment or his future employer to test him and 3/11's readiness. No ambitious officer can be seen as wanting in initiative. Or get the reputation of being "nervous in the service." Taking charge would improve his odds of being welcomed at the organization he planned to join immediately after his discharge. Given his background, he assumed it was a done deal.

How would the Skipper handle this? he asked himself. The CO—despite a left eye with a disquieting sideways cast and a crimped Celtic mouth that one of his detractors said resembled a cat's asshole—saw himself as a compelling leader of men. To his dubious subordinates, Lieutenant Colonel McCleod was a moronic, medal-hunting exhibitionist. No glory without heavy casualties—on both sides.

With that, Fred rose, put on his pistol belt, unholstered and examined his .45, chambered a round, determined it was on safe, and—holding it loosely in his right hand with his index finger outside the trigger guard—strode resolutely, he hoped, through the screen door and advanced on the mysterious aircraft, whose only sound was the faint pinging of cooling metal. It had to be obvious he was not to be fucked with.

The fuselage door slid open. A wiry figure in a brown flight suit vaulted to the asphalt and loped towards him. Why brown? Yes, it matched the chopper, but why not the highly visible orange worn by every other peacetime flyboy? Didn't he want to be spotted and rescued if he went down? Anonymity seemed to be the object. That would account for the absence of name tag, unit insignia, and any indication of rank. Odd. Most pilots were peacocks. And a lot of them, because of minimal exercise, were lard asses.

Not this guy. He was a beast. Veins popped out everywhere. Slung from his shoulder was a compact, finely machined shoulder weapon with a folding stock, an oversized magazine, an impressive-looking scope, and what appeared to be a silencer or the latest in flash suppressors. Black. Perfect for black ops. Totally badass. Fred wanted one. Nobody in the regular forces packed heat like that.

The mysterious visitor wore a sweat-stained Yankees cap and smoked aviator glasses. His hair was over his ears. Fred's was cut "high and tight." The visitor even had a nonregulation handlebar mustache.

Now what? "Halt, who goes there?" seemed ridiculous, but he was damned if he was going to be shown up on his own turf.

"That's loaded, isn't it?" said the visitor, eyeing Fred's .45.

"Who's asking?" Fred was pleased his voice hadn't cracked.

"A superior officer." While Fred hesitated, the visitor said patronizingly, "Do I look like a hostile or sound like one, Lieutenant Elder?"

"You must be confusing me with someone else, my friend," Fred retorted in his most no-nonsense tone.

"Cut the crap, Lieutenant."

"Are you in the military? I don't see any insignia, and this base is strictly off-limits to unauthorized civilians."

"That's affirmative, Lieutenant. And know this: I outrank you. By a great deal."

Fred did not dispute that claim.

"My bird and I choose to fly under the radar, Lieutenant. Now eject that round, uncock your piece, and holster it. At once, if you don't mind. I am aware of your CO's dumb-shit live ammo policy, and you're making me distinctly nervous, although, judging by what I've seen in your file, you don't always hit what you aim at."

Damned if he was backing down. "I'm calling out the guard," Fred croaked.

"For fuck's sake, Lieutenant, there's no guard, and you know it. Just a mob of shifty-eyed teenage delinquents shuffling around with their unloaded M1s. Now put your weapon back in its spit-shined holster. A holster that would, in the field, reflect sunlight like a signaling mirror."

He did so. Time to change the subject from his abject surrender. "What's that you're carrying?" Fred asked, in a voice that must, he realized, have sounded subservient.

The visitor said nothing, and his opaque lenses betrayed nothing.

He couldn't control himself. "What's its make? German?"

Continued silence.

"Can it fire fully automatic?"

The visitor cocked his head. "Wouldn't you think so, Lieutenant? Just by looking at it. Or do you think it's a muzzle loader?"

Fred resisted the urge to tug at his trousers. "Who else carries that baby? Can I get one?" He was mortified by his last question.

"Perhaps, but that's a long way off. If you're up to snuff, I may let you bust a few caps with this bad boy. But first, we've got a job to do."

"Job? What kind of a job?"

"You'll see, Tiger."

"When?"

"Now. You and I are taking a ride."

"A ride?" Something told him this would not be like a ride with Jayne Hoskins. "What are you talking about? I can't. I'm on duty." Then he got it. Initiation time.

Finally. Tonight, he'd learn the secret handshake. Maybe that wicked piece was for him. After his induction ceremony. Despite this revelation, he felt obliged to stay in character. In his most steely voice he said, "Negative. I'm Officer of the Day. You know I can't desert my post." He so wished he'd said, "Officer of the Fucking Day."

"Forget that post crap. It's been cleared."

"By whom? Regiment?"

"Roger your last."

"By Colonel Randall himself?"

"The very same. The word's been passed to your Duty NCO."

Had he played this out far enough?

"You can be extremely trying, Lieutenant. Stop pulling your pud and follow me. Chop-chop."

He followed. Reaching the helicopter, he grabbed for a handhold and, with a shove from the visitor, pulled himself up and in.

"Park yourself there and mind our little friend." Fred stumbled over something and fell into the canvas seat opposite the open door. The visitor strapped him in.

The helicopter was filthy. It stank of sweat, solvents, fuel, and something he later guessed was urine. Dirt and grease were everywhere. His uniform would never be the same.

The visitor stepped into what looked like a mountaineer's harness. It had a lead that he clipped to an anchor point on the fuselage. He snapped his weapon into a rack above the door and tapped the pilot's back.

Fred sensed something. He looked down, and staring back at him were a pair of dark, hate-filled eyes belonging to a small Asian who was trussed up like an oven-ready roast.

The visitor winked at him and said, "A little test, Lieutenant. You get to post a package. Airmail special delivery." Handing him a helmet, he said, "Put this on. That way, you and I and our chauffeur can chat with each other." Then he tapped the pilot twice.

The helicopter's engine roared, backfired, and caught. Its pendulous rotor blades awoke, shuddered, and, in seconds, clattered into a deafening orbit. The aircraft popped off the tarmac, hovered momentarily, pitched forward, and accelerated, picking up speed as it climbed.

"Can you hear me, Lieutenant?"

"Who's that?" he screamed, looking down at the captive.

"No concern of yours, Lieutenant."

"Where are we going?" He heard a snort. The pilot?

"About twenty klicks west of San Clemente Island."

"That's the middle of the ocean." His helmet was chafing.

"So it is, Lieutenant. Drop zone Zulu. Our obstinate friend's about to join some of his former compadres. Now yank that tape off his mouth."

He did so. "What's he done?" he asked.

"Ask him yourself, Lieutenant, but this boy's not very talkative. We know he speaks English, but not to us. I'd characterize his attitude as one of 'silent contempt,' or, as our Japanese allies say, *mokusatsu*. Give him this, he's one tough hombre. But take my word for it, his transgressions are legion. He richly deserves what's coming."

Fred couldn't look down.

"We'll be there in one five minutes, Lieutenant. You'll want to do the honors. Pop your cherry, so to speak."

Fred noticed there was nobody in the copilot's seat. Fewer witnesses.

The lights on San Clemente Island slid by beneath them. Next land-fall: Hawaii. Wind whipped through the cabin, suppressing the stench. There was nothing more to say. The minutes passed.

A light flashed on. "We have arrived. You get one bite at the apple, Mister."

Holy shit, it was one of those paralyzing "What now, Lieutenant?" moments. That's what the hard-ass Quantico instructors screamed at flustered second lieutenants they'd maneuvered into no-win situations. Fred was unable to speak.

"I'm not detecting much enthusiasm, Lieutenant. Think of it this way. Harvard has a fine crew. Visualize yourself tossing your winning cox into the Charles River. From a slightly higher altitude, of course."

Fred looked at his feet, shook his head, and checked the security of his harness. Would he need to defend himself? Did anyone know where he was?

"No? Are you absolutely sure about that? Okay, we're wasting fuel. Last chance to grow a pair, Stud. You've got one zero seconds. Still no? Alrighty-dighty. That's all she wrote. Time's up."

Fred tasted vomit. He closed his eyes.

"Watch and learn, young man." The visitor tapped the pilot and pressed himself against the fuselage. The helicopter banked to starboard. Steeply. Fred gasped and was thrown forward against his shoulder harness. The prisoner slid in the same direction. Towards the open door. Along a sheet of plywood tilted in that direction.

"Going, going . . ."

The prisoner was staring at him.

The visitor slammed the door closed. The helicopter reversed itself, banking hard to port. The prisoner slid back to the center of the aircraft. Using a box cutter, the visitor slashed the prisoner's bonds and, as Fred now saw, the cable securing him to the aircraft. It had been a test.

Sitting up, the prisoner rubbed his wrists and said, "Lieutenant Tran *à votre service*, as our French overlords put it."

"Say hello to your fellow lieutenant, a decorated South Vietnamese Marine," laughed the visitor. "And, while you're at it, thank Lieutenant Tran for his brilliant role-playing. At the moment, we're out of badasses in need of a dip, but I'm sure we won't be so constrained for long."

Fred felt sick.

"Don't fuckin' boot in my bird," growled the pilot, looking over his shoulder.

Fred could only nod.

"You screwed the pooch, Lieutenant. You coulda tried to shove him out the door. You coulda tried to save his ass, but you didn't do shit. Am I right?"

Lieutenant Tran's expression was indecipherable.

"I'm mighty disappointed, Lieutenant," said the visitor. "Our candidates seldom falter. You're not as advertised. Way overrated. But that's no skin off mine. As for you, you'll make a good . . . Shit, I don't know what you'd be good at."

"Roger your last," echoed the pilot.

Lieutenant Tran said nothing.

Fred remained silent on the flight back to base. He'd been gone under an hour.

They came in fast and low. The pilot lifted the helicopter's nose and dropped its tail. They lost speed instantly and touched down. Fred unstrapped and prepared to deplane. The visitor pushed him back into his seat while the pilot switched his radio to a civilian station. On came a rumba. With his left hand on the collective, his right on the cyclic, and his feet pumping the rudder pedals, the pilot and his aircraft flowed back and forth and side to side in perfect time with the music while maintaining an altitude never exceeding three feet.

When the music stopped, the visitor cried out, "Bravo, Xavier! Two ears and a tail for my squadron's top stick-and-rudder man," while the pilot—his face obscured by a helmet decorated with Tony the Tiger cutouts—bowed to the visitor, turned to Fred, and shook his head.

"Hard to do a victory roll in this bird," said the visitor.

Fred pulled himself out of his seat.

Catching Fred staring at the weapon over the door, the visitor said, "Sorry, Hoss. You gotta earn it, and you are *unfuckingsat*." Fred handed his helmet to the visitor and, keeping low to avoid a beaning, stumbled forward. The visitor grabbed him by his pistol belt and, looking him in the eye, said, "Just so we understand each other, Lieutenant, this never happened, and, in case you're wondering, you just flunked your entrance exam. Do you read me?"

Fred couldn't stop himself from nodding. The visitor released him, and he jumped heavily to the ground. His trousers were flecked with grease stains. A coating of dirt covered his shoes.

The helicopter leapt up and was gone in an instant—its sound merging into and being swallowed up by the incessant scratching of the crickets.

His stand-in was gone too. The Duty NCO handed him a letter and a fresh mug of coffee. Like all 3/11 mugs, this one bore the logo devised by its jerk-off CO: a tartan-clad highlander firing a 105mm howitzer above the words "We Cannonize On Call."

The letter was from his father reporting that Daniel Shaver, having followed him to Harvard, had joined the Corps and was reporting to OCS around Labor Day.

The following months were painful. While he never got it fully sorted out, Fred couldn't help feeling he'd let down the side. His father would have done better. What about Shaver? But it happened so quickly. Next time he'd do the right thing, or at least something.

11

DR. E

Much as it pains me to admit it, D-B is a bigger man than I. It's amazing we ever came to be friends.

In the first place, I had no right to be angry about his response to the Jayne Hoskins imbroglio. I'd have reacted in a similar fashion. Freddy was out of line, but I secretly admired his resourcefulness. I saw hope for my boy.

Back then everything about D-B irked me, and I'm afraid I didn't disguise my feelings. I saw it all as a charade. The languor. The flowing hair. The double-breasted blazers. No elbow patches for D-B. The nipped-in hacking jackets and, for certain ceremonial occasions, a beautifully sculpted morning coat, the cutaway front allowing ease of movement when on horseback. Mustn't forget the shoes. Bespoke Lobbs.[16] Worst of all: those boutonnieres. Insufferable. No, it's that signet ring. Roll out the tumbrels

D-B should have been an irresistible target for nasty teenage boys with an instinct for the jugular. But no, they guzzled his Kool-Aid. In fact, many of the boys with large allowances aped his wardrobe—not mine. As for the girls, there was always a line of them giggling outside *his* office door.

---

16 Mine were Dexters from Maine.

One of the saucier young ladies—she brought out the Humbert Humbert in a significant number of my colleagues—went so far as to mimic the things D-B did with his eyebrows, either or both of them. Our aspiring Lolita was big trouble, possessing the bewitching ability to transition from cherub to coquette to courtesan and back without uttering a word. It was all in her eyes and expressive mouth. Oh, what they seemed to imply. Or what the smitten chose to infer. A performance dauntingly advanced for someone so young. At the time, I concluded our teenage Circe would come to a bad end. Not so. At our last reunion she seemed happy and at ease. A Hera with a faithful Zeus.

If that weren't enough, D-B remains to this day feudal in outlook. Everyone at St. Matthew's, including the headmaster and, infuriatingly, me, is seen by him as socially *and* intellectually inferior. However, he means us no ill. Our status and his own were preordained, and so, like a medieval lord, he feels only sincere concern for us, his vassals. Most of my fellows are amused and delighted.

I almost forgot. D-B appears to be obscenely rich. This was apparent even before one of our sixth-formers, on an illegal trip to Boston, spotted him in the red Bentley he evidently keeps garaged on Beacon Hill. D-B's stock soared after this discovery. Another of his seigneurial gestures is to hand down barely worn clothing to his impecunious, similarly sized colleagues.

And, not that I'm obsessed with him, but what gives with those objects hanging from his watch fob? Badges of valor? Spoils from the boudoir? When I suggested the latter, he did one of his eyebrow tricks and said, "My daddy fought at Mons in 1914, but pour moi, it's Mons Veneris. And below the summit, the welcoming wetlands."

What to make of that? Braggadocio, or an effort to put the hounds off the scent?

While I've become fond of D-B, I'm losing ground to him. Should I update my fifth-century BC wardrobe? Should I wear my Purple

Heart? Not the medal itself. Just the modest ribbon in the lapel of my important-events blue blazer. It's discreet and would be a gentle reminder that D-B was never scratched. Perhaps he never left England. There's a term for that sort of thing—stolen valor.

The answer is a resounding "No!" Self-promotion is abhorrent. Besides, if asked, I'd have to admit I was wounded by a tree.

12

DANIEL

"**O**kay, Slater, here's the fucking deal," snarled Alpha Company's CO, Francis X. McCarthy—Captain Mac, as he was known behind his back. "You don't want to be here, and I sure as shit don't want you here fucking up *my* rifle company. Do I make myself clear, Mister?"

"Yes, sir!" replied Daniel Shaver in his most gung-ho voice, seasoned with a dollop of "up yours."

Captain Mac adjusted his chew, hawked, and fired a stream of brown liquid at the rat scuttling across the dirt floor of his bunker. "Didn't lead the fucker," he muttered.

The only other person in the bunker was a corporal, the captain's radioman. The captain continued, "This is a fighting outfit, and I don't babysit boot lieutenants, Slater. When I say jump, the answer's 'how fucking high.' Got that?"

"Yes, sir. It's Shaver, sir."

The radioman was staring at him insolently. The guy looked to be about forty, was missing the top half of his right ear, and was cleaning a foreign-looking pistol. A Walther? Damned if he knew.

Despite their difference in rank and the oppressive silence, it was clear the two of them were tight. Both struck Daniel as being efficient and enthusiastic takers of human life. A useful skill in their present setting.

"If I was you, Slater, I'd fucking stop staring at Corporal Szendrock. He's been taking care of business 'in every clime and place' for over twenty years, and he's fucking good at it. But here's the thing: He gets jumpy when people start asking about what he used to do. Where he fought. Who he fought. That kinda shit."

How could he stop staring? The guy was stocky with a tiny chin, huge nose, receding forehead, and protruding brows. No way were the Neanderthals extinct. And those teeth. Not a ringing endorsement of military dental work.

"It's Shaver, sir."

"You're fucking right you shave here, Slater. I'm running the leanest, meanest, hardest-charging herd of grunts in Nam. Not some hairy, hippy, fucked-up mob. Do you read me?"

It was difficult to take his mind off Captain Mac's missing finger. Combat? Or had the asshole stuck it into an unwelcoming aperture? "Loud and clear, sir."

"One other thing, Slater. You're meeting Corporal Szendrock on his way up. I'm planning to get him back to sergeant."

Szendrock grinned. Kee-rist. Those fucking teeth.

"But then some college puke like you'll bust him back to private."

Szendrock scowled. Fucking scary.

Why had he drawn Alpha Company and this crusty mustang who was equipped with every prejudice of those who'd risen through the ranks, the most significant being an indelible animus towards college "pussies," with the intensity of his loathing being directly related to the prestige of the candy-ass institution in question. Some of those below the Mason-Dixon line, like The Citadel and VMI, were marginally acceptable. Ring-knockers from the academies had to be tolerated and were sometimes grudgingly admired. Harvard was beneath contempt, a sorry collection of Commies, fags, and Commie fags. It would have been counterproductive to enlighten Captain Mac about the number of Harvard Medal of Honor winners. In the eyes of most jarheads, Captain Mac was the ideal Marine: cocky, tough, loyal, profane, and impenitently mulish.

"Where you from, Slater? Not that I give a shit, but I'm supposed to ask. Buncha crap, you ask me. Me, I'm from Southie—South Boston, to the likes of you—where you got three choices if you're not going into crime: politics, police, or the Corps. Make it four: Some misfits choose the Church." Captain Mac hawked again, this time in Daniel's direction. "And, just in case you don't know it, Slater, the Corps is about 50% Southie, 40% Johnny Reb, and 10%—does that make 100%?—assholes like you."

Daniel appreciated the irony. How could he resent being resented, particularly by someone who, for all he knew, might have begun life a rung or two above him on the ladder? It was, at last, a backhanded form of validation.

Finally, he was being taken for a Harvard man. This never happened in Cambridge, where, within a week of taking up residence in the Yard, his clothes, his haircut, his chipped tooth, and his accent branded him an untouchable to those of gentle, or somewhat gentler, birth. But the captain, whose origins couldn't have been humbler than his, had been taken in. *Perhaps*, he thought, *I'm on my way.*

Captain Mac, he learned in short order, earned his commission at the "Reservoir" after his platoon commander's frozen body, like that of a dead stag, was driven south to Hungnam on the hood of a jeep, and here he was seventeen years later, nothing more than a captain. Daniel considered and rejected the idea of reassuring the dickhead that he, Daniel Shaver, was not a lifer and wouldn't be competing with him for the coveted gold oak leaves of a major. Bad idea. The captain was a resentful prick, and for the moment, had him by the short and curlies.

Mustangs like him didn't give a rat's ass if their college-boy lieutenants got wasted. The more the merrier. Showed everyone that their outfits had been in the shit, and it opened doors for the corporals and sergeants, the real Marines. It was common knowledge that some officers' reputations were based on the rate they burned through young men wearing single bars. The thinking was it couldn't have been much of a show if too many lieutenants, who were expected to lead from the front, made it home intact.

How could he let this fuckhead know he'd been the top dog of his OCS platoon? Hadn't everyone on the parade ground, including the salty DIs, stopped to watch and holler as he and a fellow candidate enthusiastically pummeled the crap out of each other with their pugil sticks? Yes, they fucking had. He supposed he'd be recognized if he collected enough Charlie scalps.

"You know what, Slater," growled the captain, "with all the shit I've got on my plate, now I'm supposed to punch your ticket with some bona-fucking-fide grunt time. What does my company look like, a fucking kindergarten? How the fuck long have you been in this fucked-up country?"

"We could forget about the whole thing, sir. Excuse me, the whole fucking thing."

The captain shot him a look. "You best not try fucking with me, Mister." Captain Mac pointed his missing finger at an upended ammo box. "Sit!"

He sat. The captain needed a shower, and his utilities looked as though they hadn't been washed since Korea.

"Here we are," said the captain, pointing to a large-scale map hanging from his bunker's sandbagged wall. "You need a nursemaid, for Chrissake? Get out your fucking map."

Captain Mac snickered and said, "Slater, you're so fucking dumb you probably don't know which hand to wipe your ass with."

Szendrock emitted a strangled laugh.

Fuck that. Why should he take this bullshit? He was a commissioned officer and closer to being a gentleman than this knucklehead. Typical mustang crap, playing to the snuffies to make junior officers look like wimps, incompetents, or handjobs.

Before he could check himself, he fired back, "At Harvard, we were taught to use toilet paper, sir!"

That was ill-advised. Captain Mac narrowed his eyes and spat a soggy something at Daniel's boots. The captain's temples were throbbing. A vein looked ready to explode. Szendrock was coiled to pounce.

"Okay, Mister, haul out your fucking grease pencil and mark Alpha's position on your map. Yeah, right there. Here's the deal, you're going out to snoop and poop. And that's it. I'm giving you a squad-sized mob of newbies, plus a radio humper, a dog team, and a scout named Nguyen. By the way, keep an eye on that fucker. He's probably VC."

Christ on a crutch. What was he supposed to do about the scout? Evidently, his unease was obvious.

"Don't sweat it, Slater. It'll be a piece of cake. The rainy season's over, so you'll have a walk in the fucking sun. You can all pop your cherries together. You're a grunt, aren't you?"

"Yes, sir. Infantry, 0302."

"Can you call in artillery?"

Fuck yes, asshole, he thought. "Yes, sir, I can," he said.

"Well, show me. Here's your position," said Captain Mac, pointing to a place on the map. "And here's a VC patrol. You're the forward observer, and I'm the fire direction center. Now blow the fuckers away. Let's rock and roll!"

He called in the fire mission and, after two adjustments, fired for effect. The captain's absence of sarcasm and obscenities amounted, he supposed, to high praise.

"This your first time in the bush?"

"Yes, sir."

"Okay, I get it. You've been up at regiment pulling your college-boy pud."

"I've been in the regiment's S-2 section, sir. When do we move out?"

"At first light, you and *my* Marines will exit our position and proceed northeasterly—I'll get you the azimuth—approximately four klicks, that's kilometers."

He winced. "I know what a klick is, sir." Szendrock bared his yellow fangs. A sneer? A smirk? A snarl? His first day and he was about to become the laughingstock of the company.

"And see what you can see, which won't be jack shit. Nothing's happened around here in weeks. We're getting fucking bored and stale. Then you 'about-face' and get your sad ass and everyone else's back here. You can even use the same route. That's how quiet it's been, and that's why I'm not wasting a corpsman on your training hike."

"Will that be all, Skipper?"

"Getting fucking salty with that 'Skipper' shit, aren't you? And no, it's not all, not by a fucking long shot."

Time for a wake-up call. The sassy approach that was tolerated stateside didn't seem to cut it here. During OCS he'd been amused by his drill instructors' attempts to intimidate. Yes, they could make him temporarily miserable, but it was not within their remit to maim or kill him. What could they do? Send him to Nam? However, Captain Mac had countless options.

"Two things to remember, Slater. This is fucking Alpha Company, First Battalion, First Marines. Chesty's old regiment. Charlie shits his knickers when he learns he's up against us. I made my bones in this regiment. Alpha's the first. In everything. We're the best of the best. We do not fuck up or, God help us, give up. Ever. Do you read me?"

"Five-by-five, sir. Will there be anything else, sir?"

Captain Mac stood and adjusted his balls. "You fucking with me again, Slater? You think you're in the fucking Navy with all that pussy 'will there be anything else' shit? You think I've forgotten something? You think I'm fucking stupid, because I didn't go to your faggot college? That it, Slater?"

"No, sir. Absolutely not, sir." Szendrock was barely controlling himself.

"Okay, here it is, *boy*. Take care of *my* Marines or you'll be hearing from me personally. I shit you not."

"Yes, sir."

"One other thing—you can drop all those fucking 'sirs.' Any VC around these parts, they hear that crap they'll wax my hairy ass. And we sure as shit wouldn't want that, would we?"

"No, sir."

Captain Mac hauled the remains of a cigar from his breast pocket, lit it, and growled, "Okay, then, Slater. Don't screw up tomorrow. I'd say 'good hunting,' but there ain't shit out there to hunt. The fucking Army's having all the fun right now. You're leading, and I mean leading, a pussy recon patrol. If you're any damn good, which I fucking doubt, I may let you go scalp hunting."

"I'd like that, Captain."

"Goddamnit, you really do want to get my tail shot off, don't you? Okay, remember this: Stay on the ball, maintain control, keep track of people, muzzle the dog, watch the fucking scout, don't get separated, and bring every fucking one of *my* jarheads—regardless of race, color, or creed, as you pukes would say—back in one piece. Your call sign's 'Blackcoat.' No air support, but you'll have a battery of 105s from 3/11 on call if you need 'em."

Freddy's old outfit. They were bound to be fuckups.

"What if we're cut off, sir?"

"For fuck's sake, if you're in trouble, call Mommy, and she'll air drop you some tampons."

"I'm sure that won't be necessary, sir."

"Fucking well better not be. Okay, my XO will brief you on radio frequencies and the other shit. Think you can remember all that, Harvard boy?"

"Aye, aye, Skipper."

"Sweet fucking Jesus."

McCarthy handed him a tightly wrapped cylinder. "Take this with you."

He must have looked puzzled.

"It's a USMC recruiting poster. Nail it to a fucking tree in Charlie's backyard."

Szendrock screamed with delight.

———

His first trip into Indian country, and it was fucking stifling. Had to be in the nineties, temperature and humidity, both. His skivvies were riding up his ass. Like he'd been warned. Everyone was edgy. And smelly. The anxiety was contagious. Canteens had been drained, leaving nothing for the slog back. Hadn't that asshole LBJ promised to get them out of this shit?

So far, the walk in the sun had been a bitch. He'd stumbled over a root or a vine or some fucking thing, going flat on his face. There'd been a derisive laugh from one of the snuffies. Nobody had given him a hand. Just kinda stared into space. At least it wasn't a trip wire. Positioned near the head of the column with his radioman—a thick fuck named Rubino—he led from the front. It was textbook. They made decent time, and the two flankers he put out managed to maintain contact.

But Nguyen, their scout, had been gone for nearly an hour. Lance Corporal Dalton and Corporal Fritz, a German shepherd, were with him. Dalton was an unknown quantity and, for that matter, so was Fritz, just returned from retraining. As was the custom, Fritz outranked his handler. Fritz had been attached to Charlie Company but would have nothing more to do with it after seeing one of its men shoot a stray dog whose barking had given away the company's position. As for Dalton, he was more attached to Fritz than his new unit.

He resisted the temptation to recheck his pistol. That might suggest anxiety or uncertainty, the last thing he needed. Besides, he'd field-stripped and cleaned it thoroughly, if not obsessively, before they set out. Every cartridge had been wiped clean. Same with his three magazines, all of them rust-free with perfectly working springs. Ditto his shotgun.

Something made him feel he was losing control. He was afraid the men felt this. Nguyen—was everybody in this fucking country named Nguyen?—had unceremoniously told him, ordered him was more like it, to halt the patrol in a slightly elevated stand of trees roughly half the size of a football field. The grove was surrounded on all sides by dry, brown elephant grass.

"Good visibility here, no visibility there," said Nguyen, pointing. "Good shade too," he added, smiling. The fucker was always smiling.

He didn't trust Nguyen for shit, and it showed. Sergeant Foster, his number two, was totally out of order in suggesting he stop referring to Nguyen as "that beady-eyed fuck."

"He's supposed to be on our side, Lieutenant," Foster said, adding, "and he may understand more than we think."

The insolent fuck. "Not your hunt, Sergeant," he replied.

Foster gave him a sullen look and slouched off.

He didn't trust dogs either, particularly German shepherds. Ditto dog nuts like Dalton. Why had he given in to Nguyen and allowed the three of them to go wandering off the reservation? Captain Mac would have his ass.

He'd tried to befriend the dog, even patted it a few times, but the fucker put its ears back, made deep, unfriendly noises, and, like Szendrock, showed his teeth. Dalton laughed and said, "Watch it, Lieutenant. Fritz don't like Charlie or officers neither." He'd fix both of them when they got back inside the wire.

In a voice audible to everyone, Nguyen had pointed and said, "Wind blowing towards us. Dog smell VC when he gets close. We check tree line. There." Hearing nothing from him, Nguyen said, "We go. Now. Back soon." Then he motioned to Dalton, and with Fritz pulling eagerly on his leash, the two of them cocked their weapons, trotted into the unforgiving, shoulder-high grass, crouched, and disappeared.

Should he be reassured by Nguyen's superb fieldcraft? Or suspicious? Most of the South Vietnamese officers he knew were at their best in bars and cat houses but not worth shit in the boonies, which, quite sensibly, they made every effort to avoid.

Nguyen, not much taller than his rifle, was, he noticed, completely at home in the bush. He moved through it fluidly and silently, seemingly mindful of wind, light, shadows, obstacles, footing, and the presence of others. Uneasy-making.

Ah, the memories he had of their allies, the dick-off South Vietnamese Marines he trained with in Basic School. Every one of those clowns crapped out on hikes, usually in the first mile, then lay sprawled by the side of the road, waiting for the meat wagon to haul them back to the base. They were drinking, compliments of the US taxpayer, at the O-club by the time the round-eyes staggered back to the Bachelor Officer Quarters and crashed.

On weekends they'd pack up their equipment and, secure in the knowledge they'd be issued new gear on Monday with no questions asked, sell it at an Army-Navy store in DC owned by one of their compatriots. Then it was off to a Post Exchange where they scarfed up electrical appliances for which there was a ready market in Saigon. Their rooms in the BOQ, which, for political reasons, were exempt from inspection, looked like General Electric warehouses.

He'd felt comfortable with those slicked-back cowboys in their Nguyen Cao Kyish aviator shades and white silk scarves. They were dissolute good ol' boys, Far East variety. The silent, ascetic scout gave him the creeps.

Anyhow, he'd salvaged something. Despite the scout's jabbering, he hadn't allowed Nguyen to grab Rubino, his lifeline. "You spot Charlie, get your ass back here ricky-tick, and I'll call in arty," he advised Nguyen in his most colonial tone. He sensed tentative approval from the other members of the patrol. But why the fuck hadn't feckless Sergeant Foster given him a hand? Foster was a lifer, for fuck sakes. Didn't he know where his bread was buttered? Had he heard this was Shaver's first patrol? Did the prick want to show him up?

Foster had just been promoted to Sergeant E-5 and was rip-shit about having been transferred from a cushy "in the rear with the gear" billet in motor transport. Tough titty. The division was running short of infantry, and wasn't everyone—as the Marine party line went—a rifleman? Foster hadn't done dick during his dustup with Nguyen. Just shrugged, picked at his rifle with a filthy toothbrush, and continued lackadaisically deploying the men in a defensive perimeter that looked half-assed, even to him. Didn't he remember some shit about interlocking fields of fire?

What a balls-up. He was even less happy than Foster. His boss, the regimental S-2, told him, almost apologetically, it was mandatory for every junior officer to serve some bush time. In an effort to make light of what could be a death sentence, the S-2 said, "You won't be getting your end wet in that bush."

It had been a most cruel betrayal. What had he done to displease the S-2, Major Meredith Cole, University of New Hampshire '54, who, noticing Shaver was from Lower Finley, had dramatically increased his chance of survival by plucking him from a replacement draft slated to fill gaps in the shot-up rifle companies?

He remembered Cole's exact words, "My gofer lieutenant's just flown back to the World, and being a Harvard man, there's an outside chance people won't laugh in your face when you say you're an intelligence officer." Had he been spared? Negative. A few weeks later he'd been shipped off to Alpha Company.

To console him, he'd been assured his banishment wouldn't last more than a month. Major Cole didn't want anyone figuring out he had no need of an assistant. And how bad could it be? Little or nothing had happened in the regiment's area of operations for weeks, and, as was usually true at this time of year, the weather was halfway decent. Everyone was feeling fat, dumb, and happy. But it couldn't last. Body counts had dropped, and the higher-ups needed well-posed pictures of prostrate bodies to advance their careers and show dubious politicians and jealous rivals in other branches that the Crotch was not just another land army and, therefore, redundant.

There were various schools of thought about displaying the kill. Cruder types leaned towards tangled piles, while the more refined favored neat linear presentations of the sort found at the conclusion of a well-run pheasant shoot. An imaginative minority used the bodies like letters or Lincoln Logs, to spell out messages or build things. It was tough on everyone. To guarantee its survival, the Crotch had to kill more, die more, and cost materially less doing so. It was fucking inexcusable. Those pussy generals, letting their Marines mix it up while equipped with anything less than the best. Marines must make do. Bullshit!

So far, conditions hadn't changed. Contacts with hostiles were rare, and for the last month, the bulk of the regiment's casualties had come from exhausted, sometimes stoned, not wildly bright teenagers screwing up with complex, deadly machinery.

He asked himself again, "How bad could it be?" Hadn't he, Lieutenant Daniel Shaver, grown up skulking through the woods like a Penacook brave with his guide and mentor, Gideon? Under his brother's tutelage, he'd become adept at making himself inconspicuous and deadly. At Basic School, he was the best shot in his platoon and proved to be adept with maps during the field exercises.

Whenever he studied a map, the meandering contour lines, which to many looked like giant fingerprints, came alive, quickly resolving themselves into three-dimensional likenesses of his surroundings, while the symbols in the map's legend became the terrain features he saw around him. It was a gift. One of the few benefits of his upbringing. But not, he suspected, of great value on Wall Street, his next destination.

13

DR. E

I had a number of reasons for choosing to help Daniel Shaver escape what I saw as his destiny. Yes, he was a teenage monster, but somewhere beneath it all I perceived faint intimations of decency. So, I offered my assistance to this latent Polyphemus.

Any doubts I may have had about Daniel's future if he remained with his family were resolved when I saw a shirtless and hungover Gideon hotdogging through the fields on the Shavers' new John Deere, a powerful machine that could obliterate our tennis court. Pa was sheltering behind a stone wall screaming, "For Chrissake, be careful of the damn thing. It's fucking uninsured."

The exuberant Gideon flipped his father the bird just before driving the gleaming green tractor into a ditch and, from the sound of it, breaking something important.

I had a good view of this from a second-story window. Thinking Gideon almost certainly needed help, I found a first aid kit and raced downstairs.

Seeing what was happening, I stopped. There was Gideon, standing in the field with his eyes fixed on the horizon as his father beat him bloody with a broken two-by-four. After exhausting himself, father Shaver dropped his cudgel and walked silently back to his house, where, according to Daniel, he grabbed a six-pack of Gansetts, several bags of chips, and turned on the Sox.

It wasn't over. In a few days, when he was feeling up to it, Gideon, using the same piece of wood—why not, it was the obvious choice—pummeled Daniel, chipping one of his teeth in the process. Daniel demurred when I asked him if he'd cried or taken out *his* anger on the farm animals. As they say in the service, "shit flows downhill."

I continued to believe in Daniel, even though a significant number of my fellows wanted him expelled.

However, for almost every discreditable act cited by the prosecution, I countered with instances of spontaneous kindness. Exhibit A: Clarence Powers, one of Daniel's more troubled classmates. Powers was an ideal victim in an environment where the high art of bullying was, and to a certain extent still is, regarded as a time-honored way of weeding out—or shaping up—the unfit. His grades were mediocre, and Powers was small, homely, unathletic, and, therefore, friendless. But that was just the half of it.

Despite endless brushing, flossing, and rinsing, Clarence Powers had a breath capable of melting steel or reinforced concrete. He could have been used in WWII to neutralize bunkers or knock out enemy armor. To cap it off, he stammered.

Daniel learned that one of Clarence's nastiest tormentors had struck "flowers" from the opening line of a popular song, so that, as revised, it went, "Take away the breath of Powers." Clarence would be serenaded with this several times a day.

Then, like Henry V, Daniel sprang into the breach, and soon those unkind words were heard no more. Remarkably, Daniel accomplished this without the shedding of blood. A single black eye did the trick.

Was I overdoing it when I quoted Portia's "The quality of mercy is not strained" speech in my repeated arguments on Daniel's behalf?[17]

---

17 D-B eventually became a staunch ally in my campaign to save Daniel.

14

DANIEL

The Shaver boys had varied woodland routines. Sometimes they'd trap their prey. Then they'd release it, stalk it, and finally kill it—their own form of live skeet shooting. Daniel, the loyal younger brother, was an able apprentice but resented having to make do with the bolt-action, single-shot .22 while Gideon strutted about with a proven man-killer, the twelve-gauge trench gun Pa smuggled back from the Pacific. It cost Daniel another chipped front tooth before he accepted his subordinate status.

Gideon's role as oppressor and tutor ended dramatically one summer morning as he was playing the male lead in a familiar pastoral drama, *The Double-Backed Beast*. Gideon's costar was Daisy, a fickle, flighty, but attractively patterned Holstein, who, just prior to consummation, veered off script and, while intending her leading man no harm, crushed his chest with a single, unanticipated kick.

It seemed to have been going so well. Having attended to the preliminaries with Daniel's assistance, Gideon mounted a milking stool and began.

Daniel would never forget Gideon's expression of shock and surprise as, still aroused but ungratified, he began drifting off to an idyllic hereafter where farm animals were more obliging. It was shocking.

Gideon had assured him this was old hat, and on such matters Gideon was infallible.

Before racing home to alert Pa, Daniel had the foresight to attend to his brother's coveralls (he would always remember Gideon's unfocused, departing look as this was taking place) and move Daisy to the adjacent field. This may have been his brother's undoing. Gideon had died by the time he and Pa got back to him.

Though the matter was never aired, Daniel was certain Pa was one of Daisy's regulars. Pa hadn't bought the story that Gideon tripped, tumbled onto a boulder, and smashed in his chest, causing massive internal bleeding. The senior Shaver looked at his surviving son, stared affectionately at Daisy, who was grazing nearby, adjusted his trousers, and loudly passed gas.

Thereafter, whenever Daniel heard the word "cowed," he was transported back to that pasture and his dying brother.

Later in the day, while Daniel was outside readying his illegal fireworks for mischief on the Fourth, Pa shouted at him from the living room, where he was watching the Sox and guzzling Gansetts. "Hey, kid, c'mere." The game was almost over, the Sox were, as usual, getting trounced by the Yankees, and Pa was in one of his moods. Noncompliance was not an option.

Daniel presented himself to his father, who put down his beer, handed him the shotgun, and said, "Here, it's yours. It took out a lot of Nips in its day." He paused. "And here's a beer," he said, as he cracked a fresh one for himself. Daniel turned to leave before his father changed his mind, but stopped in his tracks when his old man yelled, "Fix the fuckin' rabbit ears, will ya? I can't see shit."

It was a difficult summer for the Shavers. Soon after Gideon was laid to rest in the family's shady plot off Route 139, it was Pa's turn. The way Daniel heard it, Ma had been riding Pa's ass about getting a jump on the winter's firewood. On the afternoon in question, Pa was crapped out in the hammock after his regular lunch of chips and Gansetts. This time the Tigers were kicking ass at Fenway. Verna Shaver was hard to deflect when she was in full cry, so Pa groaned, rolled out of the hammock, topped up the chain saw, and headed to the woodshed.

If he hollered, nobody heard him. Somehow, he managed to get his truck halfway to Finley Community Hospital before he went into a ditch and bled out, making a terrible mess in the cab. It's challenging to drive a standard transmission with only one functioning leg.

Pa was buried next to Gideon's still raw mound in a grave dug by the new man of the house, this time without assistance. As he watched his father's casket being lowered into the indifferent, acidic soil, Daniel realized the needles from the towering evergreens acted as mulch, suppressing unwelcome plant life and reducing the cemetery's maintenance costs to virtually nothing. One of his resourceful ancestors figured out that nature herself could provide perpetual care.

There were worse places to put down roots than among his forebears. Yes, there were Elders here, but they were outnumbered. What about markers for Pa and Gideon? He and Ma couldn't afford anything right then, so he'd placed as big a boulder as he could move at the head of each grave. He had to act before the heartless New Hampshire winter erased all signs of where they reposed. He supposed he'd continue the family tradition and go with slate even though it was prone to fracture. The high-and-mighty Elders used marble, but their earliest markers were badly discolored and virtually illegible.

15

DR. E

Thinking back to that summer, I can't help but wonder if Daniel, my ambitious protege, appreciated his debt to Daisy. She rid him of the elder brother who would have kept him in bondage, and taught him an invaluable life lesson. If you fancy animals, begin with a less daunting partner, such as a resigned, compliant ewe.

What Daniel took away from the summer's deaths was the realization he'd need a college degree if he hoped to afford premium beer. But first, St. Matthew's.

D-B's response to my veiled disclosure[18] was typically nuanced. Having considered the matter, he offered the following: "I remain dubious of bestiality. After all, what to do once that beautiful, fleeting moment's passed? A shared cigarette? On the plus side, your partner cannot claim what just occurred was nonconsensual."

D-B and I, it turns out, have rather a lot in common. Like so many men, we tend to glorify the previous generation. Unlike earlier conflicts, we saw our mechanized war as unglamorous. D-B so wished to have ridden with the Imperial Camel Corps or executed wingovers in a Sopwith Camel (Why camels? Echoes of Empire?) instead of being

---

18 It goes without saying that I concealed the parties' identities.

confined in a noisy, filthy, undergunned tank. Oh, to have been a dragoon, hussar, or lancer. To have worn rows of medals, epaulettes, dazzling sashes, and, most assuredly, a saber. To have led the life of a John Buchan hero. To have had hair's-breadth escapes. To have stuck pigs. To have saved swooning damsels from woman-eating lions and marauding elephants.

What, we wondered, will be said of us? Hard to visualize us being eulogized. But, soft! Our stock is rising. Those who weren't there are referring to our cohort as the Greatest Generation. What do they know? Who cares? It beats "Lost" and "Silent."

16

DANIEL

Yes, he, Daniel Shaver, was going to get laid *and* get ahead. The idea of the Simulator came to him while "abusing" himself, as the chaplain would have put it, beneath the covers in his unheated alcove at St. Matthew's, the half-timbered, nineteenth-century pile in Massachusetts to which he'd been exiled. And he'd thought Lower Finley was the pits. At least it had a restaurant, a town green, a cannon, a granite soldier, a crumbling bandstand, a white Congo Church, a spa with a pinball machine, and shit like that.

It was Dr. Elder's doing. He arranged for the full scholarship and talked Ma into releasing him. It hadn't been difficult. He wouldn't be missed. Gideon had been her favorite and Pa's too. Verna Shaver's only response to Dr. Elder's offer of a free ride had been "That fancy school of yours better not turn my boy into no homo."

He hated the place. No guns. No Camels. No Gansetts. No pussy. Not that he knew much about that yet. Being put back a grade was a major embarrassment. He'd be shaving, for fuck's sake, before his classmates' nuts dropped.

It was Diana, the stacked school nurse, who inspired the Simulator and was responsible for the infirmary's being chronically overbooked. Certain Masters referred to her as the "muse of moist sheets."

So, he named the Simulator in her honor. Diana, a form of training aid, was intended to bring hope to the hopeless, to encourage losers like Freddy Elder to believe that if given a chance with a live girl, they might not be called out on strikes. However, before moving to the production phase, he had to figure out what breasts really looked like. The lingerie ads pored over by him and his peers inflamed but provided no practical guidance.

Then it all clicked, and he was off to the school library, where he used his X–Acto knife to detach the relevant pages from a *National Geographic* article about sub-Saharan Africa. He took it on faith—faith being harped on in chapel—that African knockers were not materially different from Diana's. If perchance they were, none of his prospective customers would be the wiser.

He fabricated Diana using the very chain saw that felled his father and unveiled her to a rapt audience of animated adolescents soon after returning from his first Thanksgiving break. He'd given much thought to site selection. The ceremony called for an inspirational setting.

He and about twenty schoolmates gathered in Dr. Elder's recently dedicated Latin classroom. It was named in honor of Second Lieutenant Gabriel Ellsworth, St. Matthew's '39. Lieutenant Ellsworth never made it to Tarawa's seawall. By the time the remnants of his platoon reached that illusory shelter, it was commanded by a corporal, and Gabriel Ellsworth, after less than ten minutes under fire, was floating facedown in the carmine lagoon.

Daniel opened his sales pitch with the depressing observation that, given his clean-cut reputation, Gabriel Ellsworth might well have died a virgin, a fate not to be wished on anyone. Then he called for a volunteer—everyone raised a hand—and a fortunate third-former whisked away the soiled pillowcase shrouding Diana. The unveiling was greeted by gasps, whistles, laughter, and the drumming of excited feet.

Using his pointer as a gavel to restore order, he cried out, "You clowns are as horny as a herd of whitetails, am I right?" More cheers. "What you see before you is an anatomically accurate model of a young lady from her shoulders to her belly button." It surely wasn't, but who would know?

More yelps and sustained applause. No reason to admit that Diana's tired brown bra was not a trophy but a prop snitched from Ma's bureau.

"Watch this," he shouted, stepping up to Diana and undoing her single article of clothing using only the thumb and index finger of his right hand, refastening it, and repeating the feat with his left. That earned him a standing ovation. "Here's the deal. Notice those two little hooks." Everyone strained for a view. "Apply gentle pressure, and presto, you're into second base. Remember! No pinching. It'll take a while to get the hang of Diana, but when you do, you'll know it, she'll know it, and more importantly, so will your dates."

No St. Matthew's Master had ever addressed a more attentive class. It was almost too easy. "Mats"—think doormats—as St. Matthew's boys were known by their peers, were generally all of a piece. Like livestock—Daisy excluded—they were well-mannered, docile, and easily led. Most of them received large allowances. They were ready to be sheared and were always astonished when that occurred.

It being his mentor's classroom, Daniel couldn't resist ending his presentation with a nod to the classics. "If Julius Caesar had the Simulator, he'd have marched into Gaul and declared, 'Vidi, vici, veni.'" No reason to point out that, according to the pedantic Dr. Elder, the divine Diana, goddess of, among other things, domestic animals, was a prude.

Then some wiseass yelled, "If I make it to first, why can't I cut across the infield to third? Or just turn around and race home?"

Somewhat unsure of himself, Daniel replied, "It doesn't work that way, jerk. You gotta touch all the bases."

Despite the interruption, all went well. Promising his potential customers they'd be ambidextrous by Christmas and charging only a dollar for a full fifteen-minute session, he'd soon earned enough to initiate Operation Mary Foley, named in honor of the eighteen-year-old waiting tables at Lower Finley's only restaurant.

When he got home for Christmas, he bought Ma a new pair of Keds but did not return or replace her bedraggled undergarment.

17

DR. E

W hat, I frequently wonder, would have become of Daniel Shaver if I'd simply let nature run its course? Would he have been content taking over the family farm and perhaps making something of it? What if he'd married smart, sexy Mary Foley—I can think of worse fates—and returned the Shavers to something approaching respectability? But that wasn't—and isn't—Daniel Shaver. With my urging, he aimed higher. Ad astra per aspera,[19] as I liked telling him. So, perhaps unwisely, I intervened.

My biggest mistake may have been the "enrichment" trip to the Worcester Art Museum. Just as I'd taken Freddy and a pair of his classmates when they were first-formers, now it was Daniel's turn to be introduced to culture. The Antioch mosaic depicting hunters slaughtering wild animals with every weapon in the ancient world's armory—swords, spears, and bows—was a compelling way to begin. Red-blooded lads couldn't help but be energized.

I pulled up to the stately Beaux Arts palace and told Daniel and his friend, Arthur Whittall, to meet me at the gory mosaic, just inside the main door.

---

19 This well-known exhortation—to the stars through hardships, or words to that effect—also happens to be the aspirational state motto of Kansas.

Having parked and entered, I was intercepted by an elderly guard.
He looked concerned. Pointing down a corridor, he said, "They went
that way."

Nearly half an hour later, the two miscreants were discovered, riv-
eted in place, mouths agape, staring at an unclothed woman from
their hideout in the back of a life class. How could I blame them?
Even paying customers at the Old Howard, Scollay Square's famous
striptease palace,[20] weren't offered such enrichment.

While I was obliged to feign displeasure, I couldn't really blame the
boys. St. Matthew's in those days bore a remarkable resemblance to
the stalags in which Allied POWs passed their time in captivity hatch-
ing plans to escape. In this case, all was revealed with no risk of being
electrocuted on the wire, shot by trigger-happy guards, or suffocating
in a collapsed tunnel.

Driving back to St. Matthew's, I told Daniel, who was lolling in
the back seat with a Mickey Spillane, that he was fortunate not to
have suffered the fate of Tiresias, who was blinded by Athena after he
came upon her bathing naked. All I got for my apt allusion was a sour
grunt. Anyhow, I couldn't help but wonder whether I possessed any
hitherto untapped artistic talent. After all, Worcester was only thirty
miles away.

Yes, I wish I'd had a similar experience in my early teens. The
ample, slightly squishy Renoiresque model was a yummy confection,
which as we know rhymes with . . .

Stop it, you old goat.

What's more, she gave me a special look—she really did—as I was
leading away my two captives.

---

20 Yes, as a Harvard undergraduate I went there, but only infrequently, and never at the
    expense of my studies. Was I—am I?—insufferable?

18

DANIEL

That was then, but now he, First Lieutenant Daniel Shaver, USMCR, was in a shit sandwich. Thanks to Dr. Elder's friend in Harvard's admissions office who tipped the scales in his favor and convinced him to sign up for NROTC. It made sense at the time. The early '60s were quiet, and Uncle Sam picked up his tuition. But then he got stupid, and, in an effort to upstage Freddy Elder, signed up with the Marines and, dumbest of all, opted for infantry. *Not to worry,* he thought. If it hit the fan, he could always wangle a cushy tour in an embassy or a civilized duty station while the dumb-shit lifers scrambled for combat billets. Besides, why would Uncle Sam squander a Harvard man when there was a surplus of lesser beings?

Then, along came Tonkin Gulf and its aftermath. So here he was in the Crotch with crotch rot and decaying feet, a tasty snack for the insects and leeches, while back in the States, cunning undergraduates had well-connected relatives call in favors or fabricated their own disabilities.

Enough with the pissing and moaning. Nam was not the place to appear inept or play the hard-ass. It was common knowledge that dangerously incompetent or overzealous junior officers were prime fragging candidates. Time to roll his own, light up, take a nonchalant drag, and audibly exhale a well-formed smoke ring. Just as Gideon had taught him.

He unslung his twelve-gauge and checked its action. The shotgun went nicely with the devil-may-care boonie hat he'd worn in place of his steel pot. If only there'd been a sultry Ava Gardner to play opposite his dashing Stewart Granger.

The numbnuts snuffies seemed impressed. He reached into his shirt, hauled out his map, and, after studying his surroundings, marked the patrol's position with a red grease pencil. Next, he placed an X on the ominous tree line, following which he calculated the coordinates of both locations, recorded them, and directed Rubino to radio them back to Alpha and 3/11. Growing up in the weeds continued to serve him well. He was a whizz at what somebody had incongruously named "terrain appreciation."

"Hey, Lieutenant," yelled Foster, pointing to his cigarette. "Does that mean the peons can light up?" That fucker. Announcing for all to hear that he'd forgotten the snuffies. He ignored the snickers.

"That's affirmative, Sergeant."

"One other thing, Lieutenant," said the insolent Foster, this time in a quieter voice. "You might think about wrapping some electrical tape around your shiny lighter. Maybe Rubino could loan you some."

Okay, Fuckhead, he thought, *That tears it. You've just drawn an eternity of shitter burning.*

And what about Nguyen? Could that shifty-eyed fuck be trusted? He'd been with Alpha for less than a week, having been fobbed off on it by some Vietnamese politician his division commander hadn't had the balls to offend. Typical. It was all about getting his ticket punched, not fucking up worse than the Army, and hauling ass back to the World for his third star. Even worse, Nguyen was a Kit Carson scout, one of those untrustworthy mothers who'd supposedly seen the light and switched sides.

And then there was Dalton and his eager mutt. All right, technically speaking Fritz wasn't a mutt. But Dalton's priorities were fucked-up big time. He was sick of Dalton going on about the hours of praise and play that had gone into his damned dog's rehabilitation.

"Fritz is good to go, Lieutenant."

"You sure? A couple weeks ago he was as useless as tits on a boar. He fell apart outside the wire. Every fucking time. Howling. Whining. Cringing. Pissing himself. Just like a Doggie."

Dalton laughed. The Army was always fair game. "Corporal Fritz has gotten his shit together; he's fully mission-capable, sir."

Fuck Dalton, his "good dog" bullshit, and the frigging rubber ball he carried for Fritz to fetch and gnaw on. Maybe he'd like to chase a live grenade. A better name for the endlessly crapping mutt would have been "Dumpster." Yes, Dumpster it would be.

"Hey, Dalton," he'd yelled, "don't forget to bury his crap."

Dalton only nodded.

Their position shat the bed. No cover, if you didn't count the seven-foot-high termite hill, and damn little concealment. Admittedly, the trees provided welcome relief from the sun, but the place was alive with things that flew, bit, sucked, and slithered into your openings. What about snakes? He'd heard a lot about big-ass cobras, for fuck's sake. And who could forget the five-step snakes? That was as far as you got after one of *them* bit you.

Leeches? You bet your sweet ass. Some of the saltier guys even talked about tigers. About some jerk-off who got chewed to pieces while wrapped in his poncho liner. Who the fuck knew? Sure, visibility was improved by being slightly above the grass, but what the fuck was going on in that crackling brown maze? It never stopped moving. And rustling. Was it the wind? Nguyen? Dalton? Dumpster? Or a company of NVA regulars about to envelop them and clean their clocks? Nobody seemed eager to get off his butt and check things out. He sure as shit wasn't.

He was certain of it now. In addition to his creeping skivvies, he had a big mother leech up his ass. Should he drop trou, spread 'em, and have Foster burn it off with his Lucky? Show his guys he was one of them? Negative, that would be fucking undignified. And he sure as shit didn't want anyone getting the wrong idea.

None of this crap had been taught at Quantico. You were supposed to die cleanly, quietly (only snuffies whimpered for their mommies), and telegenically (not in untidy pieces) while leading your melting-pot mob up a steep, booby-trapped, heavily fortified hill in a dumb-shit, Pickett-like frontal assault with the sun in your eyes. But not this. His troops would watch and remember.

Basically, they were hunkered down on a big fucking bull's-eye. Even he realized that, but Foster didn't appear upset, so it would have been poor form for the patrol leader to look antsy by the termite hill. He'd have to remember that one. In fact, Foster had taken off his helmet, laid his rifle on his pack, and sitting with his back against a tree, was spooning out the contents of a dented green can while the snuffies shot the shit, clicked their Zippos, smoked, scratched, picked at their toes, farted, wandered off to take a dump, moaned over their skin mags, and using their packs as pillows or cushions, wolfed down whatever pogey bait they could find in their pockets. One of them was passing around a bottle of Louisiana, aka Lu-see-anna, hot sauce. Two others were squabbling over a can of peaches, while another pair was chopping up an onion to invigorate their entrees. Not that he was nervous, but he wasn't hungry either. The green can Foster gave him contained ham and limas. The fucking pits. Thanks, Sergeant.

Not one snuffy had touched his entrenching tool. Surprisingly, nobody was smoking pot or, as far as he could tell, wanking off in the weeds. Was anyone paying any fucking attention? And what about water discipline? Christ! It was a classic FUBAR.

A passing thought: Should he join his men in their farting contest? Gideon would have. But he was no Gideon. How would that be regarded? As "conduct unbecoming" or a declaration they were all in the shit together? Better not. He wasn't sure he'd win. Troop-leading was fucking complicated.

Their position looked like a hobos' camp. He got up, adjusted his boonie hat, and set off to check his men and make what he hoped weren't moronic suggestions about a defensive position and other matters from the Quantico core curriculum. And get them to put their fucking boots back on. And bury their shit. Their stink alone would give them away. And so would their cigarettes, but he wasn't certain he could make them stop smoking or get Foster to do so.

Yes, he was pleased with his rakish cover. It was clear from the looks the snuffies were giving him they envied the panache he displayed in discarding his unglamorous helmet. This was leadership writ large.

For the umpteenth time he yelled at his moronic radioman, "Keep your fucking distance, Rubino. A sniper spots your antenna next to me, and I get smoked."

Rubino grunted angrily and gave him more space.

Far to his front, Shaver heard a single shot, a faint howl, and then a second report. The perimeter came alive. Talk ceased. C-rats were tossed aside. Everyone grabbed his helmet. Why the fuck had he worn this dumbass great white hunter hat? Magazines were checked and seated, weapons were cocked, and the troops—wishing they'd dug in—tried to burrow into the stubbornly resisting earth.

Something popped in the distant tree line. Oh, crap! He knew what was coming next. He'd heard that sound before. In Virginia.

Seconds later a shell detonated close behind them, followed almost immediately by another in the grass directly to their front. Mortars. The explosions were less than a hundred yards apart. If you drew an imaginary line between them, it pointed right at the fucking tree line. Three nearly simultaneous thoughts tumbled through his mind: *We're bracketed. I need a helmet. Now what?* A momentary respite. Then multiple explosions as shrapnel and jagged pieces of wood scythed through their position.

Rather unnecessarily, Sergeant Foster screamed, "Incoming!" as successive rounds, some exploding in the treetops, savaged the grove. Everything was dust, smoke, and deafening noise. Thought was impossible. He looked over at Foster, who appeared to be trying to squeeze his entire body into his helmet. What now, Lieutenant?

"Foster," he yelled. No help there. It was his show, and he was in a cleft stick. There were few choices, all of them crappy: *advance, stay put, or bug out, no, make that pull back*. Who the fuck would advance? That would only bring you closer to the source of this lethal shitstorm and further from hot chow, warm beer, four-holers, fresh porn, and his comfy cot. Sorry, legendary Marine heroes, no bayonet charge for this stud. This was a recon patrol, and Lieutenant Daniel Shaver had reconned quite enough, thank you very fucking much. There were beaucoup unfriendlies under those trees. And, truth be told, he was experiencing a major pucker factor.

Stay here? Bull dickey! There was no frigging reason to hang on to this piss-poor hunk of Asia. None whatsoever.

What about Dalton, Dumpster, and Nguyen? Out there without a radio. Tough titty. I got mine, how you doin'? They were on their own. He remembered the old standby, "When caught in a barrage, don't just sit there; do *something*, Lieutenant, even if it's wrong."

More explosions. They were being pulverized. Hissing sounds of white-hot shrapnel. Falling branches. "Foster, we're in a fucking kill zone; we're pulling back. Now!" Why was Foster so damned relaxed? A second look told him that Foster—who was coated in dirt and almost covered by leaves, bark, and small tree limbs—wasn't pulling anything anywhere. And neither would anyone else if they didn't get their butts in gear. Speaking of Foster, he wouldn't be needing his steel pot no more. Now, where was his radioman? There. Crapped out near Foster. You might fucking know it.

What was that nasty red mound? Must have been a direct hit. No helmet. No head. The better question would have been "Who had it been?" Fucked if he could remember the guy's name, but he wasn't ending up thataway. And he wasn't crawling over there to collect dog tags. No siree. Time to beat feet.

"Rubino, get your ass over here. Chop-chop!"

"I can't. I'm hit, Lieutenant."

Shit. "Stay put; I'm coming." He crawled over. "Okay, what frequency you on? All right, just nod. Arty? Good man. Give it here."

Ah, combat. So, this was it. What the bards, who were probably playing with themselves or their pals behind the lines, had eulogized for millennia. What those bullshitting recruiters sold to retard adolescents. Screw that band of brothers crap. Love 'em? Most emphatically, no. These guys didn't mean shit to him. He'd just met 'em, for Chrissake. Die for them? Ha! Them die for him? Double ha! This sucked. Oh, to be entwined with Mary Foley on her slippery back seat.

Where was the rush of adrenalin? Was this what the lifers claimed to crave?

He was fucking outta here. Hopefully with dry knickers.

Oh, to have some flyboys on station. They could flash fry those fuckers with good old, stick-to-the-bone Dow Chemical nape.

Was he scared? Fucking-A! Rounds continued to shred the canopy and slash into the ground around him. This was a monumental clusterfuck, not an everyday one. A Mongolian clusterfuck, the worst kind. He grabbed Foster's helmet, put it on, and buckled the chin strap. Wait. Shit! Should he have done that? He didn't want to lose it, nor did he want his neck broken by a concussion if a shell exploded nearby. Fuck and double fuck! He couldn't think for shit. He unbuckled the chin strap.

Rubino was staring at him with a hard-to-read expression. Panic? Contempt? That's fucking disrespectful, Rubino. No way did Foster need his helmet.

Meanwhile, with nobody ordering them not to, the snuffies abandoned any semblance of fire discipline and, burning through their ammunition, hosed down the spooky, undulating elephant grass. Some of them were heaving their grenades. Most of them were cursing. One clown stood up and, firing from the hip, was giving it his best John Wayne. The poor elephant grass didn't have a prayer. Another bozo even tossed a red smoke grenade, giving the NVA gunners, who seemed to be firing in five-or six-round salvos, an even better aiming point. Here we be, slaughter us. Good thinking, dipshit.

The fucking shotgun was getting in his way. He tossed it aside.

Gideon and Pa would never know. Rubino was still staring at him. Fuck him, and screw old man Elder and his Norse mythology. No fighting, feasting, and fucking for him. Even if the Valkyries were nymphos.

Using Foster, Rubino, and the termite hill as a makeshift shelter, he plotted an azimuth to the tree line and, with his fingers crossed, keyed the radio's handset. Had it been hit? Would it work? It should. They hadn't gone far, and there was no high ground between them and Alpha. These new-fangled "Prick-25s" were supposed to be reliable, but what if Rubino hadn't checked the battery pack?

Static. Were they out of range? Masked by something?

Trying to remain collected, he carefully enunciated, "Ramrod Three, this is Blackcoat, over." More fucking static.

Finally, "Blackcoat, this is Ramrod Three, over."

Something tore into the termite hill, showering the three of them with dirt and bugs.

"Ramrod Three, fire mission. Grid-872146. Direction-5524. Mortar position. Adjust fire, over."

"Roger your last, Blackcoat, Grid-872146. Direction-5524. Mortar position, over."

What was the fucking holdup? Were the cannon-cockers choking their chickens? Shit! What if there'd been a fuckup in the fire direction center, or some klutz had put the wrong dope on his howitzer, screwed on the wrong fuze, or cut the wrong charge? His ass would be grass.

At fucking last! A spotter round ripped overhead and impacted short and to the right of the tree line.

He wiped sweat out of his eyes, refocused his binoculars, and concentrated on steadying the mil scale. "Left 100. Add 150. Fire for effect. And hurry the fuck up, over." Christ, he was dripping.

"Roger that, Blackcoat. Left 100. Add 150. Fire for effect, over."

Yes! The tree line was being torn to pieces. Shit was flying everywhere. Fountains of earth and what he hoped were NVA or NVA remnants were being tossed skyward, together with clumps of vegetation. Most definitely green side out. Hot damn! He observed a secondary explosion. "How do you like those 105 mike-mikes, you cocksuckers with your sorry-ass mortars?" he howled.

"Ramrod Three, repeat fire for effect, over."

"Roger your last, Blackcoat, repeat fire for effect, over."

This was more fucking like it. Payback. He could dig this shit. The enemy fire began to slacken. The snuffies were whooping, hollering, cursing, making obscene gestures, and pissing away their remaining ammo. So what? He had achieved what was known in the trade as "fire superiority." Thank Christ, no khaki-clad motherfuckers had charged out of that fucking grass.

Still no sign of the missing threesome. Shit, we might have greased them as they approached our lines. Anything that moved out there was in deep kimchi.

Something slammed into his leg. Violently. He dropped his compass. His trousers were torn open, and his leg was numb. But he could still move it. He saw blood trickling from his calf. Only a trickle. Not a geyser. And, thank Christ, nowhere near the family jewels.

Then suddenly it changed. They were under fire again, this time from a different direction with higher caliber weapons. Where the fuck was it coming from? The warrior ethos evaporated, and, once again, his snuffies were scrambling for cover. Time for him to rally the troops or some shit like that.

This wasn't a scene he was watching in an air-conditioned theater with a hand around Mary Foley's shoulder and down her warm, welcoming front. While one of her hands . . .

No, this was fucking real, and he was up to his ass in it. Serviceable young Americans were being reduced to—what were those unforgettable words?—orts and gobbets. Shit! He could be next.

It wasn't noble. It wasn't glorious. It was fucking disgusting. And scary. And those who were being methodically disassembled were not taking it well. Much yowling and a lot of inexplicable shit about wanting their mothers. What the fuck would Ma do here? Offer him a Gansett? Keep it for herself?

Get a fucking grip. While he'd dozed through most of it, he recalled a pep talk delivered by a decorated Korean War jarhead who assured them that when it hit the fan, their pride and training would kick in and they'd acquit themselves like heroes, just like the Marines who'd preceded them. Gimme a break. They could be dim, but did the brass really think that being talked at by a guy with a missing arm would boost reenlistments? If he ever got back to the World, he might look the guy up and give him some free Simulator time. Or consider him for a professional discount.

The NVA fire was relentless. Did the pricks have unlimited ammo? Shells were impacting all around him. Metal, wood, and chunks of Christ-only-knows-what were lashing the grove. When was the epiphany coming? No way was he yelling, "Fix Bayonets," springing to his feet, waving his sword, and leading a moronic charge. For openers, what would he charge at? Would a more rational course of action reveal itself? Probably not with his face buried in the dirt.

A dripping hunk of meat was clinging to his sleeve. He shuddered. It fell off.

Then he remembered another Basic School bromide. It was all about accomplishing the mission. The heavens parted. His mission was to preserve Lieutenant Daniel Shaver and all his major organs. It was self-evident his life was considerably more valuable than everyone else's. Time to haul ass, to di-di mau the fuck back to mother Alpha. Why stick around? No spoils. No fallen enemies to strip of their armor, their livestock, and their concubines.

Time slowed. The snuffies were looking his way with what-the-fuck-do-we-do-now expressions on their terrified faces.

"Follow me, we're pulling back!" he screamed.

He looked at Rubino. Blood was pumping out of his inner thigh. Wasn't there something vital down there? A vein? An artery? Was that what happened to Pa? What the fuck was he supposed to do now? Stick a cork in it? Sew it up himself? With what, for fuck's sake? The sewing kit he'd been issued in OCS? He remembered the Gunny saying, "You sorry-ass pukes don't need no wife, the Commandant issued you a sewing kit." He wasn't up for this shit. And thanks so very much, Captain Mac, for not attaching a fucking corpsman. A walk in the sun, my ass.

Rubino was having no luck with his field dressing. "Get me outta here, Lieutenant." He must have seen something in Shaver's eyes. "Please."

Sorry, Rubino, he thought, *you may be an okay dude, but we got no choppers, and, thanks to Captain fucking Mac, we got no corpsman, and you be too fucking far gone. You done pulled the short straw, amigo.*

Several more explosions. The snuffies were eating dirt. Nobody'd notice shit.

He drew his pistol. The crimson puddle beside Rubino was spreading. Christ, the guy was already body bag material. He wouldn't feel shit. Or hurt any longer. Or fall into the hands of the NVA. That would be no fucking picnic. There was no fucking choice.

He racked the slide, cocking his pistol. Rubino screamed, "No!"

He clamped his left hand over Rubino's mouth and, in the shelter of the termite hill, pressed the muzzle against his forehead.

Couldn't do it. Nor could he look into those bugged-out eyes. Rubino's flak jacket was partially unzipped. Shoving his pistol into the opening, he looked away and jerked the trigger.

Functioning as designed, the claw extractor ripped the spent shell casing from the firing chamber. Next, the ejector struck the back of the casing, pivoting it out and away from the pistol through the ejection port.

Next, the slide stopped its rearward movement. Propelled forward by a simple metal spring, it stripped an eager cartridge from the magazine, fed it into the expectant firing chamber, and locked itself into the barrel.

He pulled the trigger a second time.

Rubino twitched, sighed, and stopped thrashing. Like Gideon, he was gone. His sightless eyes said so.

Where were the fucking shell casings? Screw 'em. Thank Christ, his pistol hadn't jammed. That's why you cleaned the fucker. He'd learned that from Gideon.

He tied Rubino's field dressing around his own calf.

A last look at Foster under his shroud. Was he still alive? Was he trying to say something? Were his eyelids moving? Didn't matter with all that blood loss. He'd be toast before the NVA arrived. No time to put him out of his misery. Folks were waiting for his orders. The patrol was still in danger, and more to the point, so was he. Not the moment for indecisiveness. They'd be surrounded and cut off any minute now.

"Grab the wounded, collect the weapons, and fall back. I've got the radio," he shouted.

"What about the KIAs?" someone screamed.

"We'll get 'em later," he yelled.

There was no argument. Pouring past him like a spring flood and following the trail of trampled grass, the snuffies ran, shuffled, or hobbled for their lives, the stronger pushing past the walking wounded. Very Darwinian. It was only exhaustion, a deep stream bed, and the fear of being mistaken for NVA that made them hold up before reaching Alpha's lines. That gave him the opportunity to restore a semblance of order and radio ahead.

As it happened, everyone who'd gotten out of the grove made it safely back inside the wire under a protective umbrella of shells he'd alertly called in to conceal their movement and discourage ambushes.

He returned with dry knickers and refrained from shelling their old position. Yes, it might have destroyed some evidence and zapped any bad guys who'd gone souvenir hunting, but it would have been hard to explain later.

On the whole, nicely fucking done, Lieutenant Shaver.

He'd made masterful use of the available supporting arms, flayed the NVA in the tree line, foiled that snake Nguyen, retrieved most of the weapons, not to mention his lifeline, the "Prick-25," and, with his leg wrapped in a hard-to-ignore bloody field dressing, brought nearly every swinging dick home in one piece. A first-rate job even if there were still a few bodies out there. By his reckoning it was worth a Silver Star with a shiny "V," as in valor. Throw in a Heart if the chancre mechanics backed him up. He was a fucking hero. His looks were intact. His family jewels were hanging in there.

There'd be a fucking monument to him, or minimally a plaque, on Lower Finley's town green. Right across from the Congo Church and Foley's Restaurant. Top that, Freddy!

Captain Mac didn't see it the same way, however. Daniel was nervous. It was just the two of them in the company CP. Szendrock was nowhere to be seen. Why? The captain was muttering to himself as he cleaned his pistol. When he finished, he jammed in a loaded magazine and chambered a round. Shaver noticed he didn't put his pistol on safe. At least he'd uncocked it.

"I don't know what the fuck happened out there, Slater, but I know you'll bullshit me. You returned five Marines short. Seven, if you count Dalton and Fritz. Eight if you include the fucking scout. And what became of your dipshit boonie hat and shotgun? Whose helmet did you steal? You think I don't notice nothing?" Captain Mac glared and spat. "If I thought it would bring them back, I'd shoot you myself. I shit you not. Or maybe I'd have Corporal Szendrock do the honors. You'd never see it coming.

"Don't say another fucking word. Just get out of my sight. Haul your sorry ass back to regiment," said the company commander, drawing a bead on him with his missing finger.

Wisely, he resisted the urge to explain. But Captain Mac wasn't done with him. "You hate 'em yet, Slater?"

What the hell was he talking about?

"Shit. I knew it. You'll never be any fucking good till you really wanna close with the mothers and fuck 'em up big time. Got that, Harvard puke? Beat it. Now!"

He saluted and limped to the battalion aid station, consoling himself with the thought that Mac's temper would keep him a captain forever or, better yet, get him busted back to the ranks.

"How goes it, Leutnant?" That's what Daniel thought he heard. It was Szendrock, and he had an accent that was impossible to place. Daniel ignored him and kept walking. It wasn't until he reached the aid station that he realized the corporal hadn't even considered saluting.

As it happened, the swabbie corpsman who cleaned, stitched, and rebandaged his leg and applied a glowing Camel to his resident leech reported, after Shaver promised him a fifth of Jack Daniels, that, yes, his wound had been caused by enemy action.

The debriefing went swimmingly. The battalion S-2 was more

than happy to accept Shaver's self-deprecating estimate of having "taken out an NVA mortar platoon and five or six tubes." The reason his snuffies were out of ammo, Daniel explained, was because they fought off a probe. They obviously nailed a few, but there'd been no time to search for bodies or follow blood trails. He and the S-2 settled on a plausible body count: twenty KIAs and ten WIAs. A somewhat aggressive ratio, perhaps, but his artillery fire had been devastating. This meant he'd won decisively. Dr. Elder would be proud of him. Freddy would grind his teeth.

That night, back in his hooch, he reread Mary Foley's most recent letter. What made her care for him? Did he care for her? What would it be like to care for someone?

Daniel held up his pistol and depressed the magazine catch with his right thumb. The magazine dropped into his left hand.

Next, he drew the slide to the rear and locked it there by pushing upward on the slide stop with his right thumb. He looked in the chamber, determined the weapon was clear, and depressed the slide stop. As the slide went forward, he pulled the trigger, allowing the hammer to fall. Ritual can be comforting. Then, turning to the magazine, he stripped out the remaining rounds, discarded them, checked the spring, and reloaded with seven guilt-free cartridges.

Finally, he disassembled his pistol, reamed out its barrel, washed and oiled the other parts, and carefully reassembled it. Unsatisfied, he did it again. "Turn the page. It's done. Put it all behind you," he said to the whispering jungle, the jungle that always crept closer after dark.

———

The nearly unrecognizable bodies of Foster, Rubino, and the three snuffies—all of which had been booby-trapped—were retrieved the next day. Those who carried the body bags to the helicopter spread

the word that the NVA had stripped them clean. After double-check-
ing, he learned, to his relief, that Rubino's flak jacket had not been
recovered. He'd been brooding about that. The last thing he needed
was some troublemaker wondering out loud how the flak jacket could
have an intact front and exit holes or spent slugs wedged in the back.

Something else was bothering him. How do you inform next of
kin? Understandably, that hadn't been taught either. Then he realized
the same letter would work for all of them. "Beloved and respected by
his comrades. Died instantly and bravely in the line of duty while leading and protecting his fellow Marines. Deserves a significant medal
and the nation's eternal gratitude. Etc. Etc." Some shit like that.

He was back at regimental S-2 when they brought in what was left
of Dalton. Nguyen was never found. Nor was Dumpster. No matter.
The paperwork for his awards had been drafted, approved, and, since
regiment hadn't had anything to brag about in weeks, was moving
rapidly up the chain of command. Better yet, he'd become something
of a celebrity among the REMFs (rear echelon motherfuckers), as staff
pussies were known to those at the sharp end of the spear.

It should have been perfect, but it wasn't. He was edgy and out
of sorts. Regular attendance at Happy Hour wasn't doing the trick.
After four or five stiff ones, he found himself picking fights with bigger, badder dudes who could and, after intolerable provocation, would
pound the snot out of him. But that didn't work either.

It had nothing to do with Rubino. No reason to keep beating himself up about that. Trying to bring him back alive would have been
nuts, and almost certainly futile. In fact, given his wound, it would
have been cruel. Everyone on the patrol would have done what he did.

Ditto Foster, who'd undoubtedly bought the farm before they
hightailed it. If he hadn't made the tough choices, the entire patrol
would have been screwed. And no way could he have left Rubino to
the NVA. It was no biggie, or in snuffy speak, "Don't mean nuthin';

don't mean a damn thing." Rubino was only out there one extra day, and it wasn't like the vultures ate him, or much of him.

After several more brawls, one of which resulted in a mild concussion, it came to him. His pistol.

There was an easy and obvious fix. He disassembled it, filed off its serial number, scattered its parts in a nearby pond, and reported it stolen. Nobody said a word. Their shifty allies were always pilfering Uncle's property and passing it along to their VC cousins. He submitted the required paperwork and drew a mute replacement from the regimental armory. It even had a smoother trigger pull. Plus, it kept its thoughts to itself, hadn't observed Rubino's last moments, hadn't seen his pleading expression, and could never bear witness. For the remainder of his tour, he cut back on the booze, and, with the assistance of premium pot and a smorgasbord of pills bartered from an accommodating corpsman, he found sleep to be less elusive. However, nothing helped with the nightmares and the sweats.

It took him some time before he realized Captain Mac got it assbackwards in failing to realize that by saving the patrol from certain annihilation, he, Lieutenant Daniel Shaver, had replicated—admittedly on a smaller scale—the legendary Marine withdrawal from the Reservoir. Being a veteran of that action, Captain Mac should have applauded his masterful execution of a challenging retrograde movement. Yes, there'd been casualties, as there'd been in Korea, but you can't make an omelet without . . .

As for that business in the grove—if he'd been Rubino, he'd have welcomed the quick and painless release. He was above reproach.

19

DR. E

I was so relieved when, in 1968 (our annus horribilis), Daniel made it back from Vietnam alive and, physically, still in one piece.[21]

Daniel was, and remains, a strong flavor—perhaps too strong for those in my tame, homogeneous institution. Until I won him over, D-B considered Daniel a "rotter" and tried, repeatedly and unsuccessfully, to get him expelled.

Despite D-B's machinations, I always mustered the votes needed to save Daniel. In fact, I was vindicated when Daniel's grades got him into the Cum Laude Society. Hooray. Then, in his sixth-form year he won the Latin Prize[22] and the school's extemporaneous speaking award. I was impressed when D-B admitted he'd been wrong about Daniel.

To use military parlance, I had Daniel's "six." How could I not, since I was to blame for his being in harm's way? After all, if it hadn't been for me blathering on about my time in the Ardennes and urging him to sign up for NROTC, Daniel might well have avoided Vietnam.

---

21 I was even more thankful our country was at peace during Freddy's three years in the Corps.

22 I was upset by the inevitable—and utterly false—accusations of favoritism.

As it was, Daniel quite outdid himself with his Purple Heart—well earned, unlike mine—and his Bronze Star.

It may be nothing, but something's troubling me about Daniel. He had a rough time in Vietnam but acts as though it was a lark. He's wearing a mask and seems to have nobody in whom to confide. Nevertheless, it would be wrong of me to intrude, much less probe. Besides, one of the things I took from the Ardennes is that it's not for those who weren't there to question what took place on the battlefield or to challenge the actions, much less the motives, of the combatants. Who can predict how he'd behave in similar circumstances?

I wonder whether my response to Daniel's heroics was influenced by his being regarded as mine by everyone at St. Matthew's. I owned him, and must admit his Simulator project, his performance at the Worcester Art Museum, and several other escapades still make me cringe.

After his conversion, D-B supported my campaign to get Daniel's photograph—in his dress blues, naturally—and the velvet-lined box containing his sword, medals, insignia, and shooting badges hung in the library's main reading room. Where they remain, despite my growing aversion to that conflict and its consequences.

As for D-B—although the tales ultimately proved to be false—he was seen by others as paying too much attention to my dear Helen and other women who were underage or already taken. D-B was relentlessly charming, and St. Matthew's quivered with rumor and innuendo during the "swinging" '60s and the equally debauched '70s. If you can believe it, after Helen's leave-taking there was even some tittle-tattle about me and the vivacious—by the standards of her department—math teacher from Smith. How ridiculous. A mathematician? Not on your tintype.

20

FREDDY/FRED

F red would have been surprised and disappointed had the ancient warrior not been at his post. But there he was, days after Nixon's resignation, as he had been on all of Fred's visits to the assisted living facility where his mother had resided since 1968.

Colonel Rupert Damon, USA (Ret.), had emplaced his wheelchair in an impregnable position: the angle of the wall outside the third-floor nurses' station. His back was covered, and from there the colonel could keep his eyes peeled for Cornelia Jenkins, whose heart he believed he'd won in a bold assault modeled on those of George S. Patton, under whom he'd served with distinction thirty years earlier.

Old Blood and Guts had taught Colonel Damon it was essential to remain on the qui vive. Otherwise, in the words of the exuberant general, some German son of a bitch could "sneak up behind him and beat him to death with a sock full of shit."

The colonel's position offered an unobstructed field of fire down the corridor. This enabled him to draw a bead on would-be infiltrators and bark out in his most resonant parade ground voice, "Advance and be recognized," to those he saw as friendlies. Even in these permissive times, nobody messed with the colonel.

Why, Fred asked himself as he approached this elderly but alert sentinel, hadn't someone done up his pajama bottoms? Easy answer. Neither Mercy Williams nor any of the other large but gentle Jamaican ladies dared to risk triggering one of Colonel Damon's legendary outbursts by interrupting his fascinated examination of his now quite public private parts. Fred recalled one of the staff psychiatrists with a military background suggesting that, owing to his many crossed wires, the colonel might, in a demented flashback, confuse his short arm with a sidearm. So, in order to obviate the threat of self-mutilation, the staff had confiscated his cleaning rod, bore brush, patches, and gun oil.

That had to be it. An enraged bellow from Colonel Damon could finish off one of the frail patients lined up with him to receive their morning meds. Besides, it was likely the sympathetic attendants, knowing the colonel had been gently dropped from the garden club after ordering daily sweeps of the flower beds for mines and booby traps, were reluctant to make him button up and deprive him of one of his two last pleasures, the other being chocolate ice cream. As his father, a fan of Socrates, might have put it, "The unexamined cock is not worth crowing about."

"This may be the last time you see the colonel on the third floor, Mr. Fred," said one of the more generously proportioned helpers. He'd made a point of getting to know the ladies taking care of his mother, so he stopped and, before continuing to Room 348, said, "I'm sorry to hear that, Mercy. You've done a wonderful job making sure all of us know his daily password. Now, look after yourself and take care of that knee."

Everyone admired the layout of Essex Lodge. Realizing the residents were already or soon likely to become bewildered, the designers addressed this harsh reality by painting each floor in a soothing, edible color chosen from the natural world. In ascending order, starting with lemon on the dreaded second floor, were apricot, cherry, lime, peach, and tangerine.

Though she'd been there for six years now, Fred still wasn't sold on the for-profit establishment to which his mother had been banished by Howard Paulson.

Essex Lodge began as a real estate development whose colorful banners trumpeted the imminent availability of "luxury" condos, the only variety on offer. The project went under during a regional real estate swoon in the '60s. Unfinished and rapidly deteriorating, the land and the skeletal buildings were bought out of bankruptcy by the real estate arm of Lenox Hill Capital. Howard Paulson had an easy time selling his investors on the high returns achievable by eliminating waste, superfluous staff, and the undisciplined business practices of inattentive nonprofits. "No more mollycoddling" was his mantra.

Fred's concerns grew when he overheard a conversation in the business office where Essex Lodge was described as "a factory with an efficient disassembly line." The raw materials, referred to as "solvent, ambulatory seniors," lived relatively active lives in their apartments on the upper floors, while the finished products, more often than not newly destitute decedents, were dispatched on their final journeys from the ground floor loading dock.

In answer to his questions about life on the lower floors, he was informed, "Those living on three might, to use baseball jargon, be considered 'in the hole,' while the second floor is eternity's 'on-deck' circle, the departure lounge, the 'last stop' before the last stop." Two was where you lost your independence, dignity, and privacy. As a baseball fan, he likened third-floor residents to aging minor leaguers, always hoping to move back up to the "show," but sensing it wasn't in the cards.

While the more mobile clung to their canes, many on three used a walker or wheelchair. No more sociable meals and watered-down drinks in the main dining room on the ground floor. Those days were gone. Three had its own alcohol-free eating area with food still requiring the use of teeth. You even had some choices, except on Sundays when the big meal was bologna and American cheese on white, accompanied by those vegetables—reheated yet again—that had survived the entire week. Sunday's food, Fred noticed, looked rather like those eating it. The slow pace and the skeleton staff were harbingers of what lay ahead. Fortunately, his mother's room was close to the action: the nurses' station and the dining room.

His mother didn't live on three because she was infirm. In fact, being only forty-eight when she was admitted in 1968, she was the baby of the floor, but, given her cognitive problems, the Essex Lodge administrators had correctly decided she would be happier on the restful third floor.

Fred had given her several days to settle in before his first visit.

The door to his mother's room had been ajar, so he knocked and entered. She was staring out the window at the empty parking lot. Sensing his presence, she turned and said, "I think I love it here, Freddy. It was so . . . stressful living with . . ." She was stuck.

"Howard Paulson?"

"Yes, yes. I was always disappointing him."

"What makes you think that?"

She was quick to answer. "He told me so. Sometimes I have difficulty with names, but I can still remember a lot of things, Freddy, particularly things that happened long ago."

"Are you making friends here, Mother?"

"Yes, Freddy. Many. All the old ladies here, except for . . . you know who I'm talking about, adore me, because I help them with things. I've never been adored before."

Even though she'd walked out on him, she was the only mother he had. "That's not true, Mother. I adore you, I've always adored you, and it's wonderful to see you so happy." She lit up.

"And when I'm an old lady . . ."

"Which won't be for a long, long time."

"Some lovely young person will look after me . . . Will you visit me here, Freddy?"

"Yes I will, Mother."

––––––––

It seemed fitting his mother should end up in Massachusetts. The thirty-five-year-old Helen Elder had, during 1955, fled the Commonwealth in the passenger seat of the crimson Ferrari owned by Howard Paulson, Chairman of St. Matthew's Investment Committee and, more significantly, the founding partner of Lenox Hill Capital. Now she was back. Had his financially naïve mother somehow intuited that taking an unpaid position in St. Matthew's development office would expose her to net worths significantly higher than her husband's? Fred didn't like having these thoughts about his mother.

The newly hired Helen Elder had been struggling to overcome her aversion to chasing dollars when a frisson of excitement ruffled her quiet waters. The legendary Howard Paulson, who was single-handedly responsible for the class of 1942 being atop St. Matthew's annual giving list, declared his intention of making "a not inconsequential" gift in memory of his recently deceased wife, Stephanie. Whatever the reality of his marriage, Howard Paulson insisted it be suitably (i.e., lavishly) memorialized.

Helen Elder's boss, Reginald Feather V, an alum who'd scuttled back to St. Matthew's after making a hash of things in the business world, decided that incubating this golden egg called for a degree of warmth and flexibility not possessed by the person charged with the cultivation of Howard Paulson—an alum to neither the manner nor the manor born. Priscilla Jennings—the stern and relentlessly honest seventy-one-year-old widow of the former squash coach—was thanked for her efforts, and the Paulson file was, that very morning, transferred to the desk of vivacious Helen Elder.

After all, was Priscilla Jennings, whose forebears rowed ashore from the *Arbella*, whose grandfather founded New England's most prestigious boarding school, whose extended family had graced the pages of our country's *Debretts* since its initial publication, expected to kowtow to the likes of Howard Paulson? A rhetorical question, surely. Naturally, she ignored Reginald Feather's pleas to cultivate that jumped-up Paulson fellow. Out of the question! She made a rasping, scornful sound, arranged her nubby tweed skirt, rose to her majestic seventy-three inches, stared down her no-nonsense nose, compressed her thin lips, and eyes front, chest up, shoulders back, stalked from Feather's office.

All agreed. Bright-eyed Helen Elder, neither too meek nor too brassy, was the obvious midwife for this project, a choice enthusiastically endorsed by Howard Paulson the moment the two of them were introduced. Prior to their meeting, Helen had been thoroughly briefed by Reverend Enoch Ward, St. Matthew's headmaster.

"Applications are down, the percentage of those we are obliged to accept is scandalously high, and we have countless pressing needs, Helen," said the solemn reverend. "Our library's cramped, our gymnasium's a hangover from the days of medicine balls and Indian clubs, and our lower school's alcoves remind me of anchorites' retreats in the Hebrides."

Noticing he was appraising her, Helen stopped taking notes and looked up.

Reverend Ward droned on, "Oh, and Helen, don't muffle your lovely laugh. It's an infallible pick-me-up, a sure-fire antidote to a widower's melancholia. And something else: You might wish to consider a brighter, somewhat more fashionable wardrobe. You are *not* an Inuit."

Failing to appreciate the impact of what he'd said, the reverend continued, "This is no time for droopy or dowdy, Helen. We must not cast down our donors." He wasn't finished. "While you're about it, please reconsider those shoes. Heels, perhaps? But, please, not brown."

Helen stared back at him with fire in her eyes. Reverend Ward was unused to confrontation. He wrung his hands and looked down at his blotter.

"That will be all, Helen," he murmured. "I am sure that with God's help and yours, Howard Paulson will smile again, and St. Matthew's will flourish."

Though still new to fundraising, Helen decided it might be sensible to learn Stephanie's enthusiasms. Surely they were relevant to whatever was done in her memory. Howard Paulson was delighted by this novel approach, so different from that of the no-nonsense Priscilla. In short order, Helen discovered Stephanie Paulson had been neither bookish, athletic, nor interested in modernizing adolescents' sleeping quarters.

"What were Stephanie's interests, Mr. Paulson?" asked a somewhat tentative Helen as they strolled across the hallowed sixth-form quadrangle.

Howard Paulson sighed theatrically and, whispering in Helen's ear, said, "She . . . She loved theater. And music. And dance."

"Did she perform herself?" asked an unsettled Helen.

"No, but I had a hand in her joining the board of the Met—the Metropolitan Opera. Does that help?" said Howard Paulson, holding his ground.

"It certainly does," replied Helen, reclaiming a sliver of personal space. "Now here's a wild idea. What would she think of the Stephanie Paulson Performing Arts Center? It would be magical reflected in the waters of Hinkley Pond where the boys used to play hockey."

"That would be perfect, and, now that you mention it, I was one of those boys, Mrs. Elder. And please, call me Howard."

"Very well," said Helen, giving herself a figurative pat on the back for having studied Howard Paulson's yearbook and seen he was the hockey captain. "Why don't we look at the site?"

His response was immediate. "I thought you'd never ask."

"One other thing. If you're Howard, then I'm Helen. Okay?"

It appeared to be more than okay with Howard Paulson. He grinned. "Fair enough, and, by the way, you're a genius."

"Thank you, Mr. . . . Howard."

"There, that wasn't too difficult, was it?"

"It's challenging getting to the pond in these," she said, taking off her heels. "I hope you don't mind my bare feet."

Howard Paulson didn't mind at all. In fact, he offered to carry her shoes, an invitation Helen felt obliged to decline.

After a few moments staring at the weed-choked pond, he rested a hand on her shoulder and said, "How about this? I'm staying at The Ritz, and I'd like to take you to dinner there. The main dining room has a view over the Public Garden. Don't you love that setting?"

"I've only seen it once, Howard. Out of our price range. I'm a faculty wife."

"We shall remedy that forthwith." A pause. "The fact that you've only eaten there once. What say you to The Ritz at six this evening? I'll have O'Neill pick you up and take you home."

Now she was flustered. "O'Neill?" She sat down on a bench as she put on her shoes.

"My driver. A charming old soak. He kept himself and my father pickled during Prohibition." Helen failed to respond. "Yes, that was an attempt at humor."

"That should be fine, Howard, but I must be home by nine. In time to watch a PBS documentary on Mithridates with my husband, Frederick. I believe you've met him."

"I understand completely. I missed too many nights with Stephanie when I was starting out. Sometimes I slept on cots in the office or napped at the financial printer while finalizing a prospectus. I'll never forget the ghastly Chinese takeout in those white cardboard boxes with metal handles."

As Helen assumed, getting home by nine was fine with Dr. Elder. It would take an act of God or the public enemy for him to skip the monthly 7:00 p.m. meeting of his Punic Wars discussion group.

21

DR. E

It had been decreed by the gods. My marriage was doomed. Resisting would have increased the pain without altering the outcome.

It took just over a year and regular monthly meetings overlooking the Public Garden for the sixty-thousand-square-foot Stephanie Paulson Performing Arts Center to evolve from a concept to its lovely May 1955 dedication. All agreed the Center looked magnificent surrounded by sweet-smelling lilacs and reflected in Hinkley Pond. While the relationship between my wife and Howard Paulson pained me terribly, I am by nature a Stoic. So, I did my best to ignore the sight of her at the dedication glued to Howard Paulson in an outfit "more Ascot than St. Matthew's," as the mordant D-B put it.

Priscilla Jennings cackled but looked almost sympathetic when I suggested she reinsert herself into the project. Shortly thereafter, I threw in the sponge. Anything that might jeopardize the Paulson gift would agitate Reverend Ward and imperil my own position. The Arts Center, the cornerstone of Enoch Ward's legacy, was too big to fail. Lesser schools were pulling ahead of St. Matthew's in facilities sweepstakes.

The meetings between my wife and the man I referred to as "Croesus" grew longer and more frequent, but the Ardennes had left me fatalistic. My fighting days ended for good when, in the fall of 1945, I received an honorable discharge and my "ruptured duck" lapel pin. All reminders of those days were thrown out or entombed in the footlocker I relegated to the furthest reaches of our uninsulated attic. I never bothered to obtain, let alone wear, my Purple Heart or campaign ribbons, and I accepted, with resignation, Helen's claim that my snoring precipitated her move to the guest room. By that time, neither of us regretted this. Little had taken place in our cramped eighteenth-century four-poster for many lunar cycles. Would life have been better in a bed with fewer posts?

Such a shame. It had begun so promisingly. While a handful of my classmates yearned to tunnel out of or blow up St. Matthew's— think Guy Fawkes—I loved my time there and considered it a snug harbor in which to ride out life's storms, hopefully beside a like-minded woman with whom I'd share a mooring. Ideally, she would relish New Hampshire summers and derive satisfaction from the area's simple but sustaining pursuits. Maybe, like my mother, she would enjoy quilting. In my limited experience, quilters tend to be congenial and adaptable.

I was certain I'd struck gold with Helen Eldridge, a rare alloy of beauty, intelligence, and warmth, someone who would in time become an elegant New England matron of the sort immortalized by Copley. My heart skipped a beat when I first saw her. I am not speaking metaphorically. Just recently my cardiologist considered the matter and assured me that could well have happened.

However, in matters of the heart, I, like many unworldly men, tend to endow those to whom I'm attracted with attributes I admire. At the time I met and fixated on Helen Eldridge, she was quietly licking her wounds after the collapse of a torrid relationship with a roadster-driving Californian who could not have been more unlike the prematurely staid me. Perhaps that's what caused her to drop out of Wellesley and accept my unexpected but not—I hoped—entirely unwelcome proposal.

So much for the earthshaking movement of tectonic plates. Goodbye to life in the fast lane and its associated peaks and valleys. Reliability, sobriety, and a secure pension should never be despised or discounted. Seeking portents, but sacrificing no living creatures, I concluded the ancients would have found the similarity of our surnames, Elder and Eldridge, to be propitious. And so, we wed, less than two months after being thrown together in a mixed-doubles tournament at the Longwood Cricket Club in which, to our delighted surprise, we advanced to the semifinals. I enjoyed referring to our union as the fruit of courtly love.

Might it have turned out differently if I hadn't hit Helen in the back of her head with the first serve of the match?

Not likely. It took me a while—it always does—to realize I'd married above my pay grade. Moving off the grid would only have postponed the inevitable.

———

To revisit the past: Armed with my newly issued Harvard diploma—whose Latin[23] I found comforting—and accompanied by someone I was certain would prove to be an agreeable consort, I looked to the future. Freddy, a male heir, who assured the survival of my line, arrived in August 1941. So much for that. Having been fruitful and multiplied, I then asked myself, "What now?" The answer was provided on December 7.

I returned from the European Theater of Operations with a single mission: obtain a doctorate in classics (I'd seen enough of the twentieth

———

23 Particularly the "summa."

century) to provide for my dependents and open the door to the sort of life I, and I assumed Helen, wished to lead.[24] This degree, in a field that was attracting fewer and less able candidates, came easily, and a position at St. Matthew's became available shortly thereafter. Helen, not wishing to disappoint her returning warrior and having no conflicting ambitions of her own, acquiesced. I had found my refuge. Having survived the bellicose Hun, I vowed nothing would ever upset me. At the merest hint of stress or conflict, I could seek sanctuary in departmental gatherings or, figuratively speaking, in the tumbled ruins of Carthage.[25]

While St. Matthew's could hardly be seen as truly reflective of mid-century America, it suited *me* to a tea—ha, ha. What had worked for over a century would surely suffice for a bit longer. As one proud alum put it, "You're treated the same at St. Matt's whether your old man's worth fifty million or only five." Then there was the Head of the Upper School, who also served as Master of Fox Hounds of the local hunt. The hunt, he explained, was a resource of the community, providing it "with stirring visual images" in return for which the "fortunate" community offered up its land. As MFH said, "It works both ways. I don't hunt for my pleasure alone, but for the pleasure of the community as well." Yes, this was home.[26]

Until the descent of Howard Paulson like the proverbial shower of gold, our marriage represented the St. Matthew's norm. We husbands taught, coached, and squabbled over trifles, while the wives poured tea, sewed, improved the soil, volunteered, took adult education courses, or—Helen excepted, I assumed—discreetly sought other

---

24 My dissertation on the *Vergilius Vaticanus* (the Vatican Virgil) was, despite its challenge to several orthodox interpretations, rather well received, if I do say so myself.

25 Every schoolboy knows Cato's famous "Carthago delenda est."

26 Perhaps this was why D-B was attracted to St. Matthew's. I recall him saying he "rode to hounds with the Cattistock Hunt."

outlets. I suspect Helen may have recognized Howard Paulson as the fully realized version of her college Lothario: urbane, dashing, successful, and, with the death of his wife, ostentatiously bereft. By the time I awoke to what was happening, I could only hope the allure of Howard Paulson's appetites and assets was not irresistible. Surely habit and the needs of Freddy—and me—would keep Helen anchored to our modest three-bedroom, one and one-half bath Cape so generously provided by St. Matthew's.

Despite what might be gleaned from my dispassionate exterior, I loved—to use that fraught word—Helen and knew I'd be undone if (an unthinkable "if") she did not reciprocate my feelings. Nonetheless, I was unable to muster the energy to resist, much less counterattack. My martial spirit was interred in Germania. So, I read Polybius and awaited the unfolding of events. I was in the hands of my capricious gods. A prince of Troy was carrying off *my* Helen, but—as soon became evident—I was no Menelaus.

As for Helen, she evidently found Howard Paulson's onslaught exhilarating. None of the domesticated boys with whom she'd Charlestoned and discreetly necked had gone a step further without an almost explicit invitation. This may have been her first encounter with unconstrained desire.

I was overmatched. The most myopic oracle would have called it correctly. With his looks, his energy, his net worth—he appeared regularly in *Fortune*—and his ability to stun and subdue his prey, Howard Paulson had the gravitational pull of a supermassive black hole, capable of swallowing stars, light, and—it goes without saying—Helen. In a pinch he could even excrete the vulnerability that invariably snares the kind-hearted.

It was Helen who precipitated the denouement. She cornered me on a night I had no committee meetings, and the PBS lineup was reruns of documentaries featuring panels of former luminaries with hesitant voices and diminished powers of recall. Academics who'd become what I dread becoming.

"Fred, we really must talk."

"When?" I replied, the irritated Latin teacher being dragged from one of his favorites, *The Times Literary Supplement*.

"Right now."

"About what, Helen?" I said, setting aside *TLS* and peering, no doubt grudgingly, over my half lenses.[27]

"Can't you guess? About us!"

I'm sure I winced. "We never do that, and certainly not tonight. I've got nearly twenty papers to grade. I'll be up for hours." My put-out expression did not deflect her.

"Damnit, Fred, this is long overdue, and you're just snoozing over that . . . whatever it is."

"This is essential scholarly reading, My Dear. Look," I said, pointing. "I've just found a well-regarded new study of Pompey."

"Pompey?"

I must have looked pained. "You *must* be familiar with Pompey Magnus, Helen." What followed was so unlike her.

"Christ almighty, Fred, stop it," she said, her voice rising. "We're living a lie. Have been for years."

"Stop it yourself, Helen. You sound like a hysteric on a daytime soap opera, not someone who would, *if* she'd stuck to it, have earned at least a magna at Wellesley. Besides, if it's a lie, it's a little white one. Like everyone else's." I returned to Pompey. But Helen renewed her assault.

"You are *so* tone deaf, Fred. And stop hiding behind that . . . newspaper!"

I placed the offending *TLS* on the coffee table.

---

27 I recall, now with some amusement, Helen diagnosing me with early onset "curmud-geonitis."

"Fred, I just don't matter to you. You have no idea who I am, where I am, what I'm doing, or what I'm thinking. You have no feeling for the real world or its inhabitants."

"Of course I do. Freddy's doing well at school, and we're well-suited—aren't we?" Would that silence her? Evidently not.

"Howard says he loves me and needs me. And I believe him. He doesn't have the dead Greeks and Romans for company. Not to mention your ridiculous divinities. He's begged me to leave you. He says he'll be generous." Helen paused momentarily to regroup and reload. "He says you'll never notice. He's right. And now you'll be able to find someone who's really good at tennis and skiing. Like those athletic former girlfriends you go on about."

I set aside my reading glasses and took the plunge. "Have you made love with him?"

Helen took a step backwards. "Wow, that's getting down to brass something or other. Tackiness, maybe. But, as it happens, I have not. I'm kind of out of practice. Would it bother you if I had?"

"How can you ask, Helen?"

"I suppose that's something."

My defenses were crumbling.

I wish I'd controlled myself, but instead I began shouting. "What do you want me to say, Helen? I can't stop you, and I don't intend to make a scene. I detest this vulgar, third-rate drama." It was too painful. When could I get back to Pompey?

"We are ill-suited, Fred," said Helen. She'd never sounded sadder.

I couldn't disagree. "Think it over, Helen, get some sleep, and give me your decision in the morning."

She'd turned my flanks and penetrated my center. Unconditional surrender loomed.

By the time Helen got downstairs, I was finishing my coffee and filling my book bag.

"Where's Freddy?" she asked.

"He finished breakfast early and rushed off for school. We had a little talk."

I handed my soon-to-be ex-wife her mug. I couldn't look at her. "Here, just a splash of milk. How did you sleep?"

"How do you think I slept, but you're looking bright-eyed and bushy-tailed."

I tried to ignore her anger. "Several of the papers I graded last night are quite exceptional. I'll have to bestow more than my usual quota of As."

"That would never do."

"Why that edge in your voice, Helen?"

"Sweet Jesus, Fred. Who in God's name are you playing now? Seneca?"

"Please, Helen, that's beneath you."

"Sorry, sorry, sorry. Yes, I'm going to New York, but not until school's over. That way the gossips won't have anything to chew on until September, and you'll have Three Oaks to yourself this summer."

"How considerate."

"I'm nothing if not considerate."

"There's no need for sarcasm. It's not in your nature. And what about our son?" I didn't mention it, but what about *me*? Could I remain in faculty housing as a bachelor? Or, gods forbid, would I have to become a dorm master?

"Freddy will be just fine. He can board. As you may or may not have gathered, he's wanted to for some time. I wonder why. And if the school won't give him a free ride, Howard will gladly pick up the tab. Same with college. In fact, he'd love to."

"I bet he would, the noble Howard. And you, my dear, give new meaning to the myth of Zeus and Danae."

"Now who's being sarcastic?"

"You're right, that was unworthy of me."

"And Seneca," said Helen with the faintest of smiles.

That *was* a good one. Then it hit me again. Life without Helen would be desolate. "Yes, and Seneca. And what about vacations?" I finished my coffee and edged towards the door. As the French put it, "Sauve qui peut."

"Since he'll be at St. Matthew's for most of the year, Howard and I want him during vacations. Howard's certain his Tod and Liza, who are much older, will be fine with it. Welcoming, in fact. Howard hates his empty nest."

"How caring."

"Stop it, Fred. Don't you have a class in a few minutes?"

"Thanks for your solicitude, but what about the summers? Freddy loves New Hampshire. He'd miss our tennis. Even you enjoyed that, once."

Helen shook her head. "You *must* know Freddy's terrified of those savages."

That was too much. I set down my book bag. "Now who's being snotty and intolerant? You getting this from your rich paramour?"

"Let *me* remind *you*, Dr. Elder, you're the one who's always going on about gun-toting yokels. Okay, how about this? You can sequester Freddy in the sticks from the close of school through the Fourth. Then he comes to us. Fair? Or would you like Howard's lawyer to work it out with yours?"

"Stop threatening me, Helen. All right, I yield. I suppose that's as fair as any of this."

"I assume you've got no problem with our taking Freddy abroad. You should be proud. He really wants to see Italy. And temples. And amphitheaters. And the ruins that enthrall his father."

Anything to escape. "Twisting the knife, are we? Yes, I want my son to see the world, including the superficial world of Howard Paulson. He'll learn some valuable lessons from the two of you."

"One other thing, Dr. Elder. You may not keep Freddy in Lower Finley against his will. Agreed?"

"Must we really do this to each other, Helen? Can't we just go back to the way it was? I'd be willing to look the other way on a lot of things."

Her eyes said no. Emphatically. "Stop it, Fred. There's nothing to go back to."

"Perhaps you're right. I think it was Sassoon who wrote about his 'craving to revisit the past and give the modern world the slip.' And that, my dear, would be Siegfried, not Vidal."

"Yes, Herr Doktor Professor, believe it or not, I got it."

"Very well. I'm off." Unsure of what I wanted to hear, I said, "See you this evening?"

"I'm not certain."

It was fated. Winning Helen was a fluke. As sometimes occurs in sports, I just happened to be in the right place when, figuratively speaking, an errant shot deflected off me and into the net for a goal.

22

FREDDY/FRED

Though it had happened years earlier, Fred's memory of his mother's departure remained bitterly fresh.

Towards the end of the 1955 school year, maybe it was April, he'd come downstairs for the usual catch-as-catch-can breakfast. His mother wasn't up yet. That was normal, but his father was and that was not. Nor was his smoking. He recognized what had become a familiar smell. Whiskey. And it was only 7:30 a.m. Last night's or today's?

His father didn't seem to notice him. "Mom still asleep?" No answer. He repeated the question.

"No idea. She's not here."

"Where is she?" He should not have asked that question. His mother had told him she'd be leaving, why she was leaving, where she was going, and when she'd be back. She promised she'd be gone no more than two weeks.

His father looked up, but not at him. "Reno."

This couldn't be happening. Things were just like always. Not great, but his father hadn't seemed to mind. "When will we see her?"

"Maybe never . . . Sorry, Freddy, you'll see her soon, I'm sure."

"You won't?" He was too old to cry.

"I think not."

There was a long silence while he tried to make sense of what he'd heard. What would happen to him? "Am I going to live with Mom? The way Charley Norris lives with his mother?" He couldn't bring himself to ask whether she wanted him.

His father's head snapped up. "Not if I can help it."

This was scary. His father seldom got really angry. "You won't slug her, will you?" That was unfair. And uncalled for.

His father muttered something, shook his head, and lit another cigarette.

The weeks following his mother's departure were terrible. He'd wake in the middle of the night and check his father's bedroom. If it was empty, he'd go to the window overlooking the garage. If the car wasn't there, he'd go back to bed and try to sleep. If it was, he'd put on his slippers and retrieve his father. Sometimes the engine would be running, but thank goodness, the garage door was never closed.

Dragging his father out of the car, into the house, and then upstairs was tough. Usually, he got him no further than the living room sofa. Sometimes his father would yell at him. Once he'd thrown up on himself and the dashboard. Now and then his trousers were wet.

It was even worse when his father drank at home, made quickly forgotten promises, mumbled maudlin endearments, and dropped lighted cigarettes between the sofa cushions.

Neither his mother nor Howard Paulson wanted him anything like full time. He was sure of that. So where would he be if something happened to his father?

For a long time, he hoped his parents would get back together. Then he wondered whether it was wrong to be glad they hadn't.

He couldn't figure out why his mother wasn't more interested in him. It wasn't as though she had other kids. Was something wrong with him?

———————

For years Freddy wondered if somehow Three Oaks was the reason his parents didn't like each other. Maybe his mother would not have run off with Howard Paulson if she hadn't felt "imprisoned" (that was the word she used) in Lower Finley (she made jokes about moving to the nonexistent Upper Finley).

And what was he to think of Howard Paulson? He was a rat for having stolen his mother, but he had great seats in Yankee Stadium.

His mother hadn't given a hoot that Three Oaks had been in the Elder family for several generations or that it had been bought as a favor from the impoverished Shavers after one of them saved the life of the original Frederick Elder at Gettysburg. In fact, his mother suggested the bad blood between the families was probably triggered by the Elders underpaying for the land in the first place. She certainly seemed to enjoy calling his father a piker.

It was a drag listening to his mother grumble about broken sash cords, torn screens, and endless chores. How could his father stand it? Fred vowed to marry a girl who didn't criticize everything. It upset him to look at his mother's face when his father said something like, "Lower Finley is so much more real than . . ." There were many places his father considered less real than Lower Finley. Among them were Southampton, Newport, and Bar Harbor, all of which he'd love to see.

His mother never even pretended to like Three Oaks. How could he forget her Labor Day excitement as she began what she called her "eight months' reprieve from the decay, the mold, the isolation, and the locals."

She made it clear she found the name Three Oaks botanically inaccurate and, given their straitened circumstances, absurdly pretentious. Once, looking wistful, she said, "Nothing flourishes here. The birds and the squirrels eat our berries. The rabbits get the vegetables. The worms ruin our apples, and the deer polish off whatever's left. And now the coyotes and wolves are returning to consume our pets and, after them, us."

He had to admit she was right. The only things she hadn't mentioned were the raccoons that terrorized Marcus and the Shavers who scared the bejesus out of him.

Because of the Shavers, he'd come to dislike Three Oaks too. So, when he thought about it, he was inclined to side with his mother. But did that give her the right to leave him? No, it did not.

23

DR. E

Wasn't it only yesterday I'd been courting[28] Helen and implausibly likening myself to the passionate Gaius Valerius Catullus? I'd been introduced to Catullus by my sixth-form Latin teacher, who'd exposed—so to speak—his most gifted boys to works generally off-limits to adolescents. Should I have followed his bold example? How could I with girls in my class?

To my chagrin, I should have realized Catullus and I were temperamentally different. He'd spent his boyhood making love and writing poetry. Lucky him.

Nevertheless, like so many inept but eager swains, I spent seemingly endless hours devising unlikely schemes to lure Helen to a secluded bower where we'd do—repeatedly—what I've read is done in bowers. That being so, I was inspired by Catullus's thanks to his friend Allius for the use of his house as a place to have his way with the ardent Clodia. This is how F. W. Cornish, a staid English academic,[29] portrays Clodia stepping out of the sunlight into the refreshing shade of their secluded trysting place:

---

28 Pun intended.

29 Out of modesty, I'm using his bloodless translation rather than my poetic one.

Such an aid to me was Allius;
he opened a broad track across the fenced field,
he gave me access to a house and its mistress,
under whose roof we should together enjoy each our
   own love.
Thither my fair goddess delicately stepped,
and set the sole of her shining foot on the smooth
   threshold, as she pressed on her slender sandal.
(number 68, lines 66–72)

Was I overdoing it when I insisted dear Helen and I spend two nights in Verona during our honeymoon? I needed to visit Catullus's birthplace and explain to my bride the impact of his passionate verse. There was so much to see. I was delighted with myself when I noticed the glorious amphitheater had large incised Roman numerals above each of its portals.

Helen rolled her eyes. "What else, Fred?"

Never being one to leave well enough alone, I couldn't resist reminding Helen that Verona was the setting for *Romeo and Juliet*. I don't recall her facial expression, but her response was "That turned out well, didn't it?"

I chuckled, having no idea she was being prophetic.

So much for those bittersweet memories. The destruction of my life, brought about and financed by Howard Paulson, was swift, if not painless. The papers were drawn up as a favor to me, the pathetic cuckold, by the only "family" lawyer in the firm that represented Lenox Hill Capital in its business dealings. Even I could see the terms were reasonable. Attempting to appear unfazed and affecting a non-chalant air, I executed the surrender document on the dotted line. No, I misremember. It was a solid line.

For Freddy, his days of skimping were over. As the beneficiary of his stepfather's offhand largesse, he got a free ride to Harvard, my alma mater and Paulson's, where he signed up for Marine OCS, and I began worrying about Ares claiming my only child.

24

FREDDY/FRED

In 1965, while his fellow Marines were landing in Vietnam, Fred was promoted to captain and honorably discharged. Having been found wanting by the secretive organization he believed would embrace him, he turned once again, virtually on bended knee, to his mother's seducer. He noticed, upon gaining admission to the great man's sanctuary, that his stepfather seemed even more remote than usual.

Howard Paulson was tapping an index finger on his blotter, so Fred got right to the point. "Mother said I should contact you as soon as I got out of the Marines."

"And so you have, Freddy," replied Howard Paulson, idly spinning one of his rolodexes as he stared inquiringly at his stepson.

"Mother suggested you might have something available at Lenox Hill." No response. "Doesn't your son, Tod, work here?"

"Yes, he does, Freddy." Howard Paulson grimaced and resumed, "Lenox Hill is demanding and fiercely competitive. Our young people's schedules are brutal. They have it worse than associates in the big Wall Street law firms."

"I can work hard, Howard, and I'm highly motivated. As we say in the Corps, Ooh-Rah!"

Howard Paulson looked pained. "Really? Then I suggest you stop staring over my shoulder at the Statue of Liberty. Lenox Hill demands relentless focus and intensity. And most of all, ambition. Like Caesar, your father might add. The rewards are spectacular, but the ascent is steep and strewn with the bodies of the fallen."

He'd been watching a helicopter, not the Statue of Liberty, and trying not to think about *his* helicopter flight over the Pacific. "I'm a Marine officer, Howard."

"Good for you, Freddy." Momentary silence. "I landed on D-Day. Omaha, not Utah." Howard Paulson let that sink in. "I'm sure you took a lot of hills in Virginia and California, but what do you know about corporate finance? Most of our hires are Harvard MBAs."

Fred hung his head. "I can learn corporate finance."

"Nepotism can ruin morale if the person in question isn't up to snuff. I've been damn tough on Tod, but he's come through with flying colors. You might be out of place here, Freddy."

Howard Paulson was fidgeting. Not a good sign. "Mother wondered about that."

"Your mother's extremely perceptive, but I'm starting to worry about her memory. Her cognition. Rare in someone so young."

"What do you mean by that?"

"Nothing, Freddy. Where were we? Yes, I've been expecting this conversation, and I have something that might be perfect for you."

Thank God. "What's that, Howard?" At times he loathed himself.

"A slot in Boston. You'd be closer to your father and the school we all love."

"I kind of hoped to be in New York."

"You might still get here, Freddy, but it takes a certain type to cut it at Lenox Hill. As for the rest: They're hens in the fox house. However, you'll be pleased to hear there's an attractive opening at Old Colony Bank. Lenox Hill is its controlling stockholder, so Old Colony does my bidding."

Fred did his best to look motivated.

"Old Colony's developing a personal banking division. It caters to the rich, those we now call 'wealthy.' We're looking for up-and-coming youngsters like you with agreeable personalities to work established clubs and the 'old money' side of the street. You'd fit in well, and there'd be few late nights."

"Let me think about it, Howard. It's an interesting offer. What about salary? And benefits? And vacations?"

"We may be getting a bit ahead of ourselves," said his tight-lipped stepfather, who spun in his chair and stared out the window.

Dumb move. "You're right. As I said, let me think about it. It sounds very exciting." He was such a worm.

"No rush, Freddy," said Howard Paulson over his shoulder.

Something caught Howard Paulson's eye. "Look, Lenny's hungry!"

"Lenny?" said a mystified Fred.

"Our resident peregrine. An apex predator. There!"

He saw a speck. It seemed to be orbiting. Then it plunged.

"He's diving. Like a P-51."

There was a small explosion of pigeon feathers.

"That, young man, is Lenny of Lenox Hill, just what we're looking for here."

"Can we talk about Mother?"

"I'm concerned, Freddy. Sadly, your dear mother's begun to slip. She isn't her former self, and she's no longer up to being the first lady of Lenox Hill Capital."

"What?"

"Not the time or the place, Freddy, but have your brother give me a call when he's back from Vietnam. You made it out just in time."

"My brother?"

"Daniel Shaver. Hasn't your father practically adopted him?"

"Absolutely not!" he said. "My father may have encouraged him, but that's the extent of it. Nothing more. And he doesn't have an MBA, either."

"Let him know I'd like to see him. Combat's perfect training for this place."

As he rode down in Lenox Hill's private elevator, he realized he'd wimped out by not pressing Howard Paulson about his mother. If he had, he'd have been less shocked by what happened. But nobody, certainly not him, leaned on Howard Paulson.

Was Howard Paulson right in dismissing him? As Vietnam dragged on, Fred couldn't help but wonder how he'd have done there. His father, Howard Paulson, and Daniel Shaver all saw action and, as best he could tell, performed creditably. Would he have measured up? His tentative answer was "probably," not because he was brave or bloodthirsty but because failure would have been unendurable.

25

DR. E

Thank you, Gaius Valerius. You were there for me when I was wooing Helen, and you served as my crutch when she upended my life. Cruel Clodia. Crueler Helen. For months I saw myself as the angry, despairing Catullus. Like him, I was a romantic, doomed to a short, wretched—but memorable—life. Predictably, that phase was short-lived, and here I remain, the phlegmatic Latin teacher[30] whose doctors have, thus far, detected no portents of consumption and imminent death. I missed my chance for a melodramatic youthful departure decades ago.

During my brief turn as the bruised bard, I set aside my translation of Horace's challenging lyric poems and dashed off some agonized offerings of my own. In English.[31] Bad idea. I still wince when recalling that cloying tripe and pray—to the true gods, naturally—that I succeeded in burning the entire oeuvre plus drafts. I shudder at the vision of them falling into the hands of the teenage brutes I'm charged with civilizing. Worse still, what if my rubbish were recited to the assembled school at our annual declamation contest?

---

30 Equally fleeting and implausible was my time as a brooding Byronic hero.

31 Maybe they'd have fared better in Latin.

Immediately following Helen's perfidy, I, Frederick Agonistes Elder, spent several weeks wallowing in what may be Catullus's best-known poem (number 85). Here is F. W. Cornish's version:

> I hate and love. Why I do so, perhaps you ask.
> I know not, but I feel it, and I am in torment.

Catullus and I parted company soon thereafter. Despising Helen was too enervating. It ruined my digestion *and* my squash game. Besides, equating her with Clodia just didn't hold water (or olive oil) if even half of what Catullus said about his lover was true. Yes, I was angry with Helen, but I missed her more and would have had her back in a trice. Or sooner.

Furthermore, when I consider the evidence in a judicious manner, I must allow that Howard Paulson was a better catch. Additionally, he may have appreciated Helen more than I did or convinced her he did. Yes, I flew too close to the sun, and my wings melted.

Je regrette tout.

26

DANIEL

Daniel Shaver glimpsed the band as his aircraft flashed by the control tower. He was in no rush to deplane and risk being trampled by a stampede of sex-starved snuffies. His plane, reeking of booze and body odor, cranked a hard left onto a taxiway and left again towards the gate. Nobody was meeting him. No big deal, though. He wasn't into mushy reunions.

Assuming Moonshine, his favorite Thai bar girl, had moved on, the only people he could think of who *might* give a rat's ass whether he returned carrying his shield or stretched out on it were Dr. Elder and Mary Foley, all of whose letters he had saved. But neither of them had the money to fly west and meet him. Ma, also broke, couldn't have managed it without a keeper.

Behind him, a leathery warrant officer turned to his neighbor. "Sergeant Major, looks like we made it home in time for the election."

"Some election. It'll be Trick in a landslide."

"Enough of that shit, Lou. My question to you is, how do I get it up for someone who's damn near forty? We've been spoiled, my friend."

"Roger your last," replied the sergeant major. "So, good buddy, who's the lucky lady, if I may be so bold?"

"The wife," groaned the warrant officer.

"I guessed as much. Same here. The nights of cheap booze and silent, smiling, submissive young things are gone until our next Oki-knock-knock tour."

"Okinawa, shit. We'll probably draw another all-expenses-paid trip to scenic I Corps. No reason to think Trick'll do better at ending it than LBJ."

"You're probably right. Anyway, we damn well better look horny when we hit the tarmac."

"Or it'll hit the fucking fan."

Yes, it sucked, but better no welcoming committee than wondering whether your chiquita was going boom-boom while you were having leeches burned outta your butt. Besides, being last off the plane would give him an opportunity to show off his Harvard ring, chat up the stews, and organize something for tonight.

Already a lot of the shit was becoming indistinct. The grove. Rubino. The scout. His down time in Okinawa, after being pulled out of Nam in '67, had helped.

When he stepped off the plane, he'd be home free. Rubino was worm food. His guilt and worry were bound to pass. Everything did.

The rays from the setting sun hit him in the face as he left the stifling aircraft. None of the stews had waited to see him off. Would it have been different if they'd recognized his Harvard ring? But they were otherwise engaged. Policing up the galley. Collecting cabin trash. Readying the bird for its next flight west with a fresh consignment of clean-shaven, fresh-smelling cannon fodder. Meanwhile, the band, having sleep-walked through its standard half-hour medley of Sousa marches, was wrapping it up with a desultory rendition of the Hymn. The musicians' absence of enthusiasm matched his own.

The only civilian still waiting at the gate was a striking woman in what Shaver guessed was her early twenties—a brunette with lively dark eyes that sparkled in the late afternoon sunlight. She was holding a little girl, hardly more than a baby. A yellow plastic something was about to fall from her sparse dark hair. He'd spotted the woman through his window and wondered about the lucky guy—almost certainly an officer—she was meeting. She was better turned out than the no-bra moms in their miniskirts and puffed-up hooker hair. The brunette was staring at him. Why? Clearly, she'd mistaken him for someone else. A chance for a quickie? He looked over his shoulder. There was only one guy behind him. A Black corporal. Sure as shit, that wasn't his daughter.

She was walking towards him, no mistaking that. He did some quick calculations. How old was the child, and where had he been not quite two years ago? Yes, Nam had, to some extent, erased what preceded it, but there's no way he'd have forgotten her. She'd have been a recurrent fantasy, supplanting Diana, Mary, and even Moonshine.

Whoever she was, the unclaimed babe was easy on the eyes. But then, Daisy the Holstein would have looked appetizing right then. The mother continued to stare at him as he approached. It was difficult to read her expression. Intense, but neither a smile nor a frown.

Now he could see and, since the band had packed up and departed, hear the chanting anti-war protestors outside the cyclone fence. Some of the hairy fucks were wearing unmatched pieces of Marine uniforms. Times like this he wished he hadn't turned in his .45.

She stopped in front of him. "Lieutenant?"

"Yes?"

"Lieutenant Shaver?"

"Guilty as charged," he managed with what he hoped was an engaging grin. "How did you know?"

"I found out you'd be on this plane, and now you're the only officer left. And the right rank."

She had a pleasing low voice and an intoxicating scent. Perfume had that effect on him. If women grasped its impact, they'd wallow in it. Yes, he'd buy some for Mary Foley and throw in a case of hot sauce for her bland New Hampshire burgers.

Mom had flawless skin. He wanted to run a hand over it. "And you are?"

"Alma Rubino, and this is Harriet. She's named for Tony's mother."

Oh, fuck, fuck, and fuck again! His heart was racing. Dread doused desire. *Be cool. Bugging out would arouse suspicion.* "I am so sorry for your loss, Mrs. Rubino, and even sorrier for not recognizing you." That last bit was pitiful.

"How could you have recognized me, Lieutenant Shaver? I'm not sure Tony carried my picture, and, if he did, whether he showed it to anyone. Even Tony might not recognize me now, a tired old mom."

That sure as shit wasn't true. He made a noise signifying it was her turn to talk.

Alma Rubino fell into step beside him. Harriet—somehow her old-fashioned name fit perfectly—flashed him a gummy smile. His heart rate settled. "Could we talk for a few minutes, Lieutenant Shaver?"

"You bet, but I'm afraid it's got to be quick. I'm meeting someone." *You lying fuck.*

Her face fell. "Oh dear. Is she here now? It's she, I assume. I don't want to ruin your homecoming."

"No, it's fine. I'm meeting her downtown. She's coming in from the East. I hope you realize you have my deepest sympathy, Mrs. Rubino." He was running out of evasions.

"Thank you, Lieutenant, and thank you for your thoughtful letter. Your first name's Daniel, isn't it? Tony really admired you. He dashed off a note just before that patrol. He said it was going to be led by a Harvard man who had to be smart. He was referring to you, wasn't he?"

"Yes, he was, and yes, it's Daniel, but please call me Dan." Had she noticed his ring? Did it impress her?

"Well, Dan, maybe we could talk for a minute. How about here?"

Now what, he asked himself. "Sure thing. Can I help you with Harriet, Mrs. Rubino? And watch out for that yellow thing; it's about to fall out of her hair."

"Please, Dan; it's Alma. No, I've got her. I can feed her right here." And then she proceeded to do so. "It's okay, Dan; you don't have to hide. I'm just being a mom."

Just being a mom? Christ, he was about to explode. "Alma, I'm going to grab a Coke. Can I get one for you?"

"That would be wonderful."

He dawdled at the vending machine until he subsided. Alma Rubino finished buttoning up as he approached.

"Here you go," he blurted out. Harriet burped. Liquid dribbled from her mouth. How, in the name of all that was holy, could he think about anything but what he'd just glimpsed? A delicate tracery of blue veins resembling a network of untraveled secondary roads.

"Could I ask you to do me a favor, Dan?"

"Name it."

"Would you hold Harriet while I go to the ladies' room? I won't be a minute."

"You bet." She looked great walking away.

Harriet lunged at him and, with wide-open eyes fixed on him alone, said something that could only have been "Da, da."

"You two look pleased with each other," said Alma, on her return.

He made a face at Harriet. "Yes, we are."

"Now tell me about Tony. I met him while volunteering at the USO. We had a few dates and a hurried wedding before he shipped out. Then some R & R in Hawaii. Harriet was born right before he died. Tony and I had no idea what we were getting into. My family was upset. Both of us were trying to escape things."

"What were you trying to escape, Alma?"

"It's a long story, Dan. Maybe another time . . . if there is one."

Given what happened in the grove, how *could* there be another one?

She looked up and patted the bench.

He sat down next to her. Harriet was on her mother's far shoulder. She was watching him. He and Mom were almost touching. "What would you like me to tell you?"

"Probably what every widow needs to hear. How did he die? Did he suffer? Was he brave? Did he talk about Harriet and me? I'll need to tell her as much as I can about her daddy."

"I understand." His mind was racing. Prolonging this was crazy.

"I shouldn't say this, but every wife wants to know if her husband behaved himself overseas. No, I'm sorry. It's an unfair question. Tony'd expect you to clam up, and it doesn't matter now. Marines aren't monks."

Doing his best to maintain eye contact, he said, "Do you mind if I smoke, Mrs. Rubino?"

"Of course not. Now, how many times must I tell you, Dan, it's Alma."

"Your husband died bravely, Alma. And instantly. He was my radio-man, the best in the company. We knew each other but hadn't had much contact before the patrol." Yes, that was bullshit. He hadn't known shit about Rubino. The guy'd been dumped on him because both of them were spare parts. How the hell did *he* snag someone like her?

"Yes, I heard that. He wrote about you. Said his company just got a new lieutenant who seemed to have his stuff together, except Tony didn't use the word 'stuff.'"

"I'm flattered. That's a big compliment."

"Can you tell me about the . . . you said it was a patrol, didn't you?"

"Are you sure, Mrs. . . . . Alma? It's bound to be upsetting."

Harriet was irresistible. The yellow plastic thing—it was shaped like a flower—had fallen onto the floor. She was making wet noises and stretching towards it. He picked it up. She grabbed it in a chubby knuckleless hand, favored him with a damp smile, if that's what it was, and made a sound in her pants.

"Don't worry about me, Dan. I'm over the worst of it, and, just between the two of us, I'm still angry with Tony. His medical problems could have kept him home, but no, he wanted to be a Marine. Lots of boys grow out of that. Not Tony, and not you, I guess. I left college too. Now Harriet and I are alone. And me with no degree."

"Yeah, I made it through college and then did the same thing as Tony, but nobody was counting on me. Maybe we should change the subject." What the fuck. Guilt? Check. Desire to help? Check. Unalloyed desire? Double check. Now what?

"No, please continue, Dan. I know about your college, but what was Vietnam like for you?" She gave his leg a distracted pat. He flinched.

"Sorry," he said. "I got hit on that patrol. Did you notice this ribbon?"

She bent closer. "Yes, it's a Purple Heart. Tony got one too. But he's not alive. Are you all right now?"

"Sure. It wasn't *that* serious." The "that" was inexcusable. It wasn't one fucking bit serious. "As I wrote, we were on a patrol in Indian country—enemy territory—when we came under mortar fire. It was an ambush. Before we could pull back, Tony was hit and killed instantly, and, I promise you, it *was* instantaneous. Tony couldn't have felt anything." Was she buying it?

"Isn't that what they always tell the families?"

He moved closer. He could feel her clean, fresh breath. This was reckless.

"Maybe so. I'm not sure. I'm new to this. Probably, but it happens to be true."

"Did Tony do a good job?"

"Outstanding, as we say in the Corps. He called in the artillery fire that destroyed the mortars. He saved us. I put him in for a medal, but sometimes it takes years."

"But you got your medal, Dan. I'm sorry. That was petty. Thank you for recommending him. Getting it would mean a lot to Harriet when she's older."

She was not backing off. Anything but. Time for a new topic, but Harriet was snoring peacefully, and nothing came to mind.

"Did you bring Tony's body back?"

"Absolutely. Carried him back with us. The Corps looks after its own."

"And Sergeant Foster?"

"Uh . . . yes. How did you hear about him?"

"From his widow, Marjorie."

"Yes, Marjorie Foster."

"She lives nearby, and she's having a rough time of it with two kids. We've become close."

He was sweating. Why these pointed questions? What did she know?

"Did Tony wear—what's it called?—some kind of armor?"

"A flak jacket. I can't remember. Probably. Most of us did. Why do you ask?"

"I took a last look at Tony. I owed him that, and I couldn't bear the thought of burying the wrong man. The person showing me Tony's body said he had wounds that would be hard to explain if he'd been wearing one of those jackets."

Who had she talked to? "Uh . . . Unfortunately, flak jackets aren't foolproof. They're only good against shell fragments, not direct hits by bullets." He could tell from her expression she wasn't done.

"But there weren't any bullets, were there? Just mortars? Aren't they different?"

He should have beat feet pronto. "Yes, but they can sometimes penetrate a vest. Did you hear anything else about Tony's wounds?"

"No, I didn't."

Stop with the damn questions. "Wait a sec, now that you mention it, I recall Tony wasn't wearing a flak jacket. He said they were too damn hot and heavy. Specially if you were humping a radio. Plus, nothing had been happening in our vicinity for weeks. I couldn't change his mind."

"Couldn't you have ordered him to wear one?" She looked unconvinced. "Marines are supposed to be well-disciplined."

Was he looking squirrely? "I guess so, but your husband . . . Tony was experienced. I didn't think it was my call." He was sweating. "Where's Tony buried?"

"That big military cemetery near San Diego. I couldn't bear to cremate him. Somehow that's too final."

He'd have been fine with final.

"I'm so damn mad at him. He didn't have to be there in the first place, and he promised he'd really take care of himself."

"Alma—"

"Dan, you're looking at your watch. You're bored. You weren't expecting a grilling. You've got someone waiting. I should be ashamed. And now I'm about to cry."

Oh, God. Anything but that. "She can wait a little longer, and you're not boring me. Anything but." That was dumb.

"Good. I'm glad you can spare me some time. Women in my shoes get lonely. Can you tell me more about your wounds?"

Enough. "Maybe another time."

"That would be wonderful. And I can cook you something nice. Something Italian. Tony taught me a couple dishes. The women in my family are lousy cooks, more interested in booze. I have to watch that myself. Will you be here for a few more days? You live back East, don't you?"

Harriet opened her eyes. Thank God. A diversion. "I'm not sure."

"You're not sure about what, Dan, where you live or whether you'll be here a little longer?"

"Right now, I'm not sure about anything, Alma." He was getting in too deep. Time to bug the fuck out as he'd done in the grove.

"Would you hold Harriet again? Just for a minute. She likes you, and I've got to make another fast trip to the powder room."

What a kick, holding someone who was defenseless yet completely trusting.

A wriggling Harriet Rubino looked up at him, and then, for him alone, ran through her repertoire of grunts, gestures, facial contortions, fist pumps, and leg thrusts. He couldn't applaud, because that would mean putting her down, but he could tell she was pleased with herself. She needed no confirmation of her charm.

He wanted to whistle, clap, and throw flowers. Deservedly, she reveled in her power to delight.

Just as he was feeling confident in this new role, she suddenly and terrifyingly arched her back, transforming herself into a rigid hard-to-hold-on-to plank.

Feeling his panic, she relaxed, favored him with a wanton smile, blew a shapely spit bubble, and gurgled something he, again, took to be "Da, da." The gurgling quite undid him.

In that moment their pact was sealed. This tiny creature needed him, and damnit he needed her. He would be her champion. He would wear her yellow barrette into battle against the Moors.

Alma Rubino returned, scrabbled around in her shoulder bag, found a pencil, and scribbled something on the back of a sales slip. Yes, a familiar smell. She'd taken a pop. "Here's my address and phone number. Promise you'll get in touch. As I said, I can cook—a little. And I'm not always this blue."

It would be risky seeing her again, but Harriet decided it. "I promise," he said.

"Now, before you leave, Dan, enough with the long face. What happens next for you? I bet the ladies are lined up around the block."

"You've got that wrong, Alma. There's nobody special. Let's see, where are we now? August. I'm headed back to Lower Nowhere, New Hampshire. I'll look in on Ma and spend some time with the fancy family at the top of the hill."

"Fancy?"

"Well, fancier than the Shavers, which doesn't take much."

"And what happens after your hero's welcome in New Hampshire?"

"Back to Harvard."

"I thought you were done there."

She'd been paying attention. "Harvard Business School, it's two years."

"It must be expensive."

"It is, but I'm getting a hero's free ride from a potential employer."

"Wow, and stop making fun of yourself. You deserve it."

"You stop it, Alma. No, I take it back. Keep it coming. I love hearing that kind of nonsense."

She started repacking her bag. "One more promise, please. Let me know when you're settled. My mom's sister lives in Rhode Island. I usually visit her twice a year."

This was totally nuts. Gideon would have smacked him, but what he said was, "Say no more. When?"

"I haven't figured that out. I'll tell you when I do. You won't forget?"

Fat chance. "You'll bring Harriet, won't you?"

"I will, and now you better hand her over."

He didn't want to. She'd gone to sleep on his shoulder. Nobody'd ever done that.

He took Alma Rubino to a cab, slipped the driver a fifty, and, like an idiot, gave her a chaste but satisfying kiss. On her cheek. Could he somehow make it right? Then he took a cab to the BOQ. He couldn't get either Harriet or Alma out of his mind, so he headed to the bar figuring four drinks was the price of sleep. After three and against his better judgment, he called her.

It was late. He was afraid she wouldn't pick up. He was afraid she would. "Alma, it's me, Dan. Did I wake you?"

"You did, but that's okay, I guess."

What the fuck was he supposed to say now?

"What time is it, Dan? My God. Two, and I've got my impossible second-graders tomorrow. Have you by any chance been drinking?"

"A little, but that was some time ago, and now I'm sober as a judge." Couldn't he do better than that? "Besides, I can't sleep."

"Well, I was doing fine in that department."

"Can we talk? Can I—" He shut up before making it worse. There was no way to get around it. What he'd done in the grove was—was what? It was necessary.

What if he went over to her apartment now? What if she greeted him in a bathrobe? What if he lost it? What if she resisted? He could probably justify whatever happened—he usually did—but what if he kiboshed everything with Harriet? Sometimes he frightened himself.

"What did you say, Dan?"

"How's about I come over for an early breakfast and give you a hand with Miss Harriet?"

"Okay, but you'll need to get here by six."

"See you at O-600."

Had he been an idiot to take a pass on what might have been a fabulous roll in the hay? Or had he—quite uncharacteristically—done the decent thing? Damned if he knew, but for the first time since the grove he didn't wake up in a sweat. And, in a few days, he'd pick up where he'd left off with Mary Foley.

27

DR. E

W hat for many moons had been obvious to all finally got through to me. Helen was gone for good. Despite my years of cleaning her glasses and tucking in her clothing labels, Helen would never repudiate Howard Paulson. Her New Hampshire jelly-making days were over.

That being so, what now, aging Latin teacher? Did I desire female companionship? Roger that. Was I in a fit state to bring that to pass? Doubtful. Could I learn the right moves? Doubtfuller. If I did, was I a "player"? Doubtfullest.

Those were sorrowful days, and the nights were worse. Though my aggregate caloric intake remained essentially stable, it became more heavily weighted towards less-nourishing, sugar-laden, memory-erasing liquids.

To my surprise, D-B, without initially disclosing the basis for his understanding, said he "fully grasped" my unhappiness. Sensing my doubt about his expertise in matters of the heart, D-B said, "Allow me to explain."

I nodded.

D-B continued, "I'm not sure she's still alive, but her name was/is Daphne."

D-B and I exchanged looks. He knew I caught the allusion.

"She was the adorable daughter of my Harrow House Master, an irritable sod who endorsed corporal punishment and, I was led to believe, relished regular canings on his own trembling bum. Very public school, don't you know.[32] Alas, Daphne was underage—jailbait, as you Yanks would say."

Rather than interrupt, I nodded again.

D-B rolled on, "Fast forward, to use the current argot. I finish my education, return to Harrow as a Master, and guess who's there, still too young, but even more bewitching."

There was no reason for me to respond.

"Time passes; Daphne reaches the magic milestone, and our relationship, already deliciously complex, continues its ascent. Daphne has only amused disdain for her zit-covered peers. I, on the other hand, had bested Rommel. That's a different kettle of fish and chips. I allowed myself—reluctantly, of course—to become her idol. That, by the way, infuriated her Papa, who'd been an air raid warden. Did I go too far, I wonder, when I showed her my awards and let her play with my Webley?"

I must have looked shocked, because D-B blurted out, "That's my service revolver, you dolt!"

D-B composed himself and said, "Then, in what seemed like the blink of an eye—Daphne's were a luminous blue—it was time for my nestling to fledge. I was stricken when she opted for Radcliffe, but all was well when I broached my plan to secure employment near Cambridge—the one in *Massachusetts*."

Oh, to be a swashbuckler like D-B.

D-B cleared his throat. "St. Matthew's opened its arms and its exchequer when, in my flawless Oxbridge accent, I pitched the idea

---

32 Appropriating the name of an American securities firm, D-B mused aloud about organizing an old boys' club named Bare Sterns.

of a Humanities program. Darling Daphne was thrilled. At last she'd be free of her censorious father in an atmosphere that had mellowed considerably since the days of the witch trials. Daphne was mine. In retrospect, it's clear I was impulsive, if not utterly Mediterranean."

I sensed D-B's saga was going to end poorly, so I hurried him along.

"Then, without warning or explanation, Daphne made it clear she'd had her fill of me."

D-B looked annoyed at my reaction to what I sensed might have been an off-color double entendre.

"For God's sake, dear Freddy, get your mind out of . . . To continue, while my darling nymph didn't turn herself into a laurel tree, she did something worse. She transferred to Yale, where, I have reason to believe, she fell into the clutches of a learned lecher whose academic credentials eclipsed mine."

D-B said no more about Daphne, but some years thereafter he told me she had a granddaughter at Harvard.

Finally, D-B and I returned to *my* problems, with him offering to edit the draft of a personal ad I was about to submit to—where else?—*Harvard Magazine*. I read him my proposed opening: "Seeking a companionable lady, age irrelevant, with whom to share life in the HOV lane."

I was proud of my deft HOV allusion, but D-B, my Cyrano, reminded me of my target audience and urged me to play up my "lefty" leanings.

28

DANIEL

It had been, what? December of '58, ten years ago, and it cost Daniel almost a hundred bucks worth of cokes and burgers to break the ice. He'd been emboldened by his sessions on the Simulator. No more just staring at that lucky silver cross.

He was nearly fifteen when he came home for his first Christmas vacation. Hadn't Mary Foley winked at him the last time she caught him staring?

He opened his campaign by taking Ma to Foley's Restaurant and splurging on the $4.95 Christmas special. Ma was wearing the bright red sneakers he'd bought her with his Simulator earnings, and he was decked out in the sports jacket with elbow patches Dr. Elder had just given him. His generous 10% tip made it clear to Miss Foley that he, Daniel Shaver, was someone to be reckoned with. A sure bet to return his family to preeminence in Lower Finley.

Thank God, Mary had a car with that rarity—a working heater. All he could offer was the John Deere, which wouldn't cut it for what he had in mind. Certainly not in December.

It began well. A couple miles from the restaurant, she turned west off Route 139 onto a well-maintained dirt road. "The Rogers place," said Mary as she doused her headlights, put the car in neutral, and coasted past the shuttered lakefront cottage.

"Great spot, Mare." Summoning every ounce of suave, he added, "You come here much?" She was always criticizing his "grubby" fingernails. Would she notice he'd cleaned them?

"Don't be a shit, Danny boy. And don't be spilling the beans to anybody. At least your prick brother's not around anymore."

"Why do you still hate him? Ever go out with him?"

"Never."

He'd better knock it off about Gideon. And now for *his* big treat. "I got us a six-pack." She looked interested. He seized a can. *Two* masterful flicks of his church key—he hadn't forgotten the air hole. He presented her with a cold wet one. Only then did he open one for himself.

She examined it. "You gotta be shitting me, Danny. A Gansett. That's totally lame."

What would it take to get her in the mood?

They drank in silence. He emptied his can, emitted his deepest belch, rolled down the window, and underhanded it towards the lake, where it clanged off a rock.

"Shit, Danny, I'm freezing."

Wow! Was she ready? Already? He was one smooth dude. It took only one beer.

Daniel rolled up the window and made his move. Step one: the kiss. Safe at first. Then he snaked an arm around behind her.

She stiffened. "Christ, Danny, you're pinching me." She removed his arm. "There, it's undone. Happy now?"

"You bet, Mare."

At last. There they were. And there was the silver cross! And yes, *National Geographic* had been more or less on the money.

Actually, they were just kinda staring at him. Now what? Inspiration. As though bobbing for apples, he dove headfirst and took the cross in his mouth. Nice and warm in there.

Mary was unamused. He disgorged the icon and nonchalantly tore open the foil container he'd carried in his wallet for the last two years. The damn thing was slippery. Should he have bought the dry kind? What about one of those tickler things he'd heard of but never seen? They sure didn't sell them at Freeman's Gulf Station.

Would she lose interest while he wrestled with it? Shit! It slipped out of his hands and landed on the floor. Had she noticed? She had.

"Get ridda that filthy thing."

It was his only one. "I can wipe it off, Mare."

"Yuk. No way. You don't deserve it, but I got a couple more in the glove compartment. And no fresh comments."

Thank God. He kissed her again and took a long lead off second.

"Ouch! Jesus, Danny."

"What?"

"Your belt buckle, it's going to leave a helluva bruise. Look, Danny, it's really kinda simple, like a child's jigsaw puzzle. When you line things up, they just sorta fit together. Like they're supposed to. Now gimme your hand."

"Which one?"

"Kee-rist. The one you use to write, eat, throw, and wake up girls."

He complied. Nothing on under her skirt. Wow! Safe at third with a slick pop-up slide. What now? Continue to march. Before she changed her mind.

"Jesus, Danny, you're doin' it all wrong!"

That was a showstopper.

"Okay, Danny, feel that? Yeah. Right there. Yes. A little faster. How to go, Danny, boy! You *are* getting the hang of it."

When the hell was it his turn? "Mare, I'm about to—"

"Now, off with those ratty jeans. Turn the damn thing over, you dope. Now unroll it. All the way down, lover boy."

Jesus H. Christ. Oh, wow! Lush. Curly. Fluffy. The color of fall foliage. Kinda like Lower Finley in mid-October.

"Okay, sit still. Let me get my other leg over. There. Nice, isn't it?"

Had he scored? "Pleeese, Mare."

"I'm not too heavy, am I?"

"No, Mare. You're perfect, and I love your . . . eyes."

"I bet you don't know their color."

Oh great. Were they the same as his? "Sure, I do—greenish-blue."
She sighed and closed her eyes. Thank Christ, they were back in
business.

"Am I the prettiest girl in Dad's restaurant?"

"You are the prettiest girl in all of Lower Finley, New Hampshire,
US of A."

"I'm almost ready, Danny. You know how you can tell?"

He damn well didn't. They were aching. "This is torture, Mare."

"No, it's not. Anything but. Think about something else. I'll start.
Slowly. Like this. Feels good, doesn't it?"

"Yes!" He tried to think about the Sox. That wasn't working.

"Okay, Danny, your turn. Harder!"

Yesss! Uh-oh—

"Oh shit, Danny. You damn Shavers . . . don't leave me hanging
like this."

"Mare, I'm sorry. What'll I do?"

"Just move. I'll do it myself."

Fascinating and instructive. He studied her carefully, listened to
her ragged breathing, and watched as she opened her eyes. "You okay
now, Mare?" It had turned out fine, but he'd have to improve. Would
Dr. Elder have some advice? He was a married man. Bad idea. How
about the motorcycle guy who parked in front of Foley's? For sure, he'd
have a few tips.

"So, Danny, whadaya going to do?"

"Wipe us off?"

"You're such a jerk. I mean when you get done with school and all."

"I'm going to college. First in the family. Then I'm going to make a bundle, fix up our place, and buy the Elders' land. It used to belong to us. Pa's father told him to do it. Pa told Gideon, and now it's up to yours truly."

"But hasn't old man Elder been good to you?"

"Yeah. More than anyone but you. I'll let him stay in that dumpy house till he dies, but not Freddy. You know what else? You could live at our place and keep an eye on Ma. I'd pay you for that."

"With what, Danny?"

"You'll see. And when I'm rich, I'm going to marry you. That's a promise. Count on it!" That should keep her coming back for more.

"Danny—"

"Yeah?" Why that grin?

"I gotta tell you something, Danny. I'm sure you'll do great in college, but I'm giving you an 'incomplete' for tonight. And cut those damn nails, will ya?"

29

DR. E

Alas, my ad campaign in *Harvard Magazine* bore no fruit or *anything* remotely edible. My witty HOV lane sally elicited not a single response. Equally ineffective were my personal hygiene follow-ups, pointing out that, given my regimen of two showers a day, I was reliably clean and odorless. TMI? I considered and rejected the idea of offhandedly mentioning my summa. In retrospect, I'm glad I didn't.

In growing desperation, I offered up, "Trim, tidy, and well-groomed." Still nothing. Could the reference to my increasingly inaccessible toenails and my request for a kindly lady willing to assist with their pruning have been a trifle *de trop*? Perhaps, since the only reply I received to that was "ick." Best I not mention my recurrent rash.

And now? Short of midlife chastity,[33] what were my options? A deluge of ads in the publications of lesser institutions? Graduates of such places would surely welcome the opportunity to trade up by snagging a Harvard man of my caliber.

---

33 Like the young Augustine I choose to defer my renunciation of the flesh. Who am I kidding? Like it or not, abstinence appears to have been thrust upon me.

As a last resort, there must remain—even in puritanical Massachusetts—establishments catering to recurring, but underserved, needs. I am, it goes without saying, unfamiliar with the current landscape, and, to the best of my knowledge, the Harvard Coop does not stock guides to dens of iniquity. But the dens are out there. Aren't they? Yes, they must be.

Anent that, I still treasure the letter my Harvard father sent me the first week of freshman year. Without furnishing their names, he warned me of the "lewd and bawdy taverns to be found in and around Central Square." Taverns that he implied were "patronized by the likes of fat Jack Falstaff and poxy Doll Tearsheet." Off I dashed to—yes—Central Square, but my quest was unavailing. Thwarted again. After a thorough reconnaissance I confessed to my father, whose urbanity I so admired, that these establishments had evidently gone belly-up[34] or decamped to more tolerant locales. I was delighted by Father's merry response to my raillery. Here it is:

> My roommate, Ambrose Adams
> Was fearful of Madams:
> In a house of ill repute
> He'd go utterly mute.

I remember thinking at that time of the little red kaluta, a semelparous marsupial living in the Australian desert. The male drops dead soon after mating, reportedly due to stress. So, yes, things could have been worse.

In any case, thank you, dear Polly, for rescuing me from the realization that my pen was no mightier than my sword. I cannot imagine and could not endure life without you.

---

34 He appreciated my play on words.

30

DANIEL

What was he, the returning warrior, going to do when he got home to Lower Finley? The first order of business: expunge forever the "incomplete" he'd received from Mary Foley ten years earlier. That should be a cinch, given what exuberant Moonshine had taught him.

What then? Cover the rotting windows with new plastic? Spend a couple days with Ma and make sure Tommy Reeves was doing right by him? Tommy, a former schoolmate, had taken over his father's carpentry business and volunteered to look after the Shaver place. If he sent her money, Ma—who'd gorged her way into Type 2 diabetes—would have pissed it away on junk food, Luckies, and Gansetts. So, he opened an account with Tommy on the understanding he'd be charged the barely break-even rate paid by the other locals.

And what about Mary? No doubt recognizing his upside, she'd written him once a week for thirteen months. Somewhere along the line, the tone of her letters had changed from sassy to something he didn't feel in return. He wasn't sure how to respond, so he stopped writing. He probably should have bought her something, but he hadn't done that either, not even the cheap Asian shit married lifers used to decorate their hooches.

However he parsed them, Mary's letters seemed to be saying, "I see myself in your future, but not in the role you seem to expect." Surely she couldn't expect . . . Everyone agrees, things said right afterwards don't count.

Mustn't forget Mary's job as Ma's caregiver. She was to spend the money he sent home on insulin and semi-healthy food. He dreaded watching his mother lose limbs to a disease she might have controlled, or avoided altogether, if he'd been there to kick her ass.

———

Alma's apartment was a revelation. Nothing was torn, dirty, or busted. No Jesus staring down at him.

Nothing smelled bad. No mess. No clutter. Thankfully, she was dressed.

"Being a Marine, I assume you take it black," she said.

"That's affirmative."

She handed him a scarlet and gold mug. "One of Tony's."

There was only one response. "Semper Fi." He took a sip. Not bad.

"And Semper Fi to you, Dan."

The conversation was flagging. Where was Harriet? He pointed to a pair of framed photographs. "That's you and Tony, isn't it? And the other one's our young lady?"

"Our?"

"Sorry, yours. A slip of the tongue."

"More coffee, Dan?"

"No, I'm good." Time to come partially clean. Why? Damned if he knew. "Here's the thing, Alma. I'm not exactly what I appear to be. The term 'an officer and a gentleman' doesn't apply to everyone with a commission. Have you heard the expression 'Swamp Yankee'?"

"I'm not from the East, but yes."

Feeling better about himself, he added, "Well, my family looked up to Swamp Yankees. I'm the only one standing now. Ma's barely hanging on, and Pa's dead. Ditto my brother, Gideon. He died in an accident when I was ten."

"What kind of an accident?"

"Farm. The tractor tipped over on him."

"What about your mother?"

"She's a diabetic mess. Never took care of herself. Too many beers. Too much greasy food. Pa screwed up with a chain saw, and that was the end of him. Not a pretty story."

"Things haven't been going great for either of us."

"Whatever happens, you should know what I am and where I come from. No dough. No family. No property. No, that's wrong. I own a few hundred unproductive New Hampshire acres and a run-down farm. Plus, I've got a decent education that I'm damn well gonna monetize." Christ, he was so full of shit. The last thing he wanted was for anyone to know much about him.

Alma got up and, heading for the kitchen, said, "Keep an eye on Harriet while I make us something. Fair warning—it probably won't be as good as what you got in your mess halls."

"Enough with the modesty, your chow will be ambrosial—that's a Harvard word." Pleasing smells floated from the kitchen. He relaxed. His mind wandered.

Shortly after receiving orders to Vietnam in '66, he'd grabbed the bull, Howard Paulson, by the horns. And HP was a bull, powerful and relentlessly positive, always hammering home the message "Opportunities await the opportunistic."

He'd heard many stories, all of them derogatory, about "Money

Bags" Paulson from Freddy and Dr. Elder. He could only wonder what Howard Paulson had heard about him.

So, he rolled the dice and called on one of Wall Street's biggest hitters. In his dress blues, which he knew was pushing it. Somewhat to his surprise, Howard Paulson granted him an audience.

Howard Paulson's aerie was large and uncluttered, containing none of the trappings of success customarily displayed in the haunts of the mighty. No trophies, deal toys, plaques, or diplomas. No tributes from those seeking access or advancement. No photos attesting to his presence among the elect. No evidence of good works. Why?

Equally puzzling, Howard Paulson's gatekeepers never made his supplicants grovel.

It would not have surprised him to discover Howard Paulson had been immortalized in bronze or marble. However, apart from three telephones and several rolodexes, the only object on his eight-foot slab of rosewood was a plastic donkey standing nearly a foot tall. How odd. The man couldn't be a Democrat, could he? Howard Paulson caught him staring at it, but his face revealed nothing.

After a perfunctory offer of something to drink, Howard Paulson got down to it. "Did my stepson say I wanted to see you?"

Damn that weasel. "No sir, he most certainly did not."

"Why am I not surprised?" said Howard Paulson. "Then what brings you here?"

That was the question he'd expected. His answer was well rehearsed. "I've heard a lot about you and Lenox Hill Capital from the Elders."

Howard Paulson raised an eyebrow and grinned. "I bet you have."

Daniel grinned back. "I've read up on you—the *Fortune* piece— and done as much research as I can on Lenox Hill, which isn't a lot."

"Ah, yes, the benefits of being privately held. And what did you glean from your labors, Mr. Shaver?"

"That Lenox Hill is wildly successful, its principals have to be loaded, and I would like to sign on if and when I return in one piece."

"Could I tempt you with a position at Old Colony Bank in Boston? It's quieter and closer to home. Someone with your drive and ambition could go far there, almost certainly further than your brother."

He had expected that one, too. "Freddy is not my brother, and as to your question, perhaps if it was named 'Hard-Charging Colony Bank.'"

Howard Paulson appeared to be thinking. "That was a simple preliminary test. And, yes, you passed."

"Not intending to be rude, but it was an easy test, Mr. Paulson."

"They will become more challenging, I assure you. That said, I like your attitude, Lieutenant, and I've done some due diligence on my own. For instance, I've learned you were a townie at St. Matthew's."

"That's true, but I'm catching on fast."

"You wouldn't be here if you weren't a quick study, but, let me add, I was a townie there too."

A bond. "You'd never know it, sir." Everyone likes brownnosers. Especially those who claim not to.

"Damn straight. And in a couple years, you'll pass as well. Or, even if you don't, nobody'll dare mess—note my refined language—with you."

"Thank you, sir."

"Okay. Time to knock off that 'sir' shit. To those I respect—like you—I'm 'HP.' Just like that Limey brown sauce, I'm tart with a peppery taste."

Daniel obliged with a chuckle.

Howard Paulson rose and began to pace. "Here's what I am prepared to put on the table. Should you return from Vietnam, sound in mind and body, come see me bringing with you evidence that speaks to your effectiveness as a Marine officer."

"Yes, HP. Gladly. And sometime will you tell me about your time in World War II? I've heard you were on Omaha Beach." Howard Paulson was standing behind him. Disquieting.

"No ass-kissing, Lieutenant Shaver. Then, if you pass muster, so to speak, I am prepared to underwrite your Harvard MBA."

"You can make that happen?" Daniel said admiringly.

"Would I have said so if I couldn't? As a generous and somewhat successful alum, I have a certain amount of sway in the admissions office. Moreover, trade schools look favorably on those who've proved themselves outside academia."

"Thank you, HP." He couldn't see Howard Paulson, and he didn't want to look anxious. Best to sit still.

"Don't interrupt me, Lieutenant. I was about to say your thirteen months in Nam will be valued more highly than a like amount of trainee time among the back-slapping boobs in the Thundering Herd. One other thing: Send me your undergraduate transcript before you ship out. In the meantime, good hunting and keep your pecker up."

"Thank you, HP, I will."

"And, speaking of jarheads, I'm familiar with your green side–brown side helmet cover nonsense, so know this: Lenox Hill is green side all the way. Got that, Lieutenant?"

"Roger your last, HP."

"Before you set off, check out my view. Yes, that's the Statue of Liberty, and I'm sorry Lenny's not hungry."

What the hell did he mean by that?

———

"Come and get it," Alma called from the kitchen. She'd made him a real breakfast. Eggs. Bacon, crisp, just the way he liked it. Some fancy kind of bread he'd never seen in Lower Finley. Maybe someday Alma'd whip up a batch of "shit on a shingle." Unlike most Marines, he loved it. The best part of breakfast was feeding Harriet, who—being thrilled to see him again—gurgled, shrieked, and scattered goo over him, herself, and her encrusted highchair.

"Messy, isn't she," said Alma.

"No worse than the guys I ate with," he said, checking his watch.

Then it was off to the airport. Mother and daughter accompanied him. At the boarding gate, Alma reminded him of his promise to stay in touch and kissed him on the lips. Before he turned to leave, Harriet served up another "Da, da."

What to make of all this? Given what he'd been forced to do in the grove, might he have an obligation to Alma Rubino? And how about sweet Harriet?

―――――――

Lower Finley would have to wait. Lenox Hill had booked him onto a direct flight from San Francisco to Idlewild, now JFK. The stew was geisha-like in her attentiveness as she ushered him to his first-class seat. He surprised himself by not asking if she was a member of the thirty-thousand-feet club.

So, this was how warmongers and profiteers lived. It felt good, and it kept getting better. After deplaning, he stepped onto an escalator, and there at its base was a deferential ancient in a scally cap. He was scanning faces and holding aloft a carefully lettered cardboard sign reading, "First Lieutenant Daniel Shaver, USMC." Perfect!

―――――――

Howard Paulson advanced on him with an extended right hand. "Welcome home, Tiger. I expect your ass is dragging, but it's all been laid on in Cambridge. There's a room waiting for you at the B School, and classes begin in a couple weeks. I considered getting you an off-campus flat, but you've got to immerse yourself. Study groups and all that. It's essential to be quick out of the blocks."

"Thank you for everything, sir. The first-class ticket. The limo. I—"

"It's HP, Lieutenant. How many times do I have to tell you?"

"Sorry, HP. I am so grateful for the red-carpet treatment."

Howard Paulson cut him off again. "We're still in the courtship phase—it never lasts—and I want you feeling obligated, recognizing that Lenox Hill has a first option on your ass once you've collected your MBA."

"I get the picture, HP."

"Now, fill me in. Your letter was kinda sketchy. What about that patrol? Had some ugly ones myself. The Krauts excel at making music, beer, and war."

Daniel led him through it step by step until they got to the grove. "Then we got hit. That fucking scout . . . they'd registered their mortars on our position. We were sitting ducks. They nailed my radioman, my sergeant, and some snuffies. Turned one of them into ground beef. Must have been a direct hit. Not much left to bury."

"Sit down, Lieutenant. You're shaking." Howard Paulson spun around and opened a credenza. "Try a splash of my single malt medicine, Lieutenant."

It slid down easily. "Thank you, HP. That hits the spot."

"Sounds like a shit show. I can relate. Then what?"

"I dialed up the cannon-cockers, and we clobbered those fucking—sorry—mortars. Thought we were in the clear, but then we got pounded by heavier stuff and hauled ass. I humped the radio and helped with Rubino. But we didn't get him back in time. He was probably already gone." Howard Paulson appeared to be swallowing it.

"As I recall, Rubino was your radioman. If he was dead, you should have left him there. Don't buy that crap about never leaving the stiffs behind. And sometimes the wounded. That's Boy Scout shit. We did it all the time. Can't let yourself be slowed down. Somebody'll pick 'em up later. Remember that when you join LHC. We're not about the lame and the halt. Net-net, you were outfuckingstanding, Lieutenant."

"No biggie, HP. Anyone would have done the same thing." Time to slow down. Catch his breath. Assess the situation. Take a hard look at how Howard Paulson dressed. In two years it would be his Class A uniform. But maybe he should hold off on the cufflinks and monogrammed shirts until he got to the top.

"Not so, my friend. I saw lots of guys freeze or shit themselves. Literally. You deserve a big frigging medal. And, by the way, you look sharp in your—you jarheads call that uniform 'greens,' don't you?"

"Yes, we do." It was damn near impossible to drop the "sir."

"I like that shit on your chest. Very respectable."

"I'm told my modest Bronze Star might be upgraded, but I'm not sweating it."

"I can bird-dog that. Would look damn good on your resume. Not many dudes with big balls on Wall Street. Different but related subject, hope you got your rocks off in Frisco."

What to say? Howard Paulson might take a dim view of celibacy. "I'm afraid I didn't, HP."

"Sweet Jesus! What gives with that? You better not be some kind of pansy, Mister. No place for them here."

Whew. Howard Paulson was smiling. "Didn't have time. I looked in on Rubino's widow. Same with Marjorie Foster. I hope it helped some." Howard Paulson looked impressed. He, Daniel Shaver, was ready for Wall Street. If he could sell himself, he could sell anything.

"Christ almighty, Shaver. My mistake, but that doesn't address the issue at hand. You done anything to calm the raging beast?"

"Not yet."

"Stop looking like a virgin bride. We've got someone here who's charged with attending to visiting firemen—firewomen too, if it comes to that."

Howard Paulson handed him a business card.

"I'm good for now. There's a girl at home. She waits tables at her father's restaurant, and she'll be glad to see me." He hoped that was still true.

"You need to raise your sights, Lieutenant, if you plan to make it here. She can be dumb as a rock as long as she cleans up well and is clever with parties and small talk."

Not the response he'd expected. "I'm sure I'll meet someone in Cambridge."

"Your call, compadre, but there are a whole helluva lot of two-sack women in the People's Democratic Republic of Cambridge."

"I'm not following you, HP."

"Before you hump a two-sack woman, you put a sack over her head, and then one over yours . . . in case hers slips."

That, he felt, deserved a laugh. He obliged.

"Okay, Shaver, enough shooting the shit. Your next mission: Get your MBA, finish high in your class, and then we'll talk turkey. And, for the record, Lenox Hill has first call on your services. Yes?"

"Absofuckinglutely, as my mustang company commander would say."

"A year from now, Mister Shaver, you will have completed your summer internship at Old Colony, where Freddy Elder's working. You need to see what life's like in the slow lane. I don't want you in my shop wondering if you'd be better off with the placid herbivores at a commercial bank."

Evidently, Howard Paulson was unaware that some herbivores were anything but placid. "Speaking of Freddy, is there any news about the Elder family? Dr. Elder's done a lot for me over the years."

"Yes, there's some news. You remember Freddy's mother, Helen?"

"You're referring to Mrs. Paulson, aren't you?"

"I am, but I'm afraid dear Helen's beginning to fail. The shrinks call it 'cognitive impairment' or, less euphemistically, dementia. A damn shame. Virtually unheard of for someone who's forty-nine. Worse, it's incurable, and, unlike me, it's progressive."

—————

The first thing Daniel did when he got to Cambridge was to send Miss Harriet Rubino six yellow barrettes, a copy of *Make Way for Ducklings*, and a cute card inviting her and Alma to join him for a swan boat ride before the fall semester began. That child, if he had anything to say about it, would want for nothing.

Now, what about the Rubino mess? He tried to analyze it like a B School case, but it was a hopeless muddle. Fortunately, he had a lodestar. Harriet. They needed each other. He knew it, and so did she. His feelings towards Harriet were pure and protective and, therefore, alarming.

Clearly, there was no way to pry Harriet away from Alma, at least for now. And he wasn't sure he wanted to. If he could, how would he take care of her, and who would take over as her mother? Mary Foley? No, Harriet and her mother looked to be a package deal. What was wrong with that? Answer: plenty. Alma was sneaky smart, she was curious, and she might be a lush. He knew what they were like. Unstable. Unpredictable. Untruthful. Too many "uns."

Though the possibility of discovery was becoming increasingly remote, he couldn't let down his guard. For all he knew, he talked in his sleep. But maybe he was looking at this the wrong way. Taking responsibility for Harriet and her mother would surely make up for anything untoward that might have happened in the grove.

In addition, Alma must have needs not unlike his own, was bound to be grateful, and—truth be told—courting her provided the heightened sensations he hadn't experienced since the patrol. QED. It was a close call, but, yes, he'd play out this hand.

And, yes, after he'd made a shit pot full of moolah and needed a hedge, he'd generously earmark a superfluous tranche for deductible good deeds.

31

DR. E

It pleases me to report that Freddy came to feel quite at home in Old Colony's personal banking division. Daniel Shaver was far away in New York, and my son's bland coworkers were unthreatening. So what if they weren't the sharpest financial minds on the planet? Old Colony wasn't about brilliance; it was a reliable, respectable, old-line Boston bank.[35]

Freddy assured me his peers were, like him, attractive and amiable. Most of them sailed, golfed, and were reasonably adept with a variety of racquets, talents Freddy's division marketed to its richest—strike that—wealthiest customers. True, they may not have attended the most selective colleges, but Freddy himself acknowledged that without Howard Paulson's intervention, he might have sought refuge at a lesser Ivy.

Yes, Old Colony Bank was the perfect home for my dear son. I never had the heart to discourage Freddy from approaching the hush-hush organization he so yearned to join. Blessedly, I didn't have to. My boy's not cut out for a shadowy life of danger and intrigue—or finance—where survival and advancement demand quick thinking

---

35 Old Colony, like St. Matthew's, was established in the nineteenth century.

and an innate ability to deceive. I wouldn't dream of disillusioning him, but Freddy only thrives in conventional settings with brightly illuminated road signs.

That said, I see no reason to rain on what I suspect is Freddy's rich and varied fantasy life, which—like everyone's—no doubt features perilous missions, close calls, state-of-the-art weaponry, and heavy-lidded temptresses, by which I mean exotics who've never attended finishing schools, hoisted spinnakers, or waltzed with Daddy at established cotillions.

How, I often wondered, was my son really doing? He'd languished as an assistant treasurer for no time at all before becoming an assistant vice president.[36] According to Freddy, the elderly VP delivering his initial performance review in December of '66 told him he was "on track" and backed up this assurance with a seven-hundred-fifty-dollar raise, more, Freddy discovered, than that pocketed by those who'd joined with him. Subsequent raises were in the same ballpark. Perhaps not the best of signs.

---

36 I save Freddy's business cards. It's how I chart his less-than-meteoric progress.

32

FREDDY/FRED

Fred finally understood his mother. She wasn't a gold digger. More like a fluttering moth irresistibly drawn to handsome, high-net worth males. As he hoped, the meds she was taking appeared to have stabilized her condition. Even better, she was still happy living on the third floor. She realized she'd become "forgetful," and he sensed the busy residents on the upper floors made her anxious with their groups, committees, classes, and worthwhile projects.

"So, you have a sense of freedom here, Mother?"

"Yes, Freddy, that's what I'm trying to tell you." She concentrated and continued, "There's something else, but I can't think what it is."

This was part of their ritual. "Take your time, Mother, it'll come to you."

"Now I remember . . . will you visit me again, Freddy?" She looked frightened.

"I will, Mother."

It had taken longer than he'd hoped to establish himself at Old Colony, but now the track ahead looked clear. The senior vice president giving him his 1974 review lauded his "get up and go," telling him his proposed venture had been unanimously approved. Even better news: He now rated a female subordinate and had been moved from an interior cubicle to a semiprivate outside office with a view through an air shaft to the adjacent building. His review concluded with the SVP observing that never had such latitude been granted to someone so junior. Freddy made sure this news reached both his fathers, and from one or both of them it was certain to find its way to Daniel Shaver. Not so shabby for the unsung son of a Harvard summa.

The idea had come to him on one of his visits to Essex Lodge. Like a blinding revelation. The residents were not disintegrating, doped-up wrecks slouching groggily towards the hereafter, but low-hanging, easily harvested sources of revenue. How easy to peddle his bank's smorgasbord of services to these receptive elders with assets—almost certainly underperforming assets—stagnating in their portfolios.

After attending one or two of his presentations with the bubbly Miss Worthy—who strove to remind the attendees of their favorite grandchild while handing out gewgaws embossed with Old Colony's venerable pilgrim logo—they and their dimpled cellulite were putty in his hands, literally begging him to manage their resources and, after their demise, carry on as their executors and their children's trustees. How could he fail? Undue influence is almost impossible to prove, and his competition consisted of crafts classes, group stretching, synchronized swimming, origami, and the like. His customers were as simple and trusting as the Wampanoags and Narragansetts from whom his ancestors had wrested their slivers of what became Massachusetts and Rhode Island. No, that was a false analogy. He was caring for the Essex Lodge residents, not infecting them with smallpox. He was a fiduciary.

Fred credited an empathic nature for his understanding of the poor souls warehoused at Essex Lodge. He could read what remained of their minds. Their pleading eyes said it all. They couldn't help but notice him, a reassuringly unremarkable, nonthreatening young man of their ethnicity, and say to themselves, "Stop, please stop, young man. Don't just nod and pass on. Let me tell you about myself. I was young once, and people have always said I'm a lot of fun, even if my children appear to think otherwise.

"Oh, thank you. You're so thoughtful. I wish my son, Henry, was half as nice. Let's chat some more. I dislike sitting alone with my memories and my ceramic animals. You look like such a capable young man. Wouldn't you like to see my apartment? It's only one room, but there's a comfortable chair for you to sit in. It belonged to my late husband. Thank you, thank you. Yes, I agree, the decorations on my door are the nicest on the corridor. Yes, of course I'll call you Freddy. Those are my grandchildren. That's Henry, their father; he just can't seem to find time to get all the way up here from Manhattan. And that's his sister, Martha. She had a lazy eye as a baby, but they fixed it. Martha is still unmarried.

"Will I attend your investment classes? Of course, and I'd love to subscribe to your newsletter. I adore getting mail.

"Freddy, you are so perceptive. I've always prided myself on my business acumen. My husband, Duane, used to compliment me on it. He said I'd get along fine after he'd gone, but I'm not sure he was right about that.

"Of course I'd welcome help with my investments. How much do I have?

"Nearly a million dollars, and I've always wanted to reach that number. Can I find my latest brokerage statement . . . yes, here it is. Now let's see if I can get my fingers to work properly. See, I'm worth just a hair under a million. Not bad for an old lady, don't you think?

"You say you can get me to a million dollars pretty quickly. That would be so exciting. Yes, I'm sure there are opportunities out there. Certainly, if it makes sense to you, I'd be happy to take a more aggressive approach. Much more . . . what was the word you used? Yes, 'upside.' So, how do we begin? I need to sign a contract? That's fine, Freddy. You have one with you? Wonderful, and I agree completely, strike while the iron's hot. Where do I sign? Right there? Fine. Two copies? Certainly. I'll read my copy later. I've got plenty of time for that. When will I see you again?"

It usually went something like that.

His superiors were ecstatic with his one-stop shopping approach to financial services. Looking for a suitable analogy, he likened himself to a Norman Rockwellish general practitioner, still making house calls while the world around him was growing detached and impersonal.

As part of his self-image, he saw himself needing a bit of gravitas, so he combed a hint of gray into his mouse-brown sideburns and, in an effort to appear more seasoned and imposing, stopped shaving his upper lip. Regrettably, that strip of flesh proved to be infertile. What eventually sprouted was sparse and stunted. Worse, it was an anemic tan. Like that damn helicopter. But maybe he was being too hard on himself. Perhaps the old ladies would welcome his reassuring Anglo Saxon mien.

Looking ahead, he saw himself perfecting his routine at Essex Lodge and taking it on the road to similar facilities. Best of all, he would get to see more of his mother, who was becoming increasingly muddled.

Helen Elder, knowing her affectionate son was coming to Essex Lodge in order to spend more time with her, was moved to tears. "Oh, Freddy Darling, you're so wonderful; you're the only person I want around me. And now we'll see much more of each other. So lovely!"

"Yes indeed, Mother." And why should he feel guilty? She'd left him, hadn't she?

"And I want you to meet my new friends. I've made so many here on the third floor."

"I've met most of them already, Mother. I hope they can attend my talks."

She looked confused. "What talks, Freddy?"

"A series of lectures on investments, estate planning, and protecting yourself from the unscrupulous. I've told you about them."

"So interesting. I'll tell every single one of my friends."

"That would be wonderful, Mother. I've got someone nice helping me. A Miss Andrea Worthy. She works with me at the bank."

"You said 'Miss,' Freddy. Is she from a good family?"

"A fine family. It's been here for ages." Long enough to have atrophied.

"Is she pretty?"

That was a stretch, but okay. "She's nice looking."

Say this for warmhearted Mercy Williams, his mother was well turned out. Dresses were never her thing, but she looked clean and cared-for in a white button-down shirt, gray slacks, and a pair of light blue sneakers of the sort favored by old ladies in tennis shoes. Mercy, who'd won him over when she said she loved his mother's "little smile," had apparently followed his directions by changing her shirts daily. Her hair looked just right too—neatly brushed and, as far as he could tell, recently washed. Same with her fingernails—carefully trimmed and painted a calm, ladylike pink. What about her feet? He'd have to trust Mercy on that. Having a sister would be useful. She could attend to matters outside his comfort zone.

He was pleased with the dignified, unpainted face his mother presented to the world—so unlike the harridans who slathered on makeup long after their judgment *and* their hand-eye coordination had deserted them. Many of them looked camera-ready for a documentary on Papua New Guinea's aboriginal tribes.

"Now I've got a question for you, Mother. Are there many men living here?"

"Well, Freddy." Her wistful expression pained him. "There are certainly more of us, but yes. Plenty. Most of them are married or crazy—unfortunately for your old mom. I'm divorced, aren't I, Freddy?"

"Please, Mother, you don't want to get involved with another man, especially one with suspicious children. Don't you remember what you've been saying for years, 'Old men are only looking for a nurse or a purse.'"

"I don't know, Freddy, I get awfully lonely."

He did too. "Well, you'll be seeing a lot more of me now—and Miss Worthy."

She brightened for a moment. "I hope so, but you often say you'll come right back or call right back, and then you don't."

"Mother, you're getting a little absentminded. I always keep my promises. Always." Was he going to end up like this?

"You know what, Freddy . . . I wish I had more children. Daughters. I'm sorry, Freddy. Can I come to your talks?"

"I'd be hurt if you didn't, but why do you ask?"

"Because I worry about money too, and I don't understand it." His mother had taken it for granted, as everyone once did, that if you married a man from a good family with a Harvard degree, the money would take care of itself. Now she looked anxious. "What happens if I run out? Can I still stay here? Will they put me out on the street? Would it be better if I just *died?*"

"No, it would not. And you won't run out. Howard Paulson paid for everything upfront."

"Upfront? You know what I think when I hear the name Paulson?"

"What?" He had no idea what she might say.

"The ocean . . . long summer days . . . driving a big car up a crunchy bluestone driveway . . . two granite gateposts out by the road . . . a lot of carving on them . . . floral patterns . . . interlocking Hs. What did that mean?"

"Helen and Howard, Mother."

"Howard who? I don't remember him."

"Howard Paulson. He was your second husband; he came after Dad."

Something must have jogged her memory. "He came after that old farmhouse and the Mason jars, didn't he?"

Fred nodded.

"Did I have a third husband?"

"No, Mother, you didn't."

"Well, never mind; take my old hand, Dearie."

"It's not one bit old, Mother."

"Funny, isn't it? I remember so much about your father."

Did she remember which one was his father? "Do you still love him?"

"Should I? I'm not sure . . . but I must have once, mustn't I? I wouldn't have married him otherwise, would I? Weren't the three of us happy once?"

"Which three, Mother?"

"You and me and your father."

"Yes, we were."

"I remember you as a baby. You're my only child, aren't you?"

This was all very well, but it would be a financial catastrophe if his mother's unfiltered ramblings got back to Howard Paulson. And what if the youthful Sharon Paulson threatened separate bedrooms if he continued financing her predecessor?

"Now tell me about Miss . . . what's her name? Do you like her? Will I like her? What do you think?"

"Miss Worthy, Mother."

"I'm having difficulty with names, Freddy. I can only hold a certain number in my tired brain, and they seem to be different every day."

His father's pontificating had been bad enough, and now he was being grilled by his mother. Dr. Elder had suggested—no, it had been more than a suggestion—that it was wise to hold off on marriage if you hadn't won the girl of your dreams in a fair fight with the competition (it being a bad sign if there wasn't much competition) by the time you got out of college. Well, he hadn't. Catching a girl on the rebound was bad strategy, advised Dr. Elder, because so many decided later they hadn't been thinking clearly and should not have "settled." He should have kept still, but he'd interrupted and said, "Like Mom?"

––––––––––

Enough of that. This afternoon the curtain was rising on his Essex Lodge financial workshop, and there was no reason to think he was destined to wear horns like his father. But first, lunch with Mother. Fred set off for her room.

Ah, denial. Every door on his mother's floor was decorated—some might say overdecorated—with hopeful images. What did the residents have to be optimistic about? It was all downhill. Steeply so.

Recurrent subjects were babies (presumably grands or great-grands), puppies, kittens, bunnies, and ducklings. Fuzzy, furry, or feathery warm-blooded animals that were neither predatory nor scaly, and most significantly, had their lives in front of them. Creatures with futures.

Poor Betty Ruggles in Room 359. She was, as usual, behind or perhaps far ahead of schedule. She hadn't taken down or had just hung up her wreath, candy canes, and angels. Was the staff humoring her or just being inattentive? Mrs. Ruggles herself was fine. After all, she signed up for his workshop, and he had information suggesting she needed help with her investments.

Taped to the door of Room 348 was his mother's somewhat literal message "Please knock so I can hear you." Beneath it was a vivid color photo of a lioness and her cubs. There was something familiar about it. Yes, it came from the latest Kodak annual report. What on earth was his mother doing with annual reports? Were there rustlers on his range? He knocked.

"It's unlocked, whoever you are. I hope it's you, Freddy."

"It is, Mother, and I'm right on time." She was sitting on the edge of her bed looking out the window.

"Don't you adore robins?" Before he could assure his mother of his love of robins, she turned to face him and, in an agitated tone, said, "What have they done with Henry Fletcher, Freddy? He always sits at my table, and now he doesn't. I can't find him anywhere."

"No, Mother. Mr. Fletcher hasn't been at your table for several months. He moved to the second floor right around Christmas. I'm sure he's happy there."

She seized his right hand in both of hers. "Will you take me to see him? We had such a nice . . . friendship."

"On another visit, Mother. We're pressed for time this afternoon."

"Nobody's happy on the second floor, Freddy." His mother was right about that. "You share a room. You spend most of your time in bed. You don't last very long. Is that place to be my punishment?"

"For what, Mother?"

"For being bad, for running away with . . . what's his name, Freddy?"

Time to change the subject. "How's Colonel Damon doing, Mother? I see he's still on your floor. You told me he was on his way to two."

"Yes, indeed. He's looking happier every day. Some of us are wondering if he's taking something special, something the staff's keeping from the rest of us. He's stopped complaining about his pain."

He'd visualized this moment for years, but how could he tell her what it had been like for him when she'd ridden off with Paulson? What was the point? It would have been worse if she'd stayed with his father. "You haven't been bad, Mother, not even close, and I've spoken with Dr. Patel. He says you're staying here on three."

"That's what they always say, then they take you down there in the middle of the night when nobody's watching. Colonel Damon warned me. Said he'd rescue me. Please don't let them do that to me. I don't want to go any further down."

"Certainly not, Mother. You're staying here in Room 348 for as long as your heart desires. Dr. Patel promised. And you've decorated it so prettily. The Danish Christmas plates are just right."

"Thank you, Freddy. They keep giving me these dumb memory tests. I messed up the first one, but I'm getting better and better at them."

"That's what Dr. Patel says. Okay, Mother, enough about that. Let's get ourselves some lunch. Anything good today?"

His mother shook her head.

Lunch got off to a rocky start when Agnes Benning, one of his mother's friends, said, "You look so smart today, Helen. Maybe we can go to the library and look at the newspapers after Freddy leaves."

"You're leaving?" moaned his mother. "It'll be like Sundays . . . nobody's around."

Glaring at Mrs. Benning, he said, "We'll have a nice lunch, Mother, and then I want to see your latest painting."

"Oh, Freddy, you remembered. I'd love to show it to you."

"Are you going to Henry Fletcher's service, Helen?" asked Mrs. Benning.

At this, Helen Elder looked distressed. Did his mother understand the question? Not clear. Yes, he'd seen Fletcher's photograph (he was wearing a three-piece suit and looking authoritative; they always tried to show the deceased in their prime) as he waited for the elevator in the main lobby. That's how deaths were announced at Essex Lodge. A framed photo, a brief bio, and an announcement of the service. The photos were aligned like gravestones on a small mahogany table in the ground-floor lobby that served no other purpose. The grim reaper's bulletin board. Among other things, Mr. Fletcher's death meant a bed had become available on the second floor.

Virginia Roberts, whose gentle nature suggested a life lived for others, sprang to the rescue. Looking at Mrs. Benning, she said, "Now, Agnes, tell us about your granddaughter. I heard she got into Bates, her first choice. Such wonderful news."

He glanced around the room. By his count there were five men among the thirty-odd females. Ominous, from a male perspective. Four of them, looking unkempt and resigned, were huddled together in a corner like dazed survivors of a shattered regiment. The fifth, gussied up like a circus barker in a loud jacket and bow tie, was enthralling the seven ladies at his table, all of whom were competing for his attention.

It was difficult to suppress a sneer. He, the attentive son, was wearing a blue three-button suit with natural shoulders and cuffed trousers, complemented by a white button-down shirt (like his mother's), a subdued regimental tie, and lightly polished black wing tips. Clinging to his upper lip was his still-unnoticed mustache. He'd expected alert Mrs. Roberts to remark on it.

The meal passed without further mishaps. He was pleased when his mother turned down dessert with her usual disdain. Some things never changed, but it evoked a still-vivid childhood memory of hearing her refer to him as "Fatso" to one of her friends.

The dining room emptied, and they were standing outside in the hallway. "Remind me, Mother, which one is yours?" Pinned to the bulletin board were thirty-two watercolors of a red-and-white-striped lighthouse on a grassy promontory projecting into a sea of deepest blue. In the foreground of each was a gray shape that, in the more realistic compositions, was identifiable as a seagull.

"This one, Freddy," said his mother, placing a proud index finger on one of the more abstract renderings.

"It's superb, Mother. Wonderful brushwork. Your gull is so perfectly imagined, you expect it to spring off the paper and fly away. Some of those other paintings, you just can't tell what they're supposed to be."

"Oh, Freddy, I worked so hard to get it right. You're looking at my fourth or fifth try. Nice Claude . . . what's his last name . . . says I'm extremely talented. Borderline genius. He's said new brushes . . . he'll get them for me . . . and private lessons would coax out my talents. Says they'll cost virtually nothing. Can I afford all that?"

"I'll look into it, Mother."

"Freddy," she said, studying him. "You know how much I dislike facial hair."

33

DR. E

I remember it vividly. In 1968, Freddy brought me the heartbreaking news. Howard Paulson had institutionalized Helen, and she was doing poorly. Was there, Freddy asked, something we could do to arrest her decline and keep her on an independent living floor?

Naturally, I was willing to help. Eager, in fact. How could I not since I was, to a great extent, responsible for Helen's 1955 flight. More importantly, I had not stopped missing her, and reclaiming her, even in a semi-ruined condition, was far preferable to the aching void of her absence. I would mount my caparisoned destrier and, with a talisman from Helen streaming from my helm, spur to her rescue.[37]

But some dogs never learn. They just keep chasing cars.

Would my intervention, however ineffective, upset Paulson? Probably not. More likely, he'd be relieved if someone took Helen off his hands.

Freddy volunteered to clear my visit with the Essex Lodge medical staff. Their conclusion: Helen's memory of the recent past was gone for good, but she might be cheered and stimulated by a visit from someone who evoked distant and perhaps happier times.

---

37 D-B dubbed me a Knight of the Garter Belt.

Could I be that person?

Three days later my phone rang. It was Freddy. "Good news, it's all arranged, but Dr. Patel suggests I come along, just in case."

"Should we warn your mother?"

"Done. I told Mother you'd be coming to visit. She seemed pleased and said, 'That's nice, isn't it?' I told her it was very nice. We'll play it by ear but be prepared for a speedy exit."

———

As we stood in the hallway outside her room, Freddy assured me that, according to Mercy Williams, Helen was looking forward to my visit.

We entered Room 348. My heart was racing. It was not unlike a first date. Helen was sitting in her favorite chair, the one she insisted we bring up to Lower Finley every summer. She looked at me and smiled her little smile.

"Hello, Helen. It's wonderful to see you. You're looking lovely." I was not exaggerating.

"Yes, I remember you. You often said that to me."

"I certainly did, Helen, and it's still true."

"Yes, I do remember you, but I'm having a little trouble with your name."

"It's Frederick Elder, your old tennis partner."

"Yes, tennis. Of course. You had a nice serve, didn't you?"

"Now and then. It could be a little erratic at times, Sweetie."

"Sweetie . . . nobody's called me that in ages. You're the only one who did."

Could this be the same person who was so contemptuous of my interest in Pompey? Freddy got my attention, motioned towards the hallway, and left us alone together.

"I used to call you Sweetie a lot." Not enough, obviously. "And you used to like that."

For years I'd wanted Helen back, and now, irony of ironies, she was mine again. How the gods torment us. Menelaus sought out Helen in burning Troy. He took pity on her. How could I do less?

Helen and I sat quietly together. She was still but tranquil. The way she'd often been in our early years. Before everything collapsed. It was as though we were slowly making our way upstream to the source of things. Remember, I told myself: eye contact and general questions only. Gentle movements. Do not contradict her.

Then, out of the blue, Helen said, "That nice doctor told me I had cancer." I must have looked stricken. Helen thought for a moment. "Or maybe it was that Alzheimer thing. I can't remember now."

Freddy had been listening. He bustled back into the room.

"Now, Mother," he said, "you mustn't worry yourself. Dr. Patel assured us you had neither." Freddy gave me a look. I nodded. Helen seemed relieved.

The last thing Helen said to me that morning was, "Please . . . come see me again. Soon."

I can't recall how I phrased it, but I promised her I would.

That was it for my first visit and the resurrection of our relationship. Helen appeared happy, and, since she'd lost the ability to pretend, it seemed safe to conclude that she was. Had Paulson been expunged? Though she'll never sleep next to me again, had I won her back?

Her next departure was too awful to consider. "Lethe-wards" she'd sink. Could I at least make it more easeful?

———

Visiting Essex Lodge puts me in mind of D-B. He is so charming and talented. Yes, it's churlish, but he continues to vex me. In addition to entrancing the St. Matthew's girls and melting their mothers, twice monthly he treats the residents of a neighboring retirement community to his repertoire of ballads and swoon-inducing tenor voice whilst (his word) accompanying himself on a piano or guitar.

In response to my question about the reactions of his adoring fans, he considered that for a moment and, with his aggravating faux modesty, replied, "I seem to be well received, but I have yet to be pelted with lacey nothings or, for that matter, adult diapers." Then he winked. D-B makes it impossible to stay annoyed with him.

34

FREDDY/FRED

The unobtrusive Roberta Spinelli had been instructed to never hold calls from Lenox Hill Capital. They were to be put through immediately. Ms. Spinelli was not a looker, but she was reassuring to Fred's customers and grateful to him for rescuing her from the floaters' pool.

He picked up. "Please hold for Mr. Morgan . . . Freddy, Richard here. I've got something you cannot, I repeat cannot, afford to miss out on."

Insufferable Richard (never Dick) Morgan was one of Howard Paulson's sycophants, a Harvard B School grad barely two years Fred's senior. He embodied Churchill's description of the Germans as being at your feet or at your throat. There was much to dislike about Richard. High among them was his "my time is valuable, yours is of no account" attitude.

"I'm all ears, Richard."

"Right. First, let me congratulate you on the success of your geezers initiative at—remind me, would you."

"Essex Lodge, Richard."

"Right. Howard told me to give you an 'attaboy.' Consider it done."

What a dipshit. Damn right it's a success. He—well, all right, he and Andrea—had brought nearly seven million into Old Colony's personal banking division. None of his rivals had done anything remotely comparable, and he doubted whether Richard Morgan made *any* contribution to revenue. He was overhead.

"Thanks, Richard, and what might I do you for?"

"Other way around, my friend. It's something I've got for you: a can't-miss investment opportunity for your wealthiest and most discreet codgers. Howard's issued an 'All hands on deck' for what he predicts will be the stupendous Reagan years."

"Please refrain from disparaging my customers, Richard."

"Lighten up, Freddy. I assume you're familiar with the term 'tax shelter,' although I doubt you've ever been exposed to one."

"Please continue . . . Richie."

"Watch yourself, my friend. You are not as secure as you may think. To continue, Lenox Hill has a long-standing relationship with one of Switzerland's most prestigious banks. Founded in the latter part of the eighteenth century. Specializes in private banking and asset management. Conducts business with the utmost discretion."

"You planning to tell me its name, Richard?"

"That's on a need-to-know basis, Freddy, and at the moment you don't." Another portentous pause. "The organization of which I speak is not at present actively seeking new relationships. However, I suspect it might consider taking on a select few of your better customers, those with high six-figure, preferably seven-figure, accounts, and, as a professional courtesy, allow *you* to participate on a no-fee basis."

Hearing this crap made him wonder how *he* came across to his customers. The thought passed. Morgan carried on, asserting this unnamed bank would invest his customers' funds abroad and guarantee there would be no taxes on what was earned. And it was all copacetic under Swiss law. Morgan didn't say, and he didn't ask, whether it would pass muster in the US.

At the end of the conversation—monologue was more like it—he'd been asked if he was interested. How could he not be? Rejecting this offer would piss off Howard Paulson, and didn't he owe it to his customers to maximize their returns?

Prudently, of course.

So, yes, he was interested. Salivating was more like it. A lot in it for him. Later that day he wondered why his stepfather—if Howard Paulson was still his stepfather after dumping Mother—hadn't tipped him off to this opportunity. Too busy or concerned with maintaining deniability?

The next day Roberta Spinelli stood in his doorway. She wore a quizzical expression. "A Max Glauser is here to see you, Mr. Elder."

While he never liked to give much away, he couldn't help looking puzzled.

"He said he flew in from Zurich last night. There's nothing about him on your calendar, and he's not in your rolodex," observed Ms. Spinelli.

"Show him in, and please close the door, Ms. S."

Max Glauser did not fit Fred's evolving image of a Swiss banker. The tanned, trim, fiftyish Glauser was all Milan from his stunning coiffure to his shockingly effete, thin-soled, monogrammed slip-ons fashioned from the skin of an endangered reptile. Weighing down his left wrist was an impossible-to-miss multifunction device that looked as though it told time as an afterthought. Normally satisfied with his appearance, Fred wondered whether he could be mistaken for one of his dowdy Puritan ancestors. Or maybe someone from the mailroom.

When asked what he'd like to drink, Max Glauser replied brightly, "A cappuccino." Fred resisted the impulse to reply, "A what?"

Seeing he'd embarrassed his host, Max Glauser smoothly reversed course and gratefully accepted a regular with cream and sugar. He took a sip, nodded at Ms. S, and pronounced it magnificent. In return, he proffered a cigar. Fred declined. At that, Max Glauser produced a slim silver guillotine, rolled the cigar in his fingers, and, with practiced nonchalance, beheaded it.

Max Glauser, whose business card identified him as a managing director of EFH Privatbank Zurich AG, seemed to be in no hurry. He was taking the early evening flight home, but his morning and afternoon were entirely open.

Herr Glauser looked around and nodded approvingly at Fred's uncluttered office. Taking a leaf from Howard Paulson, Fred had, only last month, removed his Harvard sheepskin (he'd ditched his St. Matthew's diploma years earlier after hearing a secretary speaking admiringly of parochial schools), given away his Lucite deal toys, and presented his sprawling ficus tree to Ms. Spinelli. Lean and mean—if no longer green—was his new look. Semper Fi!

Max—he became Max almost immediately—was lively company and his pitch, delivered in lightly flavored English, was irresistible. "The vall of secrecy" protecting Swiss banking had never been assaulted, let alone breached, even after some troublemakers had raised questions about a handful of transactions with the Third Reich. The chance of an American customer's Swiss account being discovered were, as Max put it, "less than zero."

After an hour, Fred began to wonder whether this was to be a two-cigar conference. His overtaxed window unit had given up trying to clear the air.

Max carried on with plausible assurances that, having no offices or branches in the States, EFH's assets and those of its customers were beyond the reach of grabby US authorities. "We have no physical presence in your country, so it has no jurisdiction over us. Quite perfect, wouldn't you say? Consider me a banker without boundaries."

"And your presence in my office doesn't count?" Fred replied.

Max looked pained. "*Nein*. This is purely social. I am here to visit my new American friend. We have found that collegial face-to-face sit-downs eliminate what you Americans call 'paper trails.'"

Yes, it was quite splendid, just like Max. After he and Max parted company, Fred assured himself that he would have asked the question eventually. Max simply beat him to the punch.

"Fred, may I call you Fred, or would you prefer Freddy? You've no doubt been asking yourself how your customers—I'm going to use the future tense—will repatriate their funds. Like you, we assume they won't be making regular trips to Zurich to stock up on cuckoo clocks, Swiss Army knives, chocolates, and other high-quality products of my industrious countrymen."

"That's the whole point of the exercise, isn't it?"

"Fred, Fred. Put your mind at rest. It's quite simple. EFH maintains a single bank account here . . ."

"Where?"

Max didn't bat an eye. By now, he was working on his second cigar. "In one of your—how do you say it?—friendlier jurisdictions."

He couldn't resist. "*Sehr gut.*"

Max ignored the impertinence. "Please allow me to continue, Freddy—and into this account we transfer the funds our American friends wish to withdraw. Alternatively, you can come to Zurich, withdraw your money, and bring it home in the lining of your suitcase. Ha, ha. I joke."

Was this too good to be true? Fred pressed on. "I can see EFH is pretty well insulated. What it's doing is legal in Switzerland, and it's not subject to our laws. But what about my customers?"

The atmosphere cooled perceptibly. Max put down his cigar, smoothed an unruly eyebrow, frowned, and said, "We are not in a position to say whether your customers would be in total compliance with every inconsequential US rule or regulation. If you feel compelled to pursue this tiresome inquiry, you can always consult a US attorney, and, be advised, I have several able candidates."

Fred raised both hands, palms out.

Undaunted, Max continued, "All I can say is that we have several hundred, perhaps it is now over a thousand, US customers, all of whom are delighted with the services we provide. Be assured I could, but only at the cost of confidentiality, provide a host of testimonials."

It wasn't going as he planned. "That doesn't settle it, Mr. Glauser."

Impatience was in the air. "Mr. Elder, the question you should be asking is a practical one, namely, 'What are the real-world, as opposed to the theoretical, risks to my customers?'"

He felt chastened. "Please consider that question to have been asked."

"There are no risks. EFH is offering run-of-the-mill Swiss banking services, and the privacy of these services has never been questioned—anywhere in the world. And even if they were, your customers' names would never be revealed. Full stop."

A knock. Fred consulted his inexpensive but accurate digital watch. It was already 1:00 p.m. The conscientious Ms. Spinelli looked in, announced she was going to lunch, and asked if she could bring them something to eat.

Before Fred could respond, Max sprang to his feet, bowed, and said, "No, no, my dear. In a few moments, I shall be taking Mr. Elder to zee Cafe Locke-Ober. It comes highly recommended. Have I made a good choice, Signorina Spinelli?"

"Oh, Mr. Glauser, you have. It's one of our very best restaurants," gushed the red-faced Ms. Spinelli.

"Grazie, signorina. I only hope zat zee three of us, or better yet, just you and I can dine zere together in zee near future." Then he winked at her.

Ms. Spinelli blushed, gulped, adjusted her glasses, and backpedaled as though exiting a throne room.

Over his oysters Rockefeller, Fred acknowledged he might possibly be interested in Max's proposal and, after polishing off his baked Alaska, said, "Where do we go from here?"

"Zurich." The expansive Max continued, "You should bring Signorina Spinelli with you. I sense zere's a vild thing trapped deep within her that's struggling to escape."

"Vy don't ve leave it zere, Max?"

"Your loss, Mr. Elder. In any case, our managing directors are hosting a three-day symposium for our new American accounts. You'll learn techniques you can use on your existing customers and individuals you might wish to . . . what's the word I'm seeking?"

"Poach," suggested Fred, who by this time was annoyed the smooth-talking Swiss banker hadn't recognized and acknowledged his talents.

"Precisely," said a smiling Max.

He should have kept mum, but—after getting Max into a limo to Logan—he couldn't resist crowing to Andrea about his expenses-paid Zurich boondoggle. That did not sit well. No use telling her nobody'd pick up the tab for a second person. Instead, Andrea displayed a resourcefulness he'd never dreamed of.

Standing arms akimbo in front of his desk the next morning and smirking like the mischievous Cheshire Cat, she said, "I have worked it out with the saucy Max Glauser. He assured me EFH will happily cover both of us—he's awfully fresh, you know."

Oh God, now what?

"Maxie—he told me to call him that—asked if we'd like separate rooms and, if not, what size bed or beds."

Hoping his disapproval was apparent, Fred responded with a curt "And you answered . . . ?"

"I didn't mean anything by it, but I couldn't resist saying, 'Separate but equal and perhaps adjoining.' He seemed amused."

And then Ms. Spinelli, wearing more makeup than was proper for a Katharine Gibbs graduate, entered without knocking. She, too, was looking pleased with herself. "Herr Glauser's on the line, Herr Elder."

"That's quite enough, Ms. S."

"May I listen in?" simpered Andrea.

He glared at his subordinates, shook his head emphatically, and turned his back to them.

"Yes, Max," he said in his all-business tone.

"Freddy, you sly dog, you've surrounded yourself with zee most delectable women." Sensing there'd be no response to that sally, he continued, "You and the gemutlich Ms. Worthy are booked into the Alden, a delightful nineteenth-century hotel. Just renovated. If you can't make it happen there, Freddy . . . I hope there is nobody else on the line."

"Just zee two of us, Max."

"Are you making fun of me, Freddy?"

"Never, Max."

"As I was saying, if not there, where?"

"Please, Max—Ms. Worthy and Ms. Spinelli, would you mind giving me a moment? Thank you. Max, there is nothing between Ms. Spinelli and me. Absolutely nothing." Christ almighty, could they be listening at the door?

"Ah, Freddy, we are not, at this moment, talking about the delectable Signorina Spinelli. I am referring to the bold young lady who called me this morning. She must be such an asset."

"Yes, she bragged about it. I'm appalled."

"Initiative, Fred, initiative. I think I can promise you the door between your rooms will not be locked—on her side. Have you ever considered a threesome? I'm limber for my age."

"Stop it, Max."

"If I must. Very well, I will see you next week. Dinner after the first session is on EFH. Until then, auf Wiedersehen."

———

The first session was a stunner. Max's speakers pulled no punches. Fred and the others in the audience, all of them Americans, were dumbfounded. Andrea, who was sitting beside him in the front row, was wide-eyed. Max opened the proceedings and introduced the panel. Now and again he would catch Andrea's eye and nod appreciatively. It was obvious, probably to everyone in the room, that Max was peeking, and Andrea was delighted to oblige. Good God, was she wearing anything under her skirt?

A bespectacled, expressionless Swiss lawyer named Edgar (no surname provided) laid it out for them, going so far as to say he and his colleagues would—if requested and suitably compensated—happily prepare their customers' US tax returns.

During the Q and A, Fred raised his hand and asked the question everyone was expecting. "How do you get our customers' funds back to the US, Herr Doktor?"

"We have worked out a foolproof protocol. Would you care to hear about it?"

Everyone nodded.

"When we transfer funds to our US customers, we communicate with them in a code that changes frequently. We use different terms to refer to such things as account balances and customers' checks."

"Danke," said Fred. Andrea giggled and elbowed him in the ribs.

Thirty minutes later, Edgar No Last Name assembled his notes and announced the presentation was concluded. He favored them with an icy look and added, "Never forget the nondisclosure agreements you have signed. What you hear at these sessions must remain confidential." With obvious pleasure, Edgar added, "We Swiss are secretive. My bank's hero is William No-Tell." The anticipated laughter failed to materialize.

Max stepped to the podium, wrapped things up, and, in an arch tone, said, "In case you're wondering, Edgar zee Anonymous is descended from a distinguished line of stand-up Swiss comics." The audience groaned. Max winked at Andrea, gave everyone a jaunty wave, and started to leave.

Before he could make his escape, a young woman two rows behind Fred trilled, "We must never forget that honesty's the best policy."

Max stopped, nodded, and, with an engaging smile, replied, "Vell, vat's next best?"

————

Fred made it to the Alden's snug bar with more than fifteen minutes to spare, over-tipped the maître d', and was escorted to the secluded corner table he'd requested. The mirror over the banquette gave him a clear view of the entire room. This way Andrea wouldn't be able to sneak up on him—but in reality, she already had.

The night loomed as a fractal of the larger Andrea dilemma. Over the last several months his assistant had become persistent. She had expectations and claimed to have received "feelers" from other financial institutions. How to respond?

A promotion, a pay raise, and increased responsibility topped her wish list. She had even demanded to go to Zurich and, doing a hopeless imitation of Max, said she "vanted to play vith zee big boys."

Every rising banker needed a presentable blond minion, and Andrea, while too pushy, would suffice until he was promoted and could aim higher. Possessing little by way of personal style, she had switched from Talbots into a corporate uniform that, with its shiny gold buttons, made her look like something out of the Nutcracker Suite. Her only plus: She aroused no desire in him or anyone else, other than the indefatigable Max. If only she weren't convinced she was worth listening to.

Generous Frederick Elder, Jr., was willing to extend the olive branch. Since he'd made VP, he would recommend Andrea for AVP and take her to Zurich. Would that suffice? Evidently not. Here they were, and she was discharging a fine mist of dissatisfaction. Why else would she have required assurances they had identical rooms? He resisted the urge to torment her by claiming he'd been upgraded to a corner suite with multiple televisions and phones.

While he'd never thought of himself as catnip to the fair sex, Fred was gaining a sense of what Andrea might be up to, and he found her recent assertiveness alarming.

In the low-pulse universe of Old Colony he was a keeper, if not a trophy, and, though it pained him to admit it, they may have been well-matched. Andrea was not ill-favored, and could he reasonably expect to do significantly better? Marrying Andrea—or anyone whose family made it to North America in the seventeenth century—would delight his mother, while Dr. Elder would revert to his default position of praising him with faint damns.

Could he buy off Andrea with a one-and-done, check-the-box, not-to-be-repeated romp in the edelweiss? Fat chance. She seemed rooted in the previous generation's pre-pill weltanschauung where "penetration however slight" (to borrow an unforgettable phrase from the Uniform Code of Military Justice) was tantamount to pledging one's troth.

Yes, he was anxious. He'd erred in not choosing a lighter, brighter, less suggestive venue. The dark-paneled lounge, where he lurked like a ravenous moray eel, reeked of the illicit. He ordered a beer. Better start slowly and pray Max would join him before Andrea showed up and began pressuring him to do God-only-knows-what.

Oh, dear. There she stood, looking pleased and excited. She wiggled her fingers at him. The portrait of coy innocence.

All right, in the dim light she was passable. Yes, she was. With a little imagination and a couple more drinks . . . He stood and motioned her to the banquette. Andrea smiled demurely as he repositioned the table in front of her. Yes, she was displaying rather a lot of herself, and, though she was no Mary Foley, what he saw wasn't half bad. She matched up well with Jayne Hoskins. If the rest of her . . . He felt himself responding.

The evening got off to a predictably vapid start with the thunderingly concrete Andrea declaring it really was a small world, when they discovered her Hotchkiss cousin had grown up racing on Long Island Sound against one of his St. Matthew's classmates. Next came her interminable monologue about the perky Herreshoff 12 ½ (Andrea had cleverly named hers Luffly) on which she'd learned. Like certain turns of phrase, a Herreshoff is an encoded signal to the right sort.

By the time Max arrived, the two of them had exhausted their store of fascinating coincidences. Max, who claimed to be overbooked, couldn't stay long, but it was a lively fifty-plus minutes. And Max brought gifts. An expensive—if the label was a reliable guide—tie for him and what looked like a flagon of Chanel No. 5 for Andrea, who—upon removing the wrapping paper—flashed her most endearing smile, asked Max to order her another whiskey sour, jumped up, and carried her perfume off to the powder room. It was clear she hadn't mastered her high-heeled slingbacks.

No sooner had Andrea thumped back and flopped onto the banquette than Max inhaled deeply, sighed, and said, "Zat is so you, darling Andrea." The melting Andrea could only squirm and titter in response.

Then Max flipped an internal switch, jettisoning his Swiss banker persona like empty wing tanks. Seating himself next to Andrea, he flowed effortlessly sideways until his hip, seemingly by chance, made gentle contact with hers. Docking complete. Thereupon, he began shape-shifting, not ceasing until he became a near likeness of the dissolving Andrea. The young woman had been consumed and digested. She no longer existed as a separate organism. Fred felt obliged to add Body Language to the many tongues in which Max was fluent.

Next, taking care to avoid overt improprieties, Max let slip his questing, well-tended fingers. In an instant they were caressing and calming, stroking and soothing. It was as though Andrea had been enveloped in a cloud of adoring butterflies. Her breathing had slowed, and she was wearing an expression of sublime contentment.

Fred was irked but awestruck by this master class. Though he couldn't tell for sure without a meat thermometer, it seemed to Fred that Andrea was done to perfection and ready to be served. Nicely seared on the outside with all the juices sealed within.

Max consulted his ornate timepiece, rearranged a stray lock of Andrea's dank hair, kissed a submissive hand, flashed Fred a surreptitious thumbs-up, and said, "I must leave, dear ones."

"Oh don't, Maxie," cooed Andrea.

"I must, *Liebling.*"

Fred listened. My God, was she panting?

———

By the time Max vanished into the night, the two of them were working on their fourth drinks. Fred concluded it was time to order something solid. Everything on the menu struck them as hilarious and pregnant with multiple entendres. There was increasingly loud laughter, much sniffing by Fred of the perfume-drenched Andrea, and a certain amount of purely collegial patting. And finally, the brandy. Max was correct. Under the right circumstances, a fragrance could add a certain je ne sais quoi to almost anyone.

What now, former lieutenant? They were young. As was the evening. They were vigorous, unattached, and far from home. Max had greased the skids. It would be downright ungallant if he didn't pretend to try. Wouldn't it? Yes, it would. Besides, she looked so expectant. Didn't she? Hard to say exactly, because now and again he was seeing two of her, which degraded his analysis. What exactly was she trying to convey? Availability? Nausea? Truth to tell, he was feeling a bit off himself.

Yes, he felt something. What exactly? Desire? Really? Yes. Nothing like what he'd experienced the previous fall when, at a dinner party, he'd listened to the unbearable sound of nylon on nylon as a young tease tormented him by crossing and recrossing her legs before departing with someone else.

Sound General Quarters! Open the armory! Distribute the pistols and cutlasses! Assemble the boarding party! St. Matthew's men never fail to answer the trumpet. Remember Lieutenant Ellsworth and the valorous traditions of the Corps! But how to proceed with Max-like insouciance? Where was the "hook"?

Andrea inadvertently supplied it. She muffled a hiccup and, with a lopsided grin, said, "You know what, Fweddy, there's one of those bidet thingies in my potty."

It was now or never. He gulped and, summoning his inner Errol Flynn, whispered, "Let's *play* with it, Andrea." He leered. "Maybe you could give me a demonstration."

The night hung in the balance. Was she considering his proposal or had she drifted off? Her mouth fell open, she gradually brought him into focus, and he was certain he saw her nod. Game on.

Having received a reply he wasn't entirely sure he relished, he was honor-bound to proceed. As Cyrano put it, "Out swords, and to work withal."

He summoned the waiter with an imperious wave, paid the check, and, draping a heavy arm around her waist, propelled Andrea towards the elevator. Since they were alone on the ride up, he was obliged to kiss her. Taking careful aim, he got a corner of her face. Was she still alive? He stared owlishly. Yes, barely.

After taking giggling turns on her bathroom's suggestive fixture, the two of them, still partially clothed, steered erratically to the duvet-covered four-poster . . . or was it an eight-poster? Andrea collapsed and kicked off her strappy shoes. The skies parted: a vision. An MGM spectacular.

Suddenly, he realized what all the sighing was about in certain discreet quarters. While most feet deserved purdah, there were exceptions. And he was gazing at a lovely brace of them. By some whim of nature, Andrea's were glorious—graceful arches, sweetly sloping insteps, perfectly matched, unblemished and unbunioned. Sublime.

Just as elegant hands demand to be stroked and admired, so, too, do lovely feet, and Andrea's sang to him like Sirens calling out to be held and beheld.

But it was those naughty toesies that utterly beguiled *and* inflamed him. Neither long and reptilian nor stubby, webbed, or troll-like, they tapered symmetrically as they gently fanned outward. None of them tilted in, splayed out, or crawled atop one another. No unsightly, ill-proportioned gaps. Instead, they nestled together companionably. His classicist father would have blathered on about symmetry and perfection.

Those pert little rascals. Their spirited upward flex at the mid toe joint made them appear alert and expectant. Ready to delight and obey. But wait, they were even more bewitching when examined from below. To drink in those seductive circles of vulnerable flesh was to yearn for a game of "this little piggy." Was he a creep? Well, maybe.

No. Strike that. A connoisseur.

How to acknowledge and pay homage to such splendor? Toe sucking? Perhaps premature. Tomorrow night? What was the protocol? Do you dip them first? In what? Soy sauce? Salsa? Tabasco? Or something gentler? Guacamole? Olive oil?

Burrowing terrier-like under the stifling coverlet, an invigorated Fred tucked into Andrea as he would an artichoke, peeling off and tossing aside the outer layers while resolutely advancing towards the mouthwatering inner core, wholly disregarding the perfumed nooks and silken snuggeries where, under less pressing circumstances, he might have lingered. His last thought before losing consciousness was *I believe I got it in.*

———

The following morning, Max, his host at the preconference breakfast, looked at Fred and whispered in his ear, "Vould it be accurate to say, I varmed her up for you?"

Fred—wondering if his behavior the previous night had been less than honorable, if not criminal—sipped his Bloody Mary in silence.

"Your gentlemanly reticence is admirable."

Head throbbing, he maintained his silence, but inspired by Prince Charles's fantasy of being a cylindrical unmentionable tucked deep within Camilla, Fred saw himself as an odor-eating insole savoring the intoxicating scents released by Andrea's sandals.

"One other thing, Freddy," said Max, "you must replace that Casio. This *is* Switzerland, after all, so I will help you find a timepiece better suited to the role to which you aspire."

Talking would have splintered his throbbing skull, so he didn't.

"Freddy, just nod if you concur."

He did so. Maybe Max would be his salvation. He seemed stuck at vice president, but with the bungling Georgia peanut farmer out of office, America was poised for liftoff, as was he.

35

DR. E

Freddy, in his unlikely role of host, promised me it would be a no-stress, no-obligation cocktail reception for his trusts and estates clients,[38] the bulk of whom were solvent, bookish, unattached ladies roughly my age. A geezers' mixer. It began unpromisingly when I noticed a guest wearing, of all things, a double-knit polyester leisure suit. This was 1982 for gods' sake. How could the Harvard Club have let him through the door?

What sticks in my mind is the laser-like scrutiny I received from Freddy's assistant, a well-dressed young woman named Andrea Worthy whom my son sometimes refers to as "The Prattling Gun." Knowing Freddy, I assume he didn't tell her I was his father.[39]

Had she not been so transparent, I might have welcomed Andrea's attention. However, it was obvious she was only trying to determine my potential as a customer. You could hear the primitive gears grinding in her small, self-seeking mind. Could I be useful to her? I recall thinking, *She will go far in banking.*

---

38 Not including, thank gods, those at Essex Lodge.

39 I later confirmed this with him. It's clear I'm still seen as an embarrassment. Rightfully so, perhaps.

Ms. Worthy was like a pilot preflighting her aircraft. First, a walk-around checking my general condition, followed by an inspection of my external surfaces for buildups of grime or debris, and concluding with a thorough examination of my controls, gauges, and avionics. It was evident that, given my limited flight envelope, I was not airworthy.

Unhappily, Andrea's cold-blooded assessment appears to have been shared by the other ladies with whom I chatted. So what. None of them could hold a candle to Helen.

In an effort to distract Freddy from his failure as a matchmaker, I asked him how things were going at Old Colony. It was he who brought up Andrea.

Perhaps it was the wine talking—both of us, downcast by the evening, overindulged—but my usually reserved son had a lot to say about Andrea, most of it concerning what he saw as her misguided ambition.

We each downed a final tepid glass of white wine, and, as we were collecting our coats, Freddy startled me by announcing almost breathlessly, "She has the most beautiful feet!" As it happened, the shoes Andrea was wearing that evening precluded me from verifying this contention.

Freddy was kind enough to give me a lift home. The next morning, quite pleased with myself, I sent him a postcard reading, "I hope you've found your solemate, Dear Boy."

I still await his response.

36

DANIEL

The creaking 737 completed its base leg, stood shakily on one wing, made an abrupt ninety-degree turn, leveled off, and swung onto final. It had been an ordeal: JFK to LAX to Incheon to Noi Bai, whatever the fuck that meant. Not to worry. Reagan had just clobbered Mondale, and all was right with the world.

Had any of his fellow passengers been guests at the Hanoi Hilton? If so, this flight would have knotted their sphincters. What must it have been like flying low over the seemingly innocuous countryside that concealed the MIGs, the SAMs, and the flak that punched them out of the sky? This was where it happened, but, unlike the wounded landscape, no traces remained aloft.

The official after-action reports for the war, in which the US lost close to ten thousand aircraft, were terse but haunting. To paraphrase a tiny sampling: *The aircraft was seen to explode into four major pieces. Two parachutes were seen, but it is unlikely either survived the explosion caused by a possible direct SA-2SAM hit.* Another: *Attacking using bombs in a diving maneuver, the pilot probably had target fixation and slammed into the ground 500 feet from the target.* A third: *The pilot over-rolled his aircraft in a bombing maneuver, leading to a high-speed stall and then a spin. The aircraft hit the ground before the pilot could regain control or eject.* A fourth: *Premature detonation of a just-released bomb destroyed the plane and killed the pilot.* Sometimes Poseidon—thank you, Dr. E—claimed you: *Hit by flak immediately after dropping its bombs, the aircraft dived into the sea just off the coast; the pilot did not eject.* The recruiters never mentioned those "Oh, shit" moments to wannabe Pappy Boyingtons.

———

Had she accompanied him to Vietnam, precocious Harriet, who was riding the crest of the Reagan years and defiantly flourishing at Yale, would have missed too many classes. That was why he'd selected this trip. He didn't want her there. Something could go wrong. It had before.

He was not swayed when, in her most insistent tone, she made her final argument. "Can't you cut me some slack, Daddy? I haven't missed a single class during my last three years, and you promised to show me where Mr. Rubino died." It was nice being Daddy, and it damn well was going to stay that way.

"Someday I will, Sweetie, but I need to get a feel for the place. It wasn't exactly welcoming the last time I visited."

God knows what could happen in that shithole. Nothing must be allowed to screw things up with Harriet. Anyone else? Sure. But not with her. Or Howard Paulson.

It was bad enough for Harriet that her mother had just run off with Zack, the assistant pro at the Knickerbocker Tennis Club. From Daniel's perspective, however, it was the perfect result, the very outcome he'd hoped to orchestrate, by having the bored, heavy-drinking Alma take lessons from the blond man-boy who was obliged to make her feel trim, youthful, and—implausibly—desirable. Maybe Zack would decide that servicing the tanned, increasingly portly wife of a Lenox Hill executive director was the way to escape a lifetime of rallying with bored cougars and entitled adolescents. Harriet, who'd made fun of Zack, would never be able to stomach him as her stepfather.

It couldn't have worked out better. No custody squabbles. And given Alma's flagrant adultery and desertion, the financial consequences of the divorce would be slight. There'd been no way to dump Alma without alienating Harriet, who, months after her mother's departure, changed her name to Shaver. Finally, Alma was gone, and having generously assumed all child-related obligations, the moral high ground was his. At least that's how the Supreme Court of the State of New York would see it.

Harriet was disgusted with her mother, and so, with his status and his income climbing rapidly, he could now embark on a quest for a spouse with looks, intelligence, wit, breeding, and an inhibition-free sex drive—a consort with whom he could seize New York—a partner, who after meeting darling Harriet, would love her as he did. One other requirement: taste. Essential, as he might still be somewhat deficient in that area.

A rich wife was not a prerequisite, but he did need someone to help him spend what he'd amassed in a way that would not evoke contempt from those who'd finally shed their own upstart status. On second thought, having money would not be a disqualification as long as his pile already was, or would soon become, significantly higher than hers. Being a rich woman's plaything would not bring out the best in him. Not for him, seats on second-tier boards purchased with his wife's money. He was a top dog, not a lap dog.

————

It seemed like eons since he'd boarded the big silver bird in what was now Ho Chi Minh City, flown east to San Francisco, met Harriet, and been entranced.

Howard Paulson delivered as promised. There was a slot awaiting the decorated Marine in Harvard Business School's class of 1970, and, unlike the lippy dweebs in Harvard Square on the other side of the river, his fellow B Schoolers had been quietly respectful about where he'd been and what he might have done there—particularly on days he wore one of his miniature ribbons. Even the posturing professors, who beneath their verbal swagger were, he suspected, total pussies, avoided challenging him. Who knew what that tightly wrapped, stone-cold vet might do—frag their sorry asses or string their ears on a length of rawhide? After all, he was prone to erupt, particularly in the presence of yappy draft dodgers.

The deal was closed in Howard Paulson's roost soon after Daniel got his MBA. "You've done yourself proud. Impressive transcript—nearly as good as mine with the benefit of grade inflation—a real grasp of finance and an effective way with people. This is your last chance to opt out. I'll get you a job at Old Colony, where you can snooze with your sort-of brother, or you can join the elite at Lenox Hill. Your call, but be advised, Lenox Hill is to Old Colony as the Yankees are to the Red Sox."

"I couldn't be surer. My sleepy Boston summer sealed the deal."

"Yes, Freddy's found a home at Old Colony." Howard Paulson beamed and continued, "Now, about you, Mr. Shaver, any questions about compensation, benefits, vacation, workload, or anything else?"

"None whatsoever." Would he ever exude Paulson's worldly self-confidence? "I'm delighted with the standard rookie deal. Everything will sort itself out. If I'm of value, I'll be well treated. I do not plan to disappoint you."

"I'm sure you won't. By the way, I've found you a modest apartment. Midtown. It's furnished and convenient to the subway. It should work until you make managing director. Then it's the Upper East Side, and I'll throw in a limo and a Brit secretary whose accent will be taken for posh on Wall Street, if not the UK."

"Sounds perfect, HP."

Time for him to pipe down and listen up. Howard Paulson had already diverted several calls to unseen underlings and disposed of the few he took in less than a minute each.

The man's office was unchanged. Still austere. Daniel had figured out why. No need for ostentation. No need for his secretaries to speak in hushed tones. If you didn't know who Howard Paulson was, you had no business being here. This way, the scope of his triumphs could only be imagined.

But what about that plastic donkey? Howard Paulson observed him wondering, grinned, and said, "His name is Keynes, an ironic gift from my free-market mentor. Lift its tail, Lieutenant Shaver."

Kee-rist! Memories of Gideon and Daisy. He complied. As Keynes's tail went vertical, there was a click from within, and a thick brown cigar slowly emerged from its rear.

"That's for you. Next one's mine." Howard Paulson pointed to a massive Dunhill table lighter. "Please do the honors."

They lit up, exhaled, and looked pleased with themselves. Hot damn. He was in. He relaxed.

After a moment, Howard Paulson aimed his cigar at Daniel's forehead and said, "And now for my pregame pep talk. You ready?"

Daniel nodded and confronted the fearsome Paulson stare.

"Our business is all about getting and maintaining an edge, ferreting out intel before the schlubs. Understood?"

Without awaiting a reply, Howard Paulson took a puff, savored it, exhaled, and pushed on. "Bad news is often highly valuable. It can be used both offensively and defensively. Most people are piss-poor at selling, since it can mean acknowledging a mistake and/or taking a tax hit. But often it's the smart move."

Using his cigar for emphasis, Howard Paulson continued. "You'll need to develop your own *sources*, and I use that term advisedly. I think you'll be good at it. Otherwise, you wouldn't be here. And finally, as you may have gathered, I'm a busy man. Spare me the details of how you got your information. Just tell me the rationale for your decision, and if I agree, you get the green light."

"Yes, HP."

"Before I forget—getting advance word on the outcome of clinical trials can be invaluable."

Howard Paulson signed off. "If you live up to expectations, Daniel, someday Keynes will be yours. By the way, how's married life treating you? We haven't talked since you strapped on the ball and chain."

"Just fine. And thanks again for hosting our nuptials. Great weather and what a view. Our first time in Southampton. As for the apartment, it'll be perfect. Harriet loves being close to Central Park. There's a ride on an ancient pony that makes her feel brave."

"Your little girl's awfully bright, isn't she?"

"Absolutely. Yesterday she made up a riddle. 'Where do flowers sleep?' she asked. Without giving me enough time to figure it out, she answered, 'Flower beds.'"

"Nice. You did right in marrying Alma Rubino. You can be damn proud of yourself, and your story will play well with our customers. Undamaged young heroes are always a draw, and there are damn few of them on Wall Street. Here's another bit of unsolicited advice. Join your clubs when you're young and I can still put in a good word. It's harder when you've been around, kicked some ass, and upset the dolts who run the membership committees."

———

Howard Paulson had not been exaggerating. As advertised, his first two years at Lenox Hill were grim. Endless late nights and many cubic feet of god-awful Chinese takeout. It was worth it, however. He kept climbing while his peers fell by the side of the trail. Soon he'd be pressing Tod Paulson.

Harriet was adorable in the smocked dresses he bought her, while Alma, with time on her hands and too many credit cards in her alligator carryall, was a worry. Excluding well-earned personal time with the more personable personal assistants and interludes with Mary Foley—which he considered grandfathered—he had, by and large and without really intending to, observed his marital vows. He considered making a play for his lively B School classmate and Lenox Hill colleague, Sharon Knox, but shelved the idea after learning she was known as "Fort Knox."

Howard Paulson, once he'd assigned his serfs their huts and tiny plots, spent little time with them, so it was alarming when he popped into Daniel's cubicle in the midst of the year-end frenzy.

"I'm rushed, but I thought you needed to know."

Sometimes Paulson's intensity gave him a headache. "Know what, HP?"

"Remember what I told you about Freddy's mother a couple years ago?"

"I do. Mrs. Paulson. It was worrisome."

Howard Paulson looked solemn. "It's the former Mrs. Paulson, I'm afraid."

Why hadn't he heard? "My God, she's dead?"

"Thankfully, no, but I've had to institutionalize her. Most painful thing I've ever done."

Was the great man seeking *his* approval? "I'm sure it was, HP."

"Indeed. Early onset something or other. I'd been worried."

"You said the former Mrs. Paulson." Were the peasants on the adjacent parcels wondering why he merited a visit from their liege?

"Yes, it was the only decent thing to do. We could no longer grow together as a couple. We needed freedom to fashion new lives.

Romances flourish in nursing homes. I couldn't deny Helen that opportunity."

Holy shit, he'd have to remember that one. Not what he'd heard about nursing homes. More like a mob of heavily medicated zombies stealthily pleasuring themselves and their fellows. "I'm sure you've done the right thing, HP."

"So am I. She's getting the best possible care. Essex Lodge is state of the art, and it's providing a tidy return. I should know. We financed it. Helen's settled in nicely, made new friends, and I wish her only the best. By the way, do you know what Essex Lodge and football games have in common? No? Kickoffs!"

Daniel chuckled on cue. Should he hate himself? Fuck, no! Howard Paulson was, as always, unreadable.

"One other thing, HP?"

"Yes, Daniel."

"There's a rumor you're going to remarry."

Howard Paulson laughed. "This place—done so already. Sharon Knox, your Business School classmate. We stole away to Bermuda. Coral Beach Club. I've got a cottage there. Keep it under your steel pot. I'm breaking the news when I distribute Christmas bonuses. They'll be substantial. Even better than last year's."

———

Some weeks later he was summoned. Howard Paulson was completing a call. "That was Essex Lodge. You know what my ex said? 'Who's he? Who's Howard Paulson?' That must have tickled the Elders."

"How hurtful."

"Not really. It's what I expected. Sometimes you've just got to let go," he said, looking at the photograph of himself and the incumbent Mrs. Paulson.

"It's good you have an all-consuming job and a spirited young wife."

"Yes, thanks to Sharon, I may finally be shedding my grief. Unlike the Shah, I intend to keep her even if she fails to produce a son. What a gal. Steel-trap mind with a great aptitude for finance and fun."

How the hell was he supposed to respond to Paulson's wink?

"She is impressive," Daniel said.

"Yes, like you, a Baker Scholar at the B School. She wrote a paper about Lenox Hill." He chuckled, "Some might claim she had preferential access."

"As far as I can see, that's what separates the winners from the also-rans."

"You're catching on fast, Daniel. Now, about tonight—are the four of us still on for dinner?"

"Alma and I will be there with bells on, HP."

———

Getting suited up for the command performance, he laughed about his "with bells on" bullshit, an expression he'd picked up from an unpromising Old Colony trainee referred to as a "last-rinse WASP." Meanwhile, *he* was gaining ever greater confidence in his ability to pass.

Alma, on the other hand, seemed to be on the verge of a nervous breakdown.

She was, at that moment, completing her third change of clothes. Nothing he said could persuade her she didn't look like a frump or a call girl. He told her she'd "knock 'em dead," but she wailed, "I'm clumsy. I'm awkward. I'm from Joisey, and it fuckin' shows. We're going to be eating shit I can't pronounce in a fancy dining room on Park Avenue."

Booze did not bring out the best in her. In his most reassuring voice, he said, "C'mon, Hon, we're going to be late." He reached for her glass. "Give me that. You're over your limit."

"Don't say I never warned you, Danny. Told you I had an itty-bitty problem when we met. Didn't I? Admit it."

"Knock it off and get a grip. This is important to both of us."

Her voice rising, "For Chrissake, Danny, go without me. Tell 'em I . . . you think of an excuse. Sharon's bound to understand; she's met me."

"The Paulsons love you, Hon."

"Bullshit, Danny. I'll look like a lump while the three of you yak about debentures and shit . . . Sorry, sorry, sorry. By the way, what the fuck is a debenture? Something that goes in your mouth? Like a denture?"

"I'll tell you tomorrow; the car's here, and please, not another swallow."

Since it was early, the palatial room wasn't crowded. But those present were watching discreetly as Howard Paulson—whose generosity had underwritten the replacement of his club's deteriorating windows with ones that were maintenance-free, thermally efficient, and acceptable to the Landmarks Commission—made his regal way to the table beside the dining room's center window. The Paulson party was accompanied by an attentive retinue.

Alma managed a strangled "Yes, Mr. Paulson" when asked if she enjoyed the view down Park Avenue. Even though it was the wrong season, Daniel was relieved when she ordered a gin and tonic instead of a martini.

Maybe it would have been better if she'd stayed home, or he'd signed off on her next-to-last dress. As it was, Alma was flaunting more flesh than was de rigueur for the establishment in which they were dining, not that Howard Paulson was objecting.

And perhaps he'd overdone it by wearing his Silver Star ribbon. The urbane financier gave no sign anything was amiss, but then he never would. In fact, Howard Paulson congratulated him on getting his Bronze Star upgraded.

Coffee arrived at last. Alma had stopped drinking, and he began to think they'd escaped unscathed. Then he misstepped, wondering aloud whether someone would explain debentures "to my wife." Alma rose and announced she was going to "the john." He winced. The Paulsons chuckled supportively.

She was gone too long. The Paulsons were ominously quiet. They exchanged looks. At last! He seated Alma and gave her what he hoped would be seen as an affectionate pat.

Then it went south. Looking over her shoulder, he noticed several all-too-visible stains on the front of her dress.

———

The next morning, Howard Paulson, skipping the niceties, said, "Let me be blunt, Daniel. Much as it pains me to say this, Alma is no longer an asset to you *or* to Lenox Hill Capital."

What could he say? "I'm afraid I cannot disagree with you, HP."

"That relieves me, Daniel. I don't want to see you held back by her."

"Thank you, HP. As always, I'm grateful for your advice."

"Let me know if I can help in any way. We still have high hopes for you here."

"I shall, HP, but I've got to move gently for Harriet's sake."

"Understood."

With that, Howard Paulson turned away and took a call.

———

Now he was faced with a bus ride into Hanoi he'd heard could take over an hour. Being able to afford it, he'd flown first class and taken a pass on the hotel selected by the tour operator. Thank you, Lenox Hill Capital. Figuring the odds of surviving Uncle Ho's revenge increased with each star in a hotel's rating, he'd booked a superior room in the renovated Metropole, the erstwhile destination of early twentieth-century celebrities. Let the others, all of them former snuffies, stay at the Lotus and eat *thit cho*, aka dog. Officers should never bunk in with the "other ranks." He'd catch up with them tomorrow at their first stop, the military museum.

He'd been considering this for years, long before relations with the Democratic Republic of Vietnam began to mellow. So many vets were claiming a return to Nam had exorcised their demons—not that he needed fixing. He could live with his dreams and saw no reason to blubber about them with others. Yes, tough decisions had to be made, but unlike those sniveling, panhandling basket cases in their tattered military castoffs—many of whom were frauds—he was just fine. Rich and successful with a perfect daughter and the opportunity to trade in his starter wife. Neither broke nor broken. He hadn't been in a fistfight in—how long was it? Damned if he could remember.

Nevertheless, there was still that unfortunate incident in the grove. It was always lurking in the wings, and he could never pre-dict when it would materialize beside him. A shrink was out of the question. What would Gideon call him if he did that? But how to purge Rubino? To whom could he tell his story? Would it be privi-leged? This wasn't South Africa. There was no amnesty program in the US of A, and Harriet, who, like so many of the young, could be judgmental, probably wouldn't understand. So, how could his small lapse, if that's what it was, be forgiven without being admitted? Not, when you considered the circumstances, that it needed forgiving.

Anyway, something was drawing him back to the termite hill in the shattered stand of trees, the place where, like Ares—thank you, Dr. Elder—he'd exulted while calling down devastation on the foe. Had the termite hill survived? It had shielded him once. Might it do so again?

Not that he was looking for a hugathon with a bunch of paunchy ex-snuffies. But something had been taken from him, and he was out of ideas as to how to recover it. Were some of—all of—the other guys on the tour here for similar reasons? He was disinclined to ask and, by doing so, invite questions. Rather, he chose to see himself as a Chuck Norris action hero slipping back into Nam to retrieve something he'd left behind.

About a year earlier he'd spotted an ad for the trip: "The First Marine Division Returns to Vietnam." It was a cut-rate tour to an area bounded by the DMZ in the north and Quy Nhon in the south. Not that he had any intention of signing up and spending over two weeks with a bunch of overweight bozos and their fading tats. What, he wondered, was the current fashion in tattoos? In his day, it had been a dead heat between "Mother" and "Death Before Dishonor." Neither worked for him, but given his druthers, he'd take dishonor. As for Mother . . .

It had been eerie to flip through the itinerary. By the time he'd done so a couple times, he'd figured it out. The tour would, in fact, pass close to the grove.

So why not send for the brochure? Just for the hell of it. A few days later, it was in his hands. After sightseeing in Hanoi, the group was to fly to Hue and, two days later, head west on the once-deadly Route 9 towards the Lao border. He still remembered the charred remains of the armored vehicles that had been bulldozed off the road, sometimes with the carbonized remains of their occupants still inside.

Having studied the mailing, he went to his storage locker and unearthed the stenciled green duffel bag. He opened it, felt around inside, hauled out his map case, and dumped out its contents. There it was: grimy, stained, and still folded to show Alpha's position, the grove, and the tree line that concealed the mortars that killed Rubino, Foster, and the other snuffies. His hands were shaking. It was the first time he'd touched the map since he'd interred it. And what about the filthy compass? Yes, it still worked. Where would it lead him now?

According to his calculations, at some time on the sixth day of the tour, he'd be within a few miles of the grove. The brochure said that side trips with English-speaking local guides could be arranged at moderate cost.

It didn't please him, but he found himself running out of reasons not to go. Granted, the tour was suspiciously inexpensive, but it fell during a period when ordinarily he and Alma would be confined to the minimum-security prison off the coast of Massachusetts that went by the name Nantucket. It had been a good place to park Alma, but that was its only virtue. He loathed the seersuckers—real and would-be—who abounded there and made it clear he did not belong.

What the fuck, he thought as he mailed in his deposit. *In for a penny, in for a dong.* He recalled his pleasure when he received the list of fellow travelers. No other officers. Nobody with more than a Bronze Star.

He felt self-conscious when the van dropped him at the Metropole before taking the others to the Lotus. He'd dismissed the idea of a taxi. What if the driver hated Americans? We might have torched the guy's village. An errant US barrage might have vaporized his mother. As the uniformed doorman and porter sprang forward to abase themselves and take his bags, some wiseass snuffy called out, "Sleep tight, Lieutenant Shaver. Next stop, enlisted quarters."

Raucous laughter. He flushed but straightened his back and stepped smartly into the ornate lobby of what was once a home-away-from-home to stars like Charlie Chaplin and traitors like Hanoi Jane.

Having checked in and unpacked, he resisted the urge to sack out and decided on a brisk walk to Hoan Kiem Lake, it and the water puppets—whatever the fuck they were—being "must-sees" according to the guidebooks. He hadn't made it a block from the hotel when he began coughing, rubbing his eyes, and clearing his throat. So that's why so many of the little fuckers were wearing face masks. Kee-rist! Why the fuck did fifty-eight-plus thousand of us die for this dump?

The lake was barely two blocks away, but how to get there in one piece? There were no walk signs. No little white figures telling you when to cross. No sooner did the traffic stop flowing in one direction than an avalanche of bikes, scooters, cars, and trucks surged at you from the other. You had no time to make it to safety. With all the noise and chaos it was like being under fire. He was stymied and would have called it quits had not his hand been seized by a one-armed man who stepped confidently off the curb, guided him across the boulevard, nodded, grinned a toothless grin, and vanished.

He should never have left the hotel. The opaque green water of Hoan Kiem Lake—some lake, it was barely a pond—was lifeless. Nothing existed on it, in it, or beside it. No birds, no fish, no amphibians. Certainly not the divine golden turtle said to live there. Nothing. Little by way of vegetation—not even any insects. It might as well have been a settling pool for a chemical plant. Surely it had recovered from anything we'd done to it. But the chattering mob adored it.

What the hell did they have to be happy about? Berating himself for ever leaving the States, he fell in with the crowd and plodded along, doing his damnedest to sidestep the ever-present dog crap. Where, he wondered, were the dogs? In freezers? The place was a fucking minefield.

That evening he played it safe. No way was he leaving the hotel or sampling "Vietnamese flavors" at its suggestively named Spices Garden restaurant. Hold the pho and the unrecognizable matter suspended in its clear liquid. None of that "when in Rome" shit for him. The hotel's French restaurant, Le Something, looked tired and had long since lost its Humphrey Bogartish cachet. As for La Terrasse, he'd need a respirator if he ate outside.

It was back to the bar, where he crossed his fingers before ordering a bottled Heineken and a chicken club. All went well until his second bite when he realized he was about to eat something only consumed in the third world's most desperate corners. It was stuck! He coughed.

He gagged. His eyes watered. He panicked. Heads turned. Too late to bring it up and spit it into his napkin. Oh Christ! Heimlich time?

Terror and then a silent *Thank God.* It had gotten down. Let his gut deal with it, even if it meant E. coli. Now the question was whether the revolting object would succumb to his pampered stomach acids. He was sweating heavily. Another close call in Nam.

Pulling himself together, he waved at a typically inscrutable minion and made a scribbling motion he hoped would be translated as "Bring me my fucking check tout de suite." The language barrier fell. He signed for the beer, the charge for the sandwich having been thoughtfully waived, and fled to his room, where he consumed the reassuringly familiar and securely packaged contents of the mini bar. His last thought before falling into a troubled sleep was *Thank Christ I missed the fucking water puppets.*

The following morning he had an asthma attack during a half-hearted workout in the fitness center. By happy chance he'd brought his emergency inhaler. Having survived thirteen months here during the '60s, was he going to die in this pesthole? Okay, he'd go easy. No more workouts, which was a shame. Farewell to the spandexed cuties who'd eased his jet lag and smoothed out his kinks. Come to think of it, he had yet to see an overweight, unhealthy, or discontented-looking Vietnamese. How could that be? The place was the pits, the food was life-threatening, the air quality sucked, and everyone looked broke.

The military museum, where he joined up with the snuffies, almost made him puke. There, at its entrance, squatted a 105mm Howitzer M2 Series Towed, the type of US of A field piece that saved his ass in the grove. The fact that it had been captured from the Frogs and not us was scant consolation. It had undoubtedly supported our troops on their trek through the Pacific a decade or so earlier. Then it betrayed us by changing sides.

Worse still, the ghastly heap of mangled US aircraft: choppers, fighters, attack aircraft, tankers, transports, bombers, you fucking name it. He even spotted the distinctive tail boom of a twin-engine observation aircraft—the very model from which he'd done some occasional spotting. Always at a high altitude, you can be damn sure.

How the fuck dare they? He could hear the doomed pilots' cries as their disintegrating aircraft tumbled, spiraled, or fell like rocks while they, if still alive, frantically tried to eject. Ironic. May Day, their murderers' major holiday, may have been the last words out of their mouths.

The snuffies were like a pack of overstimulated primates, babbling endlessly and explicitly about their previous night's exploits, some even claiming to have gotten it gratis. Then came the sing-along, where they bellowed out the lyrics of the anonymous but inspired Marine who transformed the insipid "Wake the Town and Tell the People" into a rollicking call to violence.

He should have avoided the museum bookstore with their hosts' distorted version of the war. The fuckers really thought they'd won. Another indignity was an enlarged photo of the wounded John McCain being fished from the drink. They'd even misspelled his name. The so-called Fine Arts Museum was a joke. A couple rooms of undistinguished antiquities and seemingly endless galleries crammed with paintings of resolute AK-47–toting peasants. The image he'd never forget was the obviously staged photograph of a tiny woman pointing her bolt-action rifle with its fixed bayonet at the downcast American airman she was prodding off into captivity. Or did she skewer him then and there?

By the time the group sat down for another scary-looking meal, everyone was pissed off and aching for payback. Not that their hosts had much to fear from this flabby mob. If anything, they were delighted. This wasn't England in the '40s. Overpaid, oversexed, and over here were just fine. These bubbas in flowered shirts and cargo

shorts weren't the hard-charging, shifty-eyed killers who'd splashed
ashore at Chu Lai twenty years earlier in 1965.

He counted four canes, a set of crutches, a walker, beaucoup
blubber, and a couple ponytails. As for himself, not bad at all. Sure,
he'd had a thirty-inch waist when he first banged Mary Foley, but
thirty-six was nothing to be ashamed of for someone of his age and
station. His barely noticeable spare tire belonged on a racing bike,
not a tractor, for Chrissake. In fact, he was a thirty-five, but nothing
came in odd sizes.

The flight to Hue was another horror. The prick at the controls was
trying to make them boot, and he succeeded. Then, surprise, surprise,
no barf bags. The seat-back pockets were empty but for a Cyrillic card
describing their piece of crap Tupolev. So that was what he'd smelled
when they boarded. Evidently, it was worth hosing out the plane to
have fat-assed former jarheads foul themselves.

The Hue portion of the trip passed quickly, despite the moist eyes
and moments of silence in remembrance of those who'd been fucked
up retaking the Citadel. He was fixated on the grove. Nothing else
mattered. He'd already made arrangements for a local guide. What
would he do when he got there? He had no fucking idea.

———————

The guide was waiting for him at the appointed hour. Like all of them,
he was slim and ageless. Unlined skin. Fine teeth. Jet black hair. Dyed?
Hard to say. White, short-sleeved shirt. Forearms like steel cables.
Black trousers. Comfortable-looking walking shoes. They'd come a
long way from sandals hacked out of stolen Goodyears.

Now it was their former enemies who blobbed around in flip-
flops. The guide's regular features were obscured by retro sunglasses
of the kind once worn by US jet jockeys. He was driving a spotlessly

clean jeep on which one could just make out a faint "USMC." Rubbing it in, was he?

Daniel was impatient to get going. "Can't go yet, sir," said the guide.

"Why not?" he replied. "It's just the two of us."

"One more, sir. Someone from another tour wants to go where you are going. Maybe fought there like you? We thought you might enjoy company. That may be him, over there."

Coming towards him was a swaying guy with thinning hair and a beer gut—this one with a pronounced limp. Was he one of the snuffies from the patrol? Christ, that would be tricky. "Coming with us?" he yelled.

"Roger that. I heard somebody organized a side trip to the place where I took out a bunch of mortars—they had one of our patrols pinned down. Thought I'd tag along, if that's okay."

"Sure. You in the Eleventh Marines?"

"That's affirmative. Three Eleven."

"By any chance did you ever use the call sign Ramrod Three?"

"You better believe it. And you are—"

"I'm Blackcoat. Remember me?"

"Fuck, yes, Blackcoat. You never forget that shit."

Though it wasn't his thing, they hugged. Surprisingly, he didn't mind.

For some reason, he handed Ramrod a photograph. "This is my daughter, Harriet. She's a lot older now, but still a knockout. Smart, too."

"She's a wonderful-looking young woman. Here's my family."

"You must be very proud of them. Your son looks a lot like you, Ramrod."

Neither of those kids could hold a candle to Harriet. Now what? Time to hit the road before Ramrod asked about Alma. Who she was. How they met. That kinda shit.

Their guide started the jeep's engine and motioned to the back seats. He hesitated. It would be harder to rehash what happened in the grove with Ramrod if he rode shotgun. He jumped in next to the guide.

Before they set off, he said, "You might want to skip this outing, Ramrod. There's going to be some rough humping. Elephant grass. Streambeds. It could really mess up your leg."

"No problemo, Blackcoat. This side trip's the high point of the tour. It's where I kicked ass big time."

A dusty, jolting, forty-five-minute off-road drive brought them to Alpha's old position. Creepy. He felt the angry ghosts. How could he have forgotten the name of the prick mustang who'd given him such shit?

Judging from his grunting, the drive had been tough on Ramrod.

"Command post over there, piss tubes here," said the guide, pointing. "Gate through wire there. Come with me." The disrespectful fucker had dropped the "sir."

Ramrod was limping badly.

"Still want to do this?" he asked.

"Absofuckinglutely," replied the grimacing Ramrod.

"Sun strong today," said the guide offering each of them a beat-up conical hat.

"No way I'm wearing one of these fuckers," said Daniel, eyeing the old VC headgear. "I'm sticking with this." He patted his faded utility cover.

Ramrod chuckled, "So you're not going to spread shit in his rice paddy?" He leaned on the jeep and groaned. "You know something, Blackcoat, I *am* going to pass. It's too fucking hot, and I'm beat to shit. Shot my wad at the hotel last night. I'll find some shade and hang out here. I've got some skin mags and plenty of H_2O. How long'll you be?"

"Three, four hours max. I'm going to skip the mortar position you blew away. They've probably policed it up by now."

"I'll be fine here. You'll come back for me? We jarheads never leave anyone behind. Right?"

"Roger that, Ramrod." Was Ramrod being ironic? He didn't seem the sort. "We aren't the fucking Army. I remember my DI talking about the Doggies' retreat from the Reservoir. As he so eloquently put it, 'Their Second Division left behind everyone they could fuckin' find.'"

"Yup. I remember hearing that one. Okay, Blackcoat. I'll see you by 1600. Just remember the cannon-cocker's mantra, 'Shoot, move, and communicate.'"

"Roger that, Ramrod."

Their guide, who hadn't moved from the driver's seat, was staring at him with his unwavering "I hate your fucking guts" expression. He was wearing a colonial pith helmet, not the peasant covers he'd offered him and Ramrod. "Where to now, Boss?"

He did not care for that tone of voice and scowled, but the guide couldn't have cared less. "Four klicks northeast of our present position. That's four kilometers."

"I know. We walk. No roads here. Just trails through grass."

"I assumed that. Okay, let me show you." He unfolded his creased map on the jeep's hood. "Look, we're here, and I want to go there, to that stand of trees," he said, pointing. "Can you read a map?"

"Yes, I can read map, even map in English."

"It's safe walking here, isn't it?"

"Yes. Mines and booby traps were cleared or blown up long ago."

"There's nothing else, is there?"

"There should not be, but if we meet something—wild pigs, per-haps—I have pistol, a .45. You know .45, yes?" A long pause. "But if we meet ghosts . . ."

He had to stop reading shit into everything the guide said. "Where did you get that pistol?"

The guide ignored his question.

He opened his compass and shot an azimuth to the distant trees. It had gotten him to the grove once before, and it would damn well do so again. "You ready?" he asked the guide.

The guide nodded.

"We're headed to the grove I showed you on the map, and if I'm right, we take that trail over there." He could see the outline of the pistol under the guide's shirt. He did not like being unarmed.

The guide nodded again. "I lead. I think you have been here before, but is more overgrown now. That is why I brought machete. We take turns."

"No," he said. "That's what I'm paying you for." The guide nodded, giving nothing away. How old was he? His age? Older? Immortal? You could never tell with these slight, fit, ageless fucks.

As the two of them struggled through the elephant grass, he began thinking, *This was one piss-poor idea.* It was stifling and airless. Just like before. Why had he sugarcoated the bad shit? Anyway, he didn't have to sweat mines, booby traps, or, he hoped, an ambush. And he wasn't humping a ton of crap. All he carried was a light day pack containing his compass, bottled water, an energy drink, sunscreen, insect repellent, an Elmore Leonard, bumwad, a couple bandages, and some junk food from the Metropole.

There was no fucking visibility. He was completely vulnerable. Nobody walking point. Nobody covering his six. No flankers. No radio. He was cut off and isolated.

It was coming back like it was fucking yesterday: the low ridgeline, the stream bed that would be overflowing soon, the fucking wait-a-minute vines. Lucky Ramrod, he would've busted his ass. And yes. Now he remembered. The fuckhead's name was McCarthy. Captain Mac. How did he end up? On the Wall, he hoped.

Did the expressionless guide sense his panic? But it wasn't panic, merely justifiable concern. Who wouldn't be somewhat on edge in this suffocating maze?

"You want to stop, go back to Ramrod?" asked the guide.

"Negative. I just need a couple slugs of water." He shouldn't have said "need."

They moved out, with the guide making skillful use of the machete. The man was alarmingly at home here. Just like . . . what was his name? At least he wasn't the only one sweating. Which of them smelled worse? Easy, the guide. Must be the shit they ate.

Was he going to vanish like Nguyen? That was the creep's name. If so, would *he* be a late addition to the Wall? He'd been fucking stupid to let Ramrod drop out. At the very least, he should've talked one of the other snuffies into accompanying him.

He'd been brooding about the damn Wall ever since he'd gotten here. In his dreams it contained only one name—Anthony T. Rubino—carved in gigantic letters, one per panel, followed by a detailed and frighteningly accurate description of his death.

Yes, this was almost worse. He'd been jumpy the first time, but he'd been with guys who'd look out for his ass and get him home to Alpha if it hit the fan. Unless, of course, they didn't.

After twenty minutes, he called another halt, caught his breath, took a piss, applied more bug juice, and slugged down some water. He noticed the guide, who was squatting like a catcher, hadn't touched his. Fucked if he was mooching water off the prick. He shook his head when the guide thrust the machete at him. He damn well wasn't going to lose this war. Realizing Ramrod knew where he was going made him feel better. But neither of them had bothered to get the guide's name, and no American could have picked him out of a lineup.

When they resumed, he congratulated himself on figuring out how to dress: jeans, a long-sleeved denim shirt, and heavy-duty shoes.

Ramrod would've been cut to pieces in his shorts, polo shirt, and flip-flops.

Don't be nervous in the service, he kept telling himself. Despite a few short detours, they'd stayed close to the azimuth he'd plotted on the map; so, unless the compass malfunctioned, they were bound to reach the grove.

And they did.

Okay. Where was it? Over there? Yes. He walked to the termite hill and looked around. Sweet shit. The trunks still bore shrapnel scars and little had changed. Were the dead watching him?

"Does it look the same, Lieutenant Shaver?" said the guide.

He flinched and dropped his water bottle.

"You do not recognize me, do you? You think only our mothers do?"

Oh, shit! "Should I? No, I'm afraid I don't," he said, backing up and lying.

"You hurt my feelings, but do not worry, I shall not harm you. That time has passed. The gods have their plans for each of us. As I said, pistol is for wild animals, and you are not wild. I will end mystery. You knew me as 'slant-eyed fuck' or words to that effect. To my men, I was Colonel."

He backed into the anthill. "Colonel?"

"That is correct. Invisible fuckhead was colonel. You were outranked, and I am better educated than you. By the way, did you enjoy your stay at the Metropole? It is our best. And, while you are in my country, you must sample our 'ethnic' dishes. We are not known for club sandwiches."

Daniel stared at the ground. The termites were hard at it, reminding him of downtown Hanoi. But what was he looking for? As a kid he'd seen the virtually indelible blood trail left on a sidewalk by a rabbit struck by a car. Leaking badly, it made it off the street, across the grass verge, and onto the concrete, where it took shelter beside a tree and died. The blood stains remained in his mind long after they ceased to be visible. Rubino's were nowhere to be seen.

"Have you asked yourself how many generations of termites have come and gone since you and I were here? Oh, Dalton was killed by your artillery. Fritz—Dumpster to you—we cooked and ate. Tasty American dog. Better than C-rats. Now we go back. Ramrod may be wondering what has happened to us, and yes, I know about Ramrod, too."

"How did you learn all that?"

With infinite patience, "Please, Lieutenant Shaver. It is easy to collect information on our guests. I know you are what we once called 'running dog of capitalism,' and you married your radioman's widow. She needs to learn nothing about what you did at Metropole after unfortunate experience with club sandwich."

"No more about my family, Colonel." Evidently, he hadn't heard Alma'd decamped.

"Very well, but you must allow me to tell you about my discoveries after you and your patrol—how do I put it?—fled."

"Discoveries?"

"Yes. Your radioman, his name was Rubino, yes? Italian extraction, I think. Two chest wounds. But front of flak jacket was undamaged. Not so the back. Peculiar. I gave it to our fat political officer. Too big for me and bad example to my men. Their only armor was their shirts."

"Why are you here now, Colonel?"

"To reconnect with old adversary from American War."

A vulture was gliding overhead on a thermal. Less to eat these days.

"Don't be alarmed, Lieutenant. I want to give you something. Shell casing. I found it next to Rubino. From a .45. Yours? '*Qui sait?*' as our former masters might put it. This area has been fought over many times by many peoples. We captured many .45s. It is puzzle. Yes?"

"I never fired my pistol here, Colonel."

In the same calm voice, the guide said, "And why would you? We never got close to your position before you—I believe your expression is—bugged out. Now, let us get Ramrod. Marines never leave anyone behind. Oh, I forgot, Sergeant Foster lived for several hours. Prompt evacuation would have saved him. We tried, but we did not have your medical facilities."

"Colonel—"

"I am not finished, Lieutenant. I have something else of yours. It is back at jeep—your shotgun. You were proud of it. You said your father carried it in the Pacific when we both fought Japanese. I used it too. Very effective at close range. Now I return it. That will make it happy."

"Keep it."

"Here it is rude to reject gifts. Now we go. Almost forgot, your recruiting poster is on display in military museum. Did you see it?"

He had, but fucked if he'd admit it.

Screw that. He, Daniel Shaver, was running this lash-up. They'd fucking move out when he said so. He sat down in the shade of the termite hill, undid his laces, opened his pack, and started in on the snacks. Having finished, he scattered the remains on the ground, ignored the pissed-off guide, and with Elmore Leonard and his roll of bumwad sauntered off in search of privacy. He found it, hunkered down, and did his business. Take that, Nam. The poor ghosts. First, he messed up their lungs with secondhand smoke, then he did this to them. Sorry, Rubino, Foster, et al.

Despite the lousy food, his plumbing was still in decent working order. He gave the guide a cheery wave. Daniel Shaver was ready to mosey back. Would the fucker ever shut up? Evidently not.

"One more thing, Lieutenant. I found two shell casings but have misplaced second one. Can you guess where I found them?"

He could give less of a shit. "What are you getting at, Colonel?"

"Please say nothing more, Lieutenant. But take shotgun and beware of angry gods."

Fuck him. He was feeling no pain. None whatsoever. He'd taken the worst the prick could throw at him.

The hike back was a cinch. They found Ramrod, who'd saved him a beer, tapped out in the shade beside the jeep. Another bumpy ride brought them to Route 9, where they rejoined the tour. He sat in back with Ramrod, who talked nonstop about the fire mission that "had saved your ass." When they got to their hotel, Ramrod reached for his wallet.

"Lieutenant Shaver has taken care of everything," said the guide.

"Thanks, Blackcoat," said Ramrod.

He nodded. So did the guide.

"Au revoir, Lieutenant."

Au revoir, my ass, he thought.

"What's that about?" asked Ramrod.

"Fucked if I know," he snapped.

Walking to their hotel, Ramrod said, "What gives with that package he gave you?"

"Probably some cheesy souvenir."

"Can I take a look at it?"

"Nah. Not worth unwrapping. I'm chucking it."

Later, having been unable to find anything better to do, he joined the snuffies in the bar. One of them yelled, "I bet these pricks start another war so that suckers like us will come back twenty years later, stay in their fleabag hotels, get the shits, screw their broads, and pump up their fucked-up country." Nearly everyone but him roared with laughter. He declined to stay and sing.

Before crapping out, he threw the shell casing into the trash and smashed the shotgun into several pieces, which he scattered in the garbage cans outside the hotel. Then he remembered. In some Asian lands inanimate objects have resident spirits. Had he offended those inhabiting his father's prized weapon? And what about the .45 he'd thrown into a pond back in '67? Was it aware of his presence in Vietnam? Was it angry?

Fuck that angry gods shit, he thought as he went to sleep.

He dozed fitfully, wondering whether the shell casing would be discovered. That was stupid. Who'd give a shit? The fucking country was littered with brass.

That night he didn't dream about the Wall. Instead, he lingered longer than usual in the uncharted realm between sleep and full wakefulness, where random, jumbled images skittered through his mind. Then, with no warning, he was standing by a familiar moonlit pond. Something was disturbing the water. It was as though hungry predators were driving bait fish to the surface. Next, almost in unison, a seemingly ill-matched assortment of rusted objects rose from the mud where they'd been waiting, clambered up the bank, gathered in a semicircle at his feet, and began what looked like a primitive mating ritual. Seconds later, he was staring at a fully assembled United States pistol, caliber .45, M1911A1, without, he was relieved to see, a serial number.

Nguyen was staring at him from the other side of the pond.

37

DR. E

I received a disquieting call from Daniel. Just back from what he hoped would be a healing trip to Vietnam, he was on his way to visit Marjorie Foster in San Francisco. Marjorie, he reminded me, was the widow of a man killed on the patrol where Daniel won his medals, the patrol to which he frequently alludes but never really discusses.[40] Years ago, he'd told me he was helping her, but I was stunned when he announced, with justifiable pride, that his gifts were now "north of 100K a year." Amazing generosity and a noble use of his Wall Street spoils.

Our conversation was lagging when I offered, "While I have no desire to revisit the Ardennes and commune with the descendants of the tree that assaulted me, I hope you laid to rest any and all torment-ing ghosts. As we both know, that can be challenging."

Daniel mumbled something, said he was emptying his hotel room's minibar, and got to the point.

Flying back from Vietnam, he'd gotten irritated with the prospec-tus he'd been struggling to decipher. Discarding it, he reached into his

---

40 I can understand his reticence. When it "hits the fan," few of us live up to our boyhood self-images.

seat-back pocket and fished out, of all things, a one-volume *Richard III*. It was a Yale edition, but, he said, "It would have to do."

We both laughed. Then silence.

"Shakespeare didn't take long getting into it, did he?" said Daniel.

"What do you mean?" I asked.

"It spills out early in the first act, doesn't it?"

I was stuck for an answer but may have guessed what Daniel was thinking. It will be impossible to unhear what he said next. "Can there be any hope for a guy who seduces the widow of the man he's murdered? Is he *not* a 'lump of foul deformity'?"

I couldn't tackle that head-on, so I dodged. "Was it really murder?"

Getting no response, I floundered on. "I'm no lawyer, but I think it might depend on the circumstances. If—"

"Bottom line, if you please, Dr. Elder."

I felt trapped. "As I said, Daniel, I'm not a lawyer, but was the killing intentional? And, even if it was, it could, I believe, still be manslaughter. Particularly in a high-stress context."

Silence.

"Are we talking about Vietnam, Daniel?"

"Would that matter, *Doctor*?"

"Possibly. There could be extenuating circumstances. Sometimes—"

"What if it was necessary? What if there was no *fucking* alternative?"

"I'm over my head, Daniel, but would you like me to . . ."

The phone went dead.

I tried to pick up where we left off the next time we talked, but Daniel stopped me cold. "Purely hypothetical, Dr. E. Something must've gotten under my skin, and I had way too many pops on the silver bird. The stews should have shut me down before Hawaii."

38

FREDDY/FRED

Should he, dutiful Freddy Elder, feel guilty about not visiting his mother more often? A resounding "no." Even though *she* left *him*, he still loved her, and—despite an overloaded plate—he showed up several times a year. Yes, his mother would have a greater number of callers if she had a husband or more children, but she didn't and that was her doing, or undoing.

In the meantime, his Essex Lodge operation was practically running itself. Andrea, who'd transferred to Old Colony's international department, was working full time as she had been (except for a two-month break) since their daughter, Elizabeth, made her unplanned appearance eleven years earlier.

To be brutally frank, Essex Lodge was demoralizing. Was he to end his days there? If so, which dreary scenario was to be his? Which of the lumbering third-floor apparitions was to be him in the not-far-enough-away future? And what about those frightened creatures cowering in their second-floor pens?

So far, his visits had been round trips, but someday he might be holding a one-way ticket. Not yet though. He was in his prime. He was busy. He was vital. He was only fifty-one, for Pete's sake.

Life was such a crapshoot. Who, besides Max, could have guessed what would come of that night at the Alden? Max, with his knowing face, his enigmatic remarks about collateral damage, and his seminars on hyperbole, deception, avoidance, and evasion.

Max had proved to be prescient. Elizabeth, aka Betsy, arrived almost nine months to the day after that blurry *prima nocta* in Zurich. Fred had awoken scant minutes before the morning's first session, feeling as though a railroad spike had been driven through his cranium. In fact, something sharp and unyielding *was* gouging his forehead. With a groan he drew back his head. It had been pressed into the dagger-like heel of a woman's shoe wedged against the headboard. How had it gotten *there*?

Taking inventory, he found himself nauseated and dispirited, spread-eagled in a tangle of bedding, clothes, and competing scents, among which he recognized a familiar spunky bouquet that removed any doubt about the outcome of the previous night's romp. "Outcome," he mumbled to himself. A double entendre was lurking nearby.

And where was Andrea? It had to be Andrea, didn't it? Rooting around beneath the duvet, he came across his snoring, sour-smelling assistant sprawled in a distant canton of the vast bed. She needed a pedicure. And a more invigorating shade of polish. While hunting for his mislaid assistant, he'd noticed the pillows were arranged in a shape resembling a squat pagan altar. His father's influence? And what had been sacrificed? His future? Or had he finally acted out one of his lurid Mary Foley–fueled fantasies? He wished he could remember. Maybe Andrea would, and they could do it again.

His sense of malaise was lingering. Christ almighty, what had gotten into him? He knew what had gotten out, but where had it come to rest? Perhaps, like Onan's, his seed had expired on barren soil. How about atop Andrea's jiggly, milky midriff?

To horse! He roused himself and, like the Marine officer he'd been, took charge in masterful fashion, ordering room service, deconsecrating and razing the altar, dragging Andrea into reluctant consciousness, and formulating an action plan. To expel the night's toxins, he pummeled himself with unforgiving water jets while simultaneously stimulating circulation with the Alden's stiff-bristled shower brush. Ooh-Rah!

The plan was to insinuate himself into the last few minutes of the first presentation, with Andrea joining him at the 11:00 a.m. coffee break looking scrubbed and chaste. Before he ventured out, she had thoughtfully applied a dab of makeup to the angry indentation on his forehead.

At lunch, each assured the other that the previous night had been a cataclysmic, once-in-a-lifetime experience to be cherished forever— but, on no account, to be repeated in the same bacchic fashion. After all, they were bankers. There were strict rules governing deposits and withdrawals. So, they adhered to this resolution, challenging themselves during their remaining nights in Helvetia to delight one another in imaginative ways that could not result in new life.

Looking back, he could only regret failing to heed thrice-burned Max, who reminded him of the "lock" in wedlock, telling him it invariably transformed tractable subordinates into creatures who were neither. So true.

During a break, Max, looking as usual delighted with himself, said, "Freddy, here is Shelley's view of marriage:

> . . . and so,
> With one chained friend, perhaps a jealous foe,
> The dreariest and the longest journey go."

Max smirked and added, "It's quite apt, as you will soon discover."

It was something of a miracle. Shortly after being admitted to Essex Lodge, his mother's condition stabilized, and now, twenty-plus years later, she was virtually indistinguishable from most of the healthier third-floor residents.

Not that she'd recovered. She couldn't hold it in her mind she'd become a grandmother but was wily enough to study other grandparents, so she gushed convincingly whenever he reminded her that Elizabeth "was named for your mother." For this privilege, he'd taken a gamble and ceded to Andrea naming rights for any subsequent issue. Thus far, there'd been no further accidents, and the odds were good there would be none.

Having but once experienced the unquenchable white heat of passion, the young Elders progressed rapidly and without rancor or reproach—at least initially—to what Fred, in a nod to his father, referred to as "coitus infrequentus." While most couples took years to reach this detached state, he and Andrea managed it by their second anniversary. Neither had any interest in experimenting with the suggestively named products that promised to revive what, in their case, had barely existed.

His mother's inability to recognize—let alone delight in—her granddaughter may have been due to her missing Fred's modest and unpublicized wedding. It had been hosted by Dr. Elder at Three Oaks immediately after Andrea twigged to her condition. The fact of her son's marital status never made it into her long-term memory.

Fred preferred to blot out that day. His father, in heretical contravention of his beliefs, unearthed a retired Unitarian minister with a distracting lisp who managed to sort out their names if not their personal histories. Three Oaks looked ignored and unloved, just as it was when his mother and her discontent fled to Manhattan. The backyard—where their union was solemnized—was, as always, unkempt. That was what Three Oaks should have been named in the first place.

And oh, those in-laws. One look at Andrea's ill-at-ease parents made it plain there was no hope of financial or social assistance from that quarter, and—if that wasn't bad enough—their delight in Three Oaks, its furnishings, and its surroundings betrayed a discouragingly Lower Finley sensibility.

And damned if Daniel Shaver hadn't turned up accompanied by Mary Foley, who, unlike her restaurant's food, was still delectable. She barely acknowledged his existence. Why? It wasn't as though he was a Yankees fan or a Democrat. How could she have forgotten him? She who'd launched a thousand nocturnal torrents? It was insupportable.

Shaver and his concubine (Where the hell was his wife?) spent the entire service giggling and whispering, probably about him and the threadbare Reverend Rimf. Afterwards, Shaver had the nerve to bore the guests (Dr. Elder had invited many of the locals, hoping his hospitality might deter them from looting Three Oaks in the off-season) with stories about Harriet Shaver, child prodigy, who had led her class at Brearley, which, Shaver explained to his fellow rubes, was the most prestigious and priciest school in Manhattan.

Then the creep laughingly told the newlyweds their wedding might receive as much coverage in *The White Mountain Tribune* as his and Alma's had in *The New York Times*. Thoughtfully, he'd waited until the conclusion of the prosecco toasts before inviting the entire wedding party over to his ostentatiously renovated place (the asshole said he was thinking of naming it "Four Oaks") for dancing, *French* champagne, lobsters, and other costly sea life that shamed the crudites, pigs in their blankets, and bacon-swaddled pineapple chunks on offer at Chez Elder.

"If Daniel Shaver were a Roman," his father cracked, "he'd have been named 'Crassus.'" Perhaps his old man was finally beginning to get it. As for himself, he preferred to forget the sight of an animated and *barefooted* Mary Foley melting into Shaver's arms.

———

It started, as much seemed to, with a transatlantic call from the ever-affable Max. "How," he began, "is my lovely goddaughter, Betsy? And how do you see Bush versus that rascal from Arkansas?"

"Betsy's flourishing, Max, and it'll be Papa Bush in a landslide," he shot back. At the time, it had seemed prudent to override Andrea's doubts and accede to Max's stated—but, at the time, puzzling—request to become Betsy's godfather. Fred saw no reason to broadcast this news and rebuked himself for being unable to enlist Howard Paulson, as Daniel Shaver had done for the radioman's child.

"Please be assured, Frederick, I shall, in concert with lovely Andrea, attend to Betsy's religious upbringing as soon as she's grasped the fundamentals, and before she's wise enough to realize it's twaddle."

The man could grate on you. "Max, I do not mean to be gauche and American, but might it be time to get to the point of this expensive, time-consuming call?"

"Freddy, my boy, you should sharpen your marketing skills by lavishing on me the charm you reserve for your geriatrics."

"Noted, *sensei*."

"That's better. I have big plans for you and your colleague, Daniel Shaver."

"He's not my colleague. You know that, Max."

"Quibble, quibble, Mr. Elder. He works for the entity that controls your backward bank; therefore, you're colleagues of a sort."

"Please get on with it, Max. I'm really jammed today."

"That's what you always say. You must learn to make every caller feel important. If you were a woman, I'd send you to geisha school for instruction in the art of pleasing."

"I get it, Max. Really."

"Let me remind you of the occasion when, at a fête I was putting on for prospects, one of them remarked it was such fun to get together in a nonworking environment. Do you recall your graceless response?"

"I'm afraid not."

"I shall never forget it. What you said was 'This *is* work.' Nevertheless, despite your negligible social skills, I need you to assist Mr. Shaver in 'marketing,' to use that vulgar expression, my institution to high-end American prospects. Your mission is to help uncouth arrivistes pass as old money. To that end, I need to transform you and Daniel into reasonable approximations of toffs. Both of you lack the polish that makes Brits so effective at selling emerging-market expertise. They claim, with a high degree of plausibility, that having owned them for several centuries, they fully understand the enigmatic little inhabitants of their former empire."

So it was that Max dispatched him and Daniel Shaver to a gentleman's finishing school set in a vast Perthshire estate, possessing miles of grouse moors and several ponds teeming with starving, but suspicious, trout. Their four-day retreat included instruction in the subtleties of fly casting, shotgunning, Barbour wearing, and single malts. Skinning, scaling, and gutting were poorly attended electives best left to the beaters.

The final exam was a so-called "European-driven" pheasant shoot. He and Daniel occupied adjacent pegs while Max alternated between them, advising and spotting as the lumbering, ill-fated creatures were coerced, like cowardly kamikazes, into their first and only flights. It would, he thought, have been more sporting to release them on the estate and run them over with Range Rovers.

Max was ecstatic. "How glorious," he cried out to Daniel. "Splendid high shots, simple close-in crossers, and incomers. Don't you love the variety and the gratifying 'thump' as they strike the ground?"

No, he hadn't liked the thumps, and he liked even less the fact that supercilious Daniel had rung up over fifty, while he accounted for a total of fourteen—many of them still quivering. Eight of his wrecked birds had to be dispatched by the ghillies.

At the shoot's conclusion, the victors were photographed with the KIAs laid out before them in two orderly rows. The scene reminded him of a smirking, bare-chested, M16-toting, shades-wearing Daniel Shaver posing behind a mound of rigid Viet Cong.

Max chortled. "We'll have to rein in Daniel, the killing machine. We can't have him discouraging our real targets."

That evening, as they consumed a fraction of what they'd just slain, Max raised his glass of Glen something and said, "Both of you are indispensable. Daniel, your shooting will stimulate our guests' competitive instincts, and Freddy, you'll be there to reassure them there's no danger of being bottom gun."

Daniel nodded with false benevolence, raised his Thistle tumbler, and barked, "Bottoms up." Grumpily, Fred complied.

"Now then," said their host as they trimmed and lighted their cigars, "I've got a surprise." With that, he left the room and returned bearing a pair of resplendent leather cases. "Take the one with your initials on it, boys."

Daniel opened his, lifted out the gleaming shotgun, checked both chambers, snapped it shut, brought it smartly to his shoulder, and tracked an imaginary bird across the room and out an open window. When Fred tried to do likewise, Max had to duck as the barrel barely cleared his head. "Closer than you came to the pheasants," snarked a sneering Daniel.

Aware he was turning red, Fred looked at Max, and in his most virile wellie-wearing voice said, "Thanks, Max, it's beautifully balanced."

Daniel cut in, "And wasted on you, my friend."

He ignored that mean-spirited crack and, turning to Max, blurted out, "A Purdey, isn't it? For me? To keep?"

"Yes, yes, and yes," said Max, "unless you plan to file off your name."

Fred noticed an odd look on Shaver's face. Hadn't Daniel and Gideon fought over a shotgun their drunkard father smuggled back from the Pacific?

He said, "It's a twelve-gauge, Max, isn't it?"

"I'd use 'bore,' not 'gauge,' Freddy," said Max. "Remember, you're swells, or must seem so to those you're stalking."

To heck with Max. This baby damn near made up for the awesome piece he'd missed out on in '65.

———

Would Mother remember any of his recent visits or his highly edited version of the pheasant shoot? Probably not, but that still left a lot to talk about, and she always appeared interested. Selective reminiscing worked best. Thank God his old man was still okay.

Fred stepped off the elevator, and there in the lounge across the corridor was Cornelia Jenkins. She was dozing through a program on the Normandy invasion.

Next to her was the crew-cut Rupert Damon, whose head whirled around at the sound of Fred's approach. The colonel shot him a warning look. Its message was "She's lovely, she's mine, and there's nothing odd about her makeup or the sparkly evening bag that's always hanging from her wrist. So, fuck off, whoever you are!" The colonel recaptured a strand of Cornelia's wandering hair and laid a gentle hand on her bruised forearm. She acknowledged his attentiveness with a sigh.

He recalled his mother's warning. "Watch out for Colonel Damon. He'll growl if you so much as look at Cornelia Jenkins. He thinks every man wants her." Therefore, he nodded respectfully to the colonel and hurried down the corridor towards Room 348.

Such a transformation. The first time he'd seen widow Jenkins, she'd been a mess. Whenever anyone—even the kindest—encountered her, she'd run a hand through her thinning, oddly dyed hair and muster an imploring stare that asked without asking, "Aren't I still beautiful?" Only the Jamaican ladies assured her she was. Residents and visitors, including—he had to admit—himself, lowered their heads and scurried away.

It had been a mistake to linger the first time he met her. In response to his innocuous remark about the weather, she replied in a keening voice,

"I always loved him. He never loved me.

"I was lonely. He knew I was available.

"I gave up everything for him. He sold my house and kept the money.

"I have anxiety and depression. I drink too much. He doesn't care.

"I can't cope anymore. He makes fun of me.

"I must leave him. He'd like that.

"I have nothing. He doesn't either, but he spends all we have on himself.

"I don't want to hurt him, but I wish he'd have a heart attack. He hopes I'll die."

But that was before Colonel Damon met her, was beguiled, saw off his imagined rivals, and claimed Cornelia Jenkins for himself.

39

DR. E

Some months earlier I'd stopped knocking before entering Helen's room. It was pointless. She'd become quite deaf, but her seventy-two-year-old pride ruled out a hearing aid. However, on the afternoon in question I wish I'd called out to her. I could see from the doorway she wasn't on her bed or playing solitaire. I'd become accustomed to waking her from a nap and allowing her time to separate what she'd been dreaming from what confronted her. In this instance, faint bird-like sounds were coming through her bathroom's open door. Before I could close it, I heard Helen's tremulous voice. "It's starting . . ."

Polly was tugging on my sleeve, dragging me back into the corridor.

We waited until we heard sounds from Helen's bed before reentering. She looked triumphant. Then I realized she was trying to place me. "It's Fred, Helen."

She looked upset. "Of course it is. I know that perfectly well, but who's that with you? Do I know her? Do I like her? Does she like me?"

"It's Polly Spencer, Sweetheart, a friend of yours, and, yes, you do like—"

"Who is Polly Spencer, Freddy . . . I mean, Fred?"

"She's St. Matthew's librarian, Sweetie. She helped choose books for you and your book group."

"Of course, now it's coming back to me."

It wasn't coming back to her, but far be it . . .

"Hello, Polly," said a suddenly confident Helen.

"Hello to you, Helen. You're looking very pretty."

"Thank you. Now, Fred, I have a question. Is Freddy my only child?"

"Yes, Helen, Freddy is *our* only child."

"That's such a relief. I was having trouble with the names of the others."

Helen appeared to be ordering her thoughts.

"Now, Fred, how is . . . why can't I remember her name? You know, that nice little girl."

"Betsy."

Angrily, "Betsy's dead, Fred. Stop trying to confuse me."

Gently, "No, Sweetheart, we're talking about your granddaughter, not your mother."

"Of course we are, Fred," said Helen, trying to digest that confusing piece of information.

"Your granddaughter, Betsy, is doing beautifully. She's popular, she's getting good grades, and she's really cute in her braces."

I am such a liar, but Betsy in her braces did look cute in a *Silence of the Lambs* sort of way. Was I sufficiently invested in my dear grandchild, or was I as detached as her father seemed to be?

"Oh, Fred, that's wonderful news. Please bring . . . that little girl on your next visit."

"You can count on it, Sweetheart."

"Goodbye, Fred, and goodbye . . ."

"It's Polly, Helen."

"Of course it is."

———

When we reached the cafeteria on the ground floor, Polly turned to me and said, "Let's grab a coffee, Fred. That was tough sledding."

"Agreed. I'd never have gotten through it without you."

"Come off it."

"Do you think Helen sensed anything between us?"

"Don't worry, Fred. Helen's a generous soul. But, while I'm at it, thanks for at least implying there *is* something between us. That's major progress."

Polly Spencer keeps me on my toes. Smart, pretty, young.[41] And funny. She suggested I upstage Seamus Heaney by translating Book VI of the *Aeneid* into limericks. "You know what, I'm going to thank D-B for his matchmaking."

"You will do nothing of the sort."

"D-B told me you'd turned him down, but more than hinted you might not be averse to seeing more of me. I owe him."

"Please, Fred."

"It was music to me ears, Polly. I knew of D-B's interest—everyone in the school did—and figured I didn't have a prayer."

"All was not as it appeared, Dr. E. Yes, D-B seemed to be pursuing me, but it was anything but hot pursuit. His primary, if not his sole objective—we never got to that point—was to dispel one of the customary rumors that swirl around in places like St. Matthew's. The one concerning handsome bachelors who appear to have no interest in the ladies."

"You could have fooled me, Polly. In fact, the two of you did."

"That was his intention, Dr. E, but even though he lost, he scored points by appearing to try. And, if you look carefully, you'll see he has not been shattered by his rejection, which, for your information, was coming regardless of his taste in partners."

---

41 Anyone fourteen years my junior is, ipso facto, young.

"You're just saying that to cheer me up, aren't you?"

"It happens to be true, Dearie."

"Well, hanging out with me will never get you tagged as a gold digger."

"Believe me, Dr. E, I'm fine with that."

"One other thing, dear Polly, could we drop the Dr. E diminutive. It emphasizes our age difference and reminds people you were once my student."

"Very well. How about 'Dr. Eros'? On a vanity plate?"

"Stop it, and let me add that, as you must be aware, I treated you no differently from my other top students.[42] The grades you received from me were well-deserved. Every one of them.[43] Furthermore, I harbored no impure thoughts about you . . . back then. You believe that, don't you?"

"I'm afraid I do. It was painfully obvious to me at the time."

"St. Matthew's is such a gossip mill."

"Who cares? And to all busybodies from California, I say, '*Honi soit qui* Malibu.'"

That's why I'm crazy about Polly.

---

42 Am I, as usual, deluding myself? I was quite aware of this sparkling, responsive young woman who seemed to understand me so well and with whom I felt so comfortable.

43 Horrors! Was I engaged in what has come to be known as "grooming"?

40

FREDDY/FRED

Yes, he'd backed into marriage reluctantly, but once ensnared and not wanting to go through what he'd grown up with, he'd tried to make it work. Hadn't he? Perhaps matters wouldn't have reached their current state if he'd invested more time in the tedious chore of figuring out what made Andrea tick. Not that he didn't have a pretty good idea. On the other hand, Andrea made no effort to discover much about him.

So, there they were, glowering at each other from their respective bunkers on opposite sides of the 38th parallel. When they conversed, it was invariably stiff, if not adversarial. If he pushed private schools for Betsy, Andrea would object. He was elitist. Or profligate. Or some damn thing. It varied with her mood. Worse, there was no physical contact, neither amorous nor affectionate. He mentioned this but once. She replied—truthfully, he had to admit—"Well, you never touch me."

He supposed he could have done more. After all, she wasn't a boozer like Alma Shaver. But he was painfully aware people were uncomfortable in their company, put off by the put-downs, the absence of warmth, and their incessant bickering.

One word defined Andrea *and* their relationship: stalemate.

———

The call had come to him, his mother's only emergency contact person, late on a Wednesday night in the middle of an unusually taxing week.

"Mr. Elder, this is Wendell Tucker, manager of Essex Lodge. We met at last year's holiday party, where you were good enough to play Santa."

"What's happening? Is something the matter?"

"Your mother's just been taken to our infirmary."

His Thursday and Friday were totally jammed. "What's going on? And please be quick. It's what, 1:00 a.m.?"

"Your mother has formed an attachment to Maurice Henderson, one of our third-floor residents."

"Yes, I remember her mentioning him. A nice-looking man, as I recall."

"It seems Mr. Henderson's been—in the old days we'd say wooing—your mother. At his request, they were seated together in the dining room. Your mother's never looked happier. She's really quite flirtatious."

Fred didn't appreciate that last bit.

"They've been seated together for three months now. Last week, Marcia Parkhurst, Mr. Henderson's regular lady friend, returned from a stay with her Florida family, and now he's sitting next to her again. I'm afraid he's forgotten your mother. Hasn't said a word to her since Ms. Parkhurst returned."

"How awful. How's Mother taking it?"

"She can't sleep. Won't eat anything. Cries constantly. Says she doesn't want to live any longer. We may have to move her downstairs."

"Please don't. What can we do? Can I bring her something?"

"Bring her yourself and stay for a meal. Spend more time with her."

That was damn rude. "That will do, Mr. Tucker!"

"And just so you know, Mr. Elder, we get a ton of marriage proposals here. It gets overheated and confusing. Proposals are made, forgotten, remade, retracted, and, if you can believe it, modified. Our more active proposers often have multiple offers outstanding. And the same applies to the proposees, who may also be proposers. Net-net, there can be a lot of bruised feelings. Sometimes, relationships are terminated without the one being cast away noticing. Less pain that way."

So, he'd come, and she'd seemed fine. Just like a temperamental car that acts up on the road but behaves when you take it in for repair. Mr. Tucker withdrew his threat of the second floor and reseated his mother at her old table.

His mother resumed eating, but the days of a healthy, balanced diet were gone. Now every meal was hot dogs and vanilla—only vanilla—ice cream. Also, she seemed to have forgotten Maurice Henderson. That was fortunate since Marcia Parkhurst, if that was the lady sitting next to Mr. Henderson, spent the entire meal trying to stop him from eating his butter pats—with his fingers.

Still and all, he'd been more than slightly interested in his mother taking up with a lonely gentleman having no children, a short shelf life, and a net worth reputed to be north of thirty million. He recalled thinking, *Maybe I'll be able to afford a Porsche 911, like Shaver.*

If only all his visits to Essex Lodge could be this productive. Prior to setting out for Room 348, he called on Claude Prenderville and terminated his mother's one-on-one art lessons. The wavy-haired, beret-wearing fraud was selling gullible residents (including some of Fred's customers) mediocre paintings with suspiciously shiny metal plaques reading "From the Collection of Isabella Stewart Gardner." It had been an ugly conversation, but he'd reduced his mother's Essex Lodge tab by over a hundred dollars a week. Now it was time for the video, if he could get his mother to cooperate and the camera to work properly.

He'd hoped it wouldn't come to this, but the wretched James Freeman had, in effect, waved his mother's power of attorney in his face, challenging him to do something about it. Yes, he might have paid more attention to his mother, but how could Essex Lodge allow scoundrels like Freeman to peddle their wares on *his* turf? His mother was supposed to be in a safe haven, but while he was bringing financial succor to the helpless, a competitor was stalking them.

A reprobate who had the gall to say, "Mr. Elder, you have been a bad shepherd. You have ignored your mother. I will improve her investment performance and help her realize her dreams."

Justifiably indignant, he burst into Wendell Tucker's office shouting, "Are you aware your flock is being exploited by an unscrupulous huckster?"

"He's less scrupulous than you, Mr. Elder?"

Had Tucker forgotten who controlled Essex Lodge? "This churner comes from what is known in the trade as a 'bucket shop,' an under-capitalized, fly-by-night brokerage house, where high-pressure rogues peddle speculative, if not fraudulent, securities to the vulnerable. Shame on you, Mr. Tucker."

"Mr. Elder, I assumed competition among financial firms would result in cheaper, higher-quality services for the residents of Essex Lodge."

"That's logical as far as it goes, but Mr. Freeman is facing serious charges by the NASD."

"The what?"

"The National Association of Securities Dealers."

"Oh, dear. That sounds bad."

Press ahead. He had Tucker on the run. "I can assure you it is."

"Perhaps then you would assist me in expelling him, Mr. Elder. We don't want Howard Paulson hearing about this."

"Gladly, Mr. Tucker. I'd consider it my pleasure *and* my duty."

With that, he embarked on his crusade against the crafty James Freeman of North Bridge Advisors, whose offices he'd discovered over a Boston sub shop at the scruffy end of State Street. But where to start? With the drivel Freeman had furnished his innocent mother? Or the one-page bio printed on impressively heavy stock? On the bottom, in a bold hand, Freeman had scrawled, "Helen—It was wonderful meeting and visiting with you! I hope it proves to be the first of many! You have an astute financial mind, and the two of us will be a great team! Working together, you will leave your unhappy past behind and realize your long-deferred and well-deserved dreams!"

Never trust anyone who lays on the exclamation points or sends you a signed portrait of himself. Freeman's was an eight-by-ten-inch color photo, three-quarter length, a formula dating back centuries. He didn't care for anything about the man, particularly, Freeman's thriving mustache. Equally offensive were the tattersall vest and monogrammed shirt cuffs—the latter, as Max once put it, a sign of "mutton dressed up as lamb."

As intended, Freeman's likeness projected competence and confidence. Gazing outward into a prosperous future, he commanded his space and the attention of viewers, especially lonely female ones. His arms were folded loosely across his waist. He was relaxed but engaged with the viewer, photographed against a plain dark background. There were no lessons in perspective. No landscapes with a distant vanishing point. No castles. No symbolic objects denoting his station. Why wasn't he holding *The Wall Street Journal* or leaning jauntily against a ticker tape machine?

Give him this, James Freeman was imaginative. He claimed to have a degree in industrial engineering (no hint of where he'd earned it) and "soon began applying its principles of logic and discipline to create his successful investment philosophy."

What a load. But that wasn't all. "In his search for patterns in the seemingly random actions of the stock market, he discovered its 'natural laws,' fundamentals that explained the movement of prices, much the way physics reveals the patterns of matter in motion."

Yes, Fred admitted to himself, it was probably his fault. He should never have allowed his mother to retain control over the pittance she inherited from her own mother, Betsy's namesake. But he couldn't bring himself to take it away from her. Even though Howard Paulson was supporting her, having dominion over something, anything, especially those funds, meant so much to his mother. So, he gave in, figuring it was only a couple hundred thousand. After all, he controlled the bulk of her property. Let her have a little fun and retain some sense of self.

Well, now it was gone, but his mother was unrepentant. In fact, she was ebullient, and this he supposed might be preferable to her habitual gloom. "I've never felt more *empowered*," she said. Where had she come up with that cliche? "James said I should be so proud of myself for taking charge of my destiny. I am, but I sense you are upset. James warned me about this. He said you might want me to be dependent on you."

That SOB. "Mother, you've made a hash of things. Selling your dividend-paying, blue-chip growth stocks and buying trendy overpriced crap—I mean, junk—that's now worthless."

"But James told me over and over I needed to shake things up. He also said the stocks we bought together were 'down but not out.'"

Could he get that damned power of attorney revoked, or was it too late?

"James is so smart and so concerned about my welfare and happiness."

"Is he suggesting I'm not?"

She considered that. Then, quietly, "Sometimes, James says, family members have mixed motives." His mother grew wary. "Did I tell you James taped that nice picture to my door? He says I'm a lioness."

"My motives are not mixed, Mother. Please remember that."

"Oh, Freddy," wailed his mother. "I'm so confused."

He really wasn't trying to get back at her. "Mother, I've looked over these papers. Don't you recall specifying 'current income' as your return objective and 'conservative' as your risk profile?"

"I don't know, Freddy."

He put an arm around her shoulder. "Do you realize what's happened here, Mother?"

"Tell me, Freddy."

"You've lost nearly all your mom's money, and I'm not sure what to do next." He shouldn't have said that.

"Oh, Freddy, I feel so terrible. It would be better if I died, wouldn't it? I wish I knew how to die."

He considered that for a moment before blurting out, "Stop indulging yourself, Mother." Yes, that was unkind, but thankfully, it didn't seem to have registered. There were things that mustn't be said to one's aged parents, no matter what.

"I'm going to die soon, aren't I?"

Sadly, she was probably correct. "No, Mother, you are not."

"And when I do, I will miss you and James and all the nice people I'm leaving behind. Including that nice Dr. Elder. Will you miss me?"

It wasn't fair. *She* could say whatever she pleased. He could not.

"Please, Mother, you've got a long time to live." That thought exhausted him.

"I am deep in the well of worry, Freddy."

"The what? That's James Freeman talking, isn't it?" Damn him. "Mother, please stop. Here's a Kleenex. You're going to be fine. No more well of worry for you."

What made him say that? He'd been flogging North Bridge's ambulance-chasing lawyer for months and gotten nowhere. Those pricks assumed he'd have to bear the expense of chasing them, and that alone would cause delay and cost a fortune. His stern letter demanding two hundred thousand dollars in damages finally produced an offer of eight thousand.

Then he had his brainstorm.

It aroused in him something a legendary Marine warrior liked to call "the spirit of the bayonet." He transformed his mother's story into an affidavit and, instead of merely sending it to North Bridge, filmed his mother reading it aloud in her piteous, halting voice while propped up in her bed with the cherubic Mercy Williams standing protectively at her side. What a ham. His mother nailed it on the first take.

Fred sent the finished product to North Bridge's lawyer, telling him two hundred thousand dollars in five working days was the cost of keeping the video out of the hands of the SEC, the NASD, the Boston dailies, and a crusading *New York Times* journalist whose antibusiness diatribes usually infuriated Fred.

Sometimes he was impressed with himself, and this was one of those occasions. His final dustup with North Bridge's lawyer was a triumph. He set up the call on a speakerphone in one of Old Colony's conference rooms and let fly with both barrels.

First, he established that his adversary had indeed watched the video. Then Fred gently inquired, "Would you like to see my Oscar-worthy film in general circulation? Would it be good publicity for your client?"

He didn't care for the lawyer's reply. "The question *you* should be asking yourself, Mr. Elder, is 'How will your frail mother fare in *my* deposition?'"

The conversation spiraled downhill from there.

"Come, come, Mr. Elder. James Freeman is a respected investment professional with an unblemished record. He warns all his clients, particularly the elderly ones, that there are no sure things. Your mother will be seen as another sore loser."

It's not often one gets to scream, let alone scream obscenities, in a bank. Fred channeled a drill instructor in full cry. In volume, content, and duration his performance would have gotten a rousing Ooh-Rah at Parris Island and MCRD San Diego. Semper Fucking Fi! He didn't know he had it in him.

So gratifying. His rant was observed and overheard by several Old Colony employees who walked slowly past the glass-walled conference room in which he raved, frothed, and paced like a rabid beast. Even better, one of them was an EVP. The word was out. Fuck not with Frederick, formerly Freddy, Elder!

He informed his stammering foe he was mistaken if he thought Frederick Elder was going to fold his tent and slip away in the night. This project was to be his "life's mission, a sacred crusade" on behalf of his "infirm, defrauded mother." His time was not costing her a red cent. It was all on the house.

"I'll take it upstairs today," conceded his cringing adversary.

"You do that, Mister," he snapped. His summa father would be impressed. Howard Paulson would nod approvingly. Shaver would be awed. Andrea might say something positive. Maybe they'd even "do it" this year. No, probably not.

He should have known better. It's always half a loaf, if that. Even when you hold a winning hand. But he'd kicked ass big time. One hundred thousand was nothing to sneeze at.

He made sure the video reached both his fathers. Dr. Elder was impressed and laudatory. He wished he'd had a tape recorder when his father said, "Really nice job, Freddy. I'm so proud of you for looking out for your mother. She needs all the help she can get, and, much as I hate the idea, so perhaps will I. If I do, I'll know where to turn." That, combined with the realization he'd already out-earned his old man, almost made up for years of being unnoticed and underrated.

But it did not. He was an only child, and, as such, wasn't he supposed to be cosseted, pampered, and indulged? From birth! He was the last of his line. Why wasn't he named Uncas?

Nevertheless, encouraged by his father's reaction and expecting more of the same from Mr. Lenox Hill Capital, he called his stepfather. Howard Paulson's response was devastating: "Sweet Jesus, Freddy, why didn't you get me involved instead of dicking around like you did? I'd have fixed the fucker in five minutes."

"I don't understand, Mr. Paulson."

"Of course you don't. You know Lenox Hill owns Essex Lodge, don't you?"

"I do, but—"

"Which means I control what the fuck happens there. Right?"

"Right."

"Henceforth, the only financial institutions allowed on the premises will be Old Colony Bank and its affiliates. Tell that to numbnuts Tucker."

"That's brilliant, Mr. Paulson."

"No, it's frigging obvious. Okay, how much did you squeeze out of those pricks? 100K? Are you shitting me, Freddy? You're not? Sweet Jesus!"

"I thought I did—"

"You screwed the pooch. Big time. I'd have had his nuts, his license, his company's license, the full value of your mother's loss, plus a bundle for P and S."

"P and S?"

"C'mon, Freddy, pain and suffering. Daniel would have reamed Freeman a new one."

Nuts to that. No more. Before he could check himself, Fred heard what sounded like a stranger saying, "I disagree, Mr. Paulson. I did *exceptionally* well under the circumstances."

Silence.

Then, thank God, a chuckle, and in an amused tone, Howard Paulson said, "Freddy, my boy, what *did* you get up to last night?"

41

DR. E

While I deplore pointless introspection, it has become impossible to avoid concluding I'm something of an oddity. What other institution has an elderly polytheist teaching a dead language to mostly empty seats? Although I may not be as collectible as a narwhal's tusk,[44] I surely deserve a place in any respectable cabinet of curiosities.

This depressing realization derives from a plodding event hosted by the head of St. Matthew's mathematics department, an individual said to be scintillating by those of his subordinates who've not gotten tenure.[45]

Our host turned out to be fond of parlor games and practical jokes. Discerning a lull, he sprang to his feet, giggled delightedly, excused himself, and returned a moment later bearing a shiny reddish-brown object six to eight inches square.

Oh, what could it be?

We passed it from hand to hand with growing good cheer. Everyone was stumped.

---

44 They were initially said to be unicorns' horns.

45 This dinner may have given rise to the absurd rumor I was "seeing" the young calculus teacher from Smith. But yes, compared to her colleagues, she is a sparkler.

When we gave up, our host was overjoyed to announce it was a fossilized mammoth tooth. He snickered. His wife grimaced. *She* knew what came next.

Off went our host, returning in no time with a second marvel. It was made of woven reeds or grasses and was roughly the size of an ice cream cone or one of those cheery bud vases, once a fixture in VW Beetles. There were vines attached to its open end.

I inferred that a number of the males at the table, me included, harbored premonitions. Despite a stricken expression on the face of our hostess, we suppressed our worries and all of us, ladies included, entered into the spirit of the game. The delicate conversation piece was explored by sight and touch, with a number of the ladies holding it to their faces, trying, without success, to sniff out a clue.

Our host was having silent convulsions. His wife was nowhere to be seen. Soon it was revealed. The ladies had just buried their noses in a Polynesian penis shield. The young lady with whom I was said to be involved blushed becomingly.

How am I to deny the obvious analogy? Yes, I am a fossil, but I choose not to dwell on the relevance of the second item to my pre-Polly member, my bone-dry dreams, and a libido that may not have matched a giant panda's.

42

DANIEL

Mary Foley looked up at the sound of the screen door slamming, flashed her welcoming grin, tossed aside the grimy rag with which she was sloshing germs around the counter, undid a button, and skipped towards Daniel with her arms spread wide.

She laughed. "Great to see ya, Danny. How's about a big wet smooch. You gotta be needing more than skinny Alma's giving you. That's more like it. You around later? After I close up? Like old times?" Mary bounded onto the adjacent stool and undid another button.

"'Fraid not, Mare, but I'll sure take a rain check."

It was still too soon to tell the world about Alma who, after less than a year with Zack, was—on Howard Paulson's nickel—drying out in the Berkshires and making piteous noises about coming back to him. No fucking way, and Harriet was good with that.

Alma'd had her chances. He'd laid it out for her on the Tuesday after Labor Day. Before she downed her first Bloody Mary.

"Look," he remembered saying, "it's damn obvious you don't think much of me."

That got him a dirty look. Jesus, she was scary before she slapped on her primer coat.

He'd continued in his most reasonable tone, "You have a point, I suppose. I could be richer, smarter, and better looking, but I'm not *that* bad, and I *am* going to make it big."

By then, she was deep into her first Bloody. "Go fuck yourself, Danny."

"You're such a lady, Sweetheart. But you are missing the point, as you're wont to do. I may not be as supple as dim-witted Zack, but I am by far the best *you* will ever do."

He was out the door before Alma could mix another drink or fling her glass at him.

Foley's Restaurant hadn't changed. Same flaking tin ceiling, beat-to-shit linoleum, gouged countertops, wobbly stools, shakers clogged with lumps of petrified salt, ashtrays pilfered from renowned restaurants by loyal customers, and, everywhere, fading photos of forgotten teams. No, he was mistaken. Even Foley's wasn't immutable. The flypaper with its disintegrating remains was gone. Should he be alarmed?

There were two other customers: a zit-faced kid and a hollow-eyed smoker in a sweat-stained John Deere cap.

Alma had turned up her nose at Foley's. She'd eaten there once and vowed, "Never again." He hadn't been sure whether it was the food, the ambience, or Mary's invincible chest.

"C'mon, Danny. I remember when you'd almost let fly in your trou if I offered you a quickie. Am I looking old or something? I only got four years on you, for Chrissake."

"No, Mare, you're looking great. You know that. But I'm kinda stuck for time, and there's something big I gotta ask you. I'm betting you'll like it."

Smiling but persistent, Mary leaned closer. "Sure I can't talk you into it, Danny? We can yak afterwards. First things first."

He felt himself weakening.

"Promise me I'm not too fat, Danny."

"No, Mare. You're abundant . . . just the way you're supposed to be."

"Getting pretty fancy, Danny Boy. I'm abundant—what kind of a bun is that? Not sure they're on our menu. Lemme look."

"Stop with the hard time, Mare."

"Danny, we could step out back and make things right in the time it takes Sam here to burn your burger."

He'd always enjoyed Sam's greaseburgers, known throughout the Finleys as the most lethal in the Granite State. But Sam was losing it, and that boded ill for his customers. Whenever Sam saw him now, he'd flinch, stammer, "Hi, Gideon," and scamper back to the supply closet where he had his cot.

"Like I said, I gotta take a rain check, Mare."

Zits and John Deere had stopped eating and were watching them.

"Hey, Mare, cut it out. Not here. Seriously. I've spilled all over myself."

"As a kid you did that a lot. Remember that night by the lake?"

"You'll never let me forget."

"You got that right. But hey, we've been through a lotta shit together, Danny. Some might call it a "Foley à deux.""

"Jesus, Mare, that's wicked funny."

"Damnit, Danny. Stop discounting me. I watch PBS and *Masterpiece Theatre*, for Chrissake."

"C'mon, Mare. I know you're smart as hell, but you gotta stop doing what you're doing. Now!"

"Now, Danny boy, a girl can't ever be certain, but looking at those trousers, I'd say your pipe is 'calling, from glen to glen and down the mountain side.' How's about we slip out back? Or upstairs. I've done some redecorating."

"Christ, Mare, I could give a rat's you-know-what about that. I've always liked your office just the way it was. And yes, change of plans, I'm gonna cash in that rain check right now. And afterwards there's something I want you to consider. Really."

John Deere heard it all. His fork had fallen into the gravy, and he was staring at them with a slack-jawed expression before hightailing it to "Gents."

Yes, she'd redecorated, but the picture he'd given her of his Pop Warner football team still occupied the place of honor behind her desk. And there he was in the center of the front row holding the ball. Two rows behind him was Tommy Reeves, a seldom-used sub. More to the point, Mary'd replaced her beat-up couch with the Naugahyde pull-out sofa bed on which she was displaying herself so bewitchingly.

"Jesus, Mare, you're dripping like a goddamn sugar maple." With that, he shed his clothes, including his recalcitrant boxers, which had gotten snagged on something.

"Oh yes, my eager beaver, and, by the way, you're leakin' too, my friend," said the saucy girl.

What more was there to say? He looked down at himself admiringly, snapped to attention, and, bringing the command up from his diaphragm as Marines are taught, roared in a voice capable of rousing a regiment, "Preee-sent SHORT ARMS!"

––––––––––

The resourceful Mary Foley made things right for them and, before getting up, said, "Well, Danny, it's taken a while, but you're getting your first A. Don't be *too* cocky, though. It's an A minus, and, for the record, I was up for a doubleheader."

His still-warm burger was waiting for him when they returned.

"Can I ask you something, Danny?"

"After that, anything."

"Before you leave, check out 'Gents.' John Deere likes to spray paint the walls. On a good day he'll splatter the mirror."

"Sure thing, Mare."

"Thanks, but what's with that scar? Yeah, right there. I've always wondered."

He touched it. "Still shows, doesn't it? That's where brother Gideon jammed the barrel of the .22 up my nose."

"Shit, Danny."

"That's what I thought too. Gideon was always sticking things in the wrong places."

Mary adjusted his placemat, then slid him the ketchup and another Gansett. She came around the counter, lit up, patted his ass, and arranged herself on the stool to his right—the one she'd vacated fifteen minutes earlier. Both of them giggled as they watched eye-avoidant John Deere sidle back to his meal.

"Still the best chow in town, Mare. And you, my dear, are always a feast."

"I wish more people thought so. My regulars are crappin' out, and I'm getting my ass kicked by those franchise joints off the interstate. And now there's a yuppie place in what used to be the five and ten selling fancy French shit. Calls itself a 'brasserie.' Like a brassiere, ya think?"

"Mare, take this."

She counted it. "Sweet Jesus, Danny. What a wad. I know you're doing great, but I can't. You could eat at Foley's for a couple months on that."

"You think Foley's will be open that long?"

"Not sure, Danny. Like the old gray mare, Foley's ain't what she used to be. Pa's hung it up, so it's all on me and Sam. Exhausting, I'm telling ya."

"That's what I understand. Now, hear me out, Mare. I've got something for you to consider." She looked too damn expectant.

"Okay, I'm all ears. No, 'strike that,' as that sweetie Judge Hendricks used to say. Nowadays, if I'm all anything, it's tits and ass. But I am listening, believe me."

"C'mon, you got great pins."

"Yeah. Broads are the opposite of boxers. Our legs go last. So whadaya wanna tell me, high roller?"

"Wait a sec, Mare." John Deere was paying too damn much attention. He went over to the jukebox, selected "Blueberry Hill," winked at the poor fuck, and returned.

"Property values round here are rising, Mare. Lotta old crocks are retiring in these parts. I want you to sell this joint, invest the proceeds—I'll give you a hand with that—move into my place, run it, and keep an eye on Ma till she can't look after herself. Make sure she takes an occasional bath and shit like that."

Her eyes fell. "That's it, Danny? I was kinda hoping for something else."

Not the reaction he expected. Surely she couldn't . . . "You'll love living there, Mare. I've put a lotta dough into the old spread."

"Maybe."

That was too close for comfort. "Okay, Mare, listen up. Ma can be a pain in the neck, but she likes you, and I need someone I can trust keeping tabs on her. There are too many ways for her to bust her ass out there by herself. Plus, the place just got a lot bigger."

"Whadaya mean?"

"A few weeks back I bought damn near all the Elders' land from Freddy. Left him his house, for now."

"Poor Freddy—the boy from the school of soft knocks—one of my shiest admirers. I was wondering if you'd ever tell me."

"Sure, I was, but how did you find out?"

Mary Foley looked pleased with herself. "Maureen, down at the registry. Thought I might be interested, given our relationship, yours and mine."

Relationship? "This damn place. Maureen oughta keep her trap shut. And as for Freddy Elder, don't even think about it."

"Why not, Danny? It would be a corporal work of mercy, and maybe Freddy'd get an A plus. How about that?"

Enough of this shit. Time for another song. Elvis. John Deere, who was listening intently, looked agitated.

"So whadidya pay Freddy for his land? You screw him?"

"Not really. I coulda though. I paid him its assessed value, but not what it's going to be worth pretty soon. Dr. Elder transferred almost everything to Freddy a couple years ago. An estate planning move. And Freddy needed some dough. Always does."

"What for?"

"Beats me. Didn't say, but I heard down at Arnie's he was getting set to unload the whole shebang to a developer. That woulda killed his old man."

Mary gave him a look. "And you're not gonna?"

"No fucking way. The Shavers are coming back strong round here."

"Hey, I almost forgot. You buy that tennis court you and Gideon used to fuck with?"

"Yup. And as a member of the landed gentry, I intend to improve my game."

"So, I'm guessing Dr. Elder's going to be disgusted with his natural-born son for selling out and delighted with his townie almost-son for saving it. Am I right? Isn't there some Wall Street term for guys like you?"

"Yeah, I'm a white knight. Now here's the deal. I'm not telling Dr. Elder. I promised Freddy I wouldn't, and I don't want you spilling the beans. It would croak him. Freddy was supposed to grow the Elder empire."

Two things Mary Foley could not do: resist his charm or keep a secret. As intended, Dr. Elder would hear all about it on his next visit to Lower Finley.

"Okay, I get it. Mum's the word."

"Here's the deal, Mare. You can move in with Ma anytime. She'll love it. When she can't take care of herself, she's going to the place I bought in Concord. I'm not expecting you to handle diaper changing and ass-wiping."

"Then what happens to *me*?"

Don't let her change the subject. "Whatever you like. You can stay on, run the place, and look after me when I come north for some R & R."

"Same old, same old, Danny?"

"Sure, why not? And I'm improving every day. An A minus, remember."

"Easy, Tiger. Don't forget who taught ya."

"That reminds me of my drill instructor who used to say, 'I taught you everything I know, Shaver, and you don't know shit.'"

"But what about snotty A-cup Alma? She'll have a fit, me moving in. Quite the lady now, but I'm betting she had fuzzy dice and air fresheners hanging from her rearview mirror when you met her."

Zits was waving at her. Mary Foley slid off her perch, got him a huge slice of pie, returned, and remounted her stool.

"Alma and I are done. She ran off with a kid tennis pro, and now she's holed up in a ritzy drunk tank. Paulson's picking up the tab."

"You miss her, Danny? I know you loved her once."

That was easy. "Not one damn bit."

"The two of you still married?"

He gulped. "Technically, but she's a lush and we're down to now-and-then hate sex. Which can, at times, be fun."

"As they say, shit happens. And to think I once said to myself, 'If Danny ever fucks me over, I can rat him out to Alma.' Wouldn't work, would it?"

"Not really, and you'd never do anything to mess me up with Harriet."

Her mood seemed to soften. "So, what's doing with the dear kid?"

"She's no kid anymore. Just turned thirty-two, and she's on my side. Figured out her mom's a mess. Thinks Daddy's pure in heart and deed. Gotta keep it that way and protect her from dogs like me."

"Everyone here knows she means the world to you, Danny. Knew it when you told everyone she was reading at a seventh-grade level as a third-grader. What the fuck would that have been like? I knew she was smart as hell when you introduced her to dumb bunny me."

"You're a helluva smart bunny, Mare, and sure I brought her to Foley's. Finest food in the valley. Now, there *is* something else." He shouldn't have put it that way.

"Yeah?"

"Harriet really likes you. I mean it. Always asking after you."

He took her hand. She pulled it away. So much for her good mood. "Okay, new topic. C'mon, Mare, don't look so damn suspicious."

She was staring at him. "Whadaya getting at?"

"You'll be needing something for your old age. Everybody does."

"Shit, Danny, you wanna talk about money? That's what's on your mind?"

"Nothing wrong with money, Mare."

She went to the bar and returned with a Bud, for herself. She drank it all before responding. This was not going as planned.

"One other thing. I got a new secretary. Marilyn Sapers. Ask for her if you can't reach me."

"That's it? You got nothin' else to say?"

She could be impossible.

"You poking her?"

Never mention another woman in front of Mary Foley. "Christ, Mare, nothing's going on. She's got twenty years on me."

"Bet she's twenty years younger, and you're doing it on your desk with her legs over your shoulders and her bare ass on the blotter. That way, when you're done, you can just toss out the sticky top piece, and you're good to go again. Right?"

Mary Foley lit a fresh cigarette, leapt off her stool, and began pacing. "I know all about you big shots and your goddamn secretaries."

"Mare, I'm so damn harmless, Paulson put me in charge of something called 'sensitivity training.' As the old horn dog said, 'The golden age of sexual harassment's passed.'"

"I suppose you think that's funny."

Christ, she was off the reservation. No more Naugahyde nookie for him.

"You know something, Danny?"

Uh-oh. This was not the ribald, randy, ready-to-rock-and-roll Mare.

"I got feelings about us, Danny. Always have. I'm not that cow your prick brother used to bone. Wait a sec, maybe I am. But guess what? Turned out she had second thoughts too. Didn't you have something important to ask me?"

Christ, could Zits and John Deere hear this? Time to feed the jukebox.

"I started doing it way too soon. Thought it would make me popular. Big mistake. Don't get me wrong. It was fun, but I made it too easy for ya—and for a few others—but not as many as you probably think. I'm the opposite of too little and too late."

"C'mon, Mare. I've got feelings about us too."

A flash of rage. Looking him full in the face: "Bullshit! I used to think that when you were younger. You had it tough, Danny, and beneath it all there was a pretty decent kid. Then, somewhere along the line, you turned into a damn Shaver. And your money just makes you worse. You ever notice how some folks shrink, instead of grow on you?"

Oh Christ, tears. They are all so frigging moody. She'd never pulled this before. Well, not in public. Zits and John Deere flung a few crumpled bills onto the counter and banged into each other as they bugged out. He damn near joined them.

"I still do, Mare. Have feelings about you. Always have. Always will. Here, use this. Your makeup's running." Not a good look. Without her war paint, she looked like a decades-old Polaroid.

"You're not as smart as you think, Danny. You think I don't notice the nicey-nice shit stops as soon as you get your rocks off."

"We got something great going between us, Mare."

"My ass, Danny. I'm just your always-on-tap Lower Finley fuck, and that sure hasn't served me well. Has it? Look at me."

"C'mon, Mare. Here."

"Your fancy, monogrammed Fifth Avenue hanky? Sure I won't ruin it?"

"Gimme a break, Mare. My life's a mess now."

"Boo fuckin' hoo." Then, a look he'd never seen before. "One other thing, Danny. Sometimes you scare the shit outta me. You're strong, you got a temper, and you think you can buy everything, get away with anything. So, what happens after you dump Alma? Where does that leave this disappointed old townie?"

Christ, it was like an old black-and-white Western. Night's fallen. Your campfire's burned out. Your dumb-shit stallion's thinking about mares and trying to hump a saguaro. You're wrapped in your blanket. Your six-shooter and your Winchester 73 are just outta reach, and you're about to have a flash flood of a wet dream over that stacked homesteader in the gingham—or was it muslin?—dress you never got to prong 'cause you saddled up and rode off into the sunset like the dumb fuck you are. Your guard's down. Your blanket's filthy. You're cold as shit, but now you gotta get up and drop a deuce. And guess what? A passel of stinkin', sneaky Apaches come howling out of the arroyo to scalp you, chop off your dick, and boost your turquoise belt buckle. Fuck!

"And don't forget I get along great with Harriet and Ma. You've said so yourself. And, with all this new medical shit, turkey basters and such, I may not be too old to have kids of my own. Harriet would love that, a little brother or sister."

Holy crap, she'd almost forced him off his stool. He was back in Nam, trapped beside the termite hill. He'd grab his .45, put a couple slugs in her, and make a run for it.

"Geez, Mare, you'd hate living in New York, just hate it. Yankees fans everywhere."

"Ya know something, Danny? I'd love it. Lower Finley sucks. You— make that we—could get a big 'flat,' as they say on *Masterpiece*. Near Central Park. Ma'd love walking there. She could kick the crap outta the pigeons. I'll ask her."

"Let's hold off on that, Mare. Don't want to upset her. She's been here her whole life. She'd miss her friends."

"They're all dead or fucking gaga. Think we might make this work, Danny?"

"Anything's possible, Mare."

"You think on it, Danny. But spare me that honest eyes crap you've gotten so damn good at. I'm entitled to some respect, and you're not the only fish in the . . . oh, fuck it."

"Calm down, Mare. Lemme get clear of Alma and figure shit out."

Temperamental broad. Where the bloody hell did she get her unrealistic expectations? Would *two* dozen roses do the trick?

Before leaving, he steeled himself, strode into "Gents," wetted down a handful of paper towels, and looked in the mirror. Yeehaw, John Deere!

43

DR. E

Like nearly everyone, women included, I have always enjoyed the earthy Mary Foley. She's smart, funny, and—beneath her brassiness—sweet-natured. Also, she's brilliant at spotting pretense. In short—which she is not—she's a treasure. Yes, yes, I'm skirting, so to speak, the obvious. She's appealing in a most un-New-Hampshireish way. She is, in fact, wasted on northern New England with its layers of L.L. Bean and its dearth of white sand beaches where she would surf ashore on a clamshell. While I'm being uncharacteristically confessional, my Mary reveries were, I suspect, not unlike those of every other male customer.[46]

In my defense, and unlike earnest Jimmy Carter, I never indulged in indecent fantasies during the few, seemingly happy, years Helen and I were together. Nor, I might add, am I so inclined since Polly and I have taken up with each other and are covertly cohabiting. Covertly, because neither of us can abide being the subject of prurient whispering.

---

46 The original Foley's, owned by Mary's great-grandfather, opened in the nineteenth century. Gregarious Brian Foley liked to announce, as he opened a bottle of wine, that he hailed from County Cork.

That said, during the dismal interregnum between Helen and Polly, I became more fully aware of Mary's charms, and I believe she may not have been entirely indifferent to my awareness. Indeed, I like to think I became something more than just another nameless votary. She began calling me Fred, and, after word of Helen's leave-taking made the rounds, she would kiss me—on the cheek, alas—whenever we encountered one another. More significantly, I never saw her offer other men free refills or favor them with extra scoops of ice cream.

Enough. Like every old fool, I was reading too much into Mary's generous nature. I deserved a scolding. Or a cold shower.

I made a resolution: Stop peeking.

How to dispel the awkwardness that I—and perhaps Mary—was feeling? Introducing her to Polly would clear the air, and I would ascend in their estimation.

Wrong again. Mary and Polly were delighted with each other, and I was ignored. An irrelevance. In fact, Mary forgot how I took my coffee. If anything, I depreciated in value. While it's hardly a New Hampshire standby, I was the Lower Finley equivalent of chopped liver.

44

DANIEL

A year earlier, when the world was fretting about the Y2K millennium bug, Daniel might have looked more favorably on Mary's plea, but that was before Sally Lenox, whom he'd never have met absent Howard Paulson's decree that his underlings go forth and colonize—infest was more like it—New York's most prestigious cultural institutions.

Daniel moved quickly and got Howard Paulson to assign him the New York Public Library, the scene of happy afternoons with Harriet, the avid young reader.

One incident stood out. Harriet had been around eight or nine, and, on the day in question, a Lenox Hill deal had closed ahead of schedule. Rather than having a massage, Daniel sent the au pair home and picked up Harriet at school. He would never forget her delight when he let her skip ballet.

It hadn't taken many classes before both realized Harriet wasn't fated to dance Odette for the Bolshoi. She was fine with that, and so was he. Relieved, actually. Nobody was turning his girl into an anorexic wreck.

They conferred, and, yes, she'd love to explore the NYPL. She'd walked by it many times and proudly told him about Patience and Fortitude, the two weathered lions flanking its main entrance.

Harriet was ecstatic. A huge building full of books where you could read in privacy without anyone pestering you to pick up your room. They admired the Gutenberg Bible and set up shop in the main reading room, where he immersed himself in business periodicals while Harriet devoured a novel about warring gangs of cats. That day she became his "bookerina."

They stayed until almost 5:30 p.m., filled Harriet's book bag at the nearby Brentano's, and shared an ice cream cone.

Thus began a monthly ritual lasting into Harriet's teens.

So, how was he to ingratiate himself with the NYPL? Easy: money and moxie, but where to begin? That was a decision for Howard Paulson, who convened what came to be known as the "Rolodex Summit." Late one Friday, after the markets had closed and the weekend commute had begun, the firm's professionals were summoned to the main conference room with their client lists. The resourceful Ms. Sapers had done a fine job padding his. Only after the lower ranks had assembled did Howard Paulson enter, followed by his two crisply arrayed secretaries, each bearing a pair of bulging rolodexes.

It was decreed that he, Daniel Shaver, would launch his assault at the NYPL's next conservation evening. Using his assigned shred of Lenox Hill capital, he would "adopt" one or more of the library's tattered holdings. Howard Paulson told his ambassadors they must be seen as selfless emissaries, eager to commit both time and treasure (his treasure, he noted) to the public good. Moreover, it would not be held against them if others, particularly those in the media, became aware of Lenox Hill's philanthropy.

Daniel's decision to fly solo at the conservation evening was dictated by events. Alma, even when she'd been on the travel team, resented being seen as most comfortable at events where her bowling jacket was comme il faut.

There he was, his confidence inflated by a gleaming pair of double monk shoes, standing alone in the doorway of a room swarming with A-list New Yorkers determined to be observed and memorialized doing good. The ramp dropped, and, with his rifle held aloft, he splashed shoreward.

My God, a friendly voice.

"Hello, Mr. . . . . it's Shaver, isn't it? Sally Lenox, as you can see from my name tag. Apologies for the wine. Not my department."

Wow! It was something. He wasn't sure what. At the very least, desire at first sight. Oh, to wander endlessly through this ward of wounded books, manuscripts, maps, paintings, globes, and sculpture with the effulgent Sally Lenox at his elbow. She was the only thing in the room not requiring conservation, restoration, or any change whatever. He stammered out an incoherent response.

She replied in a voice so not Lower Finley, "In analyzing the list of attendees, I noticed you worked for a company named Lenox Hill Capital. It piqued my curiosity, since that eminence was the site of my family's farm at what was once known as the Five Mile Stone."

"And where was that?"

"On Fifth between Seventy-First and Seventy-Second."

"You're a Lenox Lenox?"

"Yes, I suppose you could say that. Is Lenox Hill Capital located on or in the vicinity of the terrain feature whose name it appropriated? And, by the way, great shoes."

"And, by the way, thanks. So are yours. No, it's downtown." Ms. Lenox elevated a sculpted eyebrow. He'd never considered eyebrows before. If he didn't immediately up his game, Sally Lenox, her divine scent, and her ringless ring finger would attach herself to someone more promising. The room was awash in those who did not reek of rural New Hampshire. "Do you work at the library?" he added with a touch of desperation.

"Not really, but I'm on a few lesser committees and enjoy helping out at this event, especially when an item once belonging to Uncle Jimmy needs some TLC. Can I explain what's going on?"

Had he already flunked out? The monk shoes seemed to have helped, and he'd taken the hint after Howard's dismissive comments about excess starch and contrast-collar shirts, but how could he be sure? "I'd love that."

"It's quite simple. Take item four, *The Grand Pyrate: Or the Life and Death of Capt. George Cusack, the Great Sea-Robber.* It was printed in London in 1676."

"What ails it?"

"The catalogue tells us that for a mere one thousand dollars, the book doctors will 'discard the existing degraded binding and rebind it in brown calfskin in a period-style binding.' And they'll throw in a clamshell box for good measure. Are you tempted, Mr. Shaver?"

You bet he was tempted, but not by the beat-to-shit book. Would she take it amiss if he rested his nose at the base of her neck and quietly inhaled?

"Maybe, but what about those tired-looking globes?"

"Don't be so scornful. Once they were vivid and colorful. It's the varnish. It was supposed to preserve them, but it's caused their dreary brown patina."

He decided she might not be amused by Max Glauser's quips about "highly varnished truth." So, he asked, "How old are they?" Safe but uninspired.

"Early eighteenth-century and extremely rare. Rehabbing them would set you back eleven thousand dollars."

"The pair?"

"Each."

"What happens if more than one person wants to adopt something? Do they draw straws? Do they get into a bidding war? I'm up for that."

"Most certainly not. How our patrons comport themselves outside this room is not our concern, but these gatherings are conducted with utmost decorum. The price you see in the catalogue is non-negotiable."

"I am feeling gently rebuked." So what? She could rebuke him till the cows, even Daisy, came home. He was hers in the unlikely event she fancied him. Her song was lethal. Tie him to the mast.

"Please don't, Mr. Shaver. Manners aside, rebuking a potential foster parent would be rude and counterproductive. And I didn't mean to sound pedantic about the varnish. Shall we skip ahead to the main attraction?"

If only he'd said, "No, you're the main attraction." Instead, out came, "I'd love to. Where is it? Over there by the rent-a-cops?"

"Yes. All right, here we are. Drumroll, if you please. I give you James Lenox's very own Gutenberg Bible. The first to reach the New World."

Do something, Lieutenant. Something memorable. He said nothing. Thank God she kept the ball in play.

"My great, great—I can't remember how many greats—uncle James Lenox had his agent buy it in the UK in 1847 for what was described as the 'mad price' of five hundred pounds, back when the pound was worth something."

He had to do better. "Well, aren't you something, Sally Lenox?"

"Alas, I am not. The moolah ran out several generations back, and the nouveau Fricks tore down the Lenox Library in 1913, an act of vandalism that would not be countenanced today."

"And the real estate?"

"That's gone too, except for Uncle Jimmy's subterranean crypt in a cemetery on First Street, of which I'm the chatelaine. I am here on sufferance. Just someone who doesn't wish to see her patrimony further debased."

"We shall not allow that to occur."

"Equally ghastly—having Uncle Jimmy's Gutenberg restored by the spawn of Henry Clay Frick."

This was more stressful than his first formal dance. Don't let the conversation expire. He hit an easy one back to her. "Are any of them here?"

"I shall have to whisper, but yes. Please come to the aid of a humble, virtually invisible volunteer."

He was being handled, and he loved it. Why did she bother? "If there is one thing you are not, Sally Lenox, it is invisible."

"Ah declare, Mistah Shavah, if only ah hadn't left my fan back at Tara, ah would flutter it at you and yoah rakish shoes raight now. Indeed, ah would."

"Okay, I get it. What gives with the bible?"

"The binding's shot. It needs to be taken apart, the pages stabilized and resewn and then rebound in the hide of a suitable animal, preferably a sub-Saharan goat."

"What would that set a fellow back?"

"Fifty thousand per volume."

"And how many volumes are there?"

"Only two, Mr. Shaver. Might you be interested?"

"A mere trifle. Allow me to look into it?"

"Are you pulling my leg, Mr. Shaver? If not, I think I'll have a splash of that plonk."

He knew how he'd respond if Mary Foley asked him about pulling *her* leg. "I probably am, but let me call my banker."

"Not many banks are open at this hour."

"Like New York City, the lions of Lenox Hill Capital never sleep."

Howard Paulson was awake, and when he heard the "half-assed" plan, he was awake *and* pissed off. "Are you shitting me? I authorized you to go up to 20K, not five times higher."

"Jesus Christ, HP, you can't do fuck all for that amount. We're talking about saving a frigging Gutenberg. There's less than fifty of 'em still around."

"So?"

Take a deep breath and calm down, Daniel Shaver, or you'll find yourself back in the Granite State. "You can't imagine the kudos, HP. Rescuing one of civilization's crown jewels for what amounts to peanuts. I'll act as your agent, your flunky. You'll get the glory. Your name will be on the conservation plate. It's a natural—the founder of Lenox Hill Capital saves the Lenox Gutenberg. It's a sure NYPL trusteeship, if you want it."

"I'll consider it, Shaver."

It was his last shot. "There's no time, HP. The curtain's falling. You don't want the competition grabbing it." And then a white lie: "The joint's crawling with bankers."

"Who?"

"I can't remember their names, but it's the same fat fucks we see in their about-to-burst cummerbunds in the *Sunday Styles* section of the *Times*. The poor bastards whose stringy wives sand and shellac their faces. I believe one of them runs the Thundering Herd."

"Oh Christ, I know that turkey. Think we can get the bible for a little less?"

"No, we cannot. What's your pleasure? If it's a no-go on the Gutenberg, we can salvage a pair of gloomy globes, one terrestrial and one celestial. Think of them as balance sheets, snapshots of the earth and the heavens at a particular moment in time. That do it for you?"

At last, the real Howard Paulson, the man who'd just cracked the Forbes 400. "That fucking does not. Okay, goddamnit, go for it, but this better pan out or you're in deep shit, compadre."

"Got it, HP. One other thing: You can adopt objects in your name or in honor of someone else, and the plate will include the name of the sponsor and the honoree. A twofer. Make yourself look really good. I suggest James Lenox as honoree."

"Okay, shut the fuck up. Get back in there and grab the good book. Christ, imagine me dropping 100K to repair an effing bible."

"You have made another brilliant decision, HP. Think what they'll say at St. Matthew's. You'll have a big spread in the alumni magazine." That last bit was genius. When could he get back to Sally Lenox?

"Pull your nose out of my crack, Shaver. Snag that damn bible before the thundering blob does."

"I'm on it, HP."

Praise the Lord and pass the canapes. Sally Lenox was just where he'd left her, and, better yet, she seemed okay, if not ecstatic, with his reappearance.

"And what did your sleep-deprived banker have to say?"

"It's a go, and it's being done in memory of Uncle Jimmy. Take that, Fricks."

"I am impressed and grateful, Mr. Shaver. But you better step lively. See that portly gentleman with the rug? Yes, that one. And his lovely wife, the lady with the shiny, taut skin? They look ready to pounce."

"To paraphrase the French at Verdun, 'They shall not pounce.'"

And they didn't. He made his move and secured the Gutenberg.

And there was the incandescent Sally, saying goodbye to the sulky-looking pair, who, having missed out on the Gutenberg, had jumped at the globes. The room was nearly empty. Perhaps he could leave with her. Perhaps they could have a drink together at the Saint Regis. Perhaps he could take her upstairs to the Lenox Hill apartment. Perhaps . . . Had she noticed him staring at her? He hoped not, but they usually did.

"Congratulations on a fine night's work, Mr. Shaver. You took the golden apple."

"And fatso in the Chesterfield got stuck with the his-and-her globes."

Dread silence descended. He helped her on with her coat, and he told her it was stylish. How limp. How could it not be? He tasted the metallic awkwardness of his words. No, she almost certainly didn't follow the Red Sox or guzzle Gansetts.

"I would love to hear more about the Lenox clan. You're Scots, aren't you? What would you say to a nightcap at the King Cole Bar? Have you been there?" He regretted that immediately.

"I am a New Yorker and a descendant of New Yorkers, Mr. Shaver. That said, I really can't; it's a school night."

"Literally?"

"Yes, I'm a school marm, who, in her spare time, scratches away at a novel—like English teachers everywhere. Mine's a mishmash of Homer and Edith Wharton. Enough of that. Here, I even have these tiresome cards."

Progress. Now he had her business number. "Wow, the head of the English department. I am impressed."

"Don't be. I've been there since Princeton. I'm now depressingly senior."

It was an unworthy thought, and he should hate himself for it, but he couldn't help wondering whether dames like her *ever* screwed like Mary Foley. Sally Lenox was in Grace Kelly's league, and somewhere he'd heard the Princess had been hot.

"You sure I can't change your mind about that nightcap? It's not even ten." What possessed him to keep trying? She was not a fish that could be yanked into the boat.

"That would be lovely, but, as I just said, not tonight."

Her expression was hardening. Her eyes were wandering. Time to back off. Keeping his fingers crossed, he contented himself with "Would you consider taking a rain check?"

"I will, Mr. Shaver, but I sense you are already taken, and, to be clear, I am not interested in auditioning for the role of home-wrecker or the pathetic creature who sits by her silent phone waiting longingly for a call from the dashing financier in monk shoes."

"Why do you malign me, Ms. Lenox?"

"You are a gifted actor, Mr. Shaver, but it is not within my declining powers to make anyone, let alone someone like you, feel as miserable as you are trying to appear at this moment."

"You underrate yourself, Ms. Lenox. To recapitulate: The suggestion of a drink at the Saint Regis is off the table, but would you consider a cup of coffee here and now?"

"Very well, but it must be quick."

"Agreed."

It was quick. Too quick. He discovered she'd had a fiance who'd been killed while helping an old lady, wouldn't you know it, broken down on the Wilbur Cross Parkway. How could he top that?

He talked mainly of Harriet, cleverly, he thought, resisting the temptation to run down Alma. As they drained their Styrofoam cups and rose to leave, he let it slip in his best "aw shucks" fashion that he'd "picked up a few medals in Nam." There was no reaction.

Though he'd learned little about Sally Lenox, one thing was certain: She would not be happy with the recently decided *Bush v. Gore.*

———

After torturing himself through the night over the maddeningly remote Ms. Lenox, he arose, cranked up fleet 911, and made it from the Upper East Side to Lower Finley without either coffee or a pit stop. How *does* a guy impress a dame who's been applauded and pursued since her debut in the delivery room?

He pulled into the restaurant's parking area, zipped into "Gents," checked the walls and mirror, emerged, grabbed a Gansett, and hustled Mary upstairs, holding aloft a small gift-wrapped package while whispering, "Got something special for you, Mare, but we're gonna wait until after."

———

Now he was spent, and his need for Sally Lenox marginally less acute. It was all good. He had a great view of the town green, where the tablet commemorating his valor would go.

Sprawled on his back, he was at the mercy of the bubbling Mary Foley, who, Magic Marker in hand, was releasing her pent-up, post-coital creativity.

If ever a tabula was rasa, it was he.

"Hold still, you," said the rosy-cheeked artist as she transformed his navel into a giant bloodshot eye.

"And no peeking, it's not ready for prime time."

What was up with that? Had she read about the Cyclopes at Finley High? God, she could be fun—at times.

Yes, she'd earned it. He handed Mary her present. Excitedly, she tore off the wrapping paper, pressed the metal release, and opened the cloth-covered box.

Her face fell.

Why? It was a diamond circle pin for Chrissweetsake. A Tiffany. Mid–four figures.

Maybe not the time or the place, but he *had* to tell someone. Who else but her? Surely she'd sympathize. And be damn glad she hadn't been in his boondockers. Plus she'd understand why marrying Alma had been the only decent thing to do.

"I gotta tell you something, Mare."

"Fire away," she said distractedly while studying the pin.

Christ. Why did she put it *that* way? "Remember what I told you about my radioman?"

"Yeah, sure. Rubino. You musta told me a million times. Why?"

"Well, there's a little more to it."

"Okay." Setting down the pin and selecting a brown Magic Marker, she began drawing a shaggy eyebrow while flashing her "I'm all ears" expression.

"I had to put him out of his misery."

A heavy silence. "Jesus, you mean *kill him*?"

"Yes."

She gasped, dropping the marker. "What the fuck, Danny!"

"Had to. He was a goner, and he damn well knew it. We couldn't fix him. We couldn't evacuate him. He begged me to end it. Asked me to look after his family."

Gone was the mischievous grin. "And you're telling me you obliged?"

"I had no choice."

She rolled off the bed, stepped into her slippers, threw on her terry cloth robe, and disappeared into the bathroom.

Had he been an idiot?

Mary returned, showered and fully dressed. She brought him a coffee, not the way he liked it, said, "I'm damn glad it's not a ring," and trotted downstairs.

He rinsed off Mary's artwork and, leaving the pin on her bureau, bugged out.

She'd come around.

45

DR. E

The nerve of that damnable upstart, calling Freddy at work—or anywhere else for that matter. And how did he get Freddy's direct line? Even I, his father and a longtime customer of Old Colony, don't have it. Worse yet, how dare he talk with Freddy about *me*?

Relations between me and Lucius Scully have never been cordial, and they completely unraveled when he, with his undisguised in-your-face attitude, his unprepossessing bachelor's degree,[47] his undistinguished master's, and his unfortunate background, stole the chairmanship of *my* department. This is no longer the St. Matthew's of yore.

Further, Scully, despite his first name, knows hardly any Latin, much less Greek. Then there's his pandering course, "Dissent and Diversity." With its automatic A, it's become a campus favorite—so symptomatic of these permissive times. Students queue up for his D & D drivel instead of my own traditional, rigorous offerings.

Finally, there's the matter of our relative ages. Scully, having grown up during the '60s, proclaims his allegiance to its zeitgeist by those

---

47 We got off to a bad start when Scully told me he'd gone to Ottawa and had to explain it was in Kansas, not Canada.

irritating pins adorning the grimy knapsack that bulges from his back like an overripe boil. And why, in this temperate climate, is there always a water bottle in its mesh pocket? Ridiculous! Most offensive: his rusty, dented, sticker-covered VW bus. So banal. And, lest I forget, Earth Shoes and a fanny pack, in this worrisome new century.

Some may consider it confrontational, but I am duty-bound to differentiate myself from this cipher. Students at places like St. Matthew's must be made to understand there are standards. And embrace them.

Scully is insufferable. His hobby horses are diversity and tolerance and openness to—if not outright encouragement of—unseemly attire and disruptive behavior. Chairman Scully's foe is, it goes without saying, elitism (I would say excellence) in all its guises. Such a fool, he is relentless in his assault on shibboleths long since interred.

That leaves me to retard or, if possible, reverse St. Matthew's precipitous descent into mediocrity, slovenliness, vulgarity, and what is coming to be known as political correctness.

Despite having once advised Freddy that "Our tribe dresses to the sevens or the eights, but never the nines," I have planted my standard on the sartorial high ground and enlisted D-B as my trusted consigliere. My rallying cry will be familiar to those who served: "Dress right, DRESS!"

With my classical attire reserved for ceremonial occasions, I have diversified my everyday couture. This began, innocently enough, with boldly patterned cashmere sports jackets set off by modish Italian ties, and whipcord trousers (cuffs, no pleats). One of my proudest efforts involves the revival of the white buck and the unhorsed saddle shoe. Then, I upped the ante. Delighted students applaud me striding about in opera capes and spats. Not to be overlooked is my eclectic headgear. My top hat. My deerstalker. Best yet: my eighteenth-century sword cane. I have had it restored and sharpened. Beware, knaves, cutpurses, and strident hippies.

46

FREDDY/FRED

Had his obstreperous father started down a path bound to end in involuntary commitment? Would his parents be reunited at Essex Lodge? That would be complicated.

If he'd been of an introspective bent, Fred might have asked himself what transformed his father from a self-effacing Stoic into a late-life Beau Brummell. Was it the tawny camel's hair coat Howard Paulson wore during the ruination of his mother? Parents' weekends at St. Matthew's could be combustible, as the hosts peered timidly or enviously into pastures lusher than the withered fields in which they were corralled. Resigned but resolutely cheerful faculty couples were now and again torn asunder by exposure to shimmering lives thought to have vanished with the death of Gatsby and the repeal of Prohibition. Never again would his father be out-dressed—or dressed down.

Or perhaps Dr. Elder reveled in his status as a cosseted customer in the Cambridge store where he'd earned spending money as a penurious undergraduate and now cheerfully dropped fifteen hundred dollars on bespoke sports jackets. Whatever the reason for his new plumage, he'd taken a lifelong scunner to those wearing camel's hair coats. Fred was unconsoled when someone suggested his father's peacock-like finery was preferable to his decades-long threadbare, out-at-the-elbows appearance, not to mention his Greco-Roman getups.

Recalling the unkind behavior of adolescents and their spot-on nasty nicknames, Fred cringed at the realization his father was undoubtedly being ridiculed behind his back. In addition, there could be no doubt Dr. Elder's eccentricities were compromising his son's future. Neither a St. Matthew's salary nor pension would enable Dr. Elder to carry on in this profligate fashion. Already Dr. Elder, in service to his finery, had begun deaccessioning certain family antiques, such as the exquisite Pembroke table by Chippendale that Fred had longed for since learning its value.

And, if that weren't enough, he had to live with Andrea's being promoted to SVP *and* taking over *his* bank's relationship with EFH Privatbank Zurich AG. Big deal. He'd gotten to SVP before Andrea, so from a military standpoint, he still outranked her. Annoyingly, he had no idea what Andrea was making, since she'd elected to file separately with the IRS.

No wonder his call from Lucius Scully got off to a poor start. A sour "What's up, Lucius?" is not a promising way to begin.

"I'm not sure whether it's up or down, but we need to discuss it face-to-face," Scully responded.

At least the jerk wasn't calling him Freddy. "Is it urgent?" he asked.

"Yes, it's urgent, Freddy."

When would he lose that damn name? "Will you be available this weekend?" Fred asked.

"For you, certainly. One other thing: Though it's not, strictly speaking, my business, I hope you'll drop in on your father while you're here. He misses you terribly."

The knight who'd toppled James Freeman and broken lances with Howard Paulson was taking no lip from the likes of Lucius Scully. "You're correct. It's not your business."

Fred suspected neither he nor his father looked forward to their brief and infrequent get-togethers during the school year. There were so many blackout dates. In addition to teaching, his old man coached third-form football, served on innumerable committees, led the rhetoric club, and was—since he'd founded it decades earlier—chairman for life of the Punic Wars discussion group. Croquet was, of course, seasonal, but to blot up what remained of his unallocated time, there were twice weekly rehearsals of The Matthew's Minstrels, the faculty a cappella group for which his father was the prime advocate and apologist.

Had his father overstepped with the Minstrels? Secure in the knowledge their changeless routine represented the capstone of events at which they appeared, the Minstrels would shuffle into a room, block its exits, warm up interminably, and then warble smugly—it seemed endlessly—at their captives, all the while glaring at those who dared to withhold rapturous attention. Anything, the Minstrels felt, to outshine the hearty boors in the Russian Chorus. Now Dr. Elder was encountering polite but determined resistance. One despairing Master suggested the Minstrels be renamed "Death and Taxes." For those who put their faith in the actuarial tables, the future looked equally bleak. Whenever a Minstrel joined the heavenly choir, a prescreened volunteer sprang forward to fill the void. "Just like the 'Immortals' in Cyrus's army," cackled Dr. Elder.

Yes, Fred mused. *It must involve the Minstrels.*

In any case, "dropping in" to see his father was out of the question. Dr. Elder tolerated no surprises. And anything not laid on weeks in advance was by definition a surprise. Structure was what separated the civilized from the barbarians, and deviation from fixed routines called for extensive prior vetting and much scraping of dottle from his father's shell briar pipes.

Fred needed a pretext for the visit. And why, he often wondered, was his father the only person never taken in by his subterfuges?

Without uttering a word, his old man could stare at him over his glasses, and Fred's elaborate fabrications became as sandcastles before an onrushing tide.

Why was he, an SVP at a prestigious financial institution, still so intimidated? Was it his father's casket-like, paneled study? The watchful busts of three emperors? The oppressive curtains? The mold? The heavy, tobacco-tainted air that had him clearing his throat moments after entering? The only recent change to the room was a neatly printed sign reading "Thank you for not wearing spandex." Dr. Elder's many fans pronounced it delightful. Fred winced every time he saw it. Nor could he forget the bowl of all-natural, kettle-cooked Cape Codders in a crystal bowl on his father's desk. "I'm embracing my Mr. Chips role," chortled his old man.

That Saturday, Fred found himself and Lucius Scully occupying a corner table at the Essex County Arms, a swaybacked, low-ceilinged former coaching inn. Having waded through his chowder, chicken pot pie, and rice pudding, Fred grieved over the misfortunes of the football team and, pleased with his worldliness, ordered a cappuccino. Then he fell silent, shifting to Scully the burden of prolonging their meandering parley or getting, at last, to the point. At that moment, the wan, eighteenth-century reenactor/harpist—evidently upset at having her plucking ignored and talked over—had, dabbing her eyes, hurried off for a welcome if unexpected mid-chord break. The moment had arrived.

Fred returned his cup to its saucer and stared at the chairman of the history department.

"I've asked you here to talk about your father," said Scully unnecessarily.

Fred was familiar with this ploy. His move was to wait him out. Silence can be unnerving. Trying not to stare at Scully's matted braid, he looked at him expectantly but said nothing.

"Your father has contributed so much to St. Matthew's," offered Scully.

Fred picked up his napkin, patted his lips, and put it back in his lap.

"Your father and I go back a long way together."

Fred broke his silence. "My father and I go back further." He was not accepting a laurel branch from an upstart who tried to force his father into retirement when he turned seventy-five. And here he was, despite his cane, still going strong ten years later in 2004 with only the faintest suggestion of cognitive decline.

It's never easy to dislodge a St. Matthew's Senior Master, particularly the first holder of a newly created chair. Known only by the Head, Dr. Elder's position had, in an act of expiation, been endowed by Howard Paulson, who, as a condition of his beneficence, directed that eligibility be defined to exclude everyone on the faculty but Dr. Elder.

Any remaining doubts about Dr. Elder's protected status were erased when his nearly life-size face with its "suffer the little children to come unto me" expression appeared on the cover of the *Alumni Quarterly*. Thenceforth, he was untouchable.

There was no denying the photo's impact. Except for the deletion of extraneous facial hair, the air brushing of blemishes, the restoration of amber-colored teeth, and the masking of time's depredations, the image of Dr. Elder was vividly, if not cruelly, realistic. He was staring pop-eyed at the viewer like an amphibian fixated on a succulent slug.

"Are you aware of your father's most recent transgressions?"

Fred crossed one pin-striped leg over the other but remained mute. So easy to emasculate someone with a low net worth and a stunted self-worth by bludgeoning him with a suit that screamed, "You can't afford me."

"He's begun a movement to resuscitate our football team," said Scully.

"A worthwhile undertaking, I would have thought."

"No doubt, but he's driving Coach Wollmer out of his mind."

Fred stared pointedly. "Lucius, you are extremely difficult to understand when you talk with your mouth full."

Scully colored, bit his lip, and swallowed. "Your father is agitating to bring back the single-wing. He argues that this offense, not seen in decades, would be impossible to contain. He also likes its aesthetics. He rhapsodizes about phalanxes of indomitable tiny blockers turning the foe's flank and follows with a paean to Daniel Shaver, who was once his triple-threat tailback."

Fred could play this game. He assumed the "you are beneath me" expression he'd been working so hard to perfect.

Scully sipped his tap water and continued, "Your idiosyncratic father claims this formation would enable us to compete more effectively against schools with less stringent admissions standards."

"You think there's nothing to what he says?"

Scully ignored his question. "It gets worse. Your father's been proselytizing. He's assembled some fellow geriatrics—"

"That's harsh."

"Your father and what he calls his cohort sit together in their absurd outfits . . . he's also pushing to reinstate the dress code of the '50s—most of us assume it's the 1850s. To aggravate matters, they use coxswain's megaphones to call out suggested plays. The coaches have been remarkably tolerant. They wouldn't put up with this from anyone else."

"Did you summon me here to disparage my father? Would you like someone—someone my father respects—to ask him to cool it? I'm not going to. You must know by now my father's heart's in the right place."

"Yes, his heart is, but—"

"But what?"

Scully paused for effect. "His kidneys are not."

Fred stopped cleaning his glasses. Calmly: "What exactly do you mean by that?"

"Your father's kidneys are failing."

He scowled at Scully.

"It's true. I'm distressed he hasn't told you."

"Despite occasional lapses in communication, my father and I have been and remain extremely close, thank you."

Scully looked away. "None of us would have known, but for Polly Spencer. You remember her? Our librarian. A charming lady. Reminds the kids of their moms. She came here well after your father, but before my time, back in . . . when was it?"

Good God, that little round person. "I can't remember, exactly."

"It seems they've become . . . After your mother—"

Fred gripped the arms of his chair. "We are not here to denigrate my mother."

"Please calm down, Freddy."

"It's Fred, damnit!"

"Sorry, Fred. Polly tells us—"

"Us? Is she a parrot? Is she jabbering to everyone?"

"She tells me your father's trying to decide between two types of dialysis. In one your blood is cleaned in a hospital three days a week. In the other, something's pumped into your stomach every night at home."

Doing his damnedest to ignore the discolored, neglected nails of Scully's misshapen, Birkenstocked feet, Fred replied, "Every night? What's he thinking?"

"Polly says the docs are pushing him towards the second option. Less work for them, but your father hates the idea of being 'irrigated every night like a field of lettuce.' He's an independent sort and cherishes the idea of four days of freedom. He can't stand doctors. Calls them 'chancre mechanics,' a military expression, I gather."

"What about transplants? Has he gotten himself onto any lists?"

"Polly would know. I'm afraid I don't. You should get yourself tested to see if you're a match. I have, and damnit, it's a no-go."

"You have?" Fred tried to control the twitch in his right eyelid.

"Yes, of course."

Time to shift gears. "Lucius, do you happen to know the odds of surviving kidney removal?"

"Very high, I think, but you'd have to check with the docs."

"I'm sure they understate the risks to drum up business. And how does having only one kidney change your life and your life expectancy?"

"I believe not at all, but I'm not the one to ask."

Under no circumstances would his father accept, let alone request, one of his son's kidneys. Imposing obligations on or becoming indebted to a member of the next generation would be anathema to him. In fact, taking his cue from the Stoics he so admired, his father would be loath to even discuss something like this with his son. Therefore, Fred concluded, it would be cruel to initiate the conversation and pointless to get tested.

Furthermore, if kidney failure ran in the family, wouldn't it be irresponsible to surrender one of his, particularly at this juncture? And what if his mother had passed along her dementia? No, no, he had enough on his plate, and he owed it to Betsy to remain healthy. Surrendering a kidney made no sense. He'd been issued two for a reason. That led him to wonder whether you could fly on one testicle, not that he was, at the moment, in danger of overtaxing his.

"Thank you for bringing this dreadful situation to my attention, Lucius. Now, I'd be grateful if you'd allow me and my father to handle it on our own. Please do not discuss this with anyone, including Ms. Spencer. I shall speak to her directly. As I'm sure you'd agree, this is a private matter."

"As you wish, Fred. Just know that all of us at St. Matthew's are happy to pitch in if needed."

"Thank you, Lucius. I'll bear that in mind."

He settled up with the waitress, complimented her on the authenticity of her colonial costume, and while leaving, pressed a folded twenty into the palm of the harpist, who was sulking in the taproom.

Fred was in a daze during the drive home. His cell phone rang as he was finishing his second drink at the Harvard Club. It was an unfamiliar number from his father's area code.

"Wollmer, here."

"I'm not sure—"

"Paul Wollmer, head football coach at St. Matthew's, and a great fan of your dad."

"Mr. Wollmer, I'm so sorry he—"

"Forget the 'sorry' crap, Mr. Elder. We're nuts about your dad. He can be a pain in the ass, but I love him, my assistants love him, and the kids, especially his scrappy players, love him."

"Thank you for that, Mr. Wollmer."

"You're welcome. Just so you know, your dad said he's leaving me a couple ties. Says they'll improve my luck with the ladies. I turned down one of his nutty hats. Not my size. Thank you, Jesus. Your dad's a riot." Wollmer laughed and cleared his throat. "You know what he asked our baseball coach?"

"I can't imagine."

"I wonder what the Brits make of our expression 'shagging flies'?"

"Yes, that's vintage Dad." It was intolerable being the drab banker son of a living legend who had no time for you.

"Did you hear we're dedicating our season to him?"

"No," said Fred, signaling for another drink.

"Well, we are. Now, let's cut the crap. Everyone here understands your dad's situation. We've known for some time. It's a goddamn shame no donors have turned up. But it's never too late. Right? I wasn't a match, nor was anyone on my staff, and I guess you weren't either."

"What were you saying about the season, Mr. Wollmer?" asked Fred, happy to be miles away.

"Here's the deal. We've designed a decal for the boys' helmets. Your father's initials, FRE, in a small football-shaped oval. Yours too, come to think of it. But this is about him."

Yes, he was Frederick Elder, but not *the* Frederick Elder. "Have you told him?"

"Sure. He gave it his blessing. Said there was no point doing it when he was under his stele. I had to look up 'stele.' Your dad's a kick."

"That's very thoughtful of you, Mr. Wollmer." He decided to pass on the third drink.

"A no-brainer. Least we could do for our number-one fan. I hope you, or Polly, or the Minstrels can get him to a couple early season games before it gets too damn cold."

He had no desire to cross Paul Wollmer. "I'll see what I can do."

"If he comes, we're going to surprise him with a few single-wing plays. We've been practicing his creation, The Trojan Horse. It's complicated and takes a while to develop, but the boys are totally into it."

"I'll do my best, Mr. Wollmer."

"Please do, Mr. Elder. We may not have much time."

A message was waiting for him when he got home. He could ignore it, but that would be pointless. Fred returned his father's call.

47

DR. E

I should not have lost it with Freddy, but there were extenuating circumstances. After all, without alerting me, Freddy visited St. Matthew's *and* spoke at length about *me* with my bête noire, Scully. I was upset, and D-B said I had every right to be.

Yes, I may have been somewhat unforthcoming about my medical difficulties, but surely that was my decision.

―――――――

I suspected the call was from Freddy, and I was tempted to let it ring. That would have been small-minded, but I almost wish I had. The painfulness of the conversation that followed matched my worst with Helen.

Freddy opened aggressively, expressing his annoyance—in fact it was more like outrage—at not being privy to my medical situation.

My answer was, as always, measured and modulated. "Freddy, there was no point in whining about it. Nothing was certain. Why on earth drag you through the inconclusive opening scenes of *my* drama? More to the point, why didn't you look in on *me* today? We could have talked about the dreaded 'it.'"

Freddy's conciliatory response: "I didn't want to bother you on a weekend."

And on we went.

I countered, "You should have come by. We never see each other. And my tempus is fugiting."

"I'm sorry, Dad. I know how you hate surprise visits, and I don't blame you. Your calendar's always stuffed."

"That's all it is, Freddy. Stuffing. Time fillers. Placeholders. Polly, you, and Betsy are all that's left to me, and you're the one who's always booked up. And sometimes you blow me off at the last minute." Then I overstepped. "I wish you and Andrea hadn't split up. She was good for you. She made you *somewhat* aware of others. I miss her."

"Despite what you may think, that was not my fault. Everyone but you agrees. As to that other matter, you can call me at any time."

That was not fair. "C'mon, Freddy. You say that, but you screen my calls. I wouldn't do that to you even if I knew how. Moreover, dates with you are always contingent on something better not turning up. One of my courtier friend's like that. Everything with him is conditional and transactional."

"Stop it, Dad."

"Sorry, Freddy. Must be low blood sugar or something. I skipped lunch."

"Dad, why won't you get a cell phone? I'll buy it and set it up for you."

"Ugh. The thought of scrabbling for the damn thing as it goes off in my pants . . . nuts to that. No pun intended. I have enough plumbing problems without a cheerful ring tone—is that the correct term?—coming from a dank area best kept silent. Then too, I'd never remember to charge it, carry it, or turn the damn thing off when you're supposed to. Not happening."

When Freddy, in a rare affectionate moment, suggested we talk more, I disgraced myself with "That's what your mother used to say before she hit the jackpot with him-who-will-remain-nameless."

It was time to change the subject. "Freddy, I've got a choice bit of gossip about Howard Paulson, war hero. It's nasty of me, but here it is. It seems Howard wangled his way into a logistics outfit that didn't make it to Normandy until *August* of '44. Evidently, the drive towards the front did not agree with him. His stay on the continent lasted roughly a week before one of his connections secured him a billet back in England. So much for our D-Day warrior. Zero wounds, zero med-als. Never heard a shot fired in anger. Never smelled cordite. It would seem Howard got nervous in the service."

"Okay, Dad. Enough of all this. Something's happened, hasn't it?"

"All I know and need to know is my numbers are down. Dialysis beckons, and donors, quick or dead, are as scarce as an honest banker. No offense intended, Freddy."

Everything Freddy said upset me. In answer to his innocent question about the two types of dialysis, I answered, "Far better to endure three days in a renal center followed by four exhilarating days of out-patient exhaustion, nausea, dizziness, and cramping."

"What happens now?" asked Freddy.

"I must prepare one of my arms for an ugly attachment, and that is all I am going to say about that. I sense you're beginning to squirm. I know I am."

"Surely there's some—"

"No, there's not! And for gods' sake, Freddy, don't buy me any books on this drear subject. Everything I've read is ambiguous, contra-dictory, and, beneath the positive fluff, profoundly unnerving."

Then came the $64 question.[48] "Is dialysis going to work, Dad?"

"It will for a while, but ultimately it's all in vein. Yes, Freddy, pun intended. It might get me a year or two, but what's needed is a donor, and we are not having that discussion. Understood?"

"Stop it, Dad. Do you want me to speak to Reverend Holmes?"

"No, no, Freddy. Not the Mantis. I'm sure he's heard. Everyone has."

---

48 Interesting fact: $64 was the big prize in the 1940s radio program *Take It or Leave It*.

"Is there anything else I should know, Dad?"

"Yes. In your father's house are many mansions. If it were not so, I would have told you. Wait, I just thought of a good one."

"Must you?"

"Absolutely. How about this: What would you name a portly Roman matron?"

"I'll bite."

"Rotunda."

Note to self: It was unpardonable of me, but I ignored Freddy's question about my *condition* as well as his rude suggestion that I take ownership of it. If I'd had my wits about me, I'd have channeled Kenny Rogers and, in my best Minstrels timbre, burst out with a verse or two of "I Just Dropped In (To See What Condition My Condition Was In)"! Now, I really must apologize to my boy.

48

FREDDY/FRED

In August of 2005, a little more than thirteen months after that painful phone call, Lucius Scully left Fred another voice mail. It was terse and uninformative. "Your father's been admitted to the North Shore Medical Center."

Fred got there in under an hour. Despite the IV pole and its pendulous fruit, Dr. Elder was sitting up in bed, looking pleased with himself.

"Holy shit, Dad, what's up with your choppers? You look like a Great White."

"You mean these, Freddy?" said his father, displaying a dazzling array of new teeth.

"Dad, they're unnatural."

"Au contraire, they're beautiful. Everyone says so. I'm ready for a screen test, n'est-ce pas?"

"What did they set you back, Dad?"

"Not your concern, Freddy. But since you ask: nothing."

"C'mon, Dad."

"They're a present from Daniel. He just had his capped, and his dentist gave him a fabulous deal for mine, or so he says. Volume discount. Those chipped teeth of his, while fine in the Corps, weren't cutting it—so to speak—on Wall Street."

"Please, Dad." That son of a bitch Shaver. His most recent outrage was an absurdly large slate marker over his father and Gideon. Rumor had it that a granite obelisk, visible from Three Oaks, was next.

"They don't match the rest of you, Dad. I wish you hadn't done that."

"Well, they please me, and maybe you can haul 'em out and use them yourself after I've 'passed.' I hate that word."

"What are they made of?"

"Damned if I know," replied his father. "PVC? Enough about my fangs. Tell me, what do you think of this?" said Dr. Elder, offering Fred a sleeve of his crimson smoking jacket. "Elegant, eh? Fondle the frogging. Violate the velvet. Sensuous, eh? Call me 'Hef.' Bring me my Bunnies."

"Really, Dad."

"Yes, another extravagance, but soon it too will be yours. Clever of you to be almost exactly my size."

"Don't you think—"

"I'm thinking all the time. There's nothing to do here but brood and regret. That '*Je ne regrette rien*' business is nonsense. My regrets, and they are legion, motivate me. Without them, I'd be inert. But rest assured, I am not meeting the Olympians in a worn, low-thread-count johnny that exposes my drooping posterior to the amused or revolted hospital staff."

"Who's talking about dying? What about dialysis? What about donors?"

"Freddy, here's the deal. I'm considering taking myself off the effing machine."

"I won't hear of it, Dad."

Dr. Elder scowled. "You what, Freddy?"

"I really wish you wouldn't, Dad."

"I suppose I'm glad you feel that way, but there's little point in continuing. The demand for kidneys far exceeds the supply, and the intrusive device to which I'm tethered will only keep me going for a few more months. Besides, I've bid adieu to the Minstrels, my successor's been named, and it would be thoughtless to drag them back here for another round of snuffly sayonaras. Bottom line: I have little to look forward to. Wouldn't you agree?"

His old man had a point. "You won't reconsider?"

"I'm not a complainer, but dialysis is fucking, pardon the French, painful. It's not called livealysis, and—in the hands of all but a few virtuosos—the needles are instruments of torture. I don't know why everyone doesn't give up."

"Dad—"

"Stop playing with that electronic gizmo. I've vacillated quite enough. My revels now are ended. And I'm sick of hearing about those who've gotten new kidneys. How they can pee, and eat, and who knows what else."

"Something could turn up at any time."

"Hogwash! Besides, it's not as though the days I'm not being flushed and filtered are any damn fun. I use them to recover from that accursed machine."

Enough of this. What about his lady friend? "There could be alternatives, Dad."

"What? A miracle cure? An expensive clinic in South America where I could subject myself to ghastly Dr. Mengele–like experiments and drain the family coffers for a few more months? Or maybe Switzerland. I gather you've got some contacts there."

Had his father heard about him and Max? "Why didn't you go to a Boston hospital, Dad? Instead of this bush-league joint?"

Why wouldn't his old man ever cooperate? Better care and closer to his son's condo. And it wouldn't cost much more. He'd heard about the competition for patients and the financial pressure on lower-tier hospitals, but nothing had prepared him for the large banner hanging over

North Shore's main entrance, proudly announcing it was Colorectal Cancer Awareness Month.

So, this was how it worked in the sticks. They suckered you in for something minor, put you under, and then what, really fucked you up? Anything to keep you in their clutches. Did they have specials on pre-owned hips? And what about the docs? Were they all fourth-quartile graduates of Bulgarian med schools? Did anyone have a prayer of leaving alive? The key was figuring out the financial incentives.[49]

How, in your weakened condition, did you avoid infection with hordes of helpers breathing, sneezing, hawking, and handling? Hazards were everywhere. The unclean cleaners. The ham-handed phlebotomists and their clumsy needlework. The breezy gurus and their fawning acolytes, each of whom got to probe, prod, and palpate those arrayed for their amusement. Hospitals sucked. And now they were shaking people down for contributions, the implication being: If you don't cough up enough for a new wing or shell out for a concierge plan, you can expect to crap out on a gurney in a storeroom.

Nevertheless, depressing as it was to visit this place of pain and terror, it would be worse when there was no reason to do so.

"Be right back, Dad. Gotta go down the hall."

"Use mine, Freddy. It's right here."

His father was dozing when he returned. He was unsuccessful in tiptoeing out the door.

"What happened? I thought you'd gone home, Freddy. Now listen. North Shore will be fine. Everyone's pushing us to buy local. Why not die local too?"

"You could at least have gotten yourself a private room."

"Not covered by my insurance, and secondly . . ."

---

49 Cui bono, as his father liked to say.

What was that sound? "You pick the oddest ways to economize."

"And secondly, I've become quite fond of the former Lieutenant Tyler. He's the gentleman on the other side of the curtain."

"The guy who's mumbling to himself?"

They both listened. "Yes. It sounds as though we've woken him. He's in the cockpit of Lucy Goosey, his B-17, on what turns out to be his ninth and final mission. Over the Ruhr. It was flak. Only four of them survived. One was terribly burned and died in a POW camp. As the pilot, he blames himself. The nurse's call button is his 'control column.'"

From the other side of the curtain came a shaky voice. "The stick's frozen . . . I can't hold her . . . we've lost another engine . . . Ernie's hit . . . jump, jump!"

"Can you sleep through this?"

"Yes, with a little pharmaceutical assistance."

"I wish I could do more for you, Dad."

"You've done a great deal, Freddy. What more could you have possibly done?"

"I'd have happily given you one of my kidneys if we'd been a match. Whichever one you wanted. That's a joke. Even if you'd said no." Oh shit, that was unwise.

His father looked up at him. There was that familiar light in his eyes. "You've had yourself tested, Freddy?"

The only sounds and smells came from the other side of the curtain. The sharp scent of urine, the clicking of a monitoring device, the endless news loop, and Lieutenant Tyler's barely audible cries of "Mayday, Mayday."

"As soon as I heard about this from Lucius Scully."

Dr. Elder stared at him over his glasses. As Fred learned in basic training after making the mistake of looking a drill instructor in the eye and having him scream, "You in love with me, maggot?" he focused on an imaginary spot, miles behind his father's head. The silence was oppressive. Dr. Elder relented.

"I'm so glad you weren't a match, Freddy. I couldn't have allowed them to rip out part of your body. Now, let me be clear. We will speak of this no more. And stop fussing with your tie, which, I must admit, is marginally more bracing than your played-out regimentals. A new lady friend, *peut-être*? And, while we're on the subject, lose those red suspenders. They've become a cliche. Even I know that."

"Is there anything at all I can do, Dad? I've never wanted to snoop, but are your papers in order? I can help with them."

"Ah, that indistinct boundary between concern and self-interest, but, no, I believe everything's in decent order. Short of staying alive, I've done what I can to minimize death taxes."

What a nightmare, having a polygraph for a father. "That makes sense."

"Doesn't it? Polly's been attending to these matters, since I've become so bloody—pun intended—weak."

Finally. "Polly?"

"Polly Spencer, your stepmother."

"My what!"

"You heard me, and, by the way, she'd love to be a real mother to you."

Fred got up, adjusted the venetian blind, and said, "I didn't even know the two of you were close."

"You are incurious, Freddy. Yes, we've been more than close for some time. Now we're hitched."

"Why?"

"We didn't want people trying to separate us." His father chuckled.

Was the old codger making fun of him? "What's up with that, Dad?"

"As the poet said, Freddy, 'The grave's a fine and private place, but none I think do there embrace.' Isn't that marvelous?"

Where did that come from? Damned if he'd ask.

"What's more, we look out for each other. Just last week she threw away my filthy comb and, in the sweetest voice, said, 'You're getting a little thin on top, Dr. Elder, so try this.' With that she handed me an expensive English hairbrush. On its back was an oval plaque engraved with a tender message—a message that will stay private."

"You're not wearing a wedding ring, Dad."

"Stop with the niggling. No Elder male ever did until Andrea forced one on you. Polly and I were old and lonely. Now we're just old. I credit her with partially rehabbing an organ I assumed had played its last note. Apropos of that, wanna hear my latest? Yes, you do. 'Never drive in the HIV lane.'"

When would it end? He'd never taken anything like a "gap" year. It had been work, work, work since his school days. Time for a sabbatical. How many had his old man taken? He, Frederick Elder, Jr., was young, energetic, and passionate. He'd fly down to Buenos Aires, slip into a pair of skin-tight trousers, and immerse himself in the tango. Yes, lithe partners in skirts slit to mid-thigh melting into his arms and submitting to his will. He'd master the dance's erotic language and, with his inky hair slicked back, return to Boston recharged. A wolf in wolf's clothing. And, while he was at it, how about a macho male Brazilian? Back, crack, and sack. The chicks would go bananas. Or possibly plantains. Save that one for Dad.

Or maybe he'd become a bohemian. He could learn how in Prague.

His father coughed to get his attention.

"We tied the knot while we still could. Not a slipknot this time. Right after your last visit. We didn't want anyone keeping us apart once we lost our independence." Fixing him with one of those "watch yourself" expressions, his father continued, "Sometimes relatives, even distant ones, prevent Gramps and Nana from being exploited by anyone but themselves. Lots of horror stories of helpless, unmarried love birds being kept apart in separate cages. For their own good, naturally."

A faint sound of escaping air. It was barely audible, and his father was unperturbed, so they both acted as though nothing had happened. Once you reach his age, you're entitled.

49

DR. E

"**F**reddy, your aged father can read your mind. You're saying to yourself, 'Surely the old buzzard's[50] got to be worth seven figures. Isn't everyone these days, when you add it all up?' C'mon, am I right?"

"You certainly aren't, Dad. But what about your wife? She'll need help, won't she? Where's that supposed to come from?"

"Her name is Polly, Freddy. Please refer to her as such. Secondly, you can relax. She's a lady. She doesn't have purple hair or tats. What's more, it may excite you to learn Polly's got money of her own. If there's a fortune hunter here, *c'est moi*."

"Stop it, Dad."

"I shan't. Polly's grandfather invented something having to do with light bulbs, a kind of filament, I believe. So, if you play your cards right—"

"Please, Dad."

"Whatever, as Lucius Scully would say. Self-interest aside, I hope you'll trouble yourself to befriend her. Polly's warmhearted, she means the world to me, and, to set your mind at rest, she owns a fully paid, two-bedroom corner unit at Riverside."

---

50 Why are buzzards, coots, and dodos all seen as old? Rank ageism, if you ask me.

My banker son can be a trial. At that moment Nurse Pat entered with my mid-morning rations: lifeless ginger ale and limp saltines. Abstemious fare for the resident Stoic.

It was naughty, but I chose not to resist. As Nurse Pat turned to walk away, I lunged for her starched bottom, the alluring outcrop at which Freddy'd been staring. I stopped just shy of my objective, but Freddy's horrified expression was priceless. When all else fails, you can still embarrass your children. I can't wait to tell Polly.

"Yes, Freddy. Polly and I were going to move into Riverside when the music stopped at St. Matthew's and I was heaved out of faculty housing. A critical mass of my retired pals live there. The place even has a singing group. It would have been jolly."

"I get the picture, Dad."

"Bottom line: Polly Elder will not be a financial burden. Did I tell you her dowry included Spike, her irresistibly good-natured, white-haired, curly-coated, dark-eyed rescue dog? Spike is of indeterminate age, provenance, and ethnicity. He tips the scales at a mere nine pounds, half a pound less than my M1 rifle, which was—as though I could ever forget—a 9.5-pound, gas-operated, clip-fed, semiauto-matic shoulder weapon.

"Spike is loving, self-possessed, and steadfast. He earns his keep by alerting us to perils, real and imagined. Don't begin to think of cur-tailing his thorough inspection of all things vertical against which he's planning to relieve himself.

"Playful when he awakes, Spike mauls his toys and, after a day of affectionate companionship, goes off duty following his 4:00 p.m. early dog dinner.

"The unperceptive misperceive Spike. He is not a dog. He's the earthly manifestation of a divinity and, as such, recognizes the limited nature of human understanding. He is a higher form of life. He brings Polly his leash when he needs to go out and, dragging one of his cush-ions, follows Helios from room to room.

"We know nothing of Spike's past. Being immortal, he survived his ordeal on the streets—probably hiding under cars—with his gentle but mischievous nature wholly intact. Sent here to instruct and motivate (like Chiron, the centaur), Spike is accepting of us, a more primitive species. Spike realizes I've seen through his disguise. My greatest fear is he'll move on once he concludes he's done all he can for Polly and me.

"Change of subject, Freddy. You'll need to talk with Polly about my send-off."

"You've planned that already?"

"Indeed. Not what I'd prefer, but, yes, a quickie. Polly's speaking, as is Coach Wollmer. Sign up if you'd like."

"Where? The chapel?"

"Gods forfend! I considered the gym, but then it came to me: The Stephanie Paulson Performing Arts Center. After all, your mother was its muse."

"Who's the minister?"

"Nobody. The Mantis will be beside himself, but it's going to be secular. Anything to avoid our doleful school hymn. Even though it would play to a packed house, I'm afraid our stuffy Head would draw the line at a priestess of Aphrodite in a clingy, diaphanous shift, sacrificing a bullock while assisted by a raucous supporting cast of sybaritic satyrs, cavorting centaurs, and nubile nymphs."

"This might be a good time for me to leave, Dad," said my attentive son. "You need your rest. That said, can I bring you something edible?"

"Don't bother, Freddy. Tomorrow you'll get to see Polly. Just in time, because my problems are, as they say, beginning to cascade."

50

FREDDY/FRED

The following morning, Fred glanced furtively into the rooms he passed on the way to his father's. The scenes were like those in a natural history museum. Hyper-realistic dioramas with sounds and smells. Stark tableaux representing Possible Loss, Imminent Loss, and in the case of empty, newly disinfected rooms: Recovery, or more likely, Irreparable Loss.

He knocked and entered. The curtain had been pulled, and Lieutenant Tyler's bed was empty.

"Last night Lieutenant Tyler flew his final mission."

"Fine. Now you'll sleep better. Aren't there things we should be talking about, Dad?"

"What kinds of things, my boy? Eschatological matters, perhaps?"

Why did he have to be this way? "C'mon."

"With the exception of issues pertaining to my modest estate, I am now prepared to respond to those questions you've been reluctant to ask."

"Must you be so difficult?" At that moment Fred vowed to behave the same way when his time came. Why *not* torment the next generation?

"Wouldn't you, in my circumstances?"

"We may not have much time."

"From my perspective, that's probably a plus."

"Where's Polly?"

"She's talking with the doctor. Wanted us to have a few moments together. So, you've met her?"

"Yes. She recognized me from that photograph on your desk." His father could have done worse. In a sweet, old-fashioned way she was kinda cute.

"Were you cordial?"

That was unkind. "How can you ask?"

"Okay, I'm being Mr. Grumpy. I've heard it happens when you're in the checkout line. Anyhow, I will put to myself the questions you are incapable of asking. The questions I wish I'd asked my old man under similar circumstances."

"If you must." *Here it comes,* he thought. The laying on of the guilt. Not happening. He'd behaved honorably and lovingly. Logically too. Hadn't he read that recovery from nephrectomy—Christ, what a name—could be painful and protracted? And potentially dangerous? What about the "harvesting" itself? Even dicier. Nothing's ever certain in an OR. And what if his surgeon was considering his next start-up deal, or—distracted by the scent, proximity, and touch of the nurse he was going to bang that afternoon—snipped when he should have stitched? The possible horrors were endless. It was senseless to roll the dice.

"I must. So, are you anxious? That's one of your questions, is it not?"

"Of course. Anyone would wonder." When would he let up?

"Yes, I'm anxious. Anxious that a hereafter with the Olympians will be denied. Anxious that I'll be sentenced to endless put-downs by your mother and an eternity of three-hour chapel services and departmental meetings at which Lucius Scully presides and only moo shu pork is served. Anxious I'll expire hemmed in by quarreling creditors, calculating kin, wheedling priests, and grade-grubbing students."

"That worries you?"

"Damn right."

His unflappable old man was too much.

"Be serious, Dad."

"Not a prayer."

"Will you stop with the Socratic monologue? You should be proud. You've led a worthy and productive life."

His father didn't buy it. Instead, he grew more upset. "Worthy of what, pray? Cautious and conventional, I'd say. The title of my never-to-be-written memoir is: *On the Beaten Path*. Or how about *My Slender Swath*? No? Okay then, what say you to *Lesser Than Life*?"

"Dad, you're being difficult. You don't believe that for a moment."

"My life has been orderly and phlegmatic—like an accountant's or, worse, an actuary's."

"What will you miss?"

"You, of course, but right now I'm thinking of April's daffodils trumpeting their inaudible anthems to Helios." He began to laugh.

"What's so funny, Dad? Are you laughing at me?"

"No, Freddy. I was thinking of one of my young colleagues. He's charismatic. His ridiculous courses are oversubscribed. He's the perfect family man. And now he's got something growing on his lip. He claims it's a cold sore. In fact, it's an outward and visible testimonial to his renowned mentoring skills. St. Matthew's should never have gone coed. Now we've got temptations for every taste."

"Who are you talking about?"

"Can't you guess? He's a department chair and sports a grimy gray braid. He should be . . . upbraided."

Best to ignore that one. "So, you never had a talk like this with your father?"

"The only time my father *talked* to me was when he was plastered. He gushed boozy praise and made promises he'd forgotten by sunrise. Oh, one other thing . . ."

"Yes."

"There is to be no ghoulish round-the-clock vigil. I'd prefer not to hear 'He's going; he's going now.' Like I'm taking a dump, which I dread I'll have to do at precisely that moment. Just before first light, I intend to slip away with Charon on an outgoing tide. Nobody likes to cast off with people staring at him."

"Maybe we should call it a day, Dad."

"How about something longer? Two straight days with your windy old man is cruel and unusual. One last thing: I wish I could have given you and Daniel as much as Howard Paulson has."

"Oh, Dad—"

"Polly, you're just in time. We need a break."

The tension eased. Would *he* have someone like Polly when he needed her?

"Freddy—I can call you Freddy, can't I? Don't you adore your dad's dazzling new teeth? He looks like a matinee idol."

"He does, Polly, but don't let him go on about his former girlfriends and their tediously wholesome New England talents. Now, Dad, is there anything I can bring you?"

His father giggled and replied, "Come to think of it, yes. While I may be too old to photocopy my ass, is it too late for me to try weed— that's the correct term, isn't it? I'm sure you can get some in what they used to call the Combat Zone. Stop looking that way, Polly. You knew what you were getting into. As I told you, 'My desires are varied, but not, I believe, entirely twisted.'"

"Come back soon, Freddy," said Polly. "He may be daft, but your father thought we'd get along famously. I think so too."

"I agree, Polly. See you both tomorrow. Can I bring anything? Other than weed? No? Okay."

Polly pulled him aside and whispered, "Maybe the two of us can stop your father's latest project. He wants vanity plates."

At last, an ally. "Saying?"

"EROS."

"You're on, Polly."

"One other thing, Freddy," said Polly in a quieter voice. "I've persuaded my old sweetie not to pull the plug. We're good for each other. We intend to limp along together as long as we can, and, with any luck, we'll decay at roughly the same rate. I hope you're okay with that."

Not that he had much choice. "I certainly am, Polly." Whatever the financial cost, she was bound to improve his old man's mood.

———————

As it turned out, they were impressive limpers. He would never have guessed they'd make it for a year in his stepmother's condo. Maybe there *was* something to that nonsense about the health benefits of a happy—or, at a minimum, a tolerable—marriage.

But it couldn't last forever. And it didn't. A productive day at Old Colony was interrupted by Polly's weepy phone call. "Your dad's back at North Shore Medical."

Damnit. He'd allowed himself to hope that those from whom he might inherit would thoughtfully expire when there were no death taxes. He could never catch a break.

He got to the hospital early the next day.

His father's tray table was covered with boxes and small brown envelopes. "Surprise, surprise," said his old man. "I wanted to slip this to you before Polly shows up. I'm not sure how she feels about short-changing the tax man."

What gives with that wink, and how much did his old man know about his bank's Swiss doings? "What are you up to, Dad?"

"I'm sorting through what in legal circles is called tangible personal property. I think of it as Elder residue. There's some fine men's jewelry: studs, cuff links, tie clips, and a few stunning pocket watches—one with a chain of alternating gold and platinum links. Once you've made it to the top, you might want to drape it over an ample robber-baron belly. Plenty of glitzy smoking gear and drinking paraphernalia as well."

"I spy some ladies' jewelry." That might come in handy.

"Indeed, you do. Did you happen to notice Polly's engagement ring?"

"I did not."

"It belonged to Great Aunt Winnie. And don't worry, it will find its way back to you in due course, assuming a caregiver doesn't snatch it first."

"Thank you for that, but can't we talk about something else?"

"Yes. Here, take everything. Stick it in this bag. Now, let me tell you about some of the better pieces."

"Another time, Dad. This has to be quick. I've got to prepare for a meeting tomorrow with Lenox Hill Capital." He saw the hurt on his father's face.

"Please let me apologize for all your rushing back and forth between here and Boston. If I could end this now, I would. Dying is inconvenient for all concerned. It's like a soccer game where the referee determines how much time is left, and nobody knows what he's decided until he blows the whistle."

Despite efforts to extricate himself earlier, Fred's visit extended well past his father's lunch. Dr. Elder barely picked at his food. He got down a few spoonfuls of a wan soup, but spurned the shriveled vegetables and the puckered drumstick. Both of them laughed when the attendant asked Dr. Elder if he'd like him to box up the leftovers.

"Thank you, Willie. Check with my son."

Fred shook his head.

"No need for me to save it, Willie. The food's bound to be more appetizing at my next stop. Even if everything's grilled. See you this evening."

"Lord willing and the creek don't rise, Dr. Elder."

"See, Freddy, things could be worse. As Lord Elgin might say, 'At least I've still got all my marbles.'"

———

What the fuck time was it? O-Dark-Thirty. He checked his bedside clock. Jesus H. Christ. Why hadn't he silenced his cell phone?

"Yeah?"

"Freddy, it's Polly."

"C'mon, Polly; it's hellishly late."

"Your father may be dying."

He was pooped. His old man'd had a good run and was probably crying wolf—again. Nothing he could do at this hour would change a damn thing.

"Are you with him?"

"What a question, Freddy."

"Is he comfortable?"

Pointedly. "I believe so, but don't you want to see for yourself?"

"Is he conscious?"

"Mostly, but sometimes I can't be sure."

"Does he recognize you?"

"Please, Freddy, I think so, but it's hard to say."

What was the effing point? "Okay, Polly, thanks for the heads-up. I'll be along."

"Hurry, Freddy."

Total nonsense. He got up, muted his phone, drained his crank-case—as his father liked to say—popped a Xanax, and rolled back into bed. Incomparable Polly could handle things. He was zonked. He'd heard this before. It would keep.

He arrived at North Shore well before lunch. His father's room was empty. It smelled of disinfectant. The venetian blinds were up. The windows were open. Bad optics.

51

DR. E

I was damn low at that time. What, I kept asking myself, was the point of playing out my losing hand? Polly would get over me—to the extent she needed to—in relatively short order. Daniel Shaver's risen above me, and Freddy's been irked with me for years. That's silly. He should be grateful. I cast a small shadow. I'm a low bar. I'm an easy act to follow. What's not to like?

I've had these thoughts before, but I cannot bring myself to fall upon my sword cane. Wholly apart from the pain, the likelihood of lingering in a leaking, perforated condition is unappealing.

Pills? I know several high-ranking docs. Surely they have access. What about a few handfuls of those magic meds that are maintaining so many Essex Lodge residents in an obedient, semicomatose condition?[51]

Would those opioids be my golden bough, my ticket to the beyond? Who would I meet there? Virgil? Would he be upset if I'd translated Book VI of his masterpiece into limericks? Would he accuse me of profaning Aeneas's journey? Could I chat with Catullus about

---

51 Freddy's convinced these narcotics have juiced Essex Lodge's bottom line by materially reducing the number of keepers required to maintain good order and discipline.

his amours? Better yet, Ovid. How about "deep-brow'd" Homer? Think of the fascinating women I'll meet: Helen, Clodia, Cleopatra, Elizabeth Taylor, lonely Dido, and, should she be in residence when I arrive, that incomparable Roman, Sophia Loren.

Enough dark thoughts. Away, umbrage! Begone, dudgeon! Polly has given me hope, and I owe her an epithalamium.

This morning—a revelation. My gloom, passivity, and fatalism may owe themselves to my having been, and remaining to this day, a loyal fan of the perennially disappointing Red Sox. Has the realization my team will almost certainly devise a novel way to collapse scarred me for life? Yankees fans like Paulson are not thus afflicted.

And yes, our 2004 success was nothing more than a mean-spirited prank of the gods, cynically calculated to increase the pain of subsequent swoons.

So, what to make of the fact that it's become fashionable for those who consider themselves wise and wonderful to adopt the Red Sox?[52] It's an article of faith that those who embrace perennial losers are themselves both lovable and worthy.

I wish I could buy that, but no. There's nothing *necessarily* abhorrent about winning. I'd love it. Secondly, how can one not warm to the shenanigans of Billy, Mickey, and Whitey, not to mention Yogi, an American original? And who married Marilyn? The Yankee Clipper. Not the Splendid Splinter. What team had a pair of wife swappers in its rotation? Not the stodgy Sox.

Yes, I am chained to the Red Sox genetically and geographically, but they are chronically dull. Like me.

And, just like that, the clouds lifted.

While I often regret answering my immobile phone—I believe it's called a landline—I'll have nothing to do with those intrusive devices

---

52 They also gush about "Dem Bums," the Brooklyn edition of the Dodgers. Not so much about their Los Angeles successors.

that accompany you everywhere, torment you relentlessly, place calls on their own initiative, are in essence grafted to your body, become obsolete or expire with exasperating frequency, and, once they've made you dependent, possess you utterly.

That said, I rejoice in having taken Sally Lenox's call. My reply to her "Do you recognize my voice, Dr. Elder?" was a delighted "Indeed I do, Sally. I'd recognize your lovely lilt anywhere."

Sally Lenox, a young woman of limitless potential, was among my last Greek students. She took all three years of my offerings, starting with Xenophon, which she correctly noted was taught for the purpose of rousing inattentive boys who were old enough for bloodshed but too callow to wallow in what was on their one-track minds. "Same with *The Gallic Wars,*" she'd added.

It was as though more than thirty years had dissolved in an instant and Sally was back in my classroom besting the boys. She was so obviously brilliant, there were no—could be no—sly suggestions her class-leading grades were undeserved.

Then she became all business. "Dr. Elder, I have a gigantic ask."

"Ask away, but what can *I* possibly do for *you?*"

"I'd like you to critique the novel I'm wrestling with—like a female Laocoön—and point out, as gently as possible, its manifold flaws."

"Sally, I'm a stodgy academic, and fiction's not my forte."

"You'd be ideal, Dr. Elder. My novel covers Penelope's twenty blissful years of freedom after Odysseus and his thugs sail off on their adventures. My working title is *Missus Odysseus.*"

"Well, if you think—"

"I do."

I was touched and, unheard of for me, speechless, so that's how we left it.

I couldn't wait to tell Polly about this project. When I finished gushing, she gave me a stern look—mock stern, I like to think—and asked,

"Should I feel threatened by you twinkling at your latest Calypso?" My jealous colleagues feigned indifference, but few, if any, ever had such an accomplished former student turn to *them* for advice. Even D-B was impressed. I took pains to assure him my intentions were pure. Not that he believes me.

52

DANIEL

He, Daniel Shaver, the bringer of hope, was in command as he dispensed the Dom Perignon.

Polly Elder was nicely turned out and looked nothing like a librarian. As for Dr. Elder, he hadn't seemed this excited since his third-formers took their only league title.

Freddy, arriving late, cast a disapproving look at the three revelers and—in a peevish tone—said, "How's about holding it down? This is a hospital, the last time I looked."

Blowing kisses to his wife and son, the euphoric Dr. Elder cried out, "Daniel Shaver, the esteemed hunter-gatherer, is back from a successful foraging expedition. Toasts and hosannas are in order. He's brought home, if not the bacon, something far better. I'm afraid the Dom's been consumed, Freddy, but you are more than welcome to a frothy split of North Shore's ginger ale."

"Not so fast, Dad," said Daniel, snapping open his attache case, taking out another chilled bottle, and deftly extracting its cork. "Can't fly on one wing, folks." He loved Fred's pissed-off expression when he referred to Dr. Elder as "Dad."

Raising his glass and turning to Daniel, Dr. Elder said, "Having lived to savor the slow-close toilet seat, I was—before today—reconciled to my fate. Your health, young man."

Sorry-ass Fred kept muttering.

"Jesus Christ, Freddy, stop being such a wet blanket. I'd say 'douche' if your stepmother weren't here. You're just about to get your father back."

"That's right, Freddy," chimed in Polly.

Daniel charged another flute, presented it to the sulky son, and topped up the other three. It was only then that Fred noticed his father was disconnected from the machines that had imprisoned, monitored, and sustained him. Dr. Elder was down to a single drip in a hand that was being cradled by Polly. Poor Freddy. Events had passed him by. He had no role here, and he damn well knew it.

"Anyone care to fill me in?" grumbled Fred.

"Why don't I have Daniel do the honors, Freddy," said Dr. Elder. "He's done me a huge service. In a touching display of initiative, generosity, and follow-through, he has—in effect—pulled a healthy kidney out of a hat."

"Before that, I propose a toast," said Daniel. "Here's to our favorite elder, pun intended. Bottoms up, everyone, and that includes you, Freddy."

Gazing about him, Dr. Elder intoned, "And to my two boys and dearest child bride."

Fred was beside himself. "C'mon, Dad, this is damn serious. What's going on? Tempus is, as you like to say, fugiting. And why, in God's name, are you unhooked from your machines?"

It was obvious Freddy wanted to smack him. Even though he'd put on a little weight, that would have been unwise. Aside from his net worth and medals, what did Freddy find most upsetting about him? His way with the ladies? The fact that he, laird of the Shavers, was now the largest landowner in Lower Finley? Poor Freddy invariably got it ass-backwards. Years ago, he'd touched up his sideburns with a little gray, and now he was going gangbusters with the brown dye. Always a day late.

"Let me take it from here," said Daniel. "I was just about to explain things to Dad and Polly. Give us a smile, Freddy."

Dr. Elder couldn't stop beaming. Polly was relieved. And Fred was in a snit. Perfect. Surely he, Daniel Shaver, had earned a summa.

"Take it away, Daniel. I hang on your every word," said Fred.

He'd gladly take it away. "Okay, long story short: Going the conventional route—contacting organ procurement outfits, putting your name on a million lists, dutifully waiting your turn, and keeping your fingers crossed—wasn't, if you'll pardon the French, accomplishing jack shit. Every year thousands of lazy losers die doing just that. It's the road to the rendering plant."

Nodding in agreement, Dr. Elder said, "Daniel adopted a more proactive approach, and I, for one, cannot thank him enough."

"And that approach is?" groused Fred.

"Please, Freddy," said Dr. Elder, "just listen and hold the sarcasm. Sometimes I wonder if you're even faintly interested in your old man's welfare . . . Sorry, Freddy, I didn't mean that."

"I know you didn't, Dad," replied Fred.

"Freddy, I am thrilled at the thought of peeing again and, mayhap, making recreational use of that mute organ."

There was no other way to describe it—Dr. Elder and Polly were making goo-goo eyes at each other. *More power to them*, thought Daniel.

Dr. Elder resumed. "To be free of that infernal device will be bliss. It isn't fixing me. It's barely preserving me—and not for that much longer. Soon, without so much as a by-your-leave, it will abandon me and trundle away to torture someone else."

"So, Freddy," said Daniel, "here's how it went down. No, hang on. We gotta stop shooting the breeze and meet my man Marko in Boston. It's laid on for tomorrow."

"Marko?" asked Dr. Elder. "Tomorrow?" added Polly. Fred said nothing.

"Yes. The healthy, vigorous twenty-something Marko Bajovic, an unemployed Serbian carpenter with a wife, a child, and a spare kidney, that mirabile dictu—as you, Dr. Elder, like to put it—is a perfect match."

"You're a genius, Daniel," said Polly.

"Okay, Freddy, let me spell it out for you. As you must have learned at your quiet bank, there's a market for everything. It's simply a question of finding it. Stop looking so puzzled. No, I'm not talking about the yellow pages. You've heard of the internet, have you not?"

"Stop being such a condescending asshole, Dan."

Polly gasped. Dr. Elder rolled his eyes.

"Enough, Freddy, we're all friends here," said Dr. Elder, turning to Polly for help.

Such fun. Unflustered, Daniel continued. "It was a cinch. One of my sharpest assistants went online and found four promising options in an hour. We had their medical records reviewed, settled on Marko, and negotiated our deal. Are we happy now?"

Polly and Dr. Elder nodded solemnly.

"What makes you think we can believe any of this?" asked Fred.

"Because I happen to trust Daniel and have for years," replied Dr. Elder.

"It sounds shady to me," retorted Fred. "Isn't there a law that makes trafficking in organs illegal? A federal statute, as I recall."

Dr. Elder looked unconvinced.

"Dad, there are unscrupulous people buying organs from the destitute and reselling them at obscene markups. Organized crime is getting into it, and, believe me, they can procure fresh body parts. It's a can of worms. Really."

"Aren't you missing the point, Freddy?" said Daniel, in his most conciliatory tone. "You know I'm not trafficking, but I'd do it in a heartbeat if it saved your father. Wouldn't you?"

"Boys, boys," implored Dr. Elder.

"Daniel, maybe we should shut off the champagne. Everyone's becoming a wee bit overwrought," said Polly, ever the peacemaker.

"Dad, you have nothing to worry about. It is all copacetic. Marko is an altruistic donor making you a gift, and I am thanking him for that, thanking him generously."

"How much?" said Fred.

Polly stared at Fred and shook her head.

"None of your business, Freddy, but it's not insignificant. That's why the deal's gone so smoothly. Marko and his wife are getting an all-expenses-paid trip to Disney and certain cash considerations. Half up front and the balance upon the successful transplant. Their baby's staying home. This may be their first real honeymoon."

When he thought nobody was looking, Dr. Elder topped up his glass.

"Who's picking up the transplant costs?"

"That would be me, Freddy."

"Thank you, dear Daniel," said a weepy Polly.

"It smells rotten to me. We could all get into trouble," persisted Fred.

"Please, Freddy, whatever else it is, it's brave of Marko to do this for his family. I can think of people who wouldn't have the guts," said Dr. Elder, pausing and waiting until he had their attention before adding, "Let us not despise lucre. How would it have turned out for Achilles if he'd been well-heeled?"

That didn't stop Fred. It didn't even slow him down.

"Dad, one of the many things that's bothering me is we have no damn idea whether the kidney's any good. How do we know it's been properly preserved? They have a short shelf life. I've heard twenty-four, thirty-six hours max."

"Sorry, Freddy. Got it covered. As we speak, the organ in question is still processing Marko's wastes. There is zero chance of its timing out. Next objection, Mr. Kidney Expert."

"You mean it hasn't been removed?"

"For the first time ever, go to the head of the class, Freddy Elder." He was loving it. "Marko and Dad will be in adjacent ORs. Within minutes of its being—I think the term is 'harvested'—it will be flushing out our dad."

"And everything's good to go at the hospital?"

"Please, Freddy, stop it," begged Polly.

It was time to silence this pest. Turning to Fred, Daniel said, "Have you told your father and stepmother about Andrea's big promotion and what she's getting up to in Zurich?"

Dr. Elder and Polly looked puzzled. Fred appeared stricken, but before he could answer, an attendant approached Daniel and said, "The ambulance you ordered is downstairs, Mr. Shaver."

Yes, this was the moment to launch the Semper Foundation, a marketing coup that would enrage Freddy and blow away Howard Paulson, not to mention Dr. Elder and Polly. He, Daniel Shaver, a decorated Marine veteran, was going to take the National Park Service off the hook by personally endowing the Vietnam Veterans Memorial—in fucking perpetuity. Take that, Captain Mac. Screw off, Rubino. Up yours, Nguyen. And yes, he, the heroic benefactor, would be identified. Prominently. Might *this* get him into the sack with the lambent Sally Lenox?

53

DR. E

Although it was less than a year ago, I recall little about the rest of that pivotal day. My ride to the hospital was a roller coaster of highs and lows. Polly sat beside me in our taxi, holding my hand and going on about I can't recall what. Daniel gave Freddy a lift in his Porsche. Polly and I amused ourselves by guessing what they might be saying to each other.

Everything was laid on at the hospital. No paperwork. No crowded waiting room. Major donor treatment. I suppose I should have felt guilty about that, but I was too frightened to notice.

Next, I was shown into a changing area, donned a crisp gown, and was helped onto a gurney. With Polly struggling to keep up, I was rolled to an elevator, ascended five floors, and wheeled to a door beyond which visitors were prohibited. Polly kissed me. I kissed her back. Would I ever see her again? Then, I was whisked into the place where I'd be butchered or rebuilt. A masked stranger bent over me and asked if I was ready. I must have nodded. I hope I was polite. I hope I concealed my terror. I was back in the Ardennes.

My last conscious thought: Should I survive, I will refresh my wardrobe, starting with a cloak of Tyrian purple trimmed in ermine.

I looked up and—with, I'm guessing, a bewildered expression—asked the hovering nurse, "Why am I still here? When are they doing me?"

"They have, Dr. Elder. It went perfectly, and you're looking better already."

When Polly and I saw each other, we broke down. It was several seconds before we were able to speak.

Polly recovered first. "It's wonderful, Darling. Your eyes are alive again, and you're pink, not the color of spackling compound." She sobbed, regained her composure, winked, and said, "Tell me when you think your avid organ's up for spring training."

"I shall, indeed. Now, I must thank Marko and get after that cloak."[53]

Polly looked confused.

It was unfeeling of me, but I couldn't resist. "After this, maybe I can get by with less invasive procedures. Semi-colonoscopies, perchance."

————

Sally Lenox is such an elixir!

Not long after receiving Marko's kidney—had Polly alerted Sally to my condition?—I received the following email: "Dr. Elder, I'm running behind schedule with my novel, but here's your mission, should you choose to accept it: (a) Call out every glitch, howler, and infelicity. If they're not irredeemable, suggest improvements; (b) catalogue all the ways I've butchered the Bronze Age; and (c) be merciless with my male characters. Are they, in fact, field hockey girls wearing swords? How can I forget those cranky female critics calling Hemingway's women 'men in dresses.' Maybe it no longer matters

---

53 I must ask Polly to fill in the blanks in this truncated account.

since 'binary' is so out. Now we can all be anything. Vive what difference, you might ask."

How to discharge this fraught assignment? I shall curb my tendency to push, push, push. I shall employ a light touch. I shall radiate enthusiasm. I shall stay in my own lane and try not to cause harm. It is, after all, Sally's book.

Some weeks later, I received an outline of *Missus Odysseus*. It was sketchy. The thrust was: Odysseus, indifferent to Helen's fate, but bored to distraction with olives, figs, grapes, and herbs, jumps at the chance to sign on with Agamemnon. A rollicking Med cruise with opportunities to plunder, rape, and burn—all in service to a cause however dubious—is not to be forgone.

Like the dutiful wife portrayed by Homer, Penelope sees hubby off at the harbor, returns to the palace, but—throwing away the script—orders up a case of vintage Mavrodaphne, and, along with the other women who've launched their spouses, offers a toast to gorgeous Paris, whose libido has liberated them for what turns out to be two decades.

Ten years pass.

News of Odysseus's equine ruse and Troy's fall reaches Ithaca. Gloom envelopes the women. While many hubbies are dead, the survivors will soon be home.

Not so fast—a reprieve! Like warriors through the ages, they are reluctant to resume their humdrum lives. Who can blame them? After encounters with Sirens and Cyclopes, sleepy Ithaca holds little allure. Distractions abound in the Mediterranean, and each must be savored and suitably immortalized.

Great news! Penelope and her ladies raise their overflowing kylikes to Calypso, Circe, and seductresses everywhere.

More years pass.

In Sally's proposed ending, Odysseus and Telemachus, after dealing with the suitors and the maids, undo all that Penelope did to

improve the lot of Ithacan women. Like those Taliban people we're
reading about.

I couldn't help but ask Sally about her novel's downbeat denouement. Was she having relationship problems herself? Evidently so. Her
response stunned me. "Some time ago, I met persistent Daniel Shaver,
one of your favorites, he claims. As you may have guessed, I chose
early on not to disclose my connection with you or St. Matthew's, and
I gather you've kept silent about me. Thank you. Daniel's like one of
Penelope's most unappealing suitors. I've been trying to elude him
without provoking him or having to weave a shroud, and I'd be deeply
appreciative if you'd continue to preserve my cover."

Without hesitation, I agreed. Something had told me to keep mum
when Daniel said he'd met Sally.

Then, my only contribution: "Sally dear, reread Tennyson's 'Ulysses'
and put yourself in Penelope's sandals. Tennyson may have understood
Ulysses/Odysseus, but he never figured out Penelope. Doing so suggests a more buoyant conclusion to *Missus Odysseus*."

54

DANIEL

It had been a fine day's work. Dr. Elder saved, Freddy upstaged, and now he must crow to Sally Lenox.

Daniel had never invested as much of himself as he had in his efforts to lay alongside and board Sally Lenox. It had been frustrating and time-consuming, but he was bound to prevail. He was accustomed to bloodless conquests, believing with Sun Tzu that "the supreme art of war is to subdue the enemy without fighting." Daniel's SOP was to prepare the ground for his final overwhelming assault with a barrage of gifts and ardent declarations. "You are my one and only" was a proven winner. If that failed, he could rely on his in-house stature and cast a plump worm into Lenox Hill's well-stocked secretarial pool with absolute certainty of an immediate strike. Yes, rank still had its privileges at Lenox Hill Capital.

Usually there was little sport in these outings. However, one cheeky young lady—after two lavish, but dubiously deductible, dinners—kept insisting she didn't believe in sex before marriage. Her resistance collapsed in an explosion of giggles when—after his customary warm-up—he took her hand and said, "But I am married, Lynn."

So how was he doing with Sally Lenox? Progress, if any, was negligible. She declined most of his invitations, but never in a manner suggesting she wished to be done with him. Which would, of course, have been inconceivable. In fact, just last month she expressed delight over a book he'd given her about the work of Richard Morris Hunt, one of whose architectural gems had been the mistreated Lenox Library. He eventually lured her to the King Cole Bar, where, as always, she stopped after a single glass. Now it was he, not a secretary, wriggling on a hook.

What was her game? She had neither banished nor bedded him. How could she be immune to his ardor? His charm, success, and vitality? Was she giving him the opportunity to get the picture and run up the white flag on his own? Was her plumbing out of order? Did she have an embarrassing deformity? She couldn't want him as a friend, could she? Few did.

Then it came to him. So obvious, really. Surely she'd succumb if he could spirit her off to a hideaway in the heather where their desire for one another could blossom unobserved. Their own Brigadoon in the land of her forefathers and foremothers. Christ almighty, for all he knew, there were Scots in his background. If not, he could fucking well fabricate a few. And pick a clan—an obscure but heroic one. There was certainly no shortage of alcoholic Micks, and—leaving aside pedophile priests—weren't the Harps and the Jocks basically the same?

But where could he take her? Easy. Deeside House. It was a no-brainer. When? He had a Zurich trip on tap for early August, after which it would be off to Perthshire, where he would kit her out in the Lenox tartan, fit her for wellies, kill grouse with her on the Glorious Twelfth, and, like an errant Titleist, nestle cozily in *her* gorse.

Following Zurich, he'd meet Sally's flight and drive her straight to Deeside, where he'd ply her with peaty single malts and await developments. She'd be jet-lagged, but—being a gentleman—he wouldn't press the issue. That said, if she was game, how bonny.

Would she be more inclined to yield if he, oh so modestly, told her about saving Dr. Elder's life? No reason to explain how it helped make up for—"atone" was too strong a word—what went down in Nam. And next, a modest aside about the Semper Foundation?

How much more must he do before he could claim in good faith he'd balanced the books? Easy. When he slept without interruption.

Okay, it was fine if Sally didn't wish to slaughter grouse. In fact, he'd be surprised if she did, and it would be intolerable if she turned out to be the better shot. Instead, they could bang away at clays, yank undersized trout from the hotel's stocked pond, and hunt for mishit drives in the impenetrable rough bordering the fairways of the hotel's secluded course—all this being the overture to the main event: the picnic in the glen.

The hotel would provide the wine, the packed lunch, the midge repellent, and a sunny day. He'd bring the blanket and the other essentials.

It was an easy walk to the burn, beside which were innumerable snug mossy dells where they could frolic among the ferns and flowers, unseen except by a few curious and reliably discreet highland sheep.

He yearned to have his way with her, but—perhaps even more—he wanted her to want him.

How better to pitch all but the object of this outing than an unthreatening lunch in the majestic main dining room of New York's oldest and—he would argue—most prestigious club, where, with Howard Paulson's backing, his origins were overlooked and his ascent to its presidency was swift and unimpeded?

Passing under the barrel-vaulted, coffered ceiling, he pointed out to Sally where his portrait would hang once he stepped down after what was certain to be a long and distinguished tenure.

As always, Sally Lenox was utterly at ease. She greeted the maître d' by name, nodded affably at several diners as they promenaded to

the table beside the center window, and gently inquired of a particularly stuffy member as to when the club might reexamine its policy of
excluding women from the library.

They were seated. Billowy napkins were floated gently onto their
laps. Sally Lenox was elegant and wildly desirable. In her heels she was
an inch or two shorter than he. Perfect.

"They mix a lively but innocuous spritzer. Would you care to join
me?"

"I'd love to, but I've got two classes this afternoon. My alert but
censorious girls would sniff, wonder, and gossip."

Phooey. He'd hoped it would be at least a two-glass lunch. If he
could get three into her, he'd start thinking about an upstairs bedroom.
Sally was looking wary. He suspected she suspected him of having an
agenda, as she once intimated he always did. Clearly, this was not her
first bronc busting.

No, he would save his stories about Dr. Elder's kidney and the
Semper Foundation.

Unexpectedly, Sally provided an opening. "When's your next business trip?" she asked between delicate spoonfuls of vichyssoise. She
did that, and everything else, so elegantly. Yes, he was unused to, but
intrigued by, elegance.

Daniel coughed and advanced cautiously into no-man's land. "I've
got a Zurich trip in August, after which I'm off to a magical country
hotel by Scotland's River Dee. I think you'd love it. It's hard not to."

And there it hung, the lifelike dry fly bobbing lightly on the surface
of the swift-moving burn. Would she strike or watch it drift past?

She merely observed. Nothing more than a close inspection and
maybe a gentle bump. "I might."

Onward! "I've spent a lot of time there with Lenox Hill customers.
It features trout, pheasant, grouse, and, in the autumn, stags."

"How charming. Your abattoir by the Dee."

So much for firearms. "There are lots of other things to do. The countryside is gorgeous, the villages are lively, and there's no shortage of castles—both ruined and restored like those books and globes. The hotel even has a tennis court and a scenic nine-hole course."

"Yes?"

"And, in case you're wondering if I'll ever get to the point, yes, it would make me deliriously happy if you'd join me at Deeside House. You'd adore it."

Sally raised her head and in a soothing, here-it-comes-now voice said, "I'm not sure how to put this, Dan, but we may see our *friendship* rather differently."

That wretched word. "I see it as something more than a friendship."

"I guessed as much some time ago, but I see you as a handsome, witty, talented, and ambitious friend. You're like those of my ancestors who clambered to the top in New York."

Trying not to sulk: "Well, that's nice, I suppose, but is that it?"

"It's not you, Dan, it's me. I'm still not over Stephen and his tragic death. I may never be. I'm just not ready for what you seem to want."

Christ almighty, it's what any guy would want, a recumbent, receptive Sally Lenox on a mattress of spongy moss by a burn that, like him, was about to overflow.

And damned if she wasn't cribbing from the playbook *he* used to get out of tight spots. "It isn't you, Honey; it's me." God, how he hated being the fool who made something out of nothing. That was for guys like Freddy.

What to say now? Maybe she'd eventually get over her sainted Stephen. If so, he'd damn well be at the head of the queue when it happened. He could always retract everything if he'd lost interest by the time she came to her senses. But maybe Stephen had nothing to do with it.

Was it possible Sally Lenox disliked or feared him? Or worse yet, just wasn't into him? That would smart.

"Consider it an open invitation in case you have a change of heart. Deeside House isn't going anywhere, Ms. Lenox."

She nodded, offered a fleeting smile, lowered her eyes, and continued to pick at her crab salad.

Okay, a minor setback, but there, over his shoulder, was *his* view of the Statue of Liberty, and there on *his* desk was Keynes, presented to him as the heir apparent when Tod Paulson took early retirement. Sally Lenox would soon be singing a different tune, just as sorry-ass Alma was already doing. They always came around.

He saw a number on his office phone but couldn't place it. Kee-rist, it was Alma's cell. "Zack's ditched me, Danny."

"After you bought him a 'Vette with my money? What a shame. Are you feeling unstrung . . . get it?"

"You shit. He's left me. Says I'm an old drunken pig. That isn't true, is it, Danny? You'd still like to do me, wouldn't you?"

"My answer to your second question is a resounding *no*! Your first one is more complex. From my perspective, you're not old. However, Zack would disagree. There is unanimity on the other part. So, what happened, my fair?"

"He met some rich cunt at a tournament. Says she has a great top-spin forehand. She got him a job at her club in Jersey and bought him a condo near her place."

"How nice for him. Looks like you've been priced out of the market for dim, baby-faced jocks."

"Take me back, Danny. We all make mistakes. Remember our great times together? They were great, weren't they?"

"Not all bad, but no, Alma, I don't want any part of you."

"Oh, Danny, I'm so alone."

"Well, you couldn't expect Harriet to live with you forever. She's a big girl, and she'll be running that hospital before we know it."

Three days later she called him again. Wasn't it too early for her to be plastered? He grabbed the call before it flipped over and Ms. Sapers got treated to one of Alma's boozy eruptions.

"What's up? I'm kinda busy."

"Fuck you, you're always too busy, but you're in for a surprise."

"Wha . . ." She was gone.

By the time he got home, he'd forgotten Alma's call. He poured himself a stiff one and watched the sun go down behind Central Park. If only he could get his mind off frigid Lenox, but that wasn't possible when his co-op was only a couple blocks north of the Frick—the site of Uncle Jimmy's fucking library.

At that moment his landline rang. "Remember me?"

"I'm afraid I do, Alma. You're hammered, aren't you?"

"The sun's over the yardarm. You taught me that one, remember."

"What now, my dear?"

"You know something, I couldn't be happier. Harriet's mine again. She's learned everything."

"What the hell are you slobbering on about?"

"You know damn well, but hang on while I fix myself a whitey. Only my second today."

She was such a mess with her boozer's body—a barrel-shaped trunk from which protruded four slack, wasted extremities.

"Alma, you are one dumb bitch. They're not white, they're fucking transparent. Like you. And if you keep tossing them down, you'll be planted before this fall's bulbs." And if that happened, his secret was safe.

"Naughty, naughty, you war hero, you."

"Just spit it out."

"I had a visitor today, a handsome Asian gentleman. He spoke beautiful English."

"Did he have a name?"

"His name is . . . he was your scout in Vietnam."

Now it was time to pour *himself* another.

"And what did he have to say for himself? He wanna sell you a knockoff purse?"

"I love it when you step on your dick. And now you're gonna start playing nice, like you did before you fucked me. You musta known it would come out. Always does."

He poured himself a double. Neat. The cleaning lady might find him passed out on the sofa tomorrow, but it wouldn't be the first time. "So, what came out, my dear?"

"Everything that happened there."

"Yeah? Well, the first thing you gotta know is Nguyen's a traitor and a deserter. He led us into a fucking trap. For some damn reason he has it in for me big time."

"Damn right he does. You killed his son, and you killed Anthony too."

"Maybe we did kill his son. Who the fuck knows? There was a fucking war on. But that shit about Anthony is a damn lie."

"You'd like to take a swing at me, wouldn't you? Like you done in the past."

She got that right.

"Mr. N even brought me something."

"What? Some crotchless knickers, maybe?"

"A shell casing from one of the bullets you shot into Anthony."

"That's a load of crap, Alma. You can find those things everywhere. The fucking country's littered with 'em."

"Ya know something? I could always tell when you were lying. Still can. You murdered my husband, came home, fucked me, and stole Harriet."

Technically she was correct, but he hadn't fucked her right off the bat. And he'd liked her at first. "You, my dear, were anything but unwilling."

"You son of a bitch; you took advantage of me."

"I cared for you. Still do, kind of. Besides, I told you early on I was mostly into sex and sports."

"And it's too bad you're no damn good at either!"

"You tell Harriet this crap?"

"Whadaya think?"

"That you are one nasty broad."

"Temper, temper. Remember that restraining order. I could get another one real easy—'specially if you've still got that fancy English shotgun you like to wave around."

"That restraining order was total bullshit."

"Like hell. I felt threatened. If a judge heard what Mr. N said, you'd be behind bars—for life. How would ya like that, Mr. Lenox Hill Capital?"

This was going poorly. "There's no chance of that, Alma. By the way, what's Nguyen want from me? Money?"

"No, but he did say there's no statute of limitations for murder."

If she wanted a war, he'd oblige. "Nobody'd buy that crap. Whose word would *you* take? That of some beady-eyed traitor or a war hero philanthropist with a spotless record on Wall Street?"

"Easy for me, buster. I know you. You feel nothing, do you?"

"I try not to."

Based on past performance, he reckoned he had about five minutes before she barfed, passed out, or both. "Is Harriet there?"

"Yeah, she's listening, and she doesn't want to see you or talk to you. How ya like them apples?"

He should have known. "Please put her on, Alma . . . Harriet, Sweetie, we've got to talk. After that, if you don't want to see me, it's your decision."

He heard the handset bang on a wooden surface, then muffled, angry voices.

"Harriet?"

"Yes, Mr. Shaver."

"What happened to 'Daddy'? Give me a chance, Sweetie."

In return for a promise to vanish from her life if that was what she really wanted, she agreed to meet him on neutral ground, the site of the abandoned pony ride at the southern end of Central Park—a place of happy memories. On the way he bought a couple Diet Cokes and a bag of Fritos—her favorite junk food. Harriet was waiting for him. She immediately declined both offerings.

"I hated the pony ride. It scared the piss out of me, but you never seemed to notice with all your Marine Corps crap about toughening me up."

"Why didn't you tell me, Sweetie? We could have stopped."

"I didn't dare. Sometimes you frighten me."

He could take this from anyone but her. "Please give me a chance. What did your mother say that traitor told her?"

It wasn't a pretty story, and it wasn't inaccurate.

"That's not the way it happened. The enemy mortars killed your biological father."

"Mom's always thought your story about Mr. Rubino was bullshit. Mr. Nguyen said we should exhume my father's body and settle things."

"Why would you listen to someone who only wants to hurt us? You know how much I love you."

"Wow. You don't use the 'L' word much. Anyhow, Mr. Nguyen brought this. Said he found it next to my father's body. Said it was from your gun."

"You mustn't believe him, Sweetie. Sure, it's from the kind of pistol I carried, but there were literally millions of them lying around in Vietnam."

"The only reason to believe you is because it's hard to visualize *anyone* murdering a fellow Marine and then seducing his widow."

"I've never lied to you, Sweetie."

"Maybe you never lied to me before, but I'm sure you are now. Look at you. I can tell. One other thing, I'm not your *Sweetie* anymore."

He held out the Fritos. She shook her head. "You'll always be my Sweetie. That man's probably telling the same lies to the families of many dead Americans. Doing all he can to cause misery—or be bought off."

"Mom remembers hearing about my real father's unexplained wounds. Mr. Nguyen had it right, according to Mom."

"Your mother's a drunk." He wished he hadn't said that. "She'd say anything to split us, because she knows that would hurt me more than anything."

"She has succeeded in doing so. You were my hero, and I had no use for poor Mom. Now, I never want to see you again."

Unbearable. "Don't believe Nguyen. He was trying to kill all of us, including your biological father. He just wants revenge."

"What do you mean?"

"He claims the artillery I called in killed his son."

"That doesn't mean he's lying about my real father."

"You gotta give me the benefit of the doubt, Harriet."

Harriet had never looked at him like this. "There is no doubt, Mr. Shaver."

———

So yeah, he'd lost another skirmish, but not the war. Every family has its ups and downs. In no time at all, this Nguyen crap would blow over.

And happily, there was a welcoming New Hampshire restaurant where his past was irrelevant.

Yes, there she was, behind her counter. He'd given her a heads-up he was on his way. She was so much hotter than Lenox. Sure, she was moody and getting on, but all would be well.

They'd go out back, or upstairs for that matter, and just do it. His need was urgent. There was only one customer, and Sam could damn well deal with him.

But something was amiss. Mary barely acknowledged him as he took his regular seat in the secluded booth farthest from the door. It was like a hunter's blind where Mary would sometimes attend to him while Sam torched his burger.

She was taking her damn sweet time, sauntering over to him with a menu and a half-empty glass of tap water. What the fuck? He didn't need a menu. And where were the ice cubes? And why wasn't she wearing her Tiffany pin?

No makeup, and she was dressed in a way that bordered on prim. Her hooters were hiding, and her skirt—Christ, it was wool—damn near reached the floor. His Lower Finley wench was masquerading as someone else. Who? Abigail Effing Adams?

"Long time no see," she said, without so much as a glance.

How to warm her up? "You wanna hear Dr. Elder's reaction to the kidney I got him?" Silence. "What he said was 'Praise be! Now there's something alive between my legs *and* my ears.'" Without a word, she thrust the menu at him.

"I don't need that, Mare. You know what I like and how I like it."

He'd been using that line for years. Now it didn't register. Then he noticed the ring. It was a sharp-edged, bargain basement rock. You could gut a trout with it.

"The depository's closed, Danny. Tommy's made an honest broad outta me."

"Tommy Reeves? That little twerp? You been doing him behind my back, have you?"

"None other, and you can knock off that little twerp nastiness.

He's kind, funny, and a damn sight smarter than you think. I shoulda swapped you for Tommy years ago. He's been sweet on me for ages—candy, flowers, that kinda stuff."

"I send you flowers, Mare."

"Hah! The secretary you're banging does. A dozen red roses. Every time you score. It's gotten stale, Danny. How about some variety, maybe some yellow ones." Her expression softened. "Now Tommy, he doesn't just haul it out and bang it on the counter, so to speak. He makes a girl, even an old one, feel good about herself."

"When did this start, Mare?"

"Let's see, it's been happening for a while. Haven't seen much of you since you told me—well, you know what you told me."

He did indeed.

"That's just between the two of us, Mare."

Silence.

"Christ, Mare, I've been damn busy, and I'm going through some nasty shit myself. I could use a little understanding."

"Understanding? Yeah, I felt that way lots of times. Been meaning to tell you about Tommy but wasn't sure you'd give a damn."

"C'mon, Mare; you sayin' you're not up for a quickie, for old times' sake?"

She looked him full in the face. "You don't get it, do you? And you can stop with those crinkly, twinkly George Clooney eyes. They used to melt me. No more."

Another grim silence. "You know something else, Mr. Irresistible? Tommy's never gotten an 'incomplete.' So, whadaya want to eat?"

He didn't give a shit. "The pot roast and a Gansett."

He grabbed her hand when she returned. "Sit down, will you?" She did so. "You'll visit Ma in Concord, won't you?"

"Come off it, Danny. You got enough dough to hire everyone in town to keep an eye on her."

"That's not the point, Mare. She likes you. She's used to you."

"Used to me? So are you, but here's how it's going down. Tommy's selling his business, and I'm unloading this place—giving it away, more likely. And I gotta take care of Sam."

"And then?"

"We're getting hitched, and it's off to Florida while we still got some tread on our tires. Way I see it, we got a future."

"Am I invited to the wedding?"

"Sure. You can be the 'worst man.'"

"Then what?"

"Tommy's bought us a condo in Boca. Oceanfront. Granite countertops."

"What'll you do there?"

"Shit, I dunno. Shuffleboard? Watch the beach disappear? Go to adult movies? Support my dermatologist?"

"Jeez, Mare; is this really it? Can't be. I thought we were forever."

"So did I. For a long time. You were just a kid, but remember what you said to me that first time? I do. Always will."

Damn right he did. But he was underage, and every dame knows a guy'll say anything just before *and* just after. Totally nonbinding.

A surly shrug. "You had your chances, Danny—tons of 'em. But I was your one-trick pony."

"I'm going to be real lonely, Mare."

Without looking at him, she said, "You won't have any trouble finding someone you think is better than me." Turning to face him, "Specially if you lose that sorry comb-over."

"Tommy know about us?"

"You kidding me? All of Lower Finley does—has for years. Tommy knows it's over, and he's fine with everything."

He digested that. "When you leaving?"

Now she was smiling. "Pretty damn soon. Whenever we can wrap it up here."

"Hey, how's about me visiting you in Boca? I'll charter a big-ass boat: Chef. Crew. Movies. The kind you *really* like." She made a face. "I'll cover you with sunscreen. Oh, those ticklish thighs. We'll have a blast. Like always."

"Sorry, Danny; that ship sailed. Or sank, maybe. You know something?"

He couldn't imagine.

"It's different with Tommy. He's tender. He's affectionate. You, you're like a vibrator." He raised a hand in protest. She continued, "There's something else, lover boy, another reason I'm glad we're done."

"Gimme a break, Mare."

"You know those pills you started popping a few years back?"

"Yeah?"

"Well, since then it felt like you were doing me with a Louisville Slugger."

She handed him his check. It was rolled up in the circle pin. Written in brown Magic Marker was "No Charge."

55

DR. E

My close friend, the languorous D-B, was in a gradual, but inexorable, decline. It pained him to resign from St. Matthew's, but better that than what would have befallen him had he balked. It pleases me to say I was instrumental in securing him a third-floor apartment at Essex Lodge.

It's no coincidence D-B's "flat" is only two doors away from Helen's. This would have upset me back in the day—what a hopelessly imprecise expression—when I believed D-B was pursuing her. But times change. Also, I may have been wrong about what constituted magnetic north to D-B. How could someone like him have done so poorly with the ladies?

Allow me to be clear. It was with the best intentions that I took D-B to the Yale game. It was a ritual, and I thought it would benefit him to get outside and interact with a larger, if even less diverse, cross section of humanity.

I arranged for a car to take us to Harvard Stadium and—on the way to our seats[54]—reminded D-B that boys *and girls* were now leading cheers. Evidently, this came as no surprise.

---

54 As he no doubt intended, D-B—swaddled in a rehabilitated raccoon coat—received many smiles and approving nods.

D-B seldom disappoints. He considered my observation and replied, "Ah, tyrannical desire. Such a relief to be out of his clutches."

We settled onto the cold, unyielding concrete, and—in an effort to distract him from our discomfort—I blurted out, "Look at that brunette. Yes, that one. On the far right. Doesn't she trigger the faintest tingle?" My mistake.

D-B considered what I'd said, leered devilishly, turned towards the brunette, cupped his hands, and in a voice combining parade ground volume with Oxbridge accent, bellowed, "I fucked your grand—"

I gave D-B a hard elbow to the ribs, cutting short his last word. Was it to be "mother" or "father?" I never learned.

As the group around us consisted exclusively of ancient male alums[55] who were to varying degrees impaired, the response to D-B's eruption appeared to be evenly divided between befuddlement, delight, and outrage.

Huzzah for D-B. He may have gone down in flames, but he did so with panache, as befits one of Monty's officers.

The next day, D-B was dispatched to the dreaded second floor, where I look in on him and rehash old times. He's forgotten my name but recognizes me as a pal. I raise his spirits by drawing him out about his time in the Eighth Army. He recalls those bygone days with total clarity. By mutual agreement, we do not discuss the present or Eros in any of his myriad forms.

Unlike the overwrought who kick against the pricks—as I would— D-B's gentle, accepting strain of dementia has erased his worries along with nearly everything else. He's happy as long as someone—anyone—is looking after him. Much like a trusting dog with no idea his time is almost up.

I'm happy for him, but I've lost my partner in denial.

---

55 Blessedly, I saw no familiar faces.

————————

Yes, yes, yes! Sally nailed it. The next outline of her novel—it was more like a complete draft—sang to me, and so it will to others.

In the reimagined *Missus Odysseus,* as in Tennyson's stirring poem, the restless wanderer—still put off by husbandry and domesticity—sails off on a final (we assume) adventure. Sadly, his armor appears to have shrunk *and* gotten heavier. Now he needs afternoon naps, and the nymphs—underwhelmed by his ED and general decrepitude—have headaches.

What now, Penelope? In Sally's revision, Penelope (Tennyson hurt-fully refers to her as "an aged wife") is ecstatic. Once again, she's on her own—plus she's got the palace, the throne, and company of her choice. Nothing remains of Odysseus—not a single spear or strigil.

As Sally said to me, "By all means, let Odysseus and Daniel Shaver 'drink life to the lees,' as Tennyson put it, providing they do so far across the—wait for it—'wine-dark sea.' And, while they're doing so, I'm gathering notes for my monograph about that serial rapist Zeus."

I've never thought of Zeus in quite that way, but I did not rise to Sally's bait, if that's what it was.

56

FREDDY/FRED

No, Fred never liked the 'burbs, and children were beyond him. So, it hadn't been a hardship ceding the Needham house, its furniture, Betsy, and Scout—the incumbent golden retriever—to Andrea. Sometimes he had to laugh about the wives always getting the house, the pets, and the children. Lucky them.

Even if Andrea'd worn a more vibrant shade of nail polish, it probably wouldn't have lasted once she'd become Old Colony's first female EVP—more misguided affirmative action. Surely she couldn't be in the running for president. Should that occur, there'd be an immediate run on his bank.

Separation hadn't been easy at first. The dismal apartment on the wrong side of Beacon Hill with its layers of flaking paint, loose panes, erratic plumbing, and recalcitrant elevator had not been the sort of pad to which movers and shakers enticed off-duty yoga instructors and personal trainers. If anything, it was an urban Three Oaks. It had, however, been a step up from the monk's cell at the Racquet and Tennis Club where he'd taken refuge immediately after the breakup. Well, not entirely. At least he hadn't been lonely at the R & T. Most of its residents were miscreants of his age and station who, having been cast from the marital bed, had yet to find long-term comforters. As a consequence, there were always erring husbands up for some squash before a tryst with the woman who was no longer the "other woman."

Thankfully, the memory of those bleak years was fading. Even without the proceeds from the sale of a large piece of Three Oaks, his improved financial position landed him a three-bedroom condo over-looking the Public Garden. He had no idea who would ever occupy the two extra bedrooms, but never mind. The building had uniformed doormen, a fitness center, an indoor pool, and underground parking. Plus, there were yoga classes where he could stare while pretending to stretch. In any case, he was finally in a position to entertain, even if he wasn't entirely sure who. However, there'd been a glitch with the hot tub on his balcony. The first woman to take a plunge developed a UTI within moments of immersion.

———

For several months after learning of his father's marriage to Polly, his life seemed to level off. However, nature abhors stasis. Without warning, Mother was gone, and there he was, with his father and step-mother in the front row of her memorial service.

It had been generous of Polly to help. She edited his mother's short bio and came up with a flattering, decades-old photograph to go on the lobby's mahogany table. To nobody's surprise, Howard Paulson was elsewhere, sending in his stead a floral arrangement better suited to a Kentucky Derby winner. Daniel Shaver was another MIA. His offering was equally impersonal.

The presence of his mother's tottering third-floor friends and her kindly attendants made the brief farewell marginally less forlorn.

Was he a freak or a monster to feel so little? He tended to nourish these self-pitying moods. No, he was wrong to accuse her. His mother cared for him. That's the way moms were wired. They had little choice in the matter, even if some of them had trouble with outward displays of affection.

Following the generic Protestant rite, his threesome and the recently married Colonel and Cornelia gathered for cookies, cheese, grapes, soft drinks, and a daunting mound of raw vegetables. The attendants, with the exception of Mercy Williams, had left. Fred handed her an envelope containing ten one-hundred-dollar bills. It was the least he could do. She had saved his mother from paying full freight at Howard Paulson's company store.

With great solemnity, Mercy opened the envelope, studied its contents, and gave Fred a warm, wet kiss. Dabbing at her eyes, she said, "I looked in on Missus Paulson every day after she went to the second floor. I brought her vanilla ice cream, but then she stopped recognizing me."

"How was she at the end?" Fred asked.

Mercy thought for a moment. "Your mama's hands and feet were icy cold. The last thing she said to me was 'I can't talk about this anymore. Night, night, Mercy.'"

"Anything about me?"

Mercy looked pained but said nothing.

"Then what?"

"I said, 'Sleep tight, Helen.'"

Before leaving, he noticed the Damons—she had taken his name—were polishing off the cookies.

Round and round went his gloom like a load of sodden wash. Should he see a shrink? It was their job to make you feel good about yourself. In fact, he could visualize his own Betsy pouring out exaggerated, if not wholly fabricated, tales of childhood "abuse"—an all-inclusive concept now encompassing such hurtful behaviors as reasonable parental directives, the withholding of unearned accolades, and the mildest constructive criticism. She might even trot out the familiar cliche about having been "raised by wolves." Well, that worked out just fine for Romulus, if less so for his brother.

Perhaps he would have fought harder to keep his mother on three if it hadn't been for the damn annuity. Something was up. He could tell when she started acting girlish. He got right to the point: "You want to tell me something; don't you, Mother?"

"How can you tell, Freddy?"

"It's your expression. You look as though you're about to lay an egg."

Coyly she replied, "Oh, Freddy, you'll be so pleased with me."

"I always am, Mother."

"Freddy, I'm going to use the money you got from . . . who was it?"

How could she have forgotten the creep? "Your protector, James Freeman."

"That's right. I'm going to buy one of those things that pay you money for as long as you live. Even if you live past one hundred."

"An annuity?"

"Yes, Freddy. I believe that's what he called it. I read about it in a church magazine."

Who was hustling her now? "What church, Mother?"

"Oh, please. I don't know, Freddy, but Father Michael explained it to me very carefully. He swore on his mother's memory it was completely safe, and my family would be so impressed by my . . . I can't remember what it was."

"*Mother*, what are *you* doing with a Father Michael?"

"He's so nice, Freddy. We talk every week."

"How did you meet him?"

"He came up to me after one of the services and gave me some little booklets to read. Just like Mr. Freedom. Said it was entirely up to me."

"What service, Mother?"

In a small voice, "I don't remember, Freddy. They're all pretty much the same, aren't they?"

What was he supposed to do now? Was it time for the second floor? She'd be safer there and less of a worry to him. He took both of her hands and said, "That's really smart of you, Mother, but I'll handle it from here."

"Oh, thank you, Freddy." Her little smile was almost worth the bother she caused. He'd get Mercy after her fingernails. Then came the "thefts."

On one of his last visits to three, she motioned him closer and whispered, "I've got something awful to tell you, Freddy."

"What's that, Mother?"

"I've told you about *those people*, haven't I?"

"You have, Mother, but you've got to stop talking that way. Especially in public. Times have changed." Thank God nobody seemed to have heard her.

"What are you talking about, Freddy? *Those people* are stealing my crystal. There's hardly any left. They must be stopped, made to give back every piece, and then sent to jail."

"No, Mother. Your crystal's in storage. I put it there myself. You never brought it to Essex Lodge. You must be thinking of your jelly jar collection."

"My what?"

"Your Fred Flintstone glasses. You've been breaking them and losing them for years. There aren't many left."

A week later his mother moved downstairs and immediately began accusing the lady in the adjacent bed of keeping their room too hot. The *only* thing she'd wanted in Room 221 was her lighthouse painting. Fred added a photo of himself.

Father Michael was not heard from again, and his mother died after receiving only one annuity payment.

Would he miss her? He'd certainly miss the dutiful son feeling he got from visiting her, but were these good deeds merely an effort to

take in the Essex Lodge staff and hedge his bets about the possibility
of a hereafter?

Yes, Mother had done her best. Who could expect more? As for
himself, he *had* been a good son. That is what he wanted to believe he
believed.

It was time to leave his mother's service, and there was his father
looking, as always, remote. Where was he now? Troy? Carthage?
Olympus? The Underworld?

57

DR. E

Helen's send-off was unmemorable yet painful. Blessedly, it was brief. It had to be. The space was booked for bingo fifty minutes after the "All-Faiths"[56] cleric positioned himself, fussed with his robes, and smiled benevolently as he'd been taught.

Was I being disloyal to darling Polly by rehashing my missteps with Helen? Ah, the delights of self-indulgence. So comforting to slip into one's favorite default mood; mine goes: "O what ails thee, Frederick Elder, so haggard and so woebegone?"

Who was I kidding, moping about "those happy, golden, bygone days," as mawkish Yalies describe their four-year confinement in decaying New Haven. D-B once called an evening at Chez Elder a "no-holds-barred, mixed-marital-arts cage fight." I had no idea our company was so toxic. No wonder the invitations dried up.

What exactly can one take away from these purportedly celebratory "Celebrate a Life" celebrations? Fortunately for him (in all instances, the masculine includes the feminine), the decedent is not present to grimace at the banal paeans of those shanghaied into extolling him or observe the telltale silence of those who knew him best. Even the most

---

56 All faiths but mine.

negligible are acclaimed as Renaissance Men.[57] Anent that: To what period will I be relegated? The Dark Ages?

My mind wandered as I listened to the speakers missing the point about Helen. I resisted the urge to correct them. That would have upset Polly, who, before the service, said, "I know you loved Helen, Dearest. Believe me, I'm fine with that, because you learned how to love and now we love each other."

How, I wondered, would Ingmar Bergman have staged these empty obsequies? Perhaps like this: a wintery setting swathed in umlauts and Nordic gloom. At the entrance of the drafty oaken hall sits a moody Liv Ullmann look-alike. She's the keeper of the ledger. Seated beside her: a gaunt spectral figure, more symbol than person. He's all in black. What else? The Liv stand-in respectfully addresses him as "Grim." Hoping to conceal his identity, Grim's scythe is stashed in the trunk of his Saab.

Grim rises and studies each of the congregants. After the officiant signs off, Grim approaches the chosen one from behind, taps him on the shoulder, and delivers the circular piece of high-quality rag paper on which is printed, in an ominous gothic font, "You're Next."

Oh, for those carefree years when the funerals through which I dozed had little to do with me. Now these ceremonies are endowed with a distressing immediacy.

Polly, you are to me what Opportunity is to Spirit, my solar-powered, robotic self. Which of us will go first? Me, I hope. Men generally do. That's fine since I couldn't survive your absence.

How will it end for me? A rover's last utterance should be informative and professional. Never maudlin. Something like "My battery's low, and it's getting dark."

---

57 What about talented women? Here, as elsewhere, they get short shrift, or none whatsoever.

58

FREDDY/FRED

It was indisputable. His old man could be utterly unfeeling. Was it Asperger's, the syndrome du jour? Fred had never seen his father more inappropriately expansive. It was like shouting, "Ha, ha! She may have left *me*, but I've outlived *her*." Maybe that's what happens when you got a last-minute stay of execution. After the service, his father insisted he join him and Polly for dinner at the Harvard Club. His treat.

On the way, they picked up Spike.

Fred sensed Polly's tender disapproval of his father's unseemly exuberance, no doubt wondering whether he'd carry on in this fashion if *she* predeceased him.

They parked behind the club, and—instead of going upstairs to the cavernous main dining room—Dr. Elder announced they were "flying economy" and hustled them off to his favorite booth in the Grill, above which hung a giant, sepia-toned photograph of a packed Harvard Stadium taken during the 1915 edition of "The Game." Some treat. As his father must have known, everything in the Grill tasted like undercooked cardboard. It was reasonably priced for a reason.

The deferential waiter seated them and, to his father's delight, gave Spike, who sprang into Polly's lap, a bulldog-shaped biscuit. Evidently, the "no pets" rule did not apply to everyone.

Then Fred noticed the ring. Why was his father wearing one? So unlike him. "That can't be a wedding ring, can it, Dad?"

"Certainly not," said his father. "It was D-B's. Said he bought it at an estate sale. Frightfully expensive but worth every pound, according to him. Claimed it opened doors, even New England doors. Someday it was to go to me, the Laird of Lower Finley. How could I say no?"

Best let it go, Fred thought.

After his first drink—Polly having reminded him to go easy—his father leaned back, scanned the area, got the waiter's attention, waved his empty glass, and said, far too loudly, "Thank you, Marko, for restoring circulation and hope to my morose member."

The room went silent.

Polly was vigorously shaking her head. "Please, Fred, we're not alone. Not everyone here's deaf."

His father was undaunted. Polly's mild rebuke was a challenge. "Stop raining on my parade—make that our parade—Sweetie. Aren't you glad we're doing it, even if sometimes neither of us is sure what, if anything, happened? Were I Greek, I'd take the name Testicles—you know, like Pericles."

"C'mon, Dad. TMI!"

As usual, his father ignored him.

"Polly, My Love, it's time for our long-delayed honeymoon. We'll fly to the Caribbean, and I'll buy you the merest suggestion of a bathing suit—a *dipthong.*"

Polly groaned.

"You know something, you two? My noblest-Roman-of-them-all act was a crock. Seneca, my foot. I just didn't have the balls to make a fuss, scream for painkillers, and make everyone around me feel like a crud for having a life expectancy exceeding one month."

Polly intercepted his father's second drink and returned it to the waiter, saying, "Johnny, let's save this one for later. You okay with that,

Dear?" Turning to Fred, she whispered, "Are you aware your dear papa has progressed from inhibited youth, to uninhibited middle age, to disinhibited dotage?"

"Johnny, come here, will ya," yelled Dr. Elder at the retreating waiter. The Grill fell silent.

"Johnny, I got one for you. What was Hermann Goering's favorite breakfast?"

Johnny shook his head.

"Luftwaffles," shouted his father, as the other diners, who'd been holding their breath, burst out laughing. There was even some applause, plus the obligatory eye-rolling that invariably follows a particularly lame pun.

Without missing a beat, his father took a bun from the breadbasket, placed it on the table, rotated it 180 degrees, and looked up expectantly. Without waiting for a response, he said, "That was a roll reversal." Polly laughed dutifully. Would she ever stop enabling him?

The other diners resumed eating, but it was obvious they were hoping for more. They didn't have long to wait.

"Freddy, me lad, stop with the grouchy face. Even you'd be acting out in my situation."

His father turned to Polly and declared, "Dearest Girl, while I may be losing my memory and much else, the vision I shall carry with me to whatever may be next is my first sight of your yummy, welcoming—"

"I beg you, Fred!"

Laughter from every direction.

"You gotta knock it off, Dad."

They finally ordered.

"Great choice," said Johnny to each of them.

"Johnny and I have a code," said his father. "Great choice means passable. Good choice means your survival's in doubt."

Then Polly took charge. "Time to finish up, Dearie," she said.

His father beamed. "Soon, soon, but first, My Love, a question." The room hushed.

"As you two may have observed, I am quite pleased with myself. I appear to have stared down death and never flinched. When applauded for my bravery, I go all self-deprecating, which has the intended effect of making me appear nobler still. Dr. Frederick Elder, the heroic Stoic."

"Now you're putting yourself down, Dad."

"Freddy's right, stop it. None of us has been able to sleep, worrying about you. Finish those lobster-flavored breadcrumbs, and, if you don't pipe down, I'll be obliged to ground your rambunctious soft-on."

His father guffawed. Polly continued, "Now answer me this, Fred. Would you have left *me* if Helen had asked you back?"

"Never."

"Thank you, Fred. That was the correct answer."

Disgusting. More goo-goo eyes. *Which of them was worse?* Fred asked himself.

"Apologies to all. I'm an unfeeling lout," said his father.

"No you're not, Fred. You've just lived through a nightmare."

"Be that as it may, I've shot my wad. I'm not going through anything like this again. If Marko's kidney conks out, it's time for yours truly to 'cease upon the midnight,' preferably with no pain. Should I linger, I'll summon Spike's vet and direct him to put me down."

"We'll have no more of that," said Polly.

"It would be best for everyone. It would end the drain on family resources. There are worse things than death."

Polly was about to cry.

"All right, Fred, we are changing the subject unless you'd like Johnny to bring *me* a double."

"Consider it changed, Mrs. Elder."

Oh God. His father raised his glass. Not again. Yes, again.

"To be semiserious for just a millisecond, here's to you, My Love. You hold my brittle, easily broken heart in your hands."

"As you hold mine, dear Fred."

That did it. She was crying. Spike looked up and, unbidden, began licking her face.

"All right, folks, I'll pipe down, but not before leaving you with this—"

"Must you, Fred?"

"Polly and Freddy, do either of you know what they call the last piece of wood placed on a fire? No? The epilog."

———

Ms. Spinelli knocked, entered, and told Fred he was to participate in a 2:00 p.m. conference call with Messrs. Paulson, Shaver, Morgan, and Glauser. She blushed when she said "Glauser," and added, "Please give him my *very* best." Ms. Spinelli was looking almost stylish and became a different woman whenever Max was mentioned. Allusions to the dashing banker brought touches of pink to her maidenly cheeks.

The conference call was disturbing for several reasons, the least important of which was his belief that there were more participants than the four who announced their presence. Fred was proud of his ability to sniff out silent listeners. Also, he was certain Max was in New York, not Zurich, as he claimed. Was he with Andrea? If so, good luck to him.

Howard Paulson led off by assuring them the "technicians" they'd noticed in their offices had been there to ensure they could converse without fear of being overheard. Then he got to the point: "Gentlemen, I have received word from reliable sources that unnamed persons are prying into our overseas operations. It is safe to assume we are, for no good reason, under criminal investigation."

Someone, it may have been that jerk Richard (never Dick) Morgan, tried to chime in but was immediately silenced. Howard Paulson continued, "We have absolutely nothing to worry about if we stick together and keep our traps shut." Howard Paulson let that sink in and resumed with his customary directness. "Henceforth, all communications with outsiders will be conducted through our New York counsel. Now let me introduce Attorney Theodore Stevenson, a former federal prosecutor who has seen the light, as so many do."

Yes, that made at least one additional person on the call. Were there more?

"Thank you, Howard," said someone, presumably Stevenson, who continued in what sounded like a high-hourly-rate voice. "Gentlemen, let me assure you up front that you have *nothing* to worry about. Justice has pulled in its horns after the beating it took in the Arthur Andersen and KPMG debacles. And don't forget its failure against the two Bear Stearns guys."

Howard Paulson broke in, "Mr. Stevenson—"

"Please, Howard, it's Ted."

"Ted, should we be worried about what's happening in our particular arena?"

Fred couldn't help wondering how many times this exchange had been rehearsed.

"In a word, *no*, you should not be worried. Justice is sucking wind in complex financial cases. It's lost the capability to litigate. The place has slipped since my day. It's not attracting the best and the brightest, and it screws up with comforting regularity. The boys are afraid of losing. Thanks in no small measure to me, that's why they settled against UBS and HSBC. Nobody wants a reputation-wrecking loss on his resume when he tries to move to greener pastures and represent those he formerly tormented."

"That's good to know, Ted, but the real reason I'm sleeping nights is because you're with us. When they see you, the Feds will piss themselves and fold."

"Thank you, Howard. Your confidence is not misplaced," smarmed Stevenson.

It was comforting to be on this call with the big dogs.

"What Ted may also be telling us," interrupted Daniel Shaver, who was undoubtedly sitting beside Howard Paulson, "is that harassing our comparatively modest operation isn't getting anyone to the House, let alone the White House. As I see it, we're sitting pretty."

One of the courtiers laughed appreciatively, and Howard Paulson chortled, "Nicely put, Daniel."

That damn kiss-ass. It made his blood boil, but then he remembered hearing that Harriet Shaver was once again named Harriet Rubino.

"A couple additional things in our favor," said Stevenson as the laughter subsided. "Nowadays prosecutors aren't allowed to squeeze people the way I did. You can't pressure them into waiving their attorney-client privilege, nor can you push companies to cut off legal fees when their boys are indicted."

"All right, Ted, given your ever-ascending hourly rate, we should think about wrapping this up. What's the drill if someone comes calling?"

"Very simple, Howard: We'll fight them tooth and nail. Were I feeling Churchillian, I'd enumerate all the places we'll fight. Hills. Streets. Beaches. You name it. If you're feeling anxious, just ask yourself how many financial executives have been indicted, much less convicted and imprisoned. The world's changed in your favor."

"Anything else, Ted?"

"Yes, Howard. As I've said, those gung-ho assistant US attorneys know that if they overdo it, they'll be outta luck when they come groveling for jobs in the private sector."

If they hadn't been on speakerphone, Howard Paulson might well have closed with what Fred knew to be his most deeply held belief:

Sophisticated, carefully compartmentalized, no-paper-trail, white-collar crimes committed by high-IQ MBAs continued to offer virtually risk-free opportunities for larger-than-life returns.

For the next several weeks, whenever he felt jumpy, Fred reminded himself of the conference call and the confidence displayed by Messrs. Paulson and Stevenson.

———

It began as just another unmemorable day at Old Colony, alike in all respects to—Christ, it had to be over five thousand—those preceding it. He arrived early, well ahead of Ms. Spinelli, fixed his coffee, grabbed what he always vowed was his last Danish, and noticed an email from Howard Paulson to everyone on the last conference call. "As I've told each of you," it read, "our esteemed counsel has changed his tune."

Fred took a gulp and looked for something to wipe his chin. WTF? Nobody'd told him shit since that call. Was Howard Paulson fucking with him? If so, why? Had he hit "Reply All" by mistake? Not like him to screw up.

He closed his office door and read on. "We're being investigated by an ambitious nobody, and, rather than scream about prosecutorial overreach, the expensive Theodore Stevenson suggests throwing him a bone. A small one."

Fred wanted to stop there but couldn't. In fact, he wanted to throw something, but Old Colony's cramped glass cubicles afforded no privacy. That was reserved for EVPs and above. He read on: "Someone who's expendable, who lacks the clout, the cash, and the cachet to take on Lenox Hill and doesn't have the stones to blow the whistle and incur some serious hurt."

There was no point in kidding himself. Could it be anyone else? He was wearing a blue shirt. The sweat stains would be obvious to everyone.

The email concluded, "I wish to get everyone's concurrence on next steps, including the identity of the bone. I'll be back to you in short order."

Sometimes he wished he hadn't quit smoking. The next best thing was a fast turn around the block. That didn't cut it, so he walked to the Public Garden, pivoted, and hustled back. In shirtsleeves. In March. With his tie askew and his collar button undone. Dumb. Boston's a small town. Acquaintances were bound to have spotted him and wondered.

He knew how the story would play out. Paulson and his stooges would go to the Feds, shed alligator tears, and "deeply regret" that a "few" slips "may have" occurred despite Lenox Hill's "stringent" compliance measures. Happily, it had become clear that the misdeeds were confined to a "single low-level operative" who appeared to have violated US law in a "few minor respects." As a show of good faith, this bad apple—whose identity had come to light as a result of Lenox Hill's "exhaustive" internal investigation—would be served up to the authorities. What did Howard Paulson mean by "in short order"?

Twenty-four hours passed. Nothing.

Fred surprised himself. He was calm, and, despite changing his shirt twice a day, he was not paralyzed. Quite the contrary. Energized. He'd be all set when the second shoe dropped.

Another day gone. No shoe. Howard Paulson didn't dick around. He could wait no longer. He'd lined up his ducks.

Fred, the fall guy? Wasn't happening. He hadn't felt so macho since skewering Freeman, who, at last count, was still a guest at Club Fed. Freddy might have been shitting his knickers. Not Frederick the Great.

He was no longer the guy in the chopper who'd sat, trembled, and watched.

Now it was H-Hour. History's great commanders displayed boldness, flexibility, and a knack for exploiting opportunities. As would he. The way to decisive victory was clearly marked, predicated as it was on the principle that the Feds were stalking high-value folks, not peripherals.

———

Easy peasy. First, he organized his stash of emails and taped phone calls. Then he paid a call on Assistant US Attorney Robeson, whom Stevenson had thoughtfully identified in their last conference call. Peter Robeson was thrilled to be handed Messrs. Paulson and Shaver, plus Max, if he could be served. Ms. Spinelli would hate him for that. Too bad. In return for his agreement to sing, he was offered immunity and a potentially huge whistleblower's fee. Elementary, my dear Watson. The winner is the dude who makes it to the Feds firstest with the mostest.

It would have been a cinch—and a delight—to implicate Andrea. That would croak her at Old Colony but hurt Betsy. He was a good father, so he held off.

So sweet. He'd never need to slink off to some third-world dump with no extradition treaty. He only had to wait. He'd walk away untarnished, having taken down the guys who'd stolen his mother and humiliated his father. It would cost him virtually nothing in legal fees, and he'd even gotten over his mild annoyance on learning *he* hadn't been under investigation. Better yet—his father would think differently about the felonious Daniel Shaver.

59

DR. E

I am blessed with Polly. So many fellows of my vintage are locked into marriages from which they are too dispirited or too broke to secede. Equally untenable are the intellectual mismatches where the desire that ignited the relationship has long since shriveled into boredom, regret, and, finally, recrimination. There they huddle, killing time, each hoping the other will hurry up and die.

Sadder yet, the erstwhile rakes. The ones who jauntily stockpile desirable, seemingly devoted, younger women. The Don Juans who bask in the envy of their peers and revel in their trophies but are cruelly cast aside when declining health, looks, prestige, cash flow, or net worth erode their allure. Beware the transactional. Beware, too, nonexistent or poorly negotiated prenups.

Will dear Polly, with whom I share my *Times Literary Supplement*, remain with me when so many younger, vital, solvent men would snap her up in a nanosecond?[58] While I might be kidding myself, I say "yes." I see Polly as my "Psyche true," the "loveliest vision far of all Olympus' faded hierarchy."

Whether Polly stays or leaves, my jests are not what hold us together. She endures them gamely but with visible pain. Speaking

---

58 Whatever that is. Less than a second?

of which, I've just hatched another. My colleagues, at an institution filled with children, would blanch or blush, but I can contain it no longer.

So, here it is, a device to shape your toenails—a pedofile.

No sooner had I shared this splendid pun with Polly than she turned to me and, in the merry tone I love so well, said, "Are you aware that the essential Dr. Frederick Elder has been immortalized in verse?"

I'm afraid I bit. "Catullus? No? Who then? Homer? Virgil? Ovid? Shakespeare? Still no? Very well, I'll settle for Yeats or Wallace Stevens . . . I'm not even warm?"

"I fear not, Dr. Elder. Try Edwin Arlington Robinson."

"Oh, dear. He can be terribly gloomy, but fire when ready, Sweetheart."

"I shall, and, as you know, it's meant lovingly:

> Miniver sighed for what was not,
> And dreamed, and rested from his labors;
> He dreamed of Thebes and Camelot,
> And Priam's neighbors."

Being enfolded in arid darkness, neither Opportunity, nor I, Senior Rover, will ever rust or rot. Millennia from now, Helios will unearth us, power up our twenty-first-century batteries, and reunite us (as toddlers we played together at the Jet Propulsion Laboratory) in a Martian museum celebrating the early days of interplanetary exploration. There we will care for each other and earn our keep by performing simple manual tasks—such as gathering soil samples—for the edification of inquisitive youngsters who won't realize Opportunity and I were once state of the art.

60

DANIEL

His driver was sick, so Daniel took the subway downtown. No biggie. It would be instructive to mingle with the less fortunate.

He grabbed a seat and was checking his emails when he felt a hovering presence. The train wasn't half full, so why was the grizzled wreck crowding him? But for his clean document bag, he could have been a street person.

Daniel raised his head. Staring down at him was a weathered beat-to-shit guy missing a hunk of his right ear.

Fuck me!

He was wearing a battered green utility cover and a Marine raincoat, also green, from which corporal's chevrons had been removed—you could tell by the darker green once covered by the insignia.

"Long time no see, Leutnant."

Kee-rist, the same lousy teeth. It couldn't be, but it was. "And you are?"

"C'mon, you remember me. I was Captain Mac's radioman. He bought it a couple weeks after your patrol. Missed his chance to waste you. He left that to me."

Daniel couldn't get past the guy unless he moved, and it was damn clear he wasn't going to. "What are you doing now, Corporal?"

"I deliver Wall Street shit. Kinda like a radioman. Like Rubino."

"You're a messenger?"

"Yeah, and the message to you is this: 'Captain Mac's rip-shit. Same goes for Foster, Rubino, Dalton, the snuffies, and Fritz—you knew him as Dumpster. They got it in for you.'"

"Remind me of your name, Corporal."

"Szendrock."

The subway stopped. Szendrock hoisted his document bag, growled, and said, "Don't think you've seen the last of me, Leutnant. Or Nguyen neither."

————

So be it. Everything he'd built, begged, borrowed, or stolen was down the crapper—as though it never happened. The status conferred by money, torn from him. His profile in *Fortune,* pulled. The Semper Foundation, scrapped. The membership he'd finally wangled in the top Nantucket club, revoked. The shame of being undone by Freddy Elder, pafuckingthetic.

Now what? Witnesses have accidents. Freddy couldn't testify if something happened to him before he took the stand. Oh, for a loaded .45.

And what about Paulson? He'd built a fucking Chinese wall between himself and the bad shit and probably laid the groundwork for a presidential pardon. Like they all do. He could hear him now: "How could I be expected to know that Daniel Shaver, my protege, was a cunning fraud? A leader must be able to delegate and trust those in whom he's reposed trust." Fuck! Was he the only one at Lenox Hill going down? Looked like it. No way was canny Max subjecting himself to service of process in the States.

But why piddling Lenox Hill? It's HSBC, UBS, and Credit Suisse they're after.

Turns out he was wrong. Lenox Hill, like the porridge Goldilocks ate, was just right. Neither too big to fail nor too small to ignore.

Who would stand up for him? Dr. Elder? Not after this. Who then? Alma, gone. Harriet, gone. Mare, gone. Sally Lenox never signed up. Freddy and Max, taking cover.

But wait, just suppose his beady-eyed barrister lined up a sympathetic judge, a Marine vet, say, who took into account his Silver Star, his philanthropy, his community service, and his good faith efforts to organize the Semper Foundation. How about them apples? Short sentence. Decent accommodations. Early release for exemplary behavior. Yes!

Then what? Banned from the securities business for life and back to Lower Finley with his tail between his legs? Not happening.

What about that other thing? He was so screwed. Nguyen and Szendrock were on his trail. He could hear them baying. What would Dr. Elder say? Some lame Greek shit about Nemesis?

Oh, to be back in that life class with everything in front of him.

Enough. Saddle up 911, set course for the Cape, and don't forget Purdey.

61

FREDDY/FRED

Change of frequency. It's me, Fred, oka (once known as) Freddy. I'm the Frederick Elder who was formerly seen as unexceptional.

Who'd have guessed it? Shaver must have flinched. He could nail the most skittish game bird but barely winged himself. That wouldn't cut it in the Corps. He'll be okay, though. They plucked most of the lead out of his cheek, and they're reconstructing his ear. Lucky he was so close to the muzzle. The shot had little time to disperse.

Better still, he was fine to stand trial. Given the material submitted by yours truly, he had no choice but to plead guilty and implicate everyone else—but me—in return for a five-year sentence. Best of all, my old man won't have to endure the shame of his only child's indictment and whatever followed. Our family name will remain unsullied, if unmemorable. Not that *I* did much wrong.

Shaver hasn't changed. Still trying to brazen it out. Claims his facial scars will give him a dueling society look. Dashing Daniel von Shaver from Heidelberg. Pretty lame, if you ask me. I'm betting he doesn't try again.

One thing's for sure. I'm not visiting him in prison. At his sentencing, Shaver accused me, accurately as we both knew, of tipping the Feds and almost got violent in the courtroom when I launched into Mark Antony's "lend me your ears" speech.

Another reason to steer clear of Shaver: the beat-up character in the tattered green raincoat. Intimidating. Like Shaver, he has a mangled right ear. Must be some cult. What about the trim Asian dude in shades? Both of them showed up at the trial. Shaver couldn't look at either one.

The former assistant US attorney loves me. Shaver's and Paulson's convictions earned Robeson a seven-figure guarantee to lead the new white-collar crime division of a tony Wall Street law firm. It's lucrative work, and most outfits have persuaded themselves there's no shame in doing it.

And now, the piece de resistance: Robeson showed his gratitude by fast-tracking my whistleblower reward, which continues to grow as more heads roll.

So, how do I feel about what I've wrought? Like a rat? A snitch? A squealer? No way. Resourceful. Exactly what Howard Paulson was looking for.

Yes, I *am* delighted with myself. A significant piece of my reward has gone into the acquisition of Shaver's Lower Finley real estate and the complete renovation of Three Oaks. Poor Shaver. After paying his fines, he was in no position to dicker.

What gave me the greatest pleasure was financing a real honeymoon for Polly and my old man—a week in a Hotel Grand Bretagne suite overlooking the Parthenon. Then, at last, they were off to Troy and its ghosts. All of it on me.

Another tranche went into the rehabilitation of Lower Finley's town green, the reconstruction of its bandstand (now the Elder Bandstand), and my civic-minded removal of the plaque honoring the disgraced Herr Shaver. I used a couple hundred thousand more for buying, gutting, and reimagining Foley's Restaurant, adding a bidet and a Tempur-Pedic king in the back room. Lastly, I threw in an annuity for Sam, who, after abusing his last "Live Free or Die" burger, skedaddled down to Mary in Florida.

As a nod to the healthy food nerds who are flooding the area, I tweaked the menu while retaining the traditional favorites that have sent so many locals and their clogged arteries to an early grave. Despite my meddling, Foley's is flourishing under the stewardship of Kathleen, Mary's effervescent niece. That cheeky redhead—she has such an engaging giggle—is significantly younger than I, but she knows which is the buttered side of her bread. I was delighted to foot the bill for her Manolos. The two of us have an unbreakable code. It's a go if she changes into the green pair when I drop in for a burger or something less lethal.

Well, what now? Should I seek a governmental position that accords me the right to precede my name with "The Honorable"? Such a kick! Why not?

So instructive how money changes the way you're perceived. Now I'm in demand, and, having crushed my "fuck-you number," I'm setting up shop as an angel investor.

Mustn't forget Dad. He's alternately sad and resigned about Shaver but believes he'll return from prison a changed man. Last week the two of us lunched at the Harvard Club. My idea. My treat. Weekday afternoon. Nearly empty. Our usual booth. The dreaded lobster rolls.

Before he managed his second sip, I blurted out, "There's something I've got to tell you, Dad."

He was on me at once. "Would it have anything to do with your response to my former condition, Freddy?"

How the hell did he know? "I'm afraid so, Dad."

He gave me his signature over-the-glasses, I-can-see-through-you stare, lowered his drink, and in his mildest voice said, "Thank you, Freddy, but that's bourbon under the bridge. Say no more; I'd have behaved the same way myself."

Both of us knew that wasn't true.

After what seemed like an endless silence, my old man held aloft his glass, flashed Johnny the high sign, and in his outdoor voice bellowed, "Johnny, my man, bring me another, and pour Junior a double. It flows like glue around here."

When Johnny returned with our libations (Dad's word), my father took an approving sip and surveyed the room. Hoping to distract him, I hesitantly ventured into his territory. "Dad, what breed of dog would a dominatrix own?"

Shaking his head, my father looked intrigued and delighted.

I waited until he'd just taken another mouthful before announcing, "A whippet."

Dad's response was perfect, even if most of his bourbon landed on my stylish Italian tie.

Moments later, having recovered, my incorrigible father put on his game face and said, "What would you call a pair of Bangkok dominatrices?" I shook my head.

"Thais that bind," guffawed my father.

I guffawed back without drenching him.

He was beaming.

ACKNOWLEDGMENTS

Thank you: Ann, Alex (both of you), Alki, Almyra, Carla, Don, El, Jenny, Jim, Ledge, Millie, Suz, Tima, and especially Larry, who was there. You forbearing readers are not to blame for the glitches, howlers, infelicities, and inadequacies. They are mine alone.

ABOUT THE AUTHOR

FRANK PORTER lives in Cambridge, Massachusetts, with his wife, Ann, and their small dog. He used to practice law. Now he does other things. He touched on the law in his 2018 ribald novel, *Semper Fee.*